W9-CIM-916

Fangs
and
Stilettos

FANGS and STILETTOS

ANTHONY DIFIORE

inGroup PRESS

Published by inGroup Press, a division of inGroup Marketing, LLC. Chicago, IL.
First Published 2012

Book cover and interior design by Jamie Kerry for
Belle Étoile Studios (http://www.belleetoilestudios.com).

inGroup Press and the inGroup Press logo are trademarks of inGroup Marketing, LLC.
The inGroup Press logo was designed by Shelly Rabuse (http://www.rabusedesign.com).

Library of Congress Control Number: 2012930891
ISBN-13: 978-1935725077

Visit our website: www.inGroupPress.com

Printed and bound in the United States of America

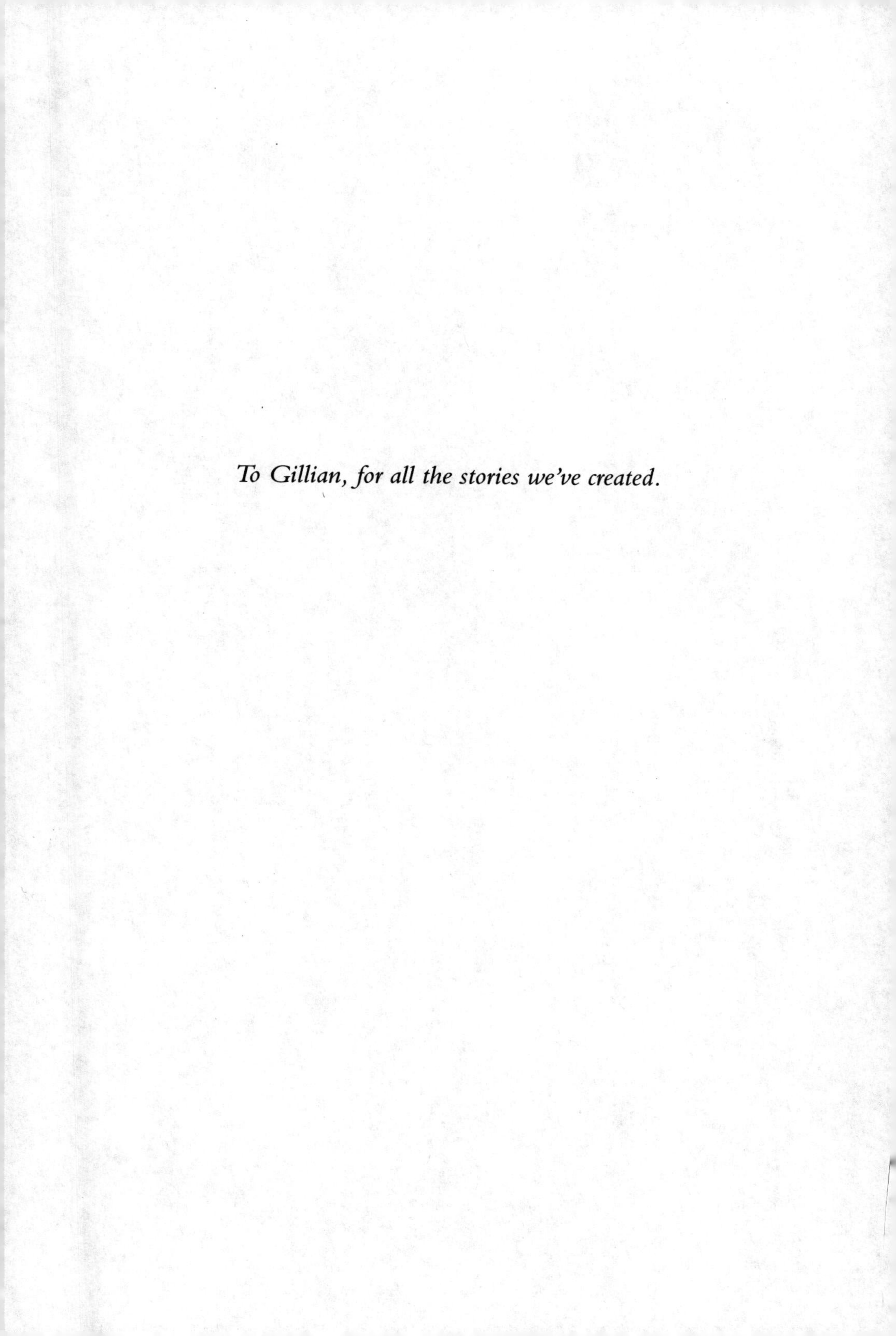

To Gillian, for all the stories we've created.

Chapter One

"NOT ALL PEOPLE IN THIS WORLD ARE GOOD," she told her infant children as she sat by the window, watching the brown Rolls-Royce driving slowly—tauntingly—down the winding road leading to her home. She knew that Candice would find her someday, but hadn't expected it to be so soon. She'd wanted to watch her kids grow up. She'd wanted to see more of the world.

"And the secret that they don't teach you when you're growing up—that they pretend isn't true—is that sometimes the bad guys win."

The woman looked into the two adjoining cribs and thought about what life might have been like had they been able to hide forever. Or what it would have been like if there was never any reason to hide at all.

"Someday, someone will tell you that you belong to an extinct race," she whispered into the cribs. "Or—if you're lucky, maybe you'll never find out."

"Are they ready?" a voice asked from the darkness of the room.

The mother nodded, and then turned again to the window.

"I don't know that they'll ever be. But if you're asking if you may take them now, then yes, you may. They're ready."

Twenty Years Later

The lives of Natasha and Marciano Genet were about to change forever, with one tiny bit of news that the twins had waited twenty-one years for.

"Do I have to get dressed up for this?" Natasha shouted from the only bathroom in the three-bedroom Philadelphia apartment, which she shared with her twin brother Marciano, or Marc, and their sister Betty. Betty wasn't their genetic sister, although the three of them had all grown up together, and were very close in age. Betty's parents adopted Natasha and Marc when they were babies, and treated them no differently than their own blood.

"No, birthday girl, it's nothing like that," Betty shouted back as she hurried around the apartment in a fit of excitement, looking for the right shoes to wear on such a special day. Not that she had as many options as her siblings. Betty wasn't nearly as fashion-forward as the twins, but at least she had them to bounce ideas off of. "Just keep it cute."

Natasha and Betty both worked for their mother, the famous French fashion designer known only as Maude. Marciano worked for her archrival, whose Philadelphia boutique was literally right across the street from Maude's. He'd been lured there with the promise of being a junior designer, although he'd primarily just been a personal assistant for his demanding boss, the designer Rafaela Simone.

"Why doesn't Rafaela know anything about this *secret*?" Marciano asked as he stepped into the bathroom wearing tight gray slacks, a white button-down shirt, and a thin black tie. No shoes though. Marciano had more shoes than Natasha and Betty combined, and the longest part of every morning was consumed by deciding which pair to wear. It was usually loafers or boat shoes on a workday. Sometimes he'd get dressy with a sharp pair of patent-leather lace-ups.

"It's kind of a family thing, but a little more than that," Betty replied.

"Well how do you know about it?" Natasha asked. "And Marc, give me some space while I'm in the bathroom, alright?"

"You're dressed," her brother replied, slightly annoyed. "We need three bathrooms!"

"It strictly has to do with you two," Betty answered, stepping out of Marc's way as he hurried back out into the hallway on his way to select the day's shoes. She walked into the bathroom—sidestepping Natasha, who was doing her hair in front of a small, rectangular mirror—in search of a brush. "It's good news, I promise. A very *good* secret."

"I don't like secrets," Natasha countered. Unlike her calm, pensive older sister, Natasha was much more of the high-anxiety type. She already knew that her entire morning was going to be consumed thinking about the secret, regardless of what other important things needed her attention. "Even good secrets. I don't like them either."

"I once heard a story about an old man," Marciano exclaimed, marching back into the bathroom as the two girls looked on in contempt, "who was given a surprise party for his seventieth birthday, and when he walked through his front door and heard everyone shouting for him, he dropped dead from a heart attack. Now, I may not be turning seventy, but today I turned twenty-one, and all I'm saying is that I have a sensitive heart. Just sayin'."

"I have no doubt that your heart is tremendously sensitive," Natasha began, starting out slow and then letting her voice rise in a fiery explosion, "but sensitive heart or not, give me some space in the stinking bathroom!"

"Stinking? What—did I forget to flush?"

Natasha and Betty simultaneously looked at the toilet with expressions of disgust.

"I can already tell it's going to be a long day," Natasha muttered.

"Well birthday girl, it'll all be worth it," Betty replied, doing her best to comfort her younger sister.

Philadelphia. Whenever Natasha would meet people who were new to Philly, they'd always sum up the city with the same choice of words: cheesesteaks, crime, and angry sports fans. And so what if it wasn't Manhattan? Natasha loved the city she'd grown up in, and she couldn't think of anywhere else she'd rather be. Then again, she also hadn't ever really traveled. But she knew she'd get out one day and see the world. And in the meantime, Philadelphia was a beautiful place to spend her early twenties.

She loved the smell of the Italian Market. She loved walking through the Bella Vista neighborhood early on a Sunday morning in search of a good brunch spot. She loved walking through Society Hill and Old City, admiring the townhomes and the way history seemed to unfold on every single block. She loved all the food carts, the fact that she could bike along the South Street Bridge into West Philly and pick up some of the best ethnic cuisine (or breakfast sandwiches) she'd ever tasted, right from one of many shiny metal vans. And she absolutely loved to walk out of her employer's boutique at lunchtime, straight into the energy of Walnut Street, and stroll up to Rittenhouse Square to watch college students, tourists, businesspeople, and starving artists weave in and out of Philly's most famous park. If she was lucky enough to get a table, and if it wasn't freezing outside, she'd snag outdoor seating at one of the restaurants that surrounded Rittenhouse.

But on that February morning, as freezing temperatures bombarded Philadelphia, Natasha couldn't stop thinking about the *secret* that had gotten Betty all excited. Natasha thought that maybe it had something to do with her and Marciano's birthday. Maybe it was a car? Maybe a new apartment that actually had more than one bathroom? That would really be something. It wasn't like her mom couldn't afford it. She was, after all, the revered and mysterious Maude, owner and lead creative designer at Maude by Maude.

Maude's story was both odd and fascinating. Born in a village in France, Maude was the only girl among seven brothers. She was the quintessential tomboy, determined to dress differently from every girl around her. Maybe it was the influence of her brothers. She'd wrestle in mud pits, forget to bathe for days at a time, and play with toads that she'd find in the backyard. Her family owned a small clothing company, and all day long she'd sew boring clothing for boring women. The same dull patterns and colors. Dreadful long blouses with long sleeves, and skirts that ended near the shins.

Sometimes at the end of her work shift, Maude would stay after all of her family members had gone home, and she'd cut up the clothing to her own liking. She'd make striking skirts that ended high above the knees, and beautiful, sleeveless evening gowns that squeezed her body. She never made anything with sleeves, unless it was a jacket. One day her mom found her hidden collection of clothing and told the family that a floozy must have broken into the factory. The locks were changed and the racy clothing was thrown away, but that didn't stop Maude from designing.

Maude's entire life changed at eighteen years old. Her brothers had all graduated from university and moved away at that point, and were working in and around France (all except for the one troublemaker, Jacque, who ended up in Quebec). Maude's mother and father could no longer handle the strains of their clothing business, and Maude could no longer handle making hideous outfits that hid rather than celebrated women's bodies. As one could guess, arguing ensued. Maude's mother wanted to leave the business behind and move to Austria. She started to routinely dress up like Julie Andrews and sing "My Favorite Things," although she'd change the words to things that she actually liked, such as corsets and Beaujolais.

Maude's father wanted to take their money and move to Rome, and open a little tailor's shop. The only problem was that he didn't know how to make suits. Nor could he speak Italian, or pinpoint Italy on a map. He assumed, however, that being old and French and distinguished-looking, if he were to open a shop in Rome, people would take him seriously.

All through her childhood and teens, Maude had never shed a single tear. Fights with her brothers wouldn't make her cry, nor would skirmishes with neighborhood kids. When her mom threw out all the clothing she'd spent months making, she just picked back up and starting to make new clothes. Her parents claimed that she never even cried as a baby! It was so stunning to them that Maude's father actually wrote a letter about his baby's mysterious disposition and was going to send it to a Parisian newspaper until Maude's mother spilled a glass of red Bordeaux on it. Dad was too lazy to write another letter, and mom was—well—she never even remembered there *being* a letter.

But the day Maude's parents told her that the clothing business was being shut down and that the three of them were moving to Italy, Maude cried. It was the first time in her entire life, and she didn't quite know what was happening to her. She'd seen other people cry, but had no idea what it felt like. And when it finally happened to her, for the very first time in her life she felt the pain of losing something important. Maude's parents were so stunned to see their daughter crying that they decided to do the unthinkable. They gave her the clothing business, and told her she could stay in France. They would move to Rome, and let her manage the clothing company.

Maude was overwhelmed. The factory she'd put years of sweat and labor into was finally her own. She had a staff. She had fabrics. She had sewing machines. She had inspiration.

Maude's parents were too far away to know what kind of clothing she'd be making. This wasn't the age when everything got tagged on Facebook, after all. And so Maude set about designing the types of clothes she liked. She made slim gowns, sleeveless dresses, short skirts, and big, sexy heels. She thought that a woman should never wear pants, and so she disposed of all of them. When her first collection hit the boutiques of Paris, shoppers were shocked. Some women were so appalled that they fainted in the arms of salesgirls. Other women were thrilled to find clothing that fit so perfectly.

It wasn't long before Maude's clothing company took off. Within three years she changed the name to Maude by Maude, jacked up the prices (the girl needed money!), introduced an haute couture collection, and moved to Paris. She opened a boutique on the rue Saint-Honoré. It wasn't long before a major fashion magazine approached her. They wanted to do a massive spread for the Maude by Maude fall/winter 1980 collection. The magazine sent Maude, her clothing, and a team of models back to her hometown to shoot pictures in and around the factory that Maude had practically grown up in. Only there was one problem. When the photographer arrived on set, he only wanted to take pictures of Maude.

And thus Maude met Claude. Claude Genet was a fashion photographer from Paris, who had always dreamed of becoming a designer. The day he arrived in Maude's old village, he fell in love at first sight. Claude told all the models to take a hike (or some French expression along the same line), and he asked that Maude model her own clothing for the shoot. The pictures were groundbreaking, and Maude's fall/winter 1980 collection went on to become the year's most popular couture.

Everyone saw that famous issue, including Maude's parents and brothers. Maude had been sending checks to her parents and brothers to give them a fair share of the business they'd worked in for so many years, but the clothing company was nothing like it used to be. And when Maude's mother saw the steamy clothing that her daughter was designing, there was no amount of Beaujolais in the world to calm her. Maude's parents demanded the return of the company.

A legal battle ensued. There was name-calling, backstabbing, heavy drinking (on Maude's mother's part), and enough lawyers to fill the fourth circle of hell. Finally, Maude had had enough. She shut down the factory, took her clothing, and moved across the pond. And no, it wasn't the English Channel. She moved across the Atlantic Ocean.

Maude hoped that maybe she could open a boutique in Manhattan. After all, she *was* famous. Or quasi famous. But Manhattan rent being sky-high, and her bank account having been depleted by legal troubles, she and Claude settled for Philadelphia. And in 1982 the couple married, and opened storefronts right next door to each other on the popular Walnut Street in Center City. Maude by Maude would produce womenswear, and Claude by Claude would produce menswear.

Five years later the couple would have their first child, a sweet little girl with blonde hair. Maude went through a period of Betty Crocker brownie binges during her pregnancy, and as a result named her daughter after the brand name. She secretly hoped that it would result in Betty being able to cook, since neither she nor Claude could use an oven without setting the house ablaze.

Two years after Betty was born, Maude and Claude adopted twins, and named them Marciano and Natasha. Being the children of fashion designers had its advantages. The three kids always had amazing outfits, although sometimes there would be major confrontations when schoolteachers demanded that the girls wear pants. Maude would never grow a taste for pants. One time she went skiing and wore leg warmers with an elastic skirt that ended just above her boots.

Natasha grew up with that behavior, and she was used to it. In fact, she couldn't imagine belonging to a normal family. And that's the first thing that popped into her mind when she walked through the doors of Maude by Maude, latte in one hand and purse in the other. Her mom was shrieking at a picture in the newspaper. She'd look at it, let out a death-curdling wail, circle around the white oval table that the newspaper was on, and then repeat herself.

"I can't open the store like this! Not today," she exclaimed with her thick French accent. Sometimes Natasha wished that she herself spoke English with a French accent. She would've loved to have grown up in Paris, had her parents managed to keep their boutique back in the early '80s.

"What's the matter?" Natasha asked as she approached Maude. She leaned in and gave her mom a kiss on the cheek, and then turned to check out the newspaper.

Candice Brown Couture was moving into town. The dreaded CBC. Candice's fashion empire had plenty of brands, but Candice's prized possession was her self-named line. It had already taken over the suburbs, and was creeping its way into big cities. And it had a whole lot of pants. Not just pants, but velour tracksuits, massive bell-bottoms, fur-lined suede boots, and maternity tops designed for women who weren't pregnant. If Maude by Maude was a celebration of the female body, then Candice Brown Couture was the total opposite. It was all about comfort. There was nothing sexy about CBC, but many women loved the ultra-relaxed outfits, and so the brand caught on.

"They'll be two blocks away!" Maude cried out, loudly enough that Natasha shot a glance to the door to make sure no one outside heard. The boutique wouldn't be open for another hour. "Soon there will be... a whole city of women walking around in velour sweat suits! I can't, I can't—" Maude looked like she was about to faint, and so Natasha grabbed the newspaper, crumpled it up, and walked it over to the trashcan.

"Don't sweat it," Natasha said. "No pun intended."

"Very funny," Maude wryly replied. "Oh my—happy birthday!"

"Aw, thanks Mom."

"Twenty-one, oh, how time flies. I recall when you designed your very first dress," Maude said, and her blue eyes lit up as she spoke. "You tore down my curtains to do it. I almost choked you with the fabric. But then I looked at it, and—well, after some minor alterations—I said: *My God. This girl has talent.*"

"Thanks Mom," Natasha said, trying to hide her laughter.

"And now look at you. A junior designer," Maude spoke with pride. "One day maybe you will take over YSL or Givenchy. But first there's something we need to discuss."

"Betty said there's a *secret*? A surprise?"

"A very big surprise. Come with me."

Maude by Maude and Claude by Claude were on the first floor of the same downtown office building, and the two fashion houses shared workspace on the second floor. Natasha worked in a little corner space where she had a great view of Walnut Street. Sometimes she'd take a break from sketching a dress and just sit by the window with coffee in hand, watching people as they walked in and out of stores. She shared an office with her sister Betty, who ran IT for the company, and managed the store website. Betty's side of the office was filled with computers, while Natasha's was filled with notepads, pencils, photographs, and fabric swatches. Their jobs had nothing in common, but they liked to keep each other company throughout the day.

Maude led Natasha up the stairs to the second floor, leading her through the workspace. It was mostly empty that morning, save for a couple people who had come in early. Betty was already in the office, typing away at one of the computers. As soon as Betty heard them coming, she sat up and smiled. It was a huge smile, like when someone has a surprise they can't wait to share. Maude casually opened the office door and led Natasha inside.

"So—," Maude began, and she hopped up onto Natasha's desk. She had surprising agility for her age, and maintained an active lifestyle. She also had the best legs that Natasha had seen on anyone over fifty. "How do I begin? Hmm..."

Natasha sat on top of a stool that she used as her office chair. It was an antique, something she'd purchased at an estate sale on the Philadelphia Main Line. Betty rolled up in her wheeled desk chair so that she was right next to her sister.

As Natasha looked into her mom's eyes, she noticed something funny. Maude's expression, which previously had some excitement to it, was growing more worrisome. Maude was never one to struggle with words, and yet she couldn't find the words to explain to Natasha what was on her mind. And it was apparent all over her face. Her lips shifted from one side to the other. Her little almond-shaped eyes would intermittently dart up to the ceiling. She couldn't stop tapping her fingers on her legs.

"Is everything okay?" Natasha asked, only because she was so worried by the way her mom was acting. She already knew that she was adopted, so what else was there to tell her? The announcement of a big gift wouldn't be hard for Maude to blurt out. Did this have to do with her real parents?

"I'm sending you and Betty to New York fashion week, and Rafaela is sending Marciano," Maude hastily told her. Natasha nearly leapt off her stool. She covered her mouth with her hands and blurted out something unintelligible.

"Isn't there something *else* you were going to tell her?" Betty asked Maude, who quickly shook her head.

"No, there's nothing else."

"What about the—"

"There's *nothing else*," Maude said as she leaned forward and dug her lean fingers into Natasha's shoulders. "You leave tomorrow morning. My runway show is scheduled for next Thursday, so you'll be there an entire week. I want you to have a beautiful week in New York City. Enjoy your birthday, have fun, and buy lots and lots of clothing."

"I'm speechless," Natasha said. She'd been secretly hoping that she'd get to go work on the Maude by Maude runway show, but an entire week in New York? She couldn't have asked for a better gift. Well, aside from an apartment or a car, or a Kelly bag. But as far as a realistic gift, New York was perfect.

"There's more. Your father and I are on the verge of opening a boutique in Manhattan. I'm nominated for Best Designer at the Fabbies next week," she said, referring to the major international fashion awards ceremony held every year, the day after New York fashion week in the winter. "If I win, our financial backers will move ahead with plans, and by the summer we'll have a store on Fifth Avenue! If that happens, I may want you girls to help run the boutique. But first you need to spend some time in New York and get a taste for it. See if you'd like to live there someday—maybe someday very soon."

Natasha was so thrilled that she missed the look of disappointment on Betty's face. There was in fact more to tell Natasha, but Maude wasn't ready to do so. At least, not yet.

"Why didn't you tell her?" Betty asked immediately after shutting the door. A weary expression came over Maude's face as she practically fell into her leather office chair.

"Be careful what you think around the office," Maude warned. "Debby in textiles is a telepath. Nosy little thing. Always snooping around for the latest gossip."

"This isn't about Debby. It's about Natasha."

"I couldn't bring myself to tell her," Maude confessed in an exasperated tone. "This whole situation has just been *wearing* on me. I know that I was supposed to tell her when she turned twenty-one, but—oh Betty, the circumstances of how they came to us!"

"Well, is Rafaela telling Marciano today?"

"No, no, I actually brought myself to call her—painful, I know—and told her not to say anything. What does she care?"

"Mom, you need to talk with them," Betty said, and sat down in one of the chairs facing Maude's desk. It was an old iron desk with an aluminum top, the kind used in garment factories from Maude's parents' era. It was a slim desk, with just a single drawer, but she preferred it to the massive desk that her husband used. "You're lucky that their powers work differently than ours. I've known for a long time that I was different."

"Because you didn't hit puberty until your twenties?"

"No! Mom—I—this is not a conversation about puberty," Betty hastily replied, her face flushed. "I'm talking about my powers."

"Natasha and Marciano are different, though," Maude countered. "You know that, my dear. They're not like you and I. Their type of supernatural is almost extinct. The less they know, the better."

"Are you afraid that if Marc and Tash know, it'll somehow lead to Caligae coming after them?"

"Why do you butcher my children's names?"

"It's—we just call each other that at home," Betty replied. "It's a one-syllable thing."

Maude yawned loudly, and raised her eyebrows. "Caligae are not people you play games with. As long as *Natasha* and *Marciano* don't know what they are, then there's less chance Candice Brown and Caligae will find them.

"I still think they deserve to know," Betty replied. She'd been so excited to share this part of her. It was hard to live with a secret that she couldn't even tell her brother and sister. She wanted more than anything for them to feel part of the family.

"Go to fashion week and have fun," Maude said dismissively. "Don't worry so much."

"Caligae headquarters are in New York. If you're so scared about them finding Marc and—*Natasha*—then why are you sending them there?"

Maude offered an ambiguous smile, as she sometimes did.

"I have friends in New York who will look after them."

"I hope so," Betty replied, her expression still full of disappointment.

"Did you hear the news?" Marciano exclaimed, bursting through the front door of Maude by Maude and shouting at no one in particular. Luckily Natasha was in the boutique helping some customers. And luckily those customers recognized Marciano as a sales attendant across the street at Haus of Simone. Marciano had scared quite a few customers in his years.

"Fashion week?" Natasha asked him, a big smile on her face.

"Yes! New York City for an entire week. I want to make a big entrance. Like, run off the train, twirl around with trunks in hand, and burst out into song," Marciano exclaimed as he began to dance around the boutique: "*Up there in the lights I'll be. Go ask the Gershwins or Kaufman and Hart!*"

"Is that from *Annie*?"

One of the old women, a shopper in Maude by Maude who didn't know any better, began to clap for Marciano.

"Please," Natasha told the lady, "don't encourage him."

"Don't rain on my parade," Marciano told her, and stopped in his tracks.

"Are you done working for the day?"

"Nah, doesn't matter that it's my birthday. I asked Rafaela if I could leave early and she told me that I can rest when I'm dead," he told his sister. "But that's okay. Tomorrow we get on the train—"

"Bus."

"The first-class—"

"It's the Chinatown bus," Natasha corrected, to which Marciano's expression slumped into a frown.

"The Chinatown bus?"

"Yep."

"Ah, well. Could be worse," he said, and then contemplated how—if it all—it could be worse. "Actually, I can't think of a worse way to travel to New York. Do you know who we're staying with?"

"Aunt Monique."

"In Tribeca? Okay, It's on. We're going to have so much fun!"

"Yeah, I'm kind of surprised that Mom is letting us stay with her," Natasha remarked. Their aunt wasn't exactly a model supervisory figure. She was an old friend of Maude's who had achieved *aunt* status after becoming the godmother to Betty. Aunt Monique was a savage cougar renowned for competing with girls far younger than she for Manhattan's finest men. Natasha had never seen her with a boyfriend older than twenty-eight.

"Exactly," Marciano replied. "Zero supervision. Just the way I like it."

"Ahem." The familiar voice of Maude could be heard in the back of the boutique. As the figurehead of the Maude by Maude fashion house walked out on the floor of her Walnut Street shop, she was greeted by shoppers the way a queen would be greeted in a royal court.

"Mom, thank you so—"

"Ah!" Maude said, holding up one finger to silence her son. "Birthday boy, you didn't *really* think I'd let you stay with Aunt Monique without proper supervision?"

"Of course not," Marciano cautiously replied. "Wait, what did you do?"

As soon as the words left his mouth, the front doors of the boutique opened, and a gush of cold wind poured into the room. Natasha was the first to look, followed by Marciano, who methodically turned on one heel and glanced over his right shoulder in fear. Standing in the doorway was a familiar face. A huge face for that matter, attached to a huge body. Towering in front of the boutique was Enya Onikova, a six foot two Russian bodyguard who worked for Maude and Claude as the sole security guard for both stores. She was the only person in Maude's employ who was allowed to wear pants, and since she had a thing for shiny tracksuits, Maude wasn't going to tell her any differently.

Enya shut both of the doors and walked into the boutique like a hired thug ready to stir up trouble. She crossed her arms as soon as she reached Marciano, and the latter trembled in fear. Enya towered over him. She had a long, blonde ponytail big enough to strangle another human. Apparently she'd done so once or twice in the past.

On that cold, windy day in early February, Enya Onikova was dressed in a gold tracksuit with a fur collar that wrapped around her neck. She wore a pair of blue wellies that she claimed were steel-toed. No one cared to find out for sure if they really were.

"I'm coming with you," Enya said in her deep, Russian accent. The message sent chills down Marciano's spine. Natasha wasn't exempt from the fear either. A week of uninhibited fun in New York City was beginning to look like a week of narrow-eyed supervision.

"Uh ... Mom, can we talk in private?" Marciano asked, but Maude immediately shook her head.

"Enya will accompany you, and that's final," she told her son. "She's just there to keep you safe. I still expect you to have fun."

Marciano slowly turned his head—a wide frown spread across his face—and looked at Enya, who had her arms folded and her chin up.

"Somehow I don't see how that'll be possible."

"Listen birthday boy, everything will be fine," Maude said as she walked toward her son in order to embrace him. She put her hands on his arms, and then leaned in to give him a kiss on each cheek. "You, Betty, Natasha, and Enya."

"How is Enya going to fit on the Chinatown bus?" he asked.

"I guess that means ... you'll have to take the train," Maude replied with a little smile. Instantly Marciano's face lit up in excitement.

Chapter Two

When Natasha, Marciano, Betty, and Enya boarded the train from Philadelphia to New York, it felt like the city of nearly nine million people was waiting for them. It was as if all five boroughs of NYC were on pause in anticipation of their arrival. But of course, New York stops for no one, and on that particular Thursday morning, something foul was brewing on Fifth Avenue.

As soon as Candice Brown's Rolls-Royce pulled up in front of the Candice Brown Couture store at the corner of 57th and Park Ave, the boutique's security guards rushed to open the door for her. It was especially windy in Manhattan that morning, which prompted Candice to walk a little faster than usual. She was dressed in a pink velour tracksuit produced by her namesake couture brand, and she was flanked by her usual cronies: Bridgette #2, a redhead with a thing for wearing spring dresses in the middle of winter, and Olympia, an old vampire who had been in Candice's employ longer than the United States had been a country. As soon as the salespeople noticed the unsavory trio they quickly averted their eyes. They knew she wasn't there to shop.

Candice took one final breath of crisp New York City air before she marched into her Fifth Avenue flagship store. She didn't acknowledge the security guards who braved the cold weather to hold the doors open; rather, she just kept walking, making her way toward a hallway behind the sales counter.

One of the sales associates manning the counter nearly tripped in a hasty attempt to get out of the fashion mogul's way. The last sales associate who got in Candice's way found herself relocated to a clearance outlet in northern Alabama that sold nothing but plus-sized sweatpants.

Candice Brown walked smoothly through the open doorway and continued down a narrow hallway until she came to a closet full of luggage tags, shoelaces, and empty cardboard boxes. Once she and her cronies were inside, she pulled down on a black luggage tag that was hanging from a metal pole, and instantly the whole room began to descend into the ground.

They were in an elevator. An elevator that had been manufactured to look like a regular closet. It was a clever little creation, and one that was only reserved for the elite members of Caligae. After all, a respectable company such as Candice Brown Couture couldn't have people walking in and out of its boutique all the time through secret back doors.

When the elevator arrived at its destination, Candice Brown inhaled the damp, thin air of Caligae's North American headquarters. The labyrinthine network of stone passages, high stalagmite ceilings, and cracked marble floors had sprung with gusto into the twenty-first century. It almost looked like someone had set up rows of computers within an ancient pyramid. The world's oldest secret society had only been in New York for a little over 150 years, and although its headquarters on the American continent didn't resemble the classical elegance of the Paris office or the dynastic tomblike tranquility of the Hong Kong office, it was successful at being very American. Every day, technology swept through headquarters and slowly replaced the old standards, leaving a hybrid workplace that meshed the old with the new in an uncompromising pursuit of innovation.

The tunnels, dark passageways, and high-security conference rooms within the subterranean workplace were buzzing with anxiety. It was the start of fashion week, and the entire office was brewing with a combination of excitement and hysteria. Fashion week for Caligae was like Christmas season for retailers. There was so much that could go wrong, and it seemed like there were so few people to perform the secret society's main task: making sure that supernatural beings didn't bother humans.

There was a slim woman with a clipboard waiting to greet Candice and her entourage as soon as they stepped off the elevator.

"Hello Miss Brown," was all she said, and she didn't expect a response. Nor did she get one. Candice knew the way to the office of Isabelle the Purple. They were sisters, after all. And she didn't need some scrawny personal assistant to give her a guided tour.

Candice rudely stepped in front of the young woman with the clipboard and marched through the offices in her fur-lined suede boots. The entire floor knew better than to stare at her. They kept on doing whatever it was they were doing, pretending she wasn't in their presence.

Candice's sister's office was located down a long, winding hallway, in a dark corner that was purposely designed to intimidate. Anyone who wanted to visit Isabelle's office would have to walk through what seemed like a dark labyrinth. There was nothing warm about it, and numerous people had at one time or another turned around midway while en route to her office. Isabelle the Purple wasn't a cruel leader, but her cold personality made subordinates uncomfortable.

The walk to Isabelle's office didn't bother Candice Brown. To her, there was nothing intimidating about her younger sister. She'd been the one to place Isabelle in command of the New York office. She'd been the one to keep her there amid all the efforts to replace her. Candice Brown attributed her younger sister's success to herself. And that's the kind of pompousness that she gave off as she opened the door to Isabelle's office, as if the very room was her own.

"My dear sister," Isabelle said, turning from her computer to face Candice. The latter waved her hand at Bridgette #2 and Olympia, motioning for them to stand guard outside the door.

"What's this nonsense about an attack in Central Park?" Candice asked her, wasting no time. Her face began to get as pink as her tracksuit.

"A werewolf that we couldn't control—"

"That you *couldn't control*?"

"Yes! It's like a switch flipped. This stuff happens, Candice," Isabelle said, nearly cowering in her seat as she tried to defend herself against her older sister. "Werewolves are volatile creatures, you know that. One minute you're discussing geopolitics and the next they're taking a leak in your kitchen sink. This one exploded, went on a little killing spree, and now everything's fine. I promise, it's covered up."

"Covered up to New York, yes, but not to supernaturals," Candice exclaimed, angrily waving a finger at a newspaper on top of Isabelle's desk. The front cover showed a picture of the crime scene, and the article criticized Caligae for not preventing the attack.

"The press! You know how they are."

"I know how they are? Caligae controls the goddamn press! And you can't even stop *them* from printing negative material about you. Let alone a werewolf in the park. Sometimes I think it was wrong of me to give you such sweeping control of an organization that is clearly too much for you to handle. Maybe if you were like Mom—"

Candice sighed, and used the opportunity to meander around the dimly lit office. She never liked that office. The entire floor was glass, and sat atop an enormous fish tank. Candice couldn't help but worry that someday she'd just fall right through, into the sea of colorful fish that swarmed underneath her feet. Candice wasn't a petite girl, after all. In fact, she guessed the fish were probably more scared of her than she was of crashing into their little home.

"The press are just getting antsy about fashion week and the Fabbies," Isabelle said in her own defense. "Come later today, they won't be writing anything about Caligae."

"Until next Friday," Candice said, and formed a devilish smile as she looked down at her feet, where yellow fish were piling up around her boots.

"I know you want to talk about the Fabbies, but I'm not ready to—"

"Stop being a big baby," Candice remarked, looking her sister square in the eye. "Are you still game with the plan?"

It was the plot for which Candice had waited four hundred years. For centuries she and her sister had managed Caligae, biding their time for a chance to break free from the great curse. Candice Brown believed that if she could spark a massive, global investigation deep into the fashion industry, then the world would find out the truth behind every fad from flannel shirts to Birkenstocks. And there was no better time to do it. They were living in the age of television, of Internet, of explosive streaming videos that could garner millions of hits in a matter of days. All that Candice needed to do was manufacture an assassination with so much media exposure that it couldn't possibly be contained.

"It's a loophole," Candice said, and quickly pointed an index finger toward the ceiling. *Loophole* had become her favorite word in recent weeks. "The curse says that we can't reveal ourselves to humans, right? But if we stage an event that garners an extreme amount of global attention, and everyone finds out about us on their own, then we've identified a loophole in the curse. Supernaturals will be free to do whatever they want, and the curse will be yesterday's news."

"This could have awful consequences," Isabelle told her sister, although she knew Candice wouldn't care about her opinion. It was like talking to a brick wall.

Isabelle was in for tough times ahead. Even though she was director of Caligae's North American operations, the overall organization had more loyalty to its founding roots than to her. Caligae was originally created to enforce the great curse, back when supernatural beings were worried that the disobedience of a few could lead to the deaths of many. Caligae kept tabs on all supernaturals. Those who bothered humans were jailed or executed. If a werewolf went on a killing spree, or a telepath started using his abilities to rack up money in a gambling den, then the organization would quickly intervene.

It was said that Mother—the first of all supernatural beings—chose the fashion industry for her great curse because it was the most harmless trade in existence. People needed to wear clothes, and so if supernaturals were tasked with designing, manufacturing, and selling clothing, they'd be doing something good for society. Mother believed that her offspring should use their powers to help rather than to disrupt human society. This was the credo of most members of Caligae, and nearly all were deathly afraid of the curse. There were hundreds of rumors, passed down from generation to generation, of those who tried to separate themselves from the fashion industry in search of a more destructive career path, and disappeared forever. Isabelle had heard these stories as a little girl, and hundreds of years later they still stuck with her.

"Curse, shmurse," Candice replied, waving her hand as if to instantly dismiss her sister's concerns. "There has never been a better time than now. Witches aren't being hung in Salem anymore, sis. People love vampires. They love supernaturals. Every other show on TV has some character with fangs. Humans *want* us to be real. And fashion is merely... *holding us back.*"

"Holding you back from what? You don't do anything to begin with."

"That's not true," Candice argued. "Being an A-list celebrity is very difficult."

"You have to try to understand my point," Isabelle calmly said after taking a deep breath. "This whole thing is a massive risk. You want to kill the winner of Best Designer and hope it inadvertently breaks the curse. But we're screwing with a two-thousand-year-old law that could wipe us all out. I don't see any gain from humans knowing who we are."

"Wah wah wah," Candice said, mimicking the sound of her sister's voice, meanwhile shaking her fists in front of her eyes to imitate crying. "You've become weak! *We've* become weak. Supernaturals are spineless. They're too busy making sequin dresses and worrying about fashion fads. Zombies don't know life outside an assembly line. They should be terrorizing cities, and instead they're making polyester socks in Indonesia. Why doesn't anyone else realize our potential beyond making clothing?"

"Because most people are happy about the way things are."

"*Happy*," Candice muttered, as if she loathed the very word. "Do you remember the great War of the Colors? Need I remind you of how supernaturals took to arms to decide the fate of Caligae? It was our finest hour. The only war that you'll never find in a history book. Queen Elizabeth was on the throne, and Europe was changing like nothing we'd ever seen before. Do you remember what you were like, little sis? You were a force to be reckoned with. You raised an undead army from the ground and fought in magnificent battles that are still whispered of among supernaturals to this very day."

"That was over four hundred years ago," Isabelle remarked. She wasn't fazed by Candice's opulent retelling of their glory days. However, she wasn't going to pursue an argument with her older sister. She'd lived for so long with the great curse that it seemed irreversible to her. In fact, she couldn't imagine a world without the great curse. It would be as if the entire North American continent sunk into the ocean. She simply couldn't comprehend what it would be like.

"At least you haven't aged much," Candice replied, and sighed in a rare moment of vulnerability. "Sometimes I forget what real skin feels like, and then I shake someone's hand, or touch someone's arm, and each time there's this moment of: *What am I*?"

Isabelle leaned forward on her desk and stared at her sister with sympathy. But just when she was about to offer kind, supportive words, Candice affixed large pink sunglasses over her eyes.

"Anyway," Candice muttered, quickly changing the subject, "the fashion show for Brown Label starts in half an hour. I can't look like a wreck in Bryant Park."

Candice let out a dramatically long sigh, and allowed her eyes to fall down upon the glass floor.

"I think you need an octopus," she remarked. "One that can read minds, or guess your body fat index."

"I don't need an octopus," Isabelle calmly told her sister. "Why do I need an octopus? You're on the verge of bringing down Caligae come next Friday. I won't even have an office for very long."

"If there's anything worse than attachment to a *thing*, it's attachment to an organization."

"Well I happen to like this organization," Isabelle replied. She rested her palms on her wooden desk, and for a moment had a strange feeling that everything around her was very finite. Having been around for so long, and in the same job for so many years, it wasn't often that she thought about mortality.

"By the way, I'm going to start coming into the office every day," Candice said, quickly and candidly dropping a bomb that Isabelle wasn't prepared to hear. "Starting tomorrow."

"You're kidding me," Isabelle said, her jaw dropping. "You haven't kept an office here in—I can't even remember the last time."

"It's been about seventy years, but I know I have an office somewhere around here. I'll be in tomorrow morning."

"So you're actually going to come in and work?"

"What, is it so shocking?" Candice replied. "Now that things are about to get crazy, I feel that as the most important supernatural in the world, I should be leading my sheep into this new world of indiscretion."

Isabelle bit her lower lip as she stared at her sister. Candice never took any part in the management of Caligae. In fact, Candice never took part in anything requiring work. Even her empire of fashion brands was managed by other people. Candice Brown had been living the high life for a long time, living in conspicuous wealth and luxury amid the occasional evil plot to destroy either the two-thousand-year-old curse, or all of mankind.

"Anyway, I'm off to the Brown Label fashion show," Candice muttered.

"Is Mauria walking?"

"Yes, she'll be modeling."

"You should feel lucky to have such a beautiful daughter!"

"Meh," Candice remarked, and Isabelle could tell she was rolling her eyes behind those bulky sunglasses that took up the entire upper half of her face. "Talk soon."

"Tell my niece I said hello," Isabelle called out, but Candice was already on her way out the door.

Marciano and the girls didn't have enough time to stop at their Aunt Monique's condo in Tribeca. They had a runway show to catch. And so with bags in hand, the four fashioned-obsessed (or three fashion-obsessed, plus one fashion-oblivious) Philadelphians walked as fast as they could from New York Penn Station to Bryant Park.

Winter wasn't slowing down Manhattan, and the city seemed alive as ever. Natasha was awestruck by the fashion. She didn't care about the skyscrapers that towered above her, or the smell of food from the steel carts on every block, or the way taxi cabs zoomed between and around each other. She just wanted to watch the people, what they chose to wear, and the way they wore it. And every once in a while she'd feel compelled to exhale in excitement when some woman would walk by in amazing clothing, like a slim-fitting camel-colored cashmere trench, or a sable fur winter hat sitting above straight brunette hair. And the shoes! Anytime a woman would pick up her legs to reveal that signature Louboutin red, Natasha would swoon.

There was something about Manhattan that just made it fun to dress up. Natasha hoped it wasn't just a tourist thing, that maybe the magic wears off once you live there long enough. But for her it was still fun. It was still exciting to arrive at Penn Station in a hot outfit, something that would prompt an *mm-hmm* of approval from other women. She didn't care if her shoes were uncomfortable to walk in. This was Manhattan! This was fashion week.

"Were two suitcases of shoes necessary?" Betty asked as she struggled to keep up with the group.

"Yes," Natasha and Marciano simultaneously replied.

Enya was carrying the bulk of the bags, and it didn't seem to faze her. On their way to the train station in Philadelphia she had told them that in her homeland she'd won a bench-pressing competition. Since her village was too poor to afford weights, they'd bench press wild animals. She'd won after pumping out ten presses on an Antarctic fur seal.

"Enya, can you help me out here?" Betty asked as she struggled with the two suitcases full of shoes. Enya shot back a narrow-eyed look, and then laughed.

"I eat luggage for breakfast," she remarked, and continued to walk without giving Betty any assistance.

"Uh—" Betty was open-mouthed, unable to produce a reply.

"We're almost there," Marciano shouted back. "I can already see the tents."

"I wonder what celebrities will be here," Natasha excitedly blurted out. "There are always celebrities at these things, right?"

"I'm sure Candice Brown will be there," Marciano replied. "It's her brand. You'd think she'd show up."

"That would be awesome. The queen of plastic surgery."

"I actually like Brown Label," Marciano remarked, to the surprise of Natasha and Betty. "They have nice sweaters. Overpriced, for sure. I think Candice thinks she's Marc Jacobs."

"She wishes," Betty said. She was practically dragging the suitcases across the pavement. "All I want to do is—sit—down."

Bryant Park looked like a zoo on the kickoff of fashion week. The park was filled with people who had braved the cold weather to come out and see America's top designers show their stuff. The weeklong event would be especially stressful on the designers because of the awards ceremony scheduled for the day after fashion week ended. That Friday night was the Fabulous Fashion Awards, a live, televised event in Central Park where awards would be given to the top members of the industry. Designers, models, photographers, and creative types nervously awaited the results of the year's most important celebration of excellence.

When the group of four arrived at their seats inside a large tent erected in the park, they breathed a collective sigh of relief. Since they were with the Maude by Maude camp, they were able to get backstage and store their bags in a safe place. There wasn't any room for bags in the sitting area, as the chairs were packed tightly together.

"You think everyone in here is like, high society?" Marciano whispered to his sisters. "Maybe there's a producer in here. I want to get cast in a reality TV show."

"Marc—maybe if you compiled your thoughts into single, distinct, clear sentences, and said them one at a time, I would know how to respond," Natasha told her twin brother.

"Don't hate me cause you ain't me," her brother defensively said. "Hey, look at that bougie down in the first row with the hat. I should've worn a hat. You know, my boss is about to release a line of hats inspired by what people's heads would look like after years of exposure to radioactive—"

"Oh my God, Marc—," Natasha interjected. "Look—front row."

"Oh wow," Betty remarked in an excited but calmer tone.

"Is that Candice Brown?" Marciano giddily whispered, and pointed in the direction of the unmistakable fashion figurehead.

Candice Brown was indeed unmistakable. Dressed in her trademark pink velour tracksuit with coffee-colored suede boots, the ultra-curvy queen of new age couture was flanked by an entourage of assistants and journalists as she walked toward her seat in the front row. Candice was the poster child of plastic surgery. She'd had so many facelifts, lip injections, and implants that people close to her whispered that she'd lost her humanity. There was little of Candice Brown's body and personality that was real or authentic. Her teeth had been replaced. Her nose had been redone numerous times. Even her hair was fake. She was the envy of bald men everywhere.

Candice Brown lived a fabulous lifestyle. She liked to surround herself with beautiful people and things. Stories of her wild partying were constantly on the gossip columns, and a young actress could get instant credibility if a picture turned up of her and Candice sitting together at the same L.A. nightclub.

The Candice Brown fashion empire reached the entire world, from suburban soccer moms to Japanese teenage girls. Her brands were all about comfort and quality. The fabrics were soft, the stitching wasn't too complicated, and the sizes were generous. Her maternity line, Baby Brown, was all the rage in Asia. She even had a successful clothing line for dogs.

"You think her daughter will be walking?" Betty asked, referring to Mauria Brown, the charmed only child of Candice. She was a stunning blonde supermodel born into wealth and prestige, who at twenty-one years old was already a fashion veteran. Candice only had one child from a short-lived marriage to her seventh (by official estimates) husband. She went on record as saying that the pregnancy was an "accident." The gossip columns loved to speculate about the relationship between Mauria and her ill-tempered mother. People said that Candice was jealous of her daughter's beauty, as she bore absolutely no resemblance to her mother. The two were rarely photographed together, yet Mauria still modeled in ad campaigns for Brown Label and Candice Brown Couture. She had been nominated for Best Supermodel at the Fabbies.

"I hope so," Natasha replied. "She's *so* pretty. Every time I see one of her spreads I wish I looked like her."

Natasha wasn't bad looking by any means, but she wasn't quite Mauria Brown. Natasha was a little too short to be a model, standing at five foot eight. She had curly brown hair that she dyed constantly, and she ate healthy so that her physique stayed slim enough to fit into her favorite designers. Natasha and Marciano shared the same pale green eyes, and the same long nose that made them look right at home in Philly's Italian Market. Marciano was one inch taller than her, so he too fell short of the height requirements for modeling, but he was far more into the design side of the industry. Still, he'd get a rush when he put on a pair of D&G boots with a 1¼-inch heel, and felt (almost) tall enough to walk the runway in New York.

The fashion show was about to commence. There was a slight confrontation between Candice Brown and Karl Lagerfeld, who had accidentally chosen to wear the same pair of sunglasses to the runway show, but the matter was quickly resolved after Candice stole a pair of shades off Tom Ford's face.

Candice Brown had hired a string orchestra to set the mood for the event, and as blue lights sprang up along the runway, the sound of violins filled the tent with an upbeat but haunting melody. It sounded like the chase scene in a horror movie, which might have been fitting for

Brown Label, since most fashion insiders found the line to be slightly horrific. Attendees were quiet as models began to walk down the runway to the sound of the violins. Natasha wondered if they got to keep the clothing they were wearing.

No one could see Candice Brown's expression, since her gigantic sunglasses covered her eyes. Her lips were pursed, and her hands were wrapped around a bag of sourdough pretzels. Candice was notorious for eating while watching runway shows, and one could tell her appreciation of the couture by how quickly she ate. Only once did she stop eating, and that was for Alexander McQueen's Highland Rape collection. It was the only time that fashion seemed to please Candice more than food.

After the fourth model, Mauria Brown walked out onto the runway. Everyone held their breath as one of the greatest models of their time moved with grace and sophistication in a pair of white heels. There was a new quietness inside the tent that acted as a sound in and of itself. Some people had come to the show just to see Mauria. She was one of those people who could look beautiful wearing a trash bag. The sloppy taupe dress that hung off her shoulders looked fabulous on her body, and she worked it for the crowd.

Natasha wanted to clap for her. She wanted to give Mauria a standing ovation. She was just perfect! The graceful way she moved was like a dolphin jumping in and out of the water. And just as Natasha interlocked her own hands to prevent herself from applauding, the unthinkable happened. Mauria tripped.

"Oh—my—" The words stumbled out of Natasha's mouth as the runway princess fell down onto her hands and knees, the taupe dress dragging across the floor. "Did you see that?" she asked Betty, tapping her sister on the leg.

"Um—Natasha—," Marciano said, his voice rising above a whisper. First Natasha turned to Betty, and then to Enya, but the girls appeared frozen in time. It was strange enough that Natasha's eyes darted around the tent. The entire crowd looked like a clever display at a wax museum. It was as if time had stopped. Even one of the models who had preceded Mauria on the runway was frozen in her trek backstage.

"What's going on?" she whispered to Marciano, who grew as nervous as she was. On the runway, Mauria was standing up and dusting herself off. The supermodel shook her dress so that it looked natural again, and pulled her hair off of her face. And that's when Candice saw them. Natasha and Candice Brown made eye contact, or at least she assumed they were making eye contact, since Candice's eyes were covered by pink sunglasses. But she saw Candice's head turn from her to Marciano, and then back again. And within an instant the entire tent was back to normal. The violins were playing again, and Mauria was moving down the runway.

"Did you see that?" Natasha whispered to Betty.

"See what?"

Marciano, who was seated on the other side of Betty, turned his head and looked at Natasha, but she was afraid to look back at him. Candice Brown was still watching them, her hands furiously submerged in the bag of pretzels.

"What happened in there?" Natasha whispered in Marciano's ear as soon as they were backstage after the show. While Betty was shyly trying to sneak peeks at famous designers and celebrities, Natasha stood by her brother and Enya with their collection of luggage. "I'm not crazy, am I?"

"Well, you *are* crazy, but that's another story. I saw the same thing," he remarked. "It's like time just—stopped."

"The only people I saw moving were Mauria and Candice. We can't be hallucinating if we both saw the same thing."

"There must be an explanation," Marciano told her, although he had no idea what that explanation could be. He'd never experienced anything like that.

"Guys, Christian Siriano is next," Betty called to them. "We have to stay."

"I think we should go to Aunt Monique's," Natasha said, her voice shaking with nervousness. Her heart was pounding in her chest.

"Are you crazy?" Betty replied. "Wait—am I crazy? Usually you're the one forcing me to go to these things."

Betty proceeded to say a bunch of things—none of which Natasha heard—in protest to leaving Bryant Park. Something else had caught Natasha's attention. Candice Brown was suddenly backstage, standing beside another person: a pretty redhead wearing a white floral dress more appropriate for spring than winter. As Natasha stared ahead at them, she saw Candice distinctly point in her direction. The eyes of the redhead followed Candice's finger.

"We've gotta go," Natasha said, barely loud enough for her companions to hear.

"Huh?" Betty said.

"Enya, grab her. We're leaving."

"But—"

Enya grabbed Betty with one arm and three bags with the other, and the four of them proceeded to hurry out of the backstage area. They needed to get to Tribeca as soon as possible.

Natasha, Betty, Marciano, and Enya hurried to the Bryant Park subway station. Natasha figured that they could hop on the orange line and just start going south. Four people plus eight people's worth of luggage was too much for just one taxi, and two cabs to Tribeca was more than they were willing to pay for. If Natasha had thought that her life was in danger, she'd have swallowed her frugality and gotten two cabs. All she wanted to do was get away from the scene, and have time to collect her thoughts. Time had literally stopped in front of them during the fashion show.

Natasha knew something was wrong the moment they got down to the subway platform and realized no one was around them. It was Thursday afternoon in one of the busiest parts of Manhattan, and not a single person nearby. There was no one waiting for trains, no homeless people sitting on the ground to escape the February cold; the entire station was barren.

Before the group of four could say anything, they heard the loud thump of boots on the stairwell leading down to the platform. Wind flew down the tunnel, shaking against the New York University sign that hung overhead. They dropped their bags and waited as long, slender white legs in brown alligator high-heeled boots emerged on the stairs, followed by the white floral-patterned dress that Natasha had seen earlier. It was the redhead who had been talking to Candice, and her pale face looked creepy in the dim lighting of the underground.

"Isn't she cold in that—," Betty began to say, but Natasha quickly hushed her. As soon as the redhead's heels touched the platform, she folded her arms and stared at the four young travelers.

"There's a train coming in four minutes," the redhead said, her arms still crossed in front of her. "Some of you may catch it, but it's unlikely that all four will. So that begs the unfortunate question: who dies first?"

Before any of them had time to react, the redhead sprang into action, racing forward and leaping off of one foot. Betty nearly toppled over the benches in the middle of the platform, but Enya charged forward. She caught the redhead's jump kick with one hand, and threw the girl backward. The redhead collided with the stairs in a loud thump that sounded like a hammer coming down upon concrete, yet within seconds she was back up, ready for more. Enya charged again, this time swinging her arms out to grab the redhead, but the latter ducked and punched the Russian bodyguard in the chest. Enya toppled backward, and just as her guard was down, the redhead kicked her in the side of the head. Enya fell to the ground, dangerously close to the edge of the platform.

Natasha wanted to help, but she had no idea how to fight. She'd never fought anyone before, nor had she witnessed a fight in real life. Marciano had already opened one of the suitcases full of shoes and was wielding a single wooden-heeled oxford as if it were a battle axe.

"Don't make me throw this at you! It's DKNY, but I'll part with it if I have to," he cried out.

"You two really don't know how to fight, do you?" the redhead taunted them, walking slowly past Enya's fallen body.

"Who are you?" Natasha asked. She stood in front of Betty and Marciano, and did her best to stand upright, but she was terrified.

"Who are *you*?" the redhead countered. "When Mauria froze time, why didn't it affect you?"

"What's she talking about?" Betty asked, frantically turning to face her twin siblings.

"I don't know!" Natasha answered. "I don't know why it didn't affect us. I don't even know what happened."

"*What* didn't affect you?" Betty asked her sister. It was rare for her to lose her cool or raise her voice, but her fears about coming to New York had come to fruition. Candice Brown had found her brother and sister.

"If you let us go, we won't tell anyone," Marciano promised, but it was clear that this girl wasn't going to let them go. The redhead looked both bloodthirsty and intrigued. If she was able to dispose of Enya with what seemed like such little effort, then Betty and the twins didn't stand a chance. They nervously watched and waited as the redhead stood there, observing them as one might look upon an endangered race.

"Are you descendants of the Thirteen?"

"I can't even name five family members, let alone thirteen," Marciano candidly answered.

"The who?" Natasha asked. She turned to Betty, who didn't look as shocked as she was by the question. Instead, Betty's face looked overwhelmed by a sad conclusion. And at that very moment, Natasha knew that Betty had kept a secret from her. "What's she talking about? Betty, what's she talking about?"

Before Betty had time to answer, Enya was back on her feet. She rammed into the redhead with her right shoulder, sending the girl flying face-first into the platform bench. Her head literally burst through the wood, sending splinters into the air. The scene made Natasha nearly jump out of her pumps. This was violence unlike anything she'd ever seen before.

As Enya approached the redhead's fallen body, a pale foot swung out and kicked the Russian in the chin. Enya stumbled backward, her long ponytail swaying as wind swept through the station. The redhead pulled her head out of the wood and wrapped her arms around the bench. As she pulled upward, she ripped the bench from its foundation, hoisting it in the air with both hands.

Enya braced herself as the redhead twirled her body once. When the latter let go of the bench, it flew through the air toward Enya. The Russian ducked the bench, but didn't have enough time to block the redhead's savage charge. When the redhead's body collided with her, Enya felt like she'd been hit by a car. She flew toward the edge of the platform, and although she tried to hang on, her body dropped onto the tracks.

The noise of the approaching train could be heard in the distance. Natasha clutched her own chest as her eyes darted back and forth between the redhead and Enya's limp body.

"You want to join her?" the redhead asked Natasha, much too calmly for a question with such dire implications.

"That's it!" Marciano hollered, and threw his DKNY oxford at the redhead, but she casually moved her head to the side, ducking the shoe.

"I might be able to stop the train," Betty said. "Just distract her."

"You're going to jump in there?" Natasha cried out.

"No!" Betty shouted without offering an explanation. She ran to the edge of the platform and sprinted in the direction of the oncoming train. Enya was still working on standing up, her legs sprawled out across the tracks.

The redhead ignored Betty and Enya, and headed for Natasha. The latter stood her ground, but her legs were trembling in fear. When the redhead got close enough, Natasha threw a punch. At least, it was what she thought a punch should be. It could have been a panicked slap. She was surprised that the weak punch even landed on the redhead's cheek, but once it did, she quickly regretted it.

"Ahh!" Natasha hollered, pulling back her hand in pain. It was as if she had punched a brick wall. The redhead let out a single laugh, and then pushed Natasha backward, causing her to topple over one of the bags of luggage.

Marciano was filled with rage when he saw what the redhead had done to his sister. He'd never witnessed anyone push his sister before, and it angered him so much that he grabbed the other black oxford and wielded it in the air. He gripped the shoe so hard that he felt like he could crush the sole, and after pulling his arm back, he swung forward and released it into the air.

The shoe flew toward its target, and Marciano's face lit up in surprise when he saw that the oxford was glowing. It was just a subtle glow, but to his amazement there was a white aura surrounding the object. The shoe collided with the redhead's chest in a blast of light, and the girl went flying backward, her body smashing into the stairs again. Natasha flung her head in amazement, staring at her brother with the same shock that was spread across his face.

The train was close. The noise of the oncoming vehicle filled the empty subway station, sending strong winds pouring through the tunnels that connected one station to the next. Betty was on the edge of the platform, holding her left hand in the air, palm facing the train, and using her right hand to motion toward Enya.

"Hurry!" she called to Enya. As the train grew near, Betty closed her eyes. Natasha and Marciano ran to the edge of the platform. They reached their hands down and grabbed onto Enya, but she was so heavy that even with all their strength they couldn't pull her up.

A loud noise shook the station. The train was screeching to a halt. Natasha turned her head and watched her older sister, whose whole body was shaking. Both of Betty's arms were flung out in the direction of the train, her palms facing outward. She thrust her arms forward, and just as she did so the train screeched to a halt short of the platform, and far enough away so that Enya had time to escape the tracks.

Natasha grabbed her older sister just as Marciano helped Enya back onto her feet.

"Watch out!" Marciano called. The redhead was also back on her feet, and the front of her floral-patterned dress was scorched. The pretentious smile had disappeared in place of a fuming expression of rage. The redhead wanted blood.

She charged at Enya, and the latter stuck her fist out. She was ready for the next round. Even though the redhead was much stronger, Enya wasn't about to get knocked onto the tracks again. But just before Enya and the redhead collided, the station went black. Pitch-black. Natasha heard the redhead scream, and when the lights went back on she saw the girl's body lying unconscious on the floor. Sparks flew from her mouth, the way a telephone pole would spark if a tree fell on its wires.

Standing above the redhead's body was someone new—someone who had appeared out of nowhere in a matter of seconds. She was an older woman, with short, wavy gray hair, and a black jacket covering a white blouse. She was panting, and her aged face looked exhausted, as if she'd just run miles to get there. The most unsettling thing about her, however, was that her eyes were pale white, with no retina to be seen. She appeared to be blind, and yet there she was, standing before them, staring in their direction.

"Come with me, immediately," the old woman said, speaking slowly and amid heavy breathing. She hurried to the edge of the platform opposite where the train had come, gliding through the air with the grace of an Olympic gymnast. "Take the stairs," she called out. "There's a passageway."

"What about our bags?" Natasha called out to her.

"Take what you can, but we must hurry," the woman shouted back. "What are you waiting for? If more people come, I won't be able to save you."

She'd said enough. The four of them grabbed whatever they could manage, and depressingly said goodbye to whatever bags of clothes they couldn't take. They weren't about to object to this woman who had just saved their lives. But they weren't about to let their guard down either.

Chapter Three

"AM I THE ONLY ONE WHO IS TERRIFIED OF rats?" Marciano asked with a cringe on his face. Each time he'd feel something brush past his skinny jeans he'd squirm, and break out into a series of noises that sounded like a talentless singer trying to imitate Christina Aguilera.

"I'm too terrified to be terrified," Natasha replied. She didn't bother to question if her words made any sentence. What she really meant was that she was more terrified of what had happened back in the subway station. Rats, sewage, foul smells, and underground homeless shantytowns couldn't faze her anymore.

"Enya, do something about these—ah!" Marciano squealed as two furry creatures ran by his right leg.

"Rats? Ha. I eat rats for breakfast."

"Really, Enya? That's kind of gross. You're gonna get like—the bubonic plague, or something," Marciano told her, but the Russian didn't nudge.

"Strong immune system," she firmly replied.

"It's not much farther! Hurry!" the old woman called back to them. Betty was walking alongside the woman, whereas Enya and the twins were trailing them. The latter group had the disadvantage of carrying bags of luggage that they were unwilling to abandon.

"I hope wherever we're going doesn't look and smell like this," Marciano whispered. "And isn't there some famous quote about the blind leading the blind?"

"I heard that," the old woman called back to them.

"Not trying to be rude—," Marciano remarked, and raised his eyebrows. "I can barely see down here as it is. How can someone who can't see get us through the tunnel?"

"Do you have to talk nonstop?" Natasha asked her twin brother.

"Yes. Yes, I do. Talking helps me deal with getting assaulted by a crazy redhead who wears a spring dress in winter!" he shot back. "When I talk nonstop, I don't have to process these things."

Up ahead, the old woman stopped in front of a rusty ladder that led up to the ceiling. She paused, and held out her hand so that tiny beams of light passed over her pale skin. She quickly recalled her arm, and then turned her head to face her companions.

"We need to go up there," the old woman told them. She was finally speaking in her normal voice, without all the panting and heavy breathing that had accompanied her in the subway station. She spoke with an English accent, but not the kind you'd hear from a London rapper or cab driver. The old woman sounded more like a stage actress who was prepared to dive into character and recite Shakespeare at a moment's notice.

"Up to the street?" Betty asked her, and the woman nodded.

"Indeed. We have a short ways to go, but can only access our destination from the street. You must go first, as I cannot be in sunlight for very long."

"What, you got a skin disease or something?" Marciano asked her before getting nudged by his twin sister.

"That's rude," Natasha whispered.

"No, I'm a vampire," the woman both bluntly and proudly answered. Once she did so, Marciano stared at her for a whole three seconds before turning on one heel in the opposite direction.

"Okay, bye! This has gotten too weird for me," he announced, and began to head back toward the subway station.

"Wait!" Betty called after him. "She's not lying."

Marciano wasn't turning around. With a duffel bag on one shoulder and a piece of wheeled luggage in his left hand, he walked briskly away from the group. Natasha was dumbfounded, and stood still next to Enya.

"Wait!" Betty called. She jogged to catch up with her younger brother. "Wait! She's not lying. There's something Mom was going to tell you guys, and she chickened out. We'll explain it to you."

"When I was eight years old I asked Mom if there was such a thing as vampires, and she said no!" Marciano called back without turning his head.

"That's because you were wetting your bed, and wouldn't get up to use the bathroom because you thought vampires were in the closet."

"Lies!" Marciano shouted, springing around. But as he stared at his older sister, he saw just how deathly serious she looked. "You're not making this up, huh?"

"I've wanted to tell you for years," Betty said, the words pouring out of her in a sudden burst of emotion. "Please, just come and listen. There's a whole world that you need to find out about."

Marciano sighed as he looked back at his sister. With crazy, eccentric parents like Maude and Claude, it was helpful to grow up with an older sister like Betty who was responsible, mature beyond her years, and seemed to have an infinite supply of love for her family members. Marciano knew that Betty would never lie to him, which made it all the more difficult to accept what was happening to him. Betty was defending an old blind woman who claimed to be a vampire. What had happened to his normal (or semi-normal) life?

After standing idle for what seemed to be a long time, Marciano reluctantly walked back to greet the group, but not before giving an accusing look in the old woman's direction.

"Don't try and bite me," he warned, waving an index finger at her. "I moisturize my neck every morning. Yeah, the lotion I use is lethal. Says right on the bottle: harmful if swallowed."

"If I bit you—lotion or not—I'd die," the old woman told him, and smiled gently enough that he couldn't tell if she was being facetious. "Now let's not waste time. Shall we?"

Betty was the first to climb the ladder, since all she brought was a computer bag. She wasn't weighed down like Enya and the twins, and therefore had the free hands to move the grate. When she reached the top of the ladder, she put her hands on the metal and slowly pushed upward. Natasha cringed when she saw her older sister's hands touch the dirty grate. Betty was always much more of a tomboy, and didn't mind getting her hands dirty.

Once the grate was pushed aside, Betty climbed through, lifting herself up onto the street. Light poured into the underground, causing the old woman to take a step back.

"We're in an alley," Betty called down. "Start handing the bags up."

Enya sprang into action, climbing up onto the middle of the ladder and carefully handing bags up through the sewer opening, where Betty pulled them onto the street. Once all the bags were with Betty, Enya climbed up, followed by Marciano. Natasha was next, and she tried to navigate the stairs with just one hand, as the other was still writhing in pain from when she punched the redhead. Finally, when it was the old woman's turn, she reluctantly stepped into the sunlight, and climbed the ladder as quickly as she could.

As soon as the old woman stepped foot on the streets of Manhattan, she backed herself against a wall in the alleyway. From within her jacket she pulled out a thin umbrella, and pressed a button to extend the black canopy.

"It's not raining," Marciano remarked.

"No, and people might think I'm crazy," the old woman answered, "but as I like to say: It's better to be crazy than dead. Not to mention—some people find it a tad disturbing to see a woman with my pair of eyes navigating the streets of Manhattan with the speed of a busy banker. The umbrella hides my face."

"Just get a pair of sunglasses, sheesh," Marciano said, which drew looks from his sisters. "What? What did I say?"

The woman lifted the umbrella over her head, and instantly began walking. The rest of the group scrambled to grab their bags and follow her. They turned out of the alleyway and were surprised to find themselves just off Fifth Avenue, right in the heart of midtown shopping. The old woman walked briskly onto Fifth Avenue, sidestepping tourists and small children. The first thing that came to mind for Natasha and Marciano was that she might be leading them to Central Park, but a look of shock sprang onto their faces when the old woman stopped suddenly, compressed her umbrella, and walked into the Versace boutique between 51st and 52nd Streets.

"Seems like an odd time to go shopping, right?" Marciano whispered to his twin sister, who nodded in agreement. But they followed anyway, carrying their bags into the store as the old woman led the way toward a wall full of men's shoes. One of the security guards at the front door, dressed in a black suit, whispered something into a microphone attached to his lapel. Within seconds an attractive young woman dressed in a black pantsuit emerged from a door located near the cashier desk. She smiled at the newcomers before closing her eyes and holding one hand out in front of her. Suddenly all of the shoppers within the exclusive boutique diverted their attention from Natasha and her companions. They scurried off to random corners of the store, moving quietly like sheep being herded by a barking dog.

"Come with me," the old woman said. She picked up a pair of Versace high-top sneakers and placed her palm where the rubber soles had sat. The entire wall of men's shoes suddenly retracted, revealing a staircase in the ground that descended deep underneath the streets of Manhattan.

"Oh—my—God," Marciano remarked as he watched the old woman slowly navigate the concrete steps into a tunnel of darkness. "She's crazy if she expects us to walk down—"

Enya gave Marciano a firm push toward the stairwell before he could finish his protest.

"Okay, okay," he said, waving one arm in the air as he dragged his bag along with his other hand. The four of them followed the steps down into the ground. After they'd walked for a while they heard the wall above them move, covering the entrance to the stairwell. They were trapped, wherever they were, in some dark passage underneath Fifth Avenue.

The passageway seemed longer than it probably was, only because no one in the group aside from the old woman knew where they were going. As they continued to follow the concrete steps deep underground, the air around them became colder and mustier.

"Isn't this a Tom Ford cologne?" Marciano asked as he sniffed the air. Natasha couldn't respond; she had an arm wrapped around her mouth and nose. She wanted to ask the old woman where they were going, but she trusted that Betty wouldn't lead them anywhere unsafe.

Once the stairs ended, the group found themselves in a small room lit by two torches that hung on either side of a metal door. The old woman grabbed hold of a rusty iron knocker, and banged it against the door twice. A second later, the huge door popped open, pushing itself backward and revealing a dimly lit space that resembled a living room.

"Is this where you live?" Marciano blurted out as soon as they followed the woman into the room. The walls were brick, and some antique sofas with exposed wooden frames sat around a cast-iron coffee table. There were paintings on the walls, but it was too dark inside to really see them. The old woman lit some candles on the coffee table, and then proceeded to walk through an opening into an attached room.

"Make yourselves at home," she called to them. She sounded more pleasant than she had back in the tunnels. There must have been something about being home that put her at ease.

Natasha laid her bags on the ground and then sat on one of the antique sofas. The fabric looked beige under the dim lights, but could've been more of a brown. Enya, Marciano, and Betty soon joined her. They waited patiently until the woman reemerged holding a silver tray containing a teapot and five cups. When she finally did, both Natasha and her brother cringed as the woman prepared to pour the contents of the teapot into the cups.

"Need a hand?" Natasha asked. She didn't want to sound rude, but she was anticipating a spill. After all, the old woman was blind. She may have walked through the streets of Manhattan, but pouring tea was another story.

"I can feel, hear, sense—quite well, actually," the woman replied, as she began to pour tea into each cup without a single spill. The twins watched on, impressed. "Vampires have strong senses to begin with. Since I cannot rely on my eyes, my other senses have benefited from an exceptional amount of use."

"Basically you're like a bat," Marciano told her. "Right? Although without the fur and the white excrement. Although I haven't been in your bathroom—"

"Is he always like this?" the woman asked Betty, who rolled her eyes and nodded affirmatively.

"Oh, dear," she replied, just as she sat the teapot back on the silver serving tray. The teapot and cups were painted china, and all from the same set. Their color was a beautiful mix of light greens, blues, and gold. "My apologies, dear, but I don't have any ice for your hand."

"It's okay," Natasha replied as she rubbed the wounded hand between her knees. "It's not broken or anything. Just hurts like a—*you know what*."

"Well you should feel very fortunate. You should all feel very fortunate. Bridgette #2 is deadly. Most supernatural beings aren't lucky enough to say they've outlived an attack by her."

"*Number two?*" Marciano tried to contain his laughter, but couldn't help himself. Betty—always the mature one—quickly nudged her younger brother.

"She's a robot," the woman said, picking up on the dirty thoughts that were streaming through Marciano's head.

"Really? What happened to Bridgette #1?"

"She's in a junkyard somewhere. Tea?"

Everyone nodded.

"So I suppose I should introduce myself," the old woman said, keeping her attention on her guests as they accepted their cups. "I've gone by many names in the past, but you may call me Elle. I've been on the run for nearly four hundred years, hiding from my difficult past, and from powerful individuals who would like to see me dead. You could say that I'm the number one fugitive of the same people who are coming after you."

"You're joking," Marciano remarked, staring wide-eyed at her. Considering they'd just been attacked by a robot in an empty Manhattan subway station, there wasn't much that he wouldn't believe at that point.

"No, I'm afraid I'm not," Elle said in a soft voice that carried some pain along with it. "How much do they know?" she asked Betty, who looked at Natasha and then back at the old woman.

"Nothing. Our mom didn't tell them yet."

"Oh, Maude," Elle said, and held a bony hand to her forehead. "So where do I begin? Natasha and Marciano. I've been keeping track of you for the past twenty-one years. Ever since I delivered you to Maude and Claude in their Philadelphia apartment. Ever since Candice Brown killed your real parents."

"You knew our real parents?" Marciano asked.

"What does Candice Brown have to do with this?" Natasha blurted out.

"I'll get to that, Natasha. Marciano, I knew your parents well. But before I tell you about them, you should know a little about the world you're living in. Six thousand years ago, on the African continent, a woman who would never age a day over twenty-one was born.

In her youth she married a villager and during her first pregnancy she had thirteen babies. Each was born with unique abilities. One of them could read minds and heal wounds. Another had sharp fangs and an aversion to sunlight. Another turned into a wolf some nights and would terrorize village animals. Another was a young girl with the strength of three grown men.

"The children eventually grew up and went out into the world, but some of them caused so much trouble that their mother spent the next four thousand years chasing down them and their descendants. She didn't want to hurt them, but she wanted to bring some kind of order to the bloodline that she'd unleashed. When she realized that she could no longer control what she'd created, she placed a curse on all of her descendants. This curse—the *great curse*—demanded that all supernatural beings must be bound to the fashion industry—"

"She had a sick sense of humor, huh?" Marciano remarked, leading to angry stares from his sisters. "What?"

"It's alright," Elle continued, and shook her head. "She—Mother, as they called her—wanted to keep supernatural beings out of trouble. She thought that if they were busy performing a public good—making clothing—then it would be better than lurking around with nothing to do other than cause mischief. The curse was vague, but just specific enough. Supernaturals were not allowed to become involved in governments, militaries, or any companies or jobs that didn't have to do with fashion. And most of all, they had to keep themselves a secret. If a supernatural revealed their abilities to a human, they'd be struck down by the curse.

"When Mother created this curse, it took all of her energy, and they say she lost her human body and simply *became* the curse. That maybe she's inside all of us.

"There was a group of supernatural beings who were deeply worried that their peers wouldn't respect the curse, and would cause harm to all of us as a result of insubordination. This group was called the Thirteen, as they were descended from the thirteenth child. This race looked like humans, lived as long as humans, and had no special, constant abilities. Yet they were the most feared, because their abilities would adjust to defend themselves against any and all supernaturals. Telepaths couldn't read their minds. Vampires couldn't bite them without losing their teeth. If an Amazonian—like Enya—engaged one in combat, the Thirteen might become just as strong, if not stronger. Yet on his own, a Thirteen would have no special strength to speak of.

"All supernatural beings feared the Thirteen. Shortly after the curse was placed, they united and formed Caligae, a secret society meant to enforce the great curse. The organization was named after the military boots worn by Roman centurions. These would be both the police and guardians of supernaturals. They would ensure that no one broke the curse, and that supernaturals adapted to normal, human society. This model worked for the next fifteen centuries. That is, until the Colors stirred up trouble."

"While the Thirteens were descendants of the thirteenth child, the Colors were descendants of the twelfth. They were unique in that they were considered the highest breed of all supernatural beings. They weren't originally called *the Colors*. For thousands of years they were just an elite bloodline. Some were vampires, some were oracles, some were sorcerers or sea people or undead. They were immune to the limitations of their breed, and had special, unusual powers not shared by anyone else.

"A bloody war erupted in 1585, and would last for thirty years. I'd worked for Caligae nearly all my life. I was a hunter. I'd sniff out disobedient supernaturals and reprimand or imprison them. Over many years, I developed a gift for foresight, which made me valuable as a hunter. I was good enough to be noticed by one of the leaders of Caligae, a quiet, sedulous vampire known as Cecilia the Red.

"Cecilia had two daughters, one of whom was very ambitious. You know her as Candice Brown. The other one was Isabelle the Purple. By the sixteenth century, the Colors had formed a sort of *secret society*. They were well organized, and named themselves after colors as a way to promulgate their own self-importance. They thought that since they were the most powerful of all supernatural beings, that they should control Caligae. They didn't see it the way the Thirteens saw it. The Thirteens believed that Caligae was an organization for protecting humans from devious creatures, and for keeping members of the bloodline within the fashion industry. The Colors saw Caligae as a governing body, a vital throne from which to wield power.

"At the time, I didn't know any better. I was brought into secret meetings with the Colors, and treated like one of them. They pretended to be my friends, and talked on and on about their goals for a *new* Caligae. In 1585, they struck. We went to war with the Thirteen, and drove them out of Caligae. They were systematically murdered—adults, children, babies. Cecilia and her daughter Candice wanted to kill them all.

"Thirty years later when the Thirteen were close to extinction, Candice turned on her own mother. She convinced her younger sister Isabelle, and a group of other Colors, that Cecilia the Red was unfit to rule. In a battle that claimed the lives of many, Cecilia was imprisoned with a devastating spell that buried her deep beneath an abandoned church in the English countryside. It was at that point that I faced my demons, and realized what kind of person I'd become. I found the remaining Thirteen and helped them to safety. Over the next four hundred years I helped the Thirteen hide, but Caligae was always on our tail. New generations of Thirteen would be born, but so many would be caught by Candice—"

Elle paused as she reflected on those most recent centuries. There was so much pain in her face. For a moment it looked like she might not be able to go on, but she lowered her head toward the silver serving tray and continued.

"In the mid-1980s, I was living in Barcelona with the last of the Thirteen. There were about twenty of them, spread out in various houses across the city and region. One of them was your mother," she said, directed toward Natasha and Marciano. "I remember when she found out she was pregnant with twins. She and her boyfriend were so thrilled. We all were beginning to get so comfortable with our lives. It had been decades since anyone from Caligae had found and murdered a Thirteen, and we finally felt safe. I felt like we had a strong team, and I didn't suspect we'd run into any trouble. One night I took the train to Sitges, so that I could walk along the beach. It was one of my favorite things to do back then. And when I returned before sunrise, they were dead.

"Candice Brown had already found most of the houses. Your mother's house was the last one to get invaded. You were so young then. Your round heads were full of little blond hairs. She wanted the two of you to be safe, and took a guess that Candice Brown probably didn't know about you. She stayed behind so that the two of you could escape with me. Together the three of us fled to America, and I placed you with two amazing people. Caligae was after me, and it would have been too dangerous to raise you myself."

"So you're saying we're Thirteens?" Natasha asked her. She was absolutely stunned. The way Elle spoke about their history was so natural, and said with such emotion, that Natasha didn't doubt its legitimacy. And yet it all seemed so outrageous!

"You are," Betty spoke up. She had tears in her eyes. "I've been wanting to tell you forever. I'm what they call an engineer. We can control the movement of energy. I've wanted to tell you since we were kids."

"Why didn't Mom tell us?" Marciano asked her.

"She was afraid to," Betty said. "She thought that if she told you, then somehow it would lead to Caligae discovering your whereabouts."

"And Candice is with this Caligae?" Marciano asked Elle, turning his attention to the old woman.

"She is. Her younger sister Isabelle is officially in charge, but Candice is the silent leader. Not all people in the fashion industry are supernatural beings, but all supernaturals work within the fashion industry, if that makes sense. Designers, models, sales associates, shoemakers, tailors, et cetera. Even the people on assembly lines at clothing factories. The security guards at boutiques," she added, and motioned toward Enya.

"So when time froze inside the—," Natasha began, partially talking to herself, before she lifted her head and looked up at Elle. "Wait a second, what happened during that fashion show? Everything froze, but Marc and I were totally conscious."

"I assume it was Mauria Brown, Candice's daughter," Elle replied. "She's a Color, just like her mom and aunt. But unlike Candice and Isabelle, who are both sorceresses, Mauria is an oracle. She can control space and time. And while her powers are young and undeveloped now, one day she will far surpass her mother and aunt. Candice knows this, and is as jealous as anyone can be. She hates her own daughter. And that's why I need you to kidnap Mauria for me."

"To do *what*?" Marciano asked, his jaw dropping. "Whoa, whoa. Elle, first you hit us with this shocker about our background, and parents, and sorcerers, and then you want us to start kidnapping people? I can't handle this. I want my life back. I'm a junior designer at Haus of Simone."

"Coffee boy at Haus of Simone," Natasha whispered.

"Watch it—," Marciano replied, and waved an index finger at her.

"But you don't seem to understand," Elle casually said. "Rafaela Simone is a supernatural. Your parents are supernatural beings. This entire industry is composed of our kind. And you and your sister are so dangerous to Candice Brown that she will stop at nothing to kill you."

"*Kill* is a strong word," Marciano replied, followed by a loud gulp.

"I've foreseen that something terrible is going to happen, very soon," Elle told them. "And you need Mauria. I don't know why yet—it's not clear to me. But something very big is just around the corner, and unless you have Mauria Brown's help, I don't foresee a bright future for us."

"So where is Caligae during all of this?" Natasha asked. "I know you said that Candice Brown and her sister are in charge. Is that whole organization going to come after us?"

"Good question. Yes and no. Caligae is split like a political congress. The Colors have forcefully been in control for four hundred years now. Many people would gladly see them replaced, but no one has the power to physically replace them. Until now." Elle let the last two words hang in the air as she sipped from her cup of tea. Natasha hadn't even tried the tea yet. She'd lost her appetite amid the shock of this old woman's revelation.

"I want to assemble a team that's capable of physically removing Candice Brown and her sister from power," Elle said. The room was dead silent. "I should have done this years ago. Instead of encouraging Thirteens to fight, I talked them into hiding, and running away. Maybe I'd seen too much bloodshed, and didn't want to face the repercussions of seeing more.

"But now it's inevitable. Candice knows you're out there. You can either run forever, or face her. I've foreseen a light at the end of the tunnel. I don't know how we get there, but kidnapping Mauria Brown is the first step along the journey."

"I'm still processing this," Marciano said, waving an index finger in a circle to the left of his head.

"You're right, my apologies," Elle quickly responded, and took one more sip of her tea before placing it back on the silver serving tray. "You need to see the world you're living in. Come with me."

She was quick for an old woman. Elle sat up with the vigor of a teenage girl and walked toward the front door of her underground home. She motioned once with her hand for them to follow, waving four pale fingers at her guests.

Marciano and his two sisters were the first to sit up, followed by Enya, whose movement caused the sofa to creak. They all followed Elle outside the front door, back into the tiny, dark area at the bottom of the stairs.

"So do you get a discount at Versace since your crash pad is underneath their menswear section?" Marciano asked. Enya gripped him by the back of the neck, causing him to squeal in panic. "Sorry—," he added in a higher pitch than usual.

Elle closed the door to her home, and waited for a moment before turning back to face her four companions.

"Betty, this might even be new to you," she remarked, and revealed a pleasant smile beneath thin, pink lips. Elle pulled on the door handle, and just when Natasha and Marciano wondered why they were going back into the old woman's home, their expressions dramatically changed upon seeing what had been revealed to them. The very same door that had led them into Elle's subterranean apartment deep beneath Fifth Avenue was suddenly wide open, and as the five of them gazed through the doorway, what they saw was not a cramped, dusty space scattered with old sofas. What they saw was a department store.

The ceiling was enormous, and the space reminded them of 30th Street Station in Philadelphia. Colorful ribbons and glass balls hung from the walls and ceiling, and three floors of shopping were wrapped around the rectangular space in the most unorthodox way. It wasn't anything like a regular mall or department store. Sets of stairs were positioned everywhere in what seemed like a random pattern of connecting one floor to the next. In some cases, shoppers had to walk all the way up from the first to the third floor, and wind around one corner of the store before finding their way down to the second floor. It seemed like a great maze of shopping, where boutiques, carts, and hundreds upon hundreds of clothing racks filled a space big enough to fit three jumbo jets.

"Betty, have you ever been to Woodsrow & Campertine?" Elle asked, but Betty just stood there shaking her head in amazement. Elle was the first to walk through the doorway. They were on a brick platform shaped like a semicircle, lined with about ten doors that acted like the exits and entrances to the department store.

"Where are we?" Natasha asked in bewilderment as she stepped out onto the platform. The rest of the crowd followed her, and shortly after they closed the door, it reopened to reveal a frumpy lady with orange curls of hair and a particularly pointy noise.

"Pardon," she said to them, and pushed passed on her way into the department store.

"Best we get off the platform," Elle advised them. Every corner of the platform descended into stairs that led down onto the main shopping floor. The words *Woodsrow & Campertine* were painted in silver on two cherrywood signs that hung from the high ceiling. Underneath the names, *est. 1819* was written in a smaller font.

Two bins full of women's bags greeted Natasha as soon as her feet hit the main floor of the department store. When she reached in to touch a black patent-leather purse, the bag instantly changed colors, completely transforming into a baby blue. It was as if the very composition of the leather had been altered with a single touch. This was a step above mood rings. This was magic.

"Ah, yes, bags for shape-shifters," Elle told Natasha, who was staring in disbelief at the blue patent-leather purse. "I've known some shape-shifters who change their outfit eight times a day. I suppose it's easy when you have that kind of power. Could you imagine? I once had a dear old friend who would go to the theatre with me, and he'd change his outfit in between acts. As if anyone really cares."

"She sounds fabulous," Marciano replied. "Did you guys see the coffins?"

"Those are for the vampires who don't know any better," Elle answered as they passed a display of blocklike coffins that had a certain cubist quality to them. "Yves Saint Laurent started the Picasso trend two years ago with a lovely ensemble of colors. Givenchy took the style into pastels, and now it's filtered down to the deep discount brands. When I was much younger I'd collect coffins like some girls collect shoes."

"So how were you able to walk along Fifth Avenue in sunlight earlier?" Natasha asked a question that had been on her mind for a while. Elle didn't seem to fit the stereotype for vampires, and one of those stereotypes was that they incinerated as soon as sunlight touched them. Natasha's image of vampires was based on some combination of Dracula and Anne Rice, and a whole lot of TV shows. Elle didn't exactly fit in. This was a fabulous old woman who lived beneath a Versace boutique, wore designer, made tea for her houseguests, and fought robots in New York subway stations.

"Old vampires are more immune to sunlight than young ones are," Enya answered before Elle had time to speak up.

"Let me guess—you used to eat them for breakfast too?" Marciano asked, which led to a scowl from the tall Russian.

"She's right," Elle said. "The older we get, the more immune we become to sunlight. It still affects me, though, just as intense heat would affect you."

"So if I ate garlic gnocchi for lunch and then breathed heavily in your face, would you start to melt?" Marciano asked her, which caused Elle to stop and pause in front of the display of coffins.

"If you ate garlic gnocchi for lunch and breathed in my face, first I'd tell you your breath stinks, and then I'd smack you upside your head."

"Oh—," Marciano timidly replied to the old woman. It wasn't the answer he sought.

"So what kind of coffin do you use now?" Betty asked Elle, as the latter continued to walk down one of the massive aisles that led through the first floor of the store.

"A classic. Bottega Veneta, with silver trim. It's vintage."

"They make coffins?" Marciano asked in surprise.

"They make everything," she casually replied, continuing to lead them straight ahead. Along the back wall were small boutiques, some with an elaborate doorway made up of metal and glass, and others wide open, exposed to the whole department store.

"Is that a werewolf?" Natasha asked, slightly fearful, as soon as she noticed a group of three large wolflike creatures covered in light-brown hair. They were huddled closely around a display of shoes. "Are those Uggs?"

"Yes and yes. Werewolves invented them, you know. And those plastic Crocs too. You know, it's tough for werewolves. Imagine if every so often your body would dramatically change, and your feet wouldn't fit in any of your shoes, and you had to walk around barefoot until you changed back to normal, only to realize that no pedicure in the world could cure the crusty, blistered feet caused by a couple days out in the wild."

"Are they dangerous?" Natasha asked as she watched the movements of the werewolves. They looked like ferocious creatures, with pointy hair, red eyes, long snouts, and slobbering, pointy teeth. And yet they acted like normal humans (sans the growling), hovering around a shoe display as they pointed and made unintelligible conversation, probably about the styles or prices.

"Uggs? Oh yes, terribly," Elle replied.

"No, I meant werewolves."

"Oh—oh, yes, they can be. A werewolf killed a human in Central Park the other night. This happens sometimes with them. Werewolves and vampires are the only supernaturals who are usually turned from human form. Sometimes the new ones experience a—well, how can I put it—*panic*. Especially if they're not into fashion! I heard once of an investment banker who was turned into a vampire and told he had to work the night shift at Macy's. I think he staked himself."

"He had a Macy's discount and he still staked himself?" Marciano asked, totally appalled. "What an ingrate."

"So how powerful is this curse?" Natasha asked. "I mean—would I catch on fire if I applied for an accounting job?"

"Not if that accounting job is for a fashion house," Elle said. "There are supernatural beings who are businesspeople, lawyers, distributors, shelf stockers—and they all work for fashion companies. I guess you could say that we've tested the limits over the past two thousand years. As long as you don't do something that's unrelated to the fashion industry, and as long as you don't directly tell humans about your abilities, then you'll be fine."

"Have you ever physically seen the curse affect someone?"

"No—no, I haven't." Elle carefully replied. "Although Caligae has done a superb job of enforcing the curse. I have no idea what would happen if one or more people broke the curse. Caligae is there to make sure we never have to find out."

"So if Caligae has been doing its job all this time, is there any reason to try and overthrow Candice Brown?"

"Yes, there are many reasons why she should be overthrown. She's evil, corrupt, and usurped control from good people. She's a plague among our kind."

"What is she? A vampire?"

"She's a sorceress, just like her sister, although she didn't age nearly as gracefully. She involved herself in so much evil magic that her body slowly deteriorated over four centuries. There was a time when Candice was too humiliated to go out in public. And then plastic surgery came along, and everything changed. They say that Candice had so much work done to herself that it interfered with her powers of sorcery. They say she can now control plastic with her mind."

"She must be fierce with a credit card," Marciano remarked. "Hey what's this place?"

They'd arrived at the back wall of the department store, lined with various boutiques of all shapes and sizes, including some that extended up to the second floor. The group was standing in front of a boutique with an elaborate entrance. The entrance itself was a stone arch with hieroglyphics scribbled on each brick, and on either side of the opening were two golden statues of gazelles with long horns that were painted blue. The inside of the shop had a clay color to it, and wooden tables that looked centuries old were scattered around in a careless layout. Some of the tables were stacked with so many random things that one could barely see the wooden surface, and others contained just a few pieces of jewelry.

"I believe you know someone in here," Elle said as she led them into the boutique. It looked right out of an Egyptian tomb, and smelled like one too. As soon as the four travelers from Philadelphia stepped into the shop they had to pinch their noses. There was a rotting quality to the store that added an additional unpleasantness surpassing even the thick layer of dust that had accumulated on every single item listed for sale.

Natasha and Marciano were wide-mouthed (they kind of had to be, since neither could breathe through their nose at that point) when they saw who was working behind the counter. Their loud and opinionated Aunt Monique was sitting behind a stone checkout counter, her legs folded, with a fashion magazine in her hands. As soon as she heard the newcomers enter her store, her eyes peeked just above the pages of the magazine. She nearly fell out of her chair when she saw her nieces and nephew.

The twins had been told that their aunt was a close family friend who had known Maude and Claude since they lived in Paris. She was their godmother, and a loud-mouthed New Yorker who would visit Philly from time to time to see the family. Whatever the twins had formerly imagined about their aunt's life in New York, seeing her in a smelly, Egyptian-themed boutique in a department store for supernatural beings was shocking to them.

"They know," were the first words that Elle said to Monique, who slowly removed the fashion magazine from her face. Her brown eyes darted back and forth between Natasha and Marciano. Monique had tan skin that seemed to blend into the clay walls. She was a compulsive tanorexic who couldn't bear to be any shade other than mocha or orange, and with her dyed and straightened blonde hair, and hoop earrings, Monique stood out like a fur coat at a PETA convention.

Maude and Claude had always told their kids—Betty included—that Aunt Monique was a fashion buyer in Tribeca who would buy clothing direct from fashion houses on behalf of department stores. The story was that they met when Monique rushed to Paris in order to procure a contract to sell the Maude by Maude fall/winter 1980 collection in a major department store chain. Supposedly there was so much interest in the fall/winter 1980 collection that Monique had to arm wrestle a buyer from Saks Fifth Avenue just for the chance to *meet* Maude.

And that was true. The rest of the story was conveniently left out. Monique was a mummy, and of the thirteen categories of supernaturals, she was considered to be an undead. Monique used to be BFFs with the Egyptian Queen Nefertiti circa 1350 BC when the queen's husband started to show interest in the future fashion buyer. Nefertiti's husband was the Pharaoh Akhenaten, a total player, who used his charming good lucks to woo many an Egyptian woman. This was common back then, since the pharaohs were allowed to have multiple wives, but Nefertiti drew the line in the sand (no pun intended) with her best friend. Even though Monique had absolutely no interest in her BFF's husband, Nefertiti's jealousy was too severe.

On a single, fateful night, Nefertiti tricked Monique into attending a party at a tomb in Amarna. Monique knew she shouldn't have attended because it was particularly humid that day, and she didn't want to mess up her hair. But, girls will be girls. She put on her finest robe, and finest pair of slippers, and headed to the tomb. When she arrived,

Nefertiti was nowhere to be found. Instead, a group of robed thugs were patiently waiting for her. Monique was mummified alive.

This didn't mean that she immediately came back to life as a mummy. Monique rested in a tomb for nearly three thousand years, until a powerful sorceress named Isabelle the Purple raised her from the dead. Isabelle was a Color, and like all members of her bloodline, she had special powers in addition to those typical of her type of supernatural. Just as Candice Brown could control plastic, and Mauria Brown could control space and time, Isabelle the Purple had the ability to raise the undead. She couldn't bring people back to life, but she could create zombies and mummies. When the War of the Colors broke out in the late sixteenth century, Isabelle created an undead army to help fight the Thirteen.

First Isabelle created zombies, which weren't of much use to her. Maybe it was because they lacked brains, or were constantly decomposing. They ended up on assembly lines in scarf-making factories.

Next Isabelle created skeleton warriors. They didn't have brains either, but they looked pretty cool, and they couldn't talk back. Unfortunately, a single Thirteen could mop the floor with about one hundred skeleton warriors. They were out.

Just when Isabelle thought that her powers to raise the undead would be useless in the war, she stumbled upon a brilliant idea. One of her lackeys had made a random comment about tomb raiders in Egypt, which led to Isabelle making a trip to the land of the pyramids. While there, she began to raise mummies from the dead. Although they had to be tightly wrapped in order to hold their bodies together, mummies were a force to be reckoned with. They were strong, ill-tempered, and could create sandstorms and curses.

Monique was one of the unlucky few to be brought back to life by Isabelle. Though she was expected to fight in a war, Monique had other intentions. She fled Egypt and lived in the über-fashionable Beirut up until the fall of the Ottoman Empire. She arrived in New York City just in time for the Roaring Twenties, started up a boutique for mummy accessories, and later became a fashion buyer for Woodsrow & Campertine when the mummy fashion market slowed down in the '70s.

She still maintained her mummy boutique, but spent far more time jetting around the globe to make sure that Woodsrow & Campertine was stocked with the hottest fashions for supernaturals.

"When did you find out?" Monique asked, the volume of her voice filling the boutique and pouring out into the department store.

"I don't know—thirty minutes ago?" Natasha replied, and shook her head in astonishment. "I'm still processing everything."

"My babies," Monique screamed and dropped her fashion magazine on the floor, just before jogging around the counter to come and hug Betty and the twins. Enya stood at the doorway with her arms folded, one eye on the department store and one on the entrance to the mummy shop.

"Your Aunt Monique is a mummy," Elle said as she watched the four of them embrace in excitement.

"What, you're pregnant now?" Marciano asked.

"No, I said a *mummy*!"

"Honey, that's why my clothes are so tight," Monique told her nephew. "This girl has to keep herself together." She tossed her blonde hair and wiped imaginary tears from her eyes. Although her body wasn't capable of crying, she still liked to pretend that she could. But after the second wipe she froze, and she turned to Elle with a sudden look of panic. "Does Caligae know about them?"

"Unfortunately they do. Or at least, Candice Brown knows about them. Maude contacted me before they left, and asked me to follow them. It's a good thing she did; otherwise there could've been an ugly situation in Bryant Park Station today."

"Oh my gawd, oh my gawd," Monique exclaimed, and dramatically waved her hands in the air. "Baby dolls, we're goin' back to my condo in Tribeca. It's the only place you'll be safe. Either there or Brooklyn, because you know Miss Brown ain't crossing the bridge."

"You don't think they'll be safer with me?" Elle asked, raising an eyebrow at Monique's antics.

"Girl, you live right next to Caligae headquarters."

"Exactly. And that's why they've never caught me."

"We'll do whatever's safest," Natasha said, butting in to give her two cents. "Our bags are still at Elle's, but—"

"Can you close up shop if we leave right now, get their bags, and head to Tribeca?" Elle asked Monique, who crossed her arms and looked around the boutique.

"Girl, do you see any customers in here? Let's ride out."

Aunt Monique hurried to gather her things and lock up the boutique, which merely involved activating a curse she'd placed on the golden gazelles that stood at the entranceway. It was more effective—albeit, more deadly—than a door. And as the group hurried back across the grand floor of the department store on their way to the exit, Natasha couldn't help but feel overwhelmed with all that was happening. A fun trip to New York fashion week had turned upside down, and instead of enjoying a siblings' outing, she was suddenly at the center of a dangerous conflict dating back to the sixteenth century.

What's worse, she supposedly had powers that she didn't know anything about! Elle had spoken with such high regard for the Thirteens, and yet she never exactly explained what they could *do*, other than that they had the natural ability to protect themselves from other supernaturals. This meant that the only time Natasha could use her powers would be during a fight, something she wasn't looking forward to. And although she hoped she'd never have to be in a situation where her powers would be triggered, somehow she knew that there would be many fights ahead, with no guarantee that she'd make it out alive.

Chapter Four

"MAURIA!"

It wasn't unusual to walk into her mother's apartment in the Upper East Side and hear screaming, but the whole point of Mauria having her own place was that she could finally have some peace and quiet. Or at least an escape from her mother. And so it was natural for Mauria Brown to stop and cringe upon hearing her mother's screeching voice within her own Greenwich Village penthouse.

"Mauria Brown!"

"Yeah?" Mauria replied in a tone laced with annoyance. She briefly wondered what would happen if she just turned around and left. Would her mom chase after her? Would she call her cell phone twenty times? If it was up to Mauria, she wouldn't even give her mom keys to her Village apartment. Candice didn't like to go south of Midtown, so why was she bothering her daughter in a place that was supposed to be peaceful and mom-free?

"You ungraceful little brat," Candice spat, marching into the living room where Mauria was hanging her winter coat on a stand-alone rack next to the front door.

"You know, I have neighbors."

"You think I'm scared of neighbors?" Candice screamed, her face nearly as pink as her hideous tracksuit. She'd changed into a cashmere tracksuit since leaving the fashion show. There was something about cashmere that calmed Candice down. Unfortunately, even *calm* Candice was intolerable.

"Apparently not," Mauria replied, and rolled her hazel eyes.

"You're a disgrace," she spat out. "I give you a prime spot in my fashion show, and you trip on the runway? What an idiot. And you're nominated for Best Supermodel next week at the Fabbies. Meh—if they only knew. I think the only reason you were given the ability to control time and space is because you're so clumsy. That's the only way you won't look like a screw-up to everyone around you."

"Are you done?" Mauria asked her. Even though she'd heard these same insults for years, they still bothered her. After all, it was her mother. Most mothers—even the awful ones—at least have some maternal love for their children. Even the strict disciplinarians and the ones with anger control management issues would have heartfelt moments with their kids. Candice Brown never had a heartfelt moment in her life. This was a woman who had buried her own mother alive. Candice didn't know anything about motherhood, and didn't care to find out. Mauria was an accident, a fact that Candice had relayed to her daughter many a time.

"Am I done? You're lucky I care at all, otherwise I wouldn't be here," Candice told her, lowering her volume but still maintaining that wicked, stabbing voice.

"Oh, I know you didn't just come here to berate me," Mauria said, turning to face her mother. "There's always a catch. If you didn't want something, you would've just called me over the phone to yell at me. So what is it?"

"You're having a party here tomorrow, right? Big fashion scene thing?"

"Yeah."

"I'm launching a new brand next fall/winter called Gold & Brown. Get it, gold and brown? Golden brown?"

"I got it," Mauria drearily replied.

"Then why aren't you laughing?"

"Well... it wasn't exactly funny—"

"I didn't ask you if it was funny!" Candice shot back. "You should laugh anyway, whether you think it's funny or not. Anyway, what do you know about *funny*?"

"Obviously more than you, otherwise your talk show would've lasted more than two episodes."

"That was a conspiracy by Leno and Letterman!" Candice grunted, pointing an angry finger at her daughter.

"Please, you weren't even in the same time slot. They had you at 3:00 a.m., and your first major guest was yourself. I remember being mortified watching that show, as you'd ask yourself a question and then hop back and forth between the desk and the guest chair to answer."

"Who could I *possibly* have interviewed that would have been more interesting than me?"

Mauria shook her head. She wasn't in the mood to debate her mom. That was and always had been a losing game.

"So Gold & Brown, okay," Mauria said, bringing up the fashion label so that Candice could make her point.

"I want you to promote it at your party. I'm sending a team of models tomorrow night to dress up in Gold & Brown outfits. I'm going to parade them around the party so that everyone can see just how wonderful my new designs are. And . . . I want you to wear a dress from the collection."

"Mom, the label is a nightmare. I've seen the sketches."

"No it's not!" Candice shot back. "It's clothing inspired by what dinosaurs would wear if they could wear clothing. Specifically pterodactyls."

"Dinosaurs didn't wear clothing, Mom."

"Well they *could* have. And my collection is going to turn heads at your party."

"Yeah, in the other direction."

Candice was fuming, and although Mauria was getting a good laugh out of her mother's frustration, she knew that she'd already lost the battle. She'd have to allow the Gold & Brown models into her party, regardless of whether or not they'd offend the crowd. Everyone knew that Candice was Mauria's mom, so they expected this sort of thing. Candice Brown never missed an opportunity to promote herself. She was like the Donald Trump of fashion. Back when Candice was launching her clothing line for infants, she used to write the name of the brand in black marker on infant Mauria's forehead. Then she'd set her loose in a shopping mall, because nothing gains publicity like a child roaming around a public setting without supervision.

"Fine," Mauria said, before Candice even had time to vocalize a response. "I'll do it. But I'm not wearing the dress with the holes for dinosaur spikes."

"Is it okay if the models squawk?"

Mauria stood there for a moment dumbfounded. How could she even respond to a question like that?

"You mean—the models are going to be walking around my party squawking?"

"Yeah, like pterodactyls."

"Do you even know for sure that pterodactyls squawked?"

"Uh, duh, of course they did," Candice replied, waving her palm in her daughter's face. She split her fingers to form an L-shape with her hand. "Loser!"

"Thanks, Mom," Mauria coldly replied, and walked past her mother on her way to the kitchen.

"Ew, are you going to eat?" Candice asked with a sudden flair of drama in her voice. She placed one hand on her rather gigantic hip and twirled on one heel so that her eyes were on Mauria. The latter's apartment had a beautiful stainless-steel kitchen that ran into the living room.

"Yes. Do you want anything?"

"Puh-lease," Candice replied, and shook her head. Even though she was a habitual eater, she never liked to reveal that to anyone. Outside of fashion shows, she had difficulty munching on sourdough pretzels and other goodies in front of people. "That's my cue to leave. Oh, and by the way, keep an eye out. There were two people in the audience at the Brown Label show. When you gracefully tripped and froze time, they were sitting there like bird brains, glancing around with wide eyes. I think we have ourselves a couple of Thirteens."

"They could just be powerful oracles or sorcerers, or—"

"They were your age," Candice interrupted. "They had to be Thirteens. The year you were born we tracked down a group of—"

"Mom, stop," Mauria said without turning to face her mother. She held up a palm in her mom's direction. "Please—I don't want to hear it. I know you've done a lot of bad stuff, so please don't talk to me about it."

"Oh, you're not your mother's daughter," Candice said, a devilish grin on her face. "Have fun at the party. Your dress will be delivered to you a couple hours before the party."

Candice blew a kiss to her daughter, which wasn't all that sincere since she was known for doing it to everyone (taxi drivers included), and with that she left the apartment.

Aunt Monique owned a two-bedroom apartment in an old textile building that had been converted into condos. It used to be a three-bedroom, but Monique had knocked one of the walls out and expanded her own master suite. She'd bought the property back in the 1960s when Tribeca real estate was inexpensive. Years later she'd often moan about wishing she had bought her entire building, given the steep rise in property values.

But Monique was satisfied. She had a beautiful place in a beautiful neighborhood, with a master bedroom that was bigger than most Manhattan apartments.

"Now be careful," Monique said as she led the group into her condominium. "This apartment is cursed up the wazoo. Uh, don't go near that," she advised Marciano.

"It's just a lamp."

"Yeah, don't touch it," she warned.

"Is it cursed?"

"No, just don't touch the lamp. It's Oscar de la Renta."

Marciano slowly backed away as Monique made room in the foyer for everyone to put their bags.

"Do mummy curses work on us?" Natasha asked Elle.

"Most don't, but some do," the old vampire replied in her ambiguous, methodical way of answering questions. "Some don't work on anyone. A curse is sort of like a—well—"

"Honey, let me explain to them. They don't have all day," Aunt Monique said, interrupting Elle midsentence. "A curse is like a lawsuit. Sometimes it gets to court, sometimes it doesn't. You can sue anybody for anything. Hell, I can sue you for taking your shoes off in my apartment, and claim you infested my carpet with foot fungus, leading to the deterioration of my hardwood floors, leading to fifty thousand dollars of property damage, leading to the loss of my social life because I can't afford to go have drinks with the girls anymore. Does that mean a judge will award me the money? Probably not. But I can still do it."

"Curses really depend on who is doing the cursing, and who is getting cursed," Elle added.

"When I was growing up in Siberia, a witch placed a curse on me for bumping into her in the supermarket," Enya said in a terrifying monotone. "The next day I buried her in the Siberian ice."

The apartment was filled with dead silence.

"Um . . . lovely story. Moving on," Betty finally said. "And on that note, I think I'm going to sleep in whichever room Enya is *not* staying in."

"I have two bedrooms. One huge one for me, and one small one for the four of you."

"What about the living room?" Marciano asked.

"No one's allowed in there," Monique replied. "Don't stand on the rug, sit on the sofa, touch the furniture or—on second thought, don't even look at the living room."

"So four of us in one bedroom?"

"I have sleeping bags. What?" Monique asked, shrugging as if it was no big deal. "Free crash pad in Manhattan. You wanna pay for a hotel? Didn't think so."

"Monique—," Elle said after releasing a long sigh. The old mummy knew what was up.

"No, the living room is off limits."

"I need to talk with them about an assignment tomorrow night. I'm not crowding into your guest bedroom. Either we do this in the living room, or in your master suite."

"What about the kitchen?" Monique protested. "Look—look, I have a kitchen. There's a kitchen table."

"I don't feel like sitting at a kitchen table," Elle replied, and did her best not to smile. "I feel like sitting on a sofa."

"Girl, you better make it quick," Monique said with a snappy voice, and rushed off to her bedroom. "Oh, the misery!"

Elle walked into the immaculate living room and her young companions followed. They spread out between two sofas, and Elle sat on an antique leather Chesterfield chair with rolled arms that could've easily been over one hundred years old. Much of Monique's apartment was furnished with items from her days in Beirut. She'd renovated the kitchen and bathrooms in the decades that she'd been living in her Tribeca apartment, but maintained a flair of classical elegance among the decorations. It was a mixture of English colonial and nineteenth century Ottoman-style, merged seamlessly to create an apartment that would look stuffy to a modernist, but absolutely delightful to someone who knew their history.

"I just wanted to sit in this chair," Elle confessed to the group, once they were all situated in the living room. They all laughed, including Elle, who didn't seem like the type who laughed a whole lot. Maybe there was a time when she did. "So I'm going to ask an enormous favor of you. I need you to kidnap Mauria Brown much sooner than expected. It has to be tomorrow night, at a party she's hosting at her Greenwich Village apartment."

Enya was the only one among the four who nodded her head. The rest sat there looking shocked. Natasha, Betty, and Marciano didn't know the first thing about kidnapping someone. If sent on a mission to kidnap, they were the kind of people who would politely approach the target and kindly ask if they'd mind getting in the back of the van that's waiting just outside. These weren't professional hostage-takers.

"I need to go to Philadelphia," Elle continued, and any smile from her face instantly faded. "Ever since you were attacked in the subway station, I've been worrying. They might not know who the two of you are, but if they identify Betty and Enya, they'll link them to your parents. Maude and Claude don't have anyone in the city to protect them, and so it's important that I go, and safely bring them up to New York. In the meantime, I need you to kidnap Mauria Brown and hold her here in your aunt's apartment."

"How do you kidnap someone?" Marciano asked in a clueless manner. "Is there like—an instructional booklet? A 'how-to'?"

"I have a source in Manhattan who tells me Candice is sending a bunch of models to the party who aren't on the official guest list. They'll be modeling some new line that Candice is debuting later this year."

"Another one?" Marciano asked, and rolled his eyes.

"Your aunt is going to make sure that the limo driver doesn't show up to work tomorrow, if you know what I mean," Elle continued. "She's going to drive you to the gathering site where the models will get dressed in their outfits, and then she'll transport the four of you, plus a carful of supermodels, to the party. Candice Brown shouldn't be there, and neither should her sister Isabelle. It'll be a young, hip *fashion-scene* crowd. When you arrive, Enya will knock out the doorman and monitor the entrance. The rest of you will be *models* at the party.

"Your goal is to get Mauria to leave in the limo with any one of you. You need to get her back to the condo. Use your powers if you have to. Mauria's powers are not very advanced yet, since Candice has never bothered to invest in proper training for her daughter. If she gives you any trouble, then that's why Enya's here."

Enya clenched her fists together, causing Marciano—seated next to her—to gulp.

"She's like a celebrity," Natasha said in protest. "How can I even approach her? I wouldn't even know what to say? This is *Mauria Brown*."

"And you're a supermodel working for her mom. So think of something. Mauria is your age. She may be a wealthy celebutante from a powerful fashion empire, but she's just a twenty-one year old girl."

"But she's like—stunning—and wears couture, and—I have curly hair that I can't do anything with, and a big nose, and—"

"Yeah, Elle, don't you think it's kind of far-fetched to be pretending that Natasha and Betty are supermodels?" Marciano asked, and immediately burst into laughter amid jabs from his sisters.

"I have a feeling that you'll be fine," Elle said, forming a little smile with her lips. "You see, Mauria's party represents the fashion establishment. Once you're inside, you're one of them. And anyone who looks at you will find the most beautiful, unique, special things about you, and they'll know instantly why you're a supermodel. Anything about you that you find ordinary or average will be completely inconsequential. Now I must go. Keep in touch, and good luck."

"When will we—"

"Your aunt has all of the information pertaining to tomorrow night. Get some rest. You'll need it."

Before Natasha could say anything else, Elle was on her way out the door, leaving them with so many questions. Natasha still couldn't fathom actually kidnapping someone. But as she turned to Marciano to ask him what he thought about the kidnapping plot, her brother's cell phone rang, causing him to leap off the sofa.

"Miss Simone?" he answered. His boss had told him on many occasions that she didn't like to hear a phone ring more than once. And if Rafaela Simone ever got voicemail—well, doomsday would ensue.

"Marciano, darling, I'll be in New York tomorrow. They were going to put me up in the St. Regis, but I absolutely hate his talk show, and so I just bought a penthouse instead. Let's do lunch on Saturday, okay dear? Okay darling, kisses."

Rafaela Simone hung up before even giving Marciano a chance to speak. Although that was typical of Rafaela. She liked her phone calls to be short, one-sided, and to the point.

"Ugh, Rafaela wants to meet up this weekend," Marciano moaned as he stared at his cell phone. "She must want something."

"Rafaela called? Oh my God, I haven't even called Mom yet," Natasha said as she stood from the sofa and hurried to grab her cell phone.

"Put her on speaker!"

"Well, today's been a little insane," Betty admitted.

"No kidding," Natasha replied as she clicked on a speed-dial button to call her mom. They had about twenty-one years to catch up on.

Chapter Five

CANDICE BROWN'S BLOODCURDLING SCREAM echoed throughout the Manhattan offices of Caligae, a place otherwise known for quiet diligence. It was early enough on Friday morning that the meeting rooms, offices, and hallways were spare, save for some of the old-timers who liked to start the workday at 6:00 a.m.

"What's that?" asked a terrified Candice Brown, covering her mouth with hot-pink fingernails.

"That's your office," replied Olympia, the ginger-haired vampire who had been in Candice's employ since Queen Elizabeth I was rocking knitted silk stockings. She was dressed rather elegantly for 6:00 a.m. at the office, and was wearing a wavy green dress with a silk headscarf that was emerald in color. Olympia was greatly feared among supernatural beings for her dangerous abilities in the field of hypnosis. Yet to Candice Brown, Olympia was just another lackey.

"But it looks so—unsightly."

"That's because it's designed for work."

With a repugnant expression spread out across her plastic-injected face, Candice Brown stepped one fur-trimmed boot into her corner office. The room was quite simple: a box with painted-gray bricks on all four walls, and a large rectangular window with a view of the main workroom. Candice's office was designed for the kind of leader who liked to keep an eye on—and be seen by—their staff. Unlike Isabelle's office, which seemed distant and detached, Candice Brown's office was intended to be visible and accessible.

Unfortunately, since Candice had never used the office, the room was pretty barren. An old wooden desk from the 1940s collected dust in one corner of the room, and a leather chair sat beside it.

"There's no television or refrigerator or pool table," Candice complained as she stepped her second foot into the room. "And it smells like barley."

"Well—," Olympia began to say, before she paused to figure out the correct wording. "Candice—most offices are designed to be free from those distractions. People are supposed to come in and work eight-hour shifts. It's generally believed that if one is tempted by forms of entertainment, they won't be as productive."

"I don't like that at all," Candice replied, dismissing Olympia's explanation. "What am I supposed to do all day? Just sit at that desk and work?"

"Well yes, that's the point. Desks are intended for sitting and working. Now, you can get up when you need to. We have a cafeteria down the hall, and two lounges: one for senior-level members, and another for visiting directors."

"Are there TVs in the lounges?"

"Um ... there are, but you probably shouldn't spend any time there," Olympia advised as she followed Candice into the dark corner office. "It's advised that you keep busy, so as to set the proper example."

"Here's what you're gonna do, ginger," said Candice, speaking with an authoritative voice that would strike fear into any lesser henchman. "You're going to get a massive, obnoxiously large flat-screen TV and put it over by the window that looks out onto the office floor. Then I want you to knock down that wall over there and extend my office by adding a gym, a shower, and a Jacuzzi. I want some sofas—either Kartell or Poltrona Frau—don't be stingy with the price tag. I need a fireplace—"

"A fireplace? But we're underground."

"I don't care if we're on the moon," Candice replied. "I want a fireplace. I want a mini-kitchen stocked with snacks. And I want a private chef to come into my office every day to prepare lunch. And it better be someone famous. They have to speak English too, because I need someone to gossip with about other people in the office."

"You're not fearful that these ... requests ... might seem *unprofessional*?" Olympia asked, gulping midsentence.

"What about prank phone calls? Can I make them?" Candice asked as she sat down in the old chair positioned in front of the desk. She stared with disinterest at the dusty, black desk phone.

"We're a two-thousand year old secret society," Olympia delicately told her superior. "No, I don't think it would be wise to make prank phone calls."

Candice rolled her eyes and tapped her pink fingernails on the desk's scratchy wooden surface.

"That's all," she remarked, and slid into a position of poor posture as she glared out the office window.

"Of course," Olympia replied, followed by a quick nod of her head. "I'll see that the renovations are hastily implemented. By the way, Bridgette #2 is being repaired, and should be back with us this weekend. In the meantime, I'm keeping my eyes and ears peeled for the two Thirteens. It would be a huge help though if Caligae could—"

"I already told you, I don't want them involved," Candice interrupted. "Too many mixed loyalties in this organization. I don't know who I can trust. It's better that you and Bridgette take care of this. I want these kids dead before the Fabbies on Friday night."

"Any particular reason that we kill them before Friday?" Olympia asked. One week didn't give her a whole lot of time to track down and kill two people who were immune to other supernaturals.

"I just want Friday night to be—*perfect*," Candice replied, and for the first time all morning, an eerie smile crawled onto her inflated lips.

It was hard for any of them to sleep that night. Maybe it was the life-threatening fight with Bridgette #2, or all the day's revelations about supernaturals, or the fact that every thirty minutes one of them would wake up to the sound of Enya sharpening her hunter's knife. Marciano was the only one brave enough to ask her *why* at 4:15 a.m. she was wide awake and handling a deadly weapon, but in her typical fashion she answered: "Because there's always a snake around every corner."

It was apparent to Natasha that her own lack of sleep showed, because Aunt Monique shrieked as soon as she stepped out of her massive master suite and saw her curly-haired niece roaming around the kitchen.

"Oh, honey, I thought you was Medusa," she remarked, and strolled into the living room in her thick cashmere robe, complete with a green facemask and moisturizing gloves. Natasha raised her eyebrows, and then pulled on a strand of her own curly hair.

"Yeah—long night."

"No kidding, girl. Lucky for you, you're gettin' the Monique makeover today."

"The what?"

"You heard me. You, your sister, your brother, and the scary one with the ponytail. I am taking you to the Meatpacking District to a makeover genius. If he can make a mummy look this fabulous, then just imagine," she said, and waved her hands as if she were about to unveil a new five-star hotel on the Vegas strip.

"Did someone say makeover?" Marciano shouted from the guest bedroom.

"The four of you are getting a complimentary makeover," Monique shouted back. "Even you, scary. We need to do somethin' bout that Siberian wind damage."

"Fine," Enya coldly replied from the bedroom, "but if they touch my feet I'll kill them."

"Oh no she didn't," Monique said, and she snapped her fingers and waved her straightened blonde hair. "Well, I'll cross ya off the list for a pedi. Now hurry up, because Aunt Monique hasn't got all day. Don't, Betty, don't get changed! Just come like that. You're getting brand-new clothes."

"New clothes?" Marciano shouted in joy.

"Do I have to repeat myself? Let's go!"

New clothes was all she had to say. Within five minutes everyone was at the door, ready to go. They exited the building with caution, and jumped into the nearest cab. Although the taxi driver protested to squeezing five people into his car, Monique yelled his ear off until finally he agreed to let them in. A tight ride later and the group arrived just outside the Christian Louboutin boutique on Horatio Street. When the door opened, Marciano was the first to stumble out, looking up at the storefront with stars in his eyes.

"We're not going in there!" Monique called to him as she fought her way out of the cab. "My friend's building is around the corner. There is no way in hell that I'm going into that—"

Monique was never able to finish the sentence. Thirty minutes and two shopping bags later, Monique was literally in (faux)tears over how much money she'd spent as she led her young companions down the street to a building of converted lofts that used to be a packing plant in the early 1900s.

"You know—," Monique said between sobs as they walked into the entrance of the loft building, "shopping is supposed to give you pleasure."

"Aunt Monique, the moment you put those shoes on and walk out your front door to attend some big event, it'll all be worth it," Marciano remarked as he patted his aunt on the back. "That's considering Candice Brown doesn't kill you first."

After Monique confused the building's doorman by wiping her dry face with a handkerchief, she tossed the piece of cotton on his desk and proceeded to shamelessly flirt before he buzzed them all up to the fifth floor. The building itself was only five floors, and so the group squeezed into a narrow elevator and headed for the top. The elevator doors opened up to a dingy hallway, complete with mothballs, crumbs, and a cheap burgundy carpet that bore many a coffee and dirt stain.

There was one hallway that ran along the building in the shape of an L, and so they turned the corner and headed toward the very last apartment on the left. The number was *507*, and the 7 looked like it was ready to fall off the oak-colored door. Monique banged on the wood and let out a masculine, "Yo! Yo, Cedric!"

"So this is the best makeover artist in the whole city?" Natasha asked with some skepticism. Where was all the glamor? It looked like there was a better chance that she'd get robbed than made over.

"Honey, he is the best. He works for Caligae, but—yo! Open up! Sorry, as I was sayin', Cedric has done everybody." Monique paused, and then placed a finger to her lips. "I mean he's been a stylist for everybody."

"We know what you mean," Betty replied, her eyebrows raised toward the ceiling.

The door opened to reveal an explosion of color. Not within the apartment, but on the person standing in the doorway. He was short, maybe five foot four or five five at most, with spiky black hair, a pretty face with dark features, and a tan that highlighted his perfect set of white teeth. He had on a red V-neck, white jeans, red high-top sneakers, and a red watch. Topping off the ensemble were frameless red sunglasses that gave him a certain touch of hipster. He looked way more Williamsburg than Meatpacking District.

"Hey girl!" he shouted as he and Monique embraced in a little ensemble of screaming and wailing.

"Oh my gawd, girl, when's the last time you cleaned?" Monique asked Cedric as soon as she looked up from hugging him and saw his apartment.

"I know, I need to do that, I've been *so* lazy lately," he replied. "So these are the nieces?"

"And one nephew," Marciano replied, holding his hand up in an unconvincing manner.

"Girl, don't kid yourself," Cedric replied, and waved his palm. "And who's the jolly giant?"

"I am Enya," the Russian replied, her arms crossed and her ponytail swaying behind her.

"I'm gonna have fun with this one. Okay girls, come in, come in," Cedric said, waving them into his apartment as he stepped over junk to try to clear some space. Cedric's apartment was tiny, just a small studio with a twin bed—a quarter of which crossed into the kitchen—and a bathroom the size of a closet.

"Is there enough space to do makeovers in here?" Natasha asked, and suddenly felt stupid when Monique raised her eyebrows and glared at her.

"Girl, what kind of question is that? Sometimes it's what you don't see that's more important than what you see, or think you can see, if you could see, but can't." Monique paused for a moment as she tried to figure out if her words of wisdom made any sense. "Aw, hell with it. Cedric, crank this baby open."

Cedric excitedly skipped over to his bed and jumped onto the narrow mattress. He fixed his frameless sunglasses so that they hung properly over his nose. Natasha couldn't help but cringe as soon as she saw the soles of his sneakers land on his mattress—she just had a thing about shoes and sheets, and had once kicked a guy out of her house for tossing shoes on her bed in a juvenile attempt at being flirtatious.

"I think what your fabulous aunt meant to say, was that sometimes you just have to take down a couple ugly walls to reveal a whole lot of beauty."

Cedric turned around so that he was no longer facing them, and he leapt into the air and clicked the heels of his high-top sneakers together. As soon as his feet came down upon the mattress, the brick walls that had enclosed the small studio space began to collapse like a deck of playing cards, falling smoothly on top of one another and flattening out. And what they revealed was astounding! An entire apartment was behind the walls, and it filled most of the fifth floor of the building. It was a massive stretch of New York loft space, with windows that ran floor to ceiling.

There were no longer any walls or rooms, just partitions and *spaces* that smoothly glided into one another. There was an area stocked with tons of shoes, and another with racks full of women's clothing, and a little spa setup with salon chairs and pedicure stations. Behind the four-hundred-square-foot space that housed Cedric's studio apartment was a stylist's dream come true. This was a makeover loft.

"Oh my God, is that a runway?" Marciano asked, eyeing an elevated catwalk in the center of the loft.

"Mm-hmm," Cedric replied. "Now Monique tells me you're going to a party at Mauria Brown's penthouse tonight?"

"Honey, it's gonna be off the wall crazy," Monique replied. "All I'm doing is being a getaway driver and I'm still excited. Gonna try and mack on some fine men on their way out of the party, know what I mean?"

Monique tapped Enya on the arm, and the Russian responded by grunting.

"I'll pick one up for you too, girl," Monique told the Amazonian. "Just don't kill him. And if you do, hide the body."

"Moving on," Cedric said, and began to clap his hands to call everyone's attention. "Nail station first, then hair, then clothing, then shoes. If you're going to be supermodels tonight in the presence of Mauria Brown, you need to know how to look, act, and be the part."

"Aunt Monique, are you getting a makeover also?" Marciano asked his aunt, who waved him off with her manicured fingernails.

"Baby doll, there's a spa bathtub and a bottle of bubbly over there with my name on it."

"Literally! She wrote her name on my bathtub last time she was here," Cedric angrily shouted out as he headed toward the nail station. "Permanent marker. Loca."

Cedric quickly got to work on Betty, the twins, and Enya. While Aunt Monique applied her spa mask, lounged in a bubbly bathtub and drank fine champagne, her houseguests got total makeovers. Even Enya didn't put up much of a fight, although when it got time to select a new wardrobe, she did give Cedric a lot of grief about there not being secret pockets and holsters for her arsenal of weapons.

After four hours of grinding, cutting, trimming, polishing, dyeing, trying on tons of clothes and shoes, cat walking, and knife throwing (on Enya's part), the group was ready for their finishing touches.

"I have some gifts for you," Cedric told them as they assembled in front of an enormous mirror positioned against a partition. "Aside from the free clothes, shoes, and my time and effort," he added, and coughed, "I have some special things that you won't find in any regular boutique. In fact, before you got here, I made a special trip to Woodsrow & Campertine just for you. And, well, for myself too," he said, and awkwardly nodded at three bags full of clothing.

"These items will help you utilize your powers to the fullest extent. Enya, I want you to come up first."

Enya—clad in a skintight elastic jumpsuit with sable fur around the collar—proudly stepped forward.

"I have two things for you," Cedric said, and sorted through a shopping bag. He first pulled out a white hairspray can. "This hair product is from a line designed exclusively for Amazonians, much like yourself. If you spray your head with this before combat, it will dramatically alter the muscle fibers in your hair follicles, sending a chain reaction through your hair that will make your ponytail about as strong as a wrecking ball. No worries though, your hair will still feel light on your head.

Enya grunted as she looked at the hairspray, and then nodded her head in approval.

"Next, I have a pair of tailor-made leather gloves. These are extremely rare, and originally designed by shape-shifters to change with their outfits, but they also will enhance the strength of your fists. For a shape-shifter it gives them a knockout punch, but for an Amazonian, you'll be able to punch through a steel vault. Hug?"

"Very funny, little man," she replied, and let out a laugh as she stepped back with her gloves and hairspray.

"Betty?"

Betty excitedly stepped forward, and tossed her blonde hair, which carried a new *vavoom* to it since her makeover.

"I have two things for you. First—" Cedric reached into a shopping bag and pulled out a beautiful, black Balenciaga bag. As soon as Betty's eyes fell upon the designer handbag, she nearly fainted in joy. "Two years ago, Balenciaga ran a line of special handbags for the engineer bloodline. You can fit anything electric in here, regardless of size. It's like a black hole. I even know an engineer who used to store her car in a bag like this because she didn't feel like paying for parking in Midtown East. If you need to transport laptops, computers—"

"Hair dryers?"

"Yes, although—well, yes—you can fit them. But, anything that's not electronic will just take up space in the bag. So before you start piling in your bottles of hand sanitizer and spare toilet-paper rolls, keep that in mind."

"Love it," Betty replied.

"I have one more thing for you." Cedric took a pair of tweezers out of his back pocket and reached into a Woodsrow & Campertine shopping bag. He quickly emerged with a pair of pink panties, dangling from the tweezers. Betty glared at him, and practically forgot that she was holding Balenciaga.

"What is that?"

"What, you've never seen panties before? This blend of nylon and spandex is going to rock your world. This is brand-new from Victoria's Secret, not even on the market yet. It's designed for engineers. There's a computer chip in the panties, and hundreds of tiny pockets that collect energy from your regular body heat. As an engineer, you can harness this energy and use the panties to fly. You can't go too high, but if you have someone chasing you then these babies can make all the difference. Oh, and dry-clean only."

Cedric released his grip on the tweezers, and the panties fell into Betty's new handbag. She stood there wide-eyed, and then shook her head and returned to her place in line.

"Marciano! Natasha!"

As soon as his name was called, Marc hurried up and stood at attention in front of Cedric, with his arms straight and his fingertips pointed at the floor. Natasha walked up next to her brother and stood at his side.

"Marciano, do you know the fashion house Lanvin?"

"Oh my God, of course!"

"Well you're not getting anything from them."

Marciano's excitement plummeted. He slumped his shoulders and hunched forward. But when Cedric's hands reappeared from digging through a shopping bag, it was like the sun was rising from beyond the mountains. Dangling in each hand was a brown suede dust bag containing a pair of shoes.

"Marciano, who is your favorite men's shoe designer in the entire world?" Cedric asked, and grinned as he watched Marc's eyebrows leap as if he were about to answer the million-dollar question on a live game show.

"Um, no-brainer. Raf Simons."

"I just met you today, and yet I feel like I've known you for much longer," Cedric said, laughing as he passed the dust bag forward. Marciano slowly accepted the bag, and his knees nearly gave out when he peeked inside. It was like that same rush of buying a hot, high-end pair of shoes at a luxury boutique, and giddily waiting for the sales associate to step around the register and hand over a fresh, crisp shopping bag. Marciano had been gifted a pair of Raf Simons black leather lace-ups, and they set his heart on fire. As he bunched his lips together and thought about all the outfits he was prepared to match the shoes with, Cedric handed the other dust bag to Natasha.

"And these are for you," he calmly said. Judging by what her brother got, Natasha knew that she was about to be gifted some serious shoes. She held her breath, and slowly opened the bag.

"Oh—my—" Natasha's mouth was open as she stared down at the sparkly blue-and-green Manolos. They were red-carpet elegant, and glimmered as the twenty-one-year-old pulled them out of the dust bag. Even Aunt Monique's eyes flung in her direction, staring at the pumps like a lion staring at a limping gazelle.

"Treat them well," Cedric said, and wiped his eyes. It was clear that he was someone who truly loved fashion. Amid all his exposure to the industry, he'd never been jaded by his access to designs and designers.

Most of all, he possessed an empathy lost on many fashion house sales associates, the kind of mutualistic joy that comes from seeing appreciation for a beautiful product.

"What do they do?" Natasha asked as she scoured each and every corner of her new shoes for some kind of hint of their special abilities. She wondered if they'd be like Marciano's black oxfords, which glowed when he threw the one shoe at the redhead back in the subway station.

"Oh—nothing," Cedric replied, and shrugged his shoulders. "I just thought they were fabulous. You're Thirteens; you don't need any special gadgets."

"I wish I knew what Thirteens actually did," Natasha said with a hint of sadness in her voice. It seemed like every other supernatural had clearly defined powers and abilities, while hers were totally ambiguous.

"Unfortunately, you'll probably find out soon enough," Cedric said, as the sad realization dawned on him too.

There was a deep feeling of nervousness within the limousine as it arrived at the pickup station for the models. Aunt Monique donned a tailored black tuxedo to look the part of the driver. She even threw in a chauffeur hat to complete the outfit.

When they arrived, Natasha, Marciano, and Betty joined the group of models just in time for the outfits to be distributed. Monique had apprehended both the limo and the Gold & Brown outfits about an hour before they were supposed to meet. Despite being thousands of years old, she still knew how to seduce a limo driver.

The outfits were abominable, and looked like a bunch of rags with random holes for spikes. (Remember, these were designed for dinosaurs, though strangely enough, human-shaped dinosaurs.) The clothing was somewhere in between caveman couture, and what a homeless person would wear in winter months. To complete the outfit, wooden muzzles with wiring in front of the teeth were distributed. The addition made the models look more like trick-or-treaters than fashionistas, but Candice Brown had assumed it would look authentic. Because, in her screwed-up head, dinosaurs wore muzzles.

Thankfully the models didn't have to put on the muzzles until they arrived at the party, so as they crowded inside the limo on the way to the event, they were at least able to talk with one another.

"So how many covers have you done?" one of the girls asked Natasha, whose mouth hung open for at least a full five seconds.

"I once covered a Stevie Nicks song at my high school junior prom," Marciano blurted out. "I got permanently banned from a hotel chain."

"I mean, like, magazine covers," the girl said.

"Um ... I'm just getting started," Natasha shyly replied.

All the models shook their heads in approval. As it turned out, this wasn't a runway couture crowd, and all of them had regular day jobs. Supermodels knew better, and Candice was too cheap to hire them for a party. But the lot was still very pretty, and it made Natasha a little nervous when she first saw the crowd of tall beauties. Something about a bunch of tall girls with size 0 waists made her feel inadequate. Natasha was rarely one to be shy, but she found herself choking up around her fellow models.

Natasha looked to her older sister for support, but Betty seemed far more lost and confused than shy. Understandably, this was a girl who hated wearing heels, and was on her way to an important party as a *model.* The fact that Betty had her legs folded and hands clasped in an introverted manner, and her eyes on the floor of the limousine, wasn't surprising to Natasha. Betty was more of a *think fast talk slow* kind of girl. As the limousine rolled along on its way to Greenwich Village, there was certainly a lot to think about.

Since Betty wasn't doing anything to lift Natasha's spirits, she looked to her twin brother, and as soon as she did, a smile poured onto her face. Marciano was wedged in between two Brazilian male models, both of whom he was shamelessly flirting with. It didn't matter that they could barely speak a word of English. Marciano used a combination of hand gestures and what he thought was Portuguese (but could have been Spanish, or Italian, or something) to communicate. For a moment he caught his twin sister's eyes, and returned her smile. It was all she needed, and Natasha took the enthusiasm and held it for the remainder of the ride.

When the limousine pulled up to Mauria's apartment building in Greenwich Village, Enya—clad in her elastic jumpsuit—leapt out of the passenger seat of the limo and opened the door for the models. She was convincing as a bodyguard. As Natasha stepped out of the limo, she nodded at the Russian, and tried to imagine her doing a job that didn't involve intimidation and limb breaking. Like, Enya as a librarian. Or Enya as a marine biologist.

Mauria Brown lived in a mid-rise apartment building that dated back to the nineteenth century. She owned a penthouse on the top level that had formerly been three apartments. The previous owner tore down the walls and joined all three units together to form a massive penthouse, complete with an outdoor terrace that overlooked the Village. When Mauria bought it, she had the interior modernized. She installed stone floors, stainless steel everything, and marble steam showers. It was a contemporary look for a classic building.

While Monique waited in the car, Enya escorted the models into the building, then waited near the doorman—a rather frumpy-looking Englishman—until all of the young men and women had packed into the two elevators. As soon as the doors were closed, a swift backhand from Enya knocked the doorman backward. Enya hadn't intended for his body to make an indent in the lobby mailbox, but such was the case. She carefully laid him underneath the doorman's lobby desk, and then sat in his chair with her arms folded.

Monique was in place, Enya was in place, and the other three were about as nervous as anyone can be. They still had no idea how to go about kidnapping Mauria Brown. They'd watched some heist movies back at their aunt's apartment for inspiration, but all of those movies involved action heroes with mad skills. The three children of Maude and Claude did not have mad skills. And as the elevator inched closer and closer to Mauria's floor, Betty and the twins began to regret ever having agreed to Elle's crazy request.

When the elevator door opened, the three of them took deep breaths. They followed the crowd of models to the front door of Mauria's apartment. They carefully affixed their wood-and-wire muzzles, tugged on their hideous outfits, and waited as the door slowly opened.

Natasha was the first to see Mauria's face when the models walked into her apartment. The celebutante daughter of Candice Brown was smiling when the door opened, and as soon as she got whiff of the outfits she gave a dreaded look that made Natasha want to turn around and run back into the elevator. Mauria was not only appalled, but totally disgusted. Her face grew red, and two of her friends tried to comfort her as the muzzled models walked into the party and immediately went to a table full of serving trays. Their instructions were to walk around the party and hand out drinks and hors d'oeuvres.

"Oh my God, Rafaela is here," Marciano whispered to his sisters, who looked up to see none other than their mother's archrival in the fashion business, and Marciano's employer.

Maude and Rafaela Simone had a feud that went back three decades, and it was mostly caused by jealousy on Rafaela's part. Both of them were of French descent. Maude grew up in the Bordeaux countryside, and opened her very first boutique in Paris, whereas Rafaela was born in the Quebec countryside, and opened her first boutique in Montreal. Maybe it was because Maude was a Parisian and Rafaela was a French Canadian. Or it could have been because Maude's breakout collection drew attention away from Rafaela, who up until that point had been gaining prominence for her provocative clothing.

The problem with Maude and Rafaela was that they were oddly similar. Neither liked pants, and neither would be caught dead wearing anything other than heels. Their minds worked alike when it came to designing clothing. They each had a thing for grunge couture and impeccably tailored dresses, and each held the principle that women should always show skin, no matter the season or weather. Even outerwear was designed with bare legs in mind.

The major problem with Rafaela was that she wasn't as consistent as Maude. She'd have her ups and downs, her creative seasons and her busts. She once released a collection of resort wear that was inspired by hot-air balloons. The whole point was that Rafaela wanted clothing that would float if set on fire. Physics was never really her forte.

Rafaela Simone was also a bit unstable. She thought that her success in the fashion world gave her a golden privilege to do whatever she wanted. Sometimes she'd crash charity events and take off with the free alcohol. Sometimes on shopping trips she'd drive her car through store windows, because she thought parking lots gave off bad energy. She also had a terrible habit of profiteering. One time she bought ninety-eight percent of the available tickets to a Kylie Minogue concert. She kept about thirty of them, and set the other three thousand on fire. She figured that the fewer tickets available, the higher the demand, and the more money she'd make off the deal. Ultimately she got arrested, and the venue merely printed more tickets.

But that was Rafaela, and people who worked with her learned to live by her rules. She was a creative genius, and had launched the careers of many aspiring designers. After she moved to Philadelphia in the 1990s (Canada revoked her citizenship), she opened a boutique directly across the street from Maude by Maude.

As much as Rafaela liked to think so, she and Maude didn't really have competing brands. Rafaela's designs were more youthful, and harnessed a mix between nightclub couture and date-night fashion. Meanwhile Maude's brand was shifting toward the successful, elegant woman. A woman in her forties would feel too old to shop at Rafaela Simone, while a young girl in her twenties might only go into Maude by Maude if she were looking for the perfect dress for a mature event. Still, Rafaela liked to think that they were archrivals. Both Rafaela and Maude were on the ballot at the Fabbies, each nominated for Best Designer. They'd each been nominated in the past, but Fabbies politics had seen that neither of them won. Finally, after many years, it was widely expected that either Maude or Rafaela would take home the grand prize.

"Just ignore her," Betty suggested. The designer was so self-absorbed that it was possible she wouldn't notice the three Philadelphia locals, since they were dressed up as models, complete with facial muzzles. Not to mention, Rafaela never noticed Betty. In fact, sometimes Rafaela would have conversations with Marciano about Betty, while the latter was standing right next to them.

The real concern was whether or not Mauria Brown would recognize them. Their faces weren't on a Wanted poster or anything, but Candice Brown had seen them, and had sent at least one assassin after the twins.

"I'll try," Marciano said. "But—" Suddenly he stopped in his tracks, and as Betty went off to carry champagne flutes around the party, Marciano's body was stiff as a nail. Natasha tapped him with her elbow.

"You okay?"

"If *okay* means I've just laid eyes upon the most beautiful man in the universe, then yes, I'm okay," he replied, and let out a long, melodramatic sigh. Natasha followed his eyes across the room to a man who was standing by himself on the terrace. The glass sliding door was closed, but he was lingering near it, looking out at the Manhattan skyline and soaking in the cold February air. Marciano was right; this guy was stunning. He was much taller than Natasha, and built like a football player. He had jet-black hair that blended into the night sky, and light skin that seemed to glow beneath moonlight. Okay, so maybe it didn't glow, but this guy had a presence, and it completely drew Natasha in.

"Go bring him some champagne," Marciano suggested. For a brief moment, Natasha forgot that she was holding the serving tray of flutes.

"No, no, I—"

"Okay, then bring him these foie gras wontons." Marciano grabbed the tray of flutes out of Natasha's hand, spilling half of the champagne on the serving tray, and he practically jabbed her with his plateful of light snacks.

"I'm not—"

"Go," he said, and playfully kneed her in the backside. Natasha stomped off toward the terrace, but not before looking back at Marciano with angry, narrowed eyes.

When she got to the sliding glass door, she held the serving tray of wontons with one hand, and opened the door with the other. She stepped out onto the terrace, turned to the stranger, and then stopped dead in her tracks.

"Okay, didn't realize it was this cold," she said to herself, and turned around to go back inside when the guy put his hand on her shoulder.

"Do you want my coat?" he asked Natasha, who turned back to face him.

"You're not wearing one?"

"It's in the coat closet. I'll trade you for that muzzle."

Natasha was mortified. She quickly closed the glass door and pulled the muzzle down around her neck. She'd totally forgotten that she was wearing the ridiculous accessory.

"You think Candice is actually going to try and sell those?" he asked her, trying not to laugh too hard at her embarrassment. "I'm Max."

"Natasha. Knowing her, probably. They'll be in a clearance bin by the end of the season."

"I'm sure you're right. Hey, let's go back inside. You look like you're freezing."

"I am," Natasha replied in between shivers. Max pulled open the door for her, and she stepped back into the apartment. Once they were both inside she relaxed a bit. Max was a tall guy, and Natasha guessed he had at least five or six inches on her.

"So you're a model, huh?"

"Well yeah—I mean I have a day job in fashion."

"Don't we all," he replied, and grinned to show a perfect set of white teeth. Natasha had already fallen in love with his eyes. Why'd they have to be blue? Every time he smiled, between the eyes and his dimples, she wanted to jump into his arms. "So what are these things?"

"Huh? Oh, the wontons? They're uh—foie gras. Duck liver."

"Looks like they're swimming in some champagne."

"Oh yeah, my uh—one of the models, my brother, spilled champagne and I guess it got into the tray," she replied, and frowned as she looked at the wet wontons. She hoped that the champagne flavor might actually improve the taste. "So uh—do you know Mauria?"

"I guess you could say that I'm a friend of the family," he replied, slowly shaking his head as he thought about the best way to phrase his response. "I know her mom a lot better," he added, which surprised Natasha, since he looked like he wasn't much older than Mauria.

"Well, Max, I probably have to hand these wine-soaked wontons out, huh? I'd love to stay and flirt, but—"

"Are we flirting?" he jokingly asked her, and smiled again to reveal those dimples and white teeth.

This was the part that Natasha wasn't very good at. The one-liners. Cute guys seemed to have an effect on her wit. Any good opportunity for a one-liner and she'd crumble up under pressure. What's worse, she ran the risk of saying something stupid. *Are we flirting?* Damn, he was good. And instead of thinking of a good comeback, all she wanted to do was stare into those blue eyes.

"Well, I am," she said, and nodded her head. She didn't need a one-liner. She was just going to tell the truth. Max smiled as soon as she said it, and Natasha instantly felt a whole lot of pressure wear off.

Unfortunately, when she turned around, her anxiety went straight back up. Rafaela had cornered Marciano and Betty, and was blabbing to them about her upcoming fashion show on Thursday. Rafaela Simone was a difficult person to back away from, and so Natasha didn't expect any graceful escapes from her brother or sister. That meant it was up to Natasha to track down Mauria, and somehow get her downstairs.

As she walked back into the crowd, she kept her eye out for Mauria. She'd been wearing a white dress that was from the same hideous Gold & Brown label, although Mauria seemed to pull it off. She could pull anything off.

Natasha couldn't find her anywhere, and just when she began to worry that Mauria had checked out of her own party, she overheard two girls talking about the hostess.

"Oh my gawd, can you believe she's crying in the bathroom right now? Like, grow up."

"Oh my gawd, like, totally. It's just a guy."

Luckily a couple of idiots had saved Natasha from performing a manhunt in Manhattan. Although she had no idea which bathroom Mauria was in (she assumed there were many), she discreetly placed her serving tray full of wontons back on a table of hors d'oeuvres, and headed for a quiet hallway that was vacant of partygoers.

Natasha passed a guest bedroom and an office before she came to a white door. It was the only one in the hallway that was shut. Natasha gently touched the handle and twisted ever so slightly to see if it was locked. It was.

"I'm sorry!" a gentle, female voice called from beyond the door. Within seconds the door had opened, and Natasha found herself staring into a bathroom the size of most bedrooms. Mauria was standing in front of a long mirror that stretched across two wide sinks. She was rinsing her face with water, and her cheeks and eyes were red enough that it was obvious she'd been crying. "I'm sorry," she repeated.

"No, don't be sorry," Natasha warmly said. She hurried into the bathroom and shut the door. How could she possibly kidnap someone who was crying their eyes out? "What's the matter?"

"It's stupid."

"Nothing that makes you cry is stupid," Natasha replied, and then thought about what she'd said. "Except made-for-TV movies. I hope you're not crying over one of them."

"No, no—," Mauria replied, and it looked like she was going to laugh, before some more sobs overtook her. "It's a . . . a stupid *guy*. Just some guy. He didn't show up."

"Oh—guy trouble. Well you'd be better off talking to my brother about that. I'm not really that experienced—"

"Tell me," Mauria said, practically springing up from the sink as water ran down her cheeks and onto her white dress, "if you're dating a guy for two weeks, and you tell him you have a really important party at your house on a Friday night—and it's not like he's working tonight—then wouldn't you expect him to be there? I mean really. No phone calls, no texts, no nothing—he just blows me off."

"Maybe he didn't want to meet your friends?"

"Why wouldn't he want to meet my friends?"

If the two gossiping girls in the living room were any indication, then Natasha was about to take the boyfriend's side. But instead she kept her mouth shut, and thought of something else to say.

"Maybe he's just not ready for this kind of commitment. Or maybe he's just an ass!"

"Whatever the reason, I'm done with him," Mauria coldly said. "I already deleted him from my cell phone."

"Well then, see, no worries! Don't let a guy bring you down. This is your party. And you have this fabulous apartment, and fabulous life—why do you care about some meathead?"

Mauria pursed her lips and formed a little smile, which instantly made Natasha feel better. Somehow it still didn't ease her concerns about kidnapping the young blonde heiress, but it was at least a start. She thought about suggesting that they go for a walk, or leave the party. All Natasha had to do was get Mauria down in the lobby, where Enya could toss her into the back of the limo. Yet for some reason Natasha was hesitant to turn the girl over to the Russian bodyguard waiting downstairs. There was something slightly warm and vulnerable about the blonde model, who stood a few inches taller than Natasha.

"I'm sorry you have to wear that outfit," Mauria said with a lot of sincerity in her voice. "My mom is unbelievable. Look at this hideous thing I have to wear. No wonder that guy didn't want to show up."

"Why, because of your outfit? Don't be silly."

Mauria shrugged her shoulders, and turned back to face the mirror. As she wiped her cheeks, she glanced at Natasha through the reflection on the glass.

"You took your muzzle off," she said. Her face lit up when she said it, like when someone laughs before they've even begun to tell a joke.

"Yeah—probably the weirdest thing I've ever worn. And that includes a period when I was seventeen and got into tie-dye unitards. I wore them with heels to a beach party and was photographed. My life was over for the next six months."

"It's no big deal," Mauria replied, and gently waved her hand. "Everyone has their fashion faux pas moments. And plus, you had to wear the muzzle to get in here."

"Yeah, it was part of the costume. All those darn prerequisites. It was harder to get into this party than it was to get into college. Not saying I went to an easy-A school, but—"

"No," Mauria interrupted her, and the smile disappeared from her face, "I meant that dressing up as a model was the only way for you and your brother to get into my party."

Suddenly Natasha wasn't in the joke-telling mood anymore. Mauria didn't turn around, but she watched Natasha through the mirror, keeping both of those hazel eyes on her.

"I don't know what you're talking about." Natasha rushed the words out of her mouth, and she knew it sounded fake. If only she was good at one-liners. She tried to think of the best fictional spies, and what they would've said. Maybe a good *Well, well, Miss Brown, cheerio and well done*, would've been sufficient. Of course, it would've been in a thick British accent, and Natasha would be wielding a glass of scotch.

Mauria finally turned from the sink and looked down at Natasha with a devious smile. She reached out her hand and touched Natasha's forehead, letting two fingers slide from her hairline down to her nose.

"It's exciting for me, you know? You're like an endangered species. I've never met one of you before, and I've met every type of supernatural in our world."

"How did you know it was me?" Natasha asked. A silly question, but it was the first thing that came to mind.

"I'm an oracle," Mauria said. She dropped her hand to her side, but was still standing face-to-face with Natasha. "Don't you know anything about oracles?"

"Not really."

"You know about Mother, and her thirteen children, right? One of them was an oracle. A girl. She could heal people by touching them. She could hear people's thoughts. When she got older she could move things with her mind, and affect the weather with her moods. Pretty cool, huh? Six thousand years of cross-bloodline breeding has changed the abilities of today's oracles. Some of them are just healers. Some are telepaths. Luckily I'm a Color, so I'm the closest thing you'll find to the original oracle. I knew it was you as soon as you and your brother walked into my apartment. As soon as I saw those God-awful outfits and those muzzles."

"You read my mind?"

"No, I can't. You're a Thirteen. And that's precisely how I knew. But what I really want to know is, why are you coming after me? Why not my mom?"

Natasha didn't know what to say. Elle had some great strategy in mind that she hadn't fully shared with the group. Her vague demand to "capture Mauria" came without further explanation, other than that Elle foresaw that they needed her for something big in the very near future.

"I'm working for powerful people who want to remove your mother and aunt from power," Natasha said, and after she delivered the line she felt like it could've been from a spy movie. That seemed like something that a secret agent would say. Maybe they wouldn't be dressed like a hobo, but at least they could've voiced the same answer.

"You don't need powerful people. You're a Thirteen. There are two of you!" Mauria remarked, and this seemed to give her some wicked delight. "I'll give you my mom's address. Go knock on her door and tell her she's banned from Caligae."

"It's not that simple."

"I have a feeling that you don't know what you're doing. Why'd you come here? To capture me? To use me against my own mother? I guarantee that she won't even know I'm missing."

"I'm just following orders. Now you can either come the hard way, or the easy way."

Mauria lost her smile for a moment, and she stared intensely at Natasha for a full five seconds before bursting into laughter.

"The hard way? This party is brewing with supernatural beings. There's no way you're going to get me out of here."

Natasha didn't even see it coming. It felt like a sweep of wind against her cheek. In less than the time it took her to blink, Max was in the bathroom, standing in front of Natasha, with Mauria unconscious in his arms.

"What did you—"

"Your brother and sister are in the limo," Max said. "Jump in my arms. We're taking an ... *alternative* way out."

"You mean you want me to jump on top of her?"

"What, you want me to make two trips?"

"Hmph," she grunted as she pushed herself off of one heel and leapt into his arms. "Think you're the big guy on campus, huh? Two supermodels in your arms."

"Very funny," he replied, and just as quickly as he'd rushed into the bathroom, they soared out an open window. It happened so quickly that Natasha didn't even feel the fall from the top story of the mid-rise apartment building down to the street. But as soon as Max's feet landed on the pavement and Natasha stepped on the ground, she felt an instant dizzying sensation that caused her to fall onto the side of the limo.

"Never do that again," she moaned.

"Get in!" Marciano shouted from within the limousine. Max hurried in, still carrying Mauria's body, and Natasha followed. As soon as the door was closed, Aunt Monique cranked up her reggae music on the limo's sound system and stomped on the gas pedal.

Chapter Six

AUNT MONIQUE HAD TURNED HER GUEST bathroom into a holding cell. She figured it was the best place for it in the apartment, since at least then Mauria could shower and use the toilet as often as she wanted. Monique stocked the room with towels and food. The only downside was that her guests no longer had their own bathroom, which meant they had to step foot in the master suite and use Monique's bathroom. This didn't sit well for the mummy, and Natasha overheard her use Elle's name along with at least a few expletives.

Mauria was still unconscious when they arrived in the Tribeca apartment, and so they put her in the bathroom and locked the door. Once everyone had adjusted to having a kidnapped stranger locked in the guest bathroom, their curiosity instantly turned to Max. While the group sat around the kitchen table (the living room was still forbidden) having late-night coffee, Marciano was the first one to break the silence.

"So who are you and why are you so attractive?" he asked, the way someone might ask their professor a question in class. Marciano didn't even crack a smile. He sat there at the table with his chin rested on one fist, staring into Max's deep blue eyes.

"A friend, and good genetics. In that order."

"A friend of whom?"

"Of yours. I work for Caligae, but—well, one thing you should know about Caligae, if you don't already, is that it's a *huge* organization.

It's split across all continents, and there's a leader—a Color—for each one. Isabelle the Purple is the director of North America, and Candice is sort of the silent boss of the whole thing. I work for one of the Colors who is trying to remove Candice and Isabelle from power. You and I have the same goal and the same enemies, so I'd say that makes us friends."

"Speak for yourself," Enya coldly replied, lowering a mug of hot chocolate from her lips. "I say who is a friend and who isn't. The last person to claim they're a friend of mine ended up six feet under the cold Siberian ground."

"Because he called you a friend?"

"No, because of tuberculosis, but that's not the point," Enya replied. "Don't be presumptuous."

"Good word choice, Enya!" Marciano applauded her.

"Thank you. It was on my *Word of the Day* app. I had to use it in a sentence, otherwise I do not remember."

"Max, what we really want to know is—how do you know about us, and who sent you?" Natasha asked him, steering the conversation back to his origins.

"My boss knows all about you," he replied, maintaining a serious expression. "She sent me here to help you."

"Who is she?" Betty asked him. "Why isn't she here?"

"She's not allowed on American soil. She's not allowed anywhere in North America. Or Europe. She's the Caligae director of Antarctica."

"You're telling me that this secret society has an office in Antarctica?" Natasha asked. Unless they were fighting rogue penguins and global warming, she didn't get the point of an Antarctic branch.

"None whatsoever, except for her," Max answered. "During the War of the Colors, there was only one Color—a cousin of Candice Brown and Isabelle the Purple—who stood up for the Thirteen. She was the only one to fight alongside them against her own bloodline. Her name is Dorina White. When the War of the Colors was over and the Thirteen had been driven out of Caligae, Candice and Isabelle cut a deal with Dorina. Since she was—and I believe, still is—more powerful than the sisters, they let her in on a devious plan.

"Candice and Isabelle wanted to kill their own mother, Cecilia the Red, and they needed help. Cecilia was a vampire Color with extraordinary power. She was a warrior, a soulless being constructed of pure evil. When Dorina White was approached with this intriguing offer, she thought that Candice and Isabelle had seen the light. Maybe the sisters weren't as bad as she thought. Dorina was sadly mistaken.

"As soon as she helped them defeat Cecilia the Red, the tables were turned on her. Since Candice and Isabelle weren't strong enough to kill her, they appointed her to the Antarctic territory, hoping she'd waste away in isolation. Dorina White didn't want to wage another war, and unfortunately the sisters had the loyalty of the other continents. There was nothing she could do but join them and accept the position.

"Candice grew more and more harsh as time went on. She began to exclude Dorina from important meetings, and spread vitriol about her to the other Colors. Finally she was banned from leaving Antarctica altogether. That hasn't stopped Dorina. Since she has no Caligae members directly under her employ, she's taken to hiring mercenaries and double agents to carry out her bidding. Her spies have infiltrated New York, Paris, and Hong Kong. I'm one of them. I've been working undercover in Manhattan for over sixty years. I'm a vampire.

"Sixty years? Come again?" Natasha said, blinking repeatedly. She wondered if she'd heard him correctly. Maybe he had meant to say *six*.

"What made this Dorina White finally act now, after all this time?" Betty asked him.

"It's only because of Natasha and Marciano. As soon as she learned that they were here in New York, and reunited with Elle, she knew that a plot was being hatched. Dorina has waited hundreds of years to seize upon this moment. I'm here on her behalf, to do whatever you need."

"Now wait a minute," Marciano said, and waved a single finger in the air. "My momma didn't raise no idiot. Nobody as attractive as you is ever good news. How do we know that we can trust you? How do we even know that Dorina White is real?"

"You don't, and you don't. In that order. The fact is, I'm here to help. Either I can help directly, by getting involved in whatever you're planning, or I can help indirectly, like I did tonight. I had no idea that you wanted to kidnap Mauria. For all I knew, you just wanted to fish around for information. But as soon as I learned of your intentions, well—she's out cold, in your bathroom now, right?"

Everyone nodded, except for Monique, who had lost track of the conversation and was busy doing a crossword puzzle on the kitchen counter.

"How about you sleep on it," Max suggested after some silence.

"We need to talk to Elle about all this," Natasha said, and sat back on the dining room chair in exhaustion. "I wish she'd call us."

"Have you tried Mom again?" Betty asked her.

"I texted as soon as we got back. Nothing yet. I'll call before bed, but she's usually good about this stuff. Elle said she'd be with her . . . I don't know. I don't know what to do."

"Sleep on it," Max repeated, and smiled. Though that was much easier said than done.

Saturday morning hit them like a brick in the face. Especially Marciano, who had promised Rafaela that he'd meet up with her for lunch. She'd bought an apartment right on Park Avenue, and asked to meet with her employee in a coffee shop on the adjacent block. Marciano didn't know what was so important that she couldn't have told him at Mauria's party, but apparently it was something that wasn't for anyone else's ears.

By the time Marciano arrived at the coffee shop, Rafaela Simone had already been escorted out by security for throwing sugar packets at the baristas. She immediately told Marciano that she was both famished and fatigued, and would never throw sugar packets when in a normal state of mind. Normally, she'd just throw a coffee mug.

Since Rafaela wasn't having much luck with coffee shops, the designer and her young associate ended up in a hotel lobby on Park Avenue, where she decided she was going to order food and then charge it to someone's room.

"Yes darling, I'll have a cappuccino, three macaroons that match the color of my outfit, and a portabella sandwich, but hold the portabella," she told the friendly female server, who rushed off to fulfill the order. Rafaela leaned back into the cushion of a wing chair. She tossed her black hair, which fell just short of her shoulders. She usually went for a spiky haircut, or something short and wavy, but between fashion week and a big nomination for Best Designer of the Year, Rafaela wanted to try something different. She also didn't want to look too much like Candice Brown, since they both had the same jet-black hair. Though, Candice's looked more like tarantula legs.

"How did you like the party last night?" Marciano asked her, which led Rafaela to stare at him blankly.

"What party?"

"Uh . . . Mauria Brown's party. You were talking to Betty and I for at least fifteen minutes."

"Do you think I can keep track of every party I'm invited to? If only you knew. Now darling, I have an important, top-secret matter to discuss with you."

"All ears!"

"Please don't use stupid expressions in front of me," Rafaela coldly told him, causing Marciano to sink a little bit in his wing chair. The pretty server hurried back with a tray that contained a French press, a coffee mug, a cup of cappuccino, three macaroons that matched Rafaela's outfit, and a portabella sandwich (sans the portabella). Rafaela waved her off and grabbed at a macaroon. "Now—," she said as she stuffed the cookie in her mouth, "let's discuss the Fabulous Fashion Awards. I'm nominated for Best Designer. So is your mother. We each have a runway show on Thursday, the closing day of New York fashion week. I need my show to look a million times better than Maude's."

"Okay, I'm following."

"By now you've heard that your mom is on the verge of opening a store on Fifth Avenue. It'll be her first venture into Manhattan fashion. I already have boutiques in Vegas and Beverly Hills, so Fifth Avenue is no big deal."

"I thought your stores are in Oxnard and Reno?"

"See Marciano, this is the kind of ignorant speech that's going to get you fired," she said, waving a bejeweled finger at him. "I too have a potential store on Fifth Avenue, set to open right across the street from the Maude by Maude boutique. Candice Brown has invested in my brand. It's a fabulous deal. She helps me get onto Fifth Avenue, and I design a collection for Candice Brown Couture. I already know what I'm going to do. I've been watching lots of reality TV lately, and I'm really inspired by worthless, depressed people and relapsed alcoholics.

I'm designing a couture collection that will focus on clothes for people who don't want to get out of bed in the morning."

"So... they'll have to put on the clothing the night before?" Marciano timidly asked his employer.

"I hate questions more than I hate my ex-husband," Rafaela snapped at him. "This isn't a game show, Marciano darling, it's reality. And the reality is that I want you to sabotage the Maude by Maude fashion show on Thursday."

"Uh... you realize she's my mom."

"I don't care if she's your fairy godmother. My show is already a disaster and it hasn't even happened yet. I can't beat her fair and square, so I need you to ruin her show. If you do, I will let you design an entire collection exclusively for my Fifth Avenue boutique. It will be called: Haus of Simone by Marciano."

She knew exactly what to say to make his eyes light up. Marciano had taken a big risk with his job at Rafaela's fashion house, when he could have easily worked for his mother. But Marciano was definitely the most rebellious and free-spirited of his siblings. When offered a position to work at Maude by Maude as a junior designer, he instantly turned it down. After interning as a tailor at Claude by Claude, he got his degree in fashion design and immediately signed up with Rafaela. She hadn't given him the hands-on work that he really yearned for, but this was finally a golden opportunity. Even though Rafaela was a little crazy, Marciano loved her brand and its emphasis on high fashion for young people. With his own small-production label at twenty-one years old, he'd be on a hot track for success in the industry. That was considering he was still alive after New York fashion week.

"So you actually want me to sabotage my mom's fashion show?" Marciano asked her. He knew what she'd said, but he just wanted to hear it again. This was a pretty serious request.

"Yes. Destroy the set, interrupt the show, sabotage the clothing—whatever you think will secure me the Best Designer award. The judges will vote on Thursday night, after watching all the shows.

"I'm not sure that I'd want to sabotage anyone's show, let alone my own mom's."

"Marciano darling, don't be a fool," Rafaela remarked as she held her cup of cappuccino up to her long, red lips. "*Haus of Simone by Marciano.* Just imagine it. How many kids your age are selling a high-end fashion line at a premier boutique on Fifth Avenue? This is a quick ticket. And who cares about Maude's runway show. Maybe she'll win next year."

"But if she doesn't win Best Designer, I don't know that her Fifth Avenue store will even get the right amount of funding to open."

"And why is that my problem? Darling, a macaroon?"

Marciano felt sick to his stomach. He certainly wasn't hungry for macaroons. What's worse, he was actually considering Rafaela's tempting offer. Although it seemed heinous and horrible, the payoff would be huge. And after all, Maude had a Parisian boutique at his age. So why couldn't he have a Fifth Avenue collection? He wished that he could just say *no* and walk away from the offer, but he needed to think deeply about it. There was no telling if he'd get a comparable offer anytime in the near future.

"No macaroons for me," he softly replied, and looked down at the French press he'd ordered with a noticeable frown.

"Can I count on you, Marciano darling?"

Marciano slowly shook his head.

"She's unbearable!" Natasha said, grabbing her own curly hair with both hands. Enya didn't seem to mind. She was too busy sitting in front of the guest bathroom, sharpening her knife and humming a Russian lullaby. Aunt Monique was at work in Woodsrow & Campertine, and Max had gone with her to rest during daylight, leaving Natasha and her sister to tend to the kidnapped princess.

"My coffee is cold!" Mauria shouted from the bathroom. "And it isn't the right color. Go to the hardware store and bring me a bucket of paint chips. I'll select one, and you need to match the color of my coffee to said paint chip. Then I want you to pour the coffee on your finger, and if it hurts really, really bad, you know it's the right temperature."

"I can't take this anymore," Natasha said in frustration. Betty was in the kitchen making lunch, and all she did was shake her head and continue to prepare sandwiches. Mauria wasn't trying to escape or anything, but since she'd woken up she demanded food, magazines, a portable TV, a spa mask, and a number of other frivolous things. She complained about the products in the bathroom, the food she was given, and even the smell of dust coming from the heating vent. She demanded that fresh flowers be delivered to the bathroom once every six hours. Betty had to make a discreet trip to Barney's to pick up the correct facial mask and cleanser that Mauria "needed to survive"—her exact words.

Mauria Brown was a nightmare. She was more spoiled than anyone Natasha had ever met. She seemed impossible to please. And to top it all off, Natasha couldn't reach her parents in Philadelphia. Numerous calls to the office had only produced vague responses. No one seemed to know where Maude and Claude were. Apparently they'd left a note at the office saying that they were going on vacation and would be back after fashion week. Betty and Natasha just hoped that Elle had gotten to them in time, and that the three were safe somewhere, hiding out from Candice Brown.

"Can we go back to my apartment?" Mauria shouted. "I promise I won't run away. This bathroom is cheap, and I'm *over* Tribeca. I want to be back in the Village in my apartment. Just put me under house arrest. You can disable the phones and Internet and whatever—just get me out of here."

"Do you hear this?" Natasha asked her sister, and Betty nodded her head. It was impossible not to hear. "I don't know if I can put up with this much longer. And we're supposed to help out at Mom's runway show on Thursday. That's five days away, and I can't even imagine keeping her here that long."

"I'm sure we'll hear from Elle soon," Betty said in her best attempt to comfort her younger sister.

"But we don't even know what we're supposed to do! All she told us was to kidnap Mauria and keep her here. What's the point?"

"Unfortunately we weren't told what the point is," Betty replied. "Sis, don't sweat it. Everything will be okay."

But that wasn't the answer that Natasha was looking for. She wanted Elle to reappear and tell them exactly what to do. Marciano was better at handling these crazy situations, but Natasha was a lot more structured—she needed to know all the details, the timeline, and how every piece connects. The lack of understanding frustrated her.

Natasha sat down at the kitchen table and rested her head in her arms.

"I'm just tired," she said to Betty as she closed her eyes and shook her head. "I was so excited when Mom told me about this trip. I thought it was going to be a fun week in New York. I mean, I'm sure she expected that for us. No one knew that Mauria was going to trip on the runway and freeze time, and that Candice Brown would see us. But all this stuff about Colors and Thirteens and—you know, I still feel like a regular girl. I can't make a subway train screech to a halt by waving my hand in the air. I don't have fangs. I don't understand what exactly I'm supposed to do.

"I felt like an idiot this morning while I was taking a shower. I tried holding my hands out like they do in those superhero movies, when they're about to shoot a bolt of lightning, or make something move with their mind. I threw my palms out and tried to make the water move. I tried to open and close the shower curtain with my mind. I'd even say catchphrases, just to see if it worked. Of course, I just looked like an idiot. But you see how weird it is for me? Huh, Betty?"

Natasha didn't hear any response, and so she peeked her head out from her folded arms and looked up into the kitchen. And as soon as she did, her eyes lit up. Betty was frozen. Her entire body was stiff, her eyes focused on a sandwich that she was in the middle of cutting.

"Oh no, oh no—"

Natasha jumped to her feet from the kitchen table and ran into the hallway where the guest bathroom was located. Enya was the same state as Betty, frozen in time as she was sharpening her rather long and intimidating knife. The bathroom door was wide open, and Mauria was nowhere in sight.

"Uh oh," Natasha exclaimed as she stood breathless in the doorway.

Mauria couldn't freeze time for very long, and so as soon as her feet hit the Tribeca pavement she released her hold and hailed the nearest taxi cab. Freezing time was like running a triathlon condensed into a two-minute time period. It took a lot out of Mauria, and she felt exhausted as soon as she slumped into the back of a yellow cab. She gave the driver her mother's address on the Upper East Side.

Mauria was relieved to be out of the Tribeca apartment. And although her abilities had saved her from her kidnappers, she wished she could do more with her powers. There was another oracle who was also a Color, but Mauria had never met her. She knew that her name was Dorina White, and that supposedly she was Mauria's aunt, but was holed up in Antarctica due to a centuries-old conflict with Candice Brown. Mauria had thought about running off to Antarctica before, not because she loved snow and glaciers, but because she wanted to meet someone who could help her develop her powers.

Mauria had stumbled upon the ability to freeze time almost by accident. It was just an instinctual thing, almost like closing one's eyes before getting splashed in the face with water. She'd read about the great oracles of antiquity, and yearned to be like them. One was rumored to be able to travel through time, although supposedly she sent herself far into the future and never returned.

As soon as the taxi arrived at Candice Brown's apartment building, Mauria waved at the doorman to pay the driver. Since Candice hated to carry cash on her, she'd give the doorman a bunch of money every month and ask him to pay her taxi fares. Mauria would abuse this privilege as often as she could for a free taxi ride. Sometimes she wasn't even planning on visiting her mother and she'd still take a free taxi up to the Upper East Side.

Candice Brown's apartment was something of a spectacle, an architectural landmark that had appeared in just about every reputable design magazine on the planet. She owned a two-story apartment in a modern Upper East Side high-rise. She'd purchased the space from the developers when it was unfinished, and she sent in a team of architects and interior designers to craft a luxurious pad worthy of being called her home.

If one word could be used to sum up the two-story apartment, it would be *plastic*. Literally, plastic. Candice used plastic everywhere. The walls, the furniture, the staircases, bookshelves, dining room table—nearly everything in the apartment except for stemware, flatware, and kitchen accessories. That was all Tiffany, of course.

Candice's home looked like a Kartell showroom. It put a whole new twist on the word *modern*. When her house was being designed and furnished, if a certain piece of plastic furniture didn't exist, she'd commission someone to make it. As a result, she had a totally custom apartment that was unlike any other property in Manhattan.

For Candice, the best thing about the apartment wasn't the fact that it was unique or high-end, or that it impressed guests, but rather that it was a playground for her special powers. Candice Brown—like her sister Isabelle—was born a sorceress. She was never as talented in the arts of witchcraft as her younger sister, and was always left feeling inadequate. She relied more on her craftiness than her abilities in sorcery. In fact, it was several hundred years before Candice Brown stumbled by accident upon the key to unlocking her true potential: plastic.

Candice didn't age as well as Isabelle, and her consistent use of malicious sorcery had aged her in an unfavorable way. One of the only reasons she established an office in North America in the mid-nineteenth century was because she wanted to get far away from the European social circles. Candice moved to New York and became a recluse for many decades, sometimes refusing to leave her home for weeks at a time. It wasn't until the advent of plastic surgery that she saw a glimmer of hope for herself.

When Candice began to undertake plastic surgery to *fix* her appearance, the unexpected happened. Not only did the surgeries change her emotional condition, but they affected her sorcery. She started to lose her old, familiar powers, and found herself with a new ability. For the first time ever, she could control plastic. She could mold it, melt it, move it—do whatever she wanted to plastic material by controlling its polymers. She could even change her own body. As she replaced more and more of herself with plastic, her own body became a playground for experimentation. She created a look—a new identity—that she found to be fabulous. And thus, she took on a new name, and re-emerged not just into the social circles of supernatural beings but also into the public eye, as Candice Brown.

Since Candice loved to feel powerful, her apartment in New York was designed for her own self-indulgence. She could take down the apartment's walls with her mind, or turn a chair into a piano. She could create whatever she wanted out of her home, and at any moment. When Mauria lived with her, there was absolutely no privacy. There was no way that Mauria could lock her bedroom door and have alone time, because Candice could literally melt the door, or the entire room for that matter.

As Mauria Brown entered her mother's apartment, she tried not to make any noise. She gently shut the front door and walked slowly through the foyer into an empty space designed for entertaining guests, with windows that looked out onto Central Park.

There was noise in the apartment, coming from the second floor. One of the problems with the plastic design was that noise traveled. Mauria used to be able to listen in on her mom's telephone conversations, until the latter got hint of her daughter's nosiness. For subsequent phone calls, Candice would enwrap her bedroom with thick layers of plastic. It was the only time Mauria would get any peace and quiet.

As Mauria neared the first set of stairs leading up to the second floor, she paused. She could hear her mother talking to her aunt. Mauria didn't know whether she should interrupt them or listen in on the conversation. Her curiosity won.

"Apparently your daughter disappeared during her own party last night," Mauria heard Isabelle say, in that typical voice that always sounded monotone and uninterested.

"Maybe she met a guy," Candice replied.

"She never returned home. No word to anyone, and no one saw her leave. Doesn't that seem strange to you?"

"Maybe she'll run away for a while, leave me in peace," Candice said, which instantly stung Mauria. It still hurt to hear her own mother talk like that. "What's more important is the Fabbies. Did you review my acceptance speech in case I win the Fashion Icon award? Was it too modest?"

"You really should just strike the word *modest* from your vocabulary," Isabelle suggested. "Why don't you just give a quick thank-you and walk off stage?"

"And waste an opportunity to bask in my own self-importance? You must be kidding me. Well—just hire me a speechwriter."

"You had the last three executed," Isabelle reminded her sister.

"Well, you should've seen their sentence structure."

"No, I read the speeches. They were perfectly fine. They just weren't outrageous and self-indulgent," Isabelle said.

"Well then my self-written speech will just have to do," Candice replied, and took the opportunity to let out a dramatic sigh. "After all, I'm an excellent writer. You remember my memoir?"

"Your memoir was touching, yes, within the first five pages. But you seem to forget that the book quickly turned into medieval fiction before ending up a Cape Cod murder mystery by page 83."

"Oh, well," Candice dismissively replied, and swatted at her sister with pink fingernails. "I had a dream about dragons and wanted to squeeze them into the biography."

"Just—just do whatever you want," Isabelle said, her voice growing increasingly aggravated. "Sometimes they don't even give away the Fashion Icon award until after Best Designer. If that's the case, then there won't be any acceptance speech. Is Olympia or Bridgette #2 carrying out the assassination?"

"Neither. Neither of them know anything about this."

"You can't be serious," Isabelle replied. She was shocked, especially in the case of Olympia, who had been in Candice's employ since the War of the Colors. She had served their mother, Cecilia the Red, before the war. If anyone could be trusted, it would be Olympia.

"I've already arranged for an assassin. I don't want Olympia or Bridgette #2 involved, because they'll get traced right back to me. I've found someone competent, and if they screw up, I won't get caught."

"I certainly hope that they're competent."

"Don't you worry. Everything will go according to plan. The news stations are gonna eat this up. Every time I've killed a fashion designer I've hoped for a strong reaction from the feds, and they never give me anything. This time will be different. This time, millions of live viewers from across the globe are going to see something that will forever be burnt into their retinas."

"Have you thought more about what will happen to Caligae once all the investigations begin?" Isabelle asked her sister.

"Caligae will be safe. The assassination is going to look like a big conspiracy within the fashion world. After Friday night, I'll have white FBI vans following me around, and so will every major designer and fashion mogul in the country. It'll only be a matter of time before the government uncovers the truth behind this industry. And wham—then we're exposed. We have our coming-out party, sing some Diana Ross—we'll finally get to be ourselves in public."

"And you really think that this will bypass the curse?"

"Of course!" Candice replied with arrogance in her voice. "Technically, we're not giving away our secret. All we're doing is carrying out a highly public assassination. But today with TV, Internet, blogs, and CSI units, there's no way that our secret won't get out. So we kill whoever wins Best Designer at the Fabbies, and then we sit back and relax."

Mauria Brown had heard enough. She raced out of her mother's apartment, and back onto the streets of Manhattan.

Chapter Seven

MAURIA WAS FREEZING, BUT SHE DIDN'T want to hop in a taxi because she didn't really have anywhere to go. She didn't want to go to her own apartment, and she didn't have any real friends who she could call. All she could do was walk down Fifth Avenue alongside Central Park, heading south toward the Village. There were plenty of clothing stores on her way, and so she decided she was going to pick up a brand-new coat and make the best out of her long walk. Maybe some retail therapy would do her good, and she could wrap her brain around the conversation she'd overheard between her aunt and mother.

It was difficult to grow up as the daughter of Candice Brown, and Mauria could only equate it to being the child of a cruel dictator. Candice was a cold woman with an awful reputation, who had led Caligae with an iron fist since seizing power in the sixteenth century. Other supernaturals assumed that Mauria was just as bad as her mother, and so people kept away. Mauria never had friends while she was growing up, and most of the girls who would hang out with her did so because they wanted something. Mauria had thought that college would bring her a new group of girlfriends, non-supernaturals who wouldn't care what family she came from. Unfortunately, college coincided with Mauria's modeling career. Her school was in New York City, but she lived off-campus. She'd show up for classes and then leave, without ever getting to join a social group or make friends. Candice Brown forced her daughter to do as much modeling as possible, and she used Mauria in campaigns for nearly every fashion line that she either owned or invested in. Mauria was a twenty-one-year-old workaholic who appeared to live a glamorous life, but in reality yearned for a life more like regular girls her age have.

"Uh … Mauria?" she heard someone say on the street. It was a guy's voice. Mauria was used to ignoring people. She'd get recognized a lot in public for all of her modeling work, especially by men. She kept on walking, but stopped abruptly near the corner of Fifth Avenue and East 62nd Street when she heard, "Aren't you supposed to be in a guest bathroom right now?"

Mauria swung around to see Natasha's brother standing a few feet away with his hands in a dark gray double-breasted nylon trench. Mauria thought about running down the street toward Caligae headquarters, but she didn't want to look crazy sprinting down Fifth Avenue. Freezing time wouldn't do her any good either. But as she stood there facing him, something about the puppy-dog look in Marciano's eyes felt welcoming. There was something warm about him, and instead of feeling intimidated, she began to relax for the first time since leaving her mom's apartment building.

"You want to get coffee?" he asked her.

"How about a coat, and then coffee," Mauria suggested, holding her arms close to her chest in an indication of how cold she was.

After a quick stop at Bergdorf Goodman, Mauria and Marciano ended up over on Columbus Circle. They found a café and bakery inside the Time Warner Center, where they intended to sit down for some coffee. However, given their moods, coffee quickly turned into champagne mimosas. Thirty minutes later, the two were practically crying in each other's arms.

"I can't believe she'd talk to you like that," Marciano said as he laid a comforting hand on Mauria's shoulder. "You're beautiful, and you can do anything you want. Don't let her anger bring you down. Maybe it's just a power trip for her. Or maybe she's jealous of you."

"You're right," Mauria said as she wiped tears from her eyes. "Next time I'm going to tell that flight attendant that I'm not paying baggage fees. So what if I travel with enough suitcases to fill a Boeing 757?"

"Right on, sister. There's no shame in trying to be fabulous," he said. "Now what were you saying about your mother?"

"Oh—I don't want to talk about her," Mauria said, quickly dismissing the subject.

"No, you started to say something earlier. I mean—you've gotta know your mom isn't a good person. We were told to kidnap you—not because anyone wanted to harm you, but because this crazy old vampire who lives under Versace said that with your help, we could remove Candice from power."

"There's a vampire that lives under Versace?"

"Yeah, and she's like a million years old. And I think she gets a discount."

"Wow, that's pretty cool," Mauria remarked, and took another gulp of her mimosa. "Refill!"

"Easy, tiger," Marciano said, a little shocked by the way she was slamming down drinks. They were starting to get nasty looks from the staff. "We're gonna switch to coffee!" he called to one of the servers, who rolled her eyes. "So—your mom."

"What about her?"

"You said you walked in on—"

"I don't want to talk about it."

"Mauria," Marciano said, the way a teacher would call out a misbehaving student's name in a classroom.

"Oh fine—I walked in on her and my aunt planning something really evil and messed up. And, well, my mom doesn't love me. She treats me awful. She's always name-calling, and forcing me to do these modeling gigs, and telling me that I'm not worthy of being a Color. And now they want to kill whoever wins Best Designer at the Fabbies."

Marciano nearly choked on his croissant.

"Kill the who? What?"

"Whoever wins Best Designer. They want to spark a huge investigation into the fashion industry. You know about the great curse, right? We're not allowed to tell people about us, but if they find out on their own, the curse somehow doesn't apply. It sounds like my mom wants everyone to know about us. I can't figure out why—"

"Well I certainly can," he replied. "Then she can use her powers to do whatever she wants. This is really dangerous, Mauria."

"Tell me about it."

"And my mom is nominated on Friday."

"Your who?"

"Maude is our—well, our adopted mom, but it makes no difference to me. She's raised us since we were babies—Natasha and I. She's nominated for Best Designer."

"Oh wow—," Mauria remarked, and raised her eyebrows. She went to take another gulp of her mimosa before realizing that it was empty. A coffee had been placed in front of her, and she looked down at it with contempt. "Really? Caffeine?"

"We live in Philly, and only found out about being Thirteens like—a couple days ago. This is all so new to me. I work for Rafaela Simone, and today she approached me, asking if I'd sabotage my own mom's show."

"Well, it might just be a smart idea," Mauria replied, which surprised Marciano. "Whoever wins Best Designer is going to get—" Mauria didn't say it, but she made a slashing sound as she flung her hand in front of her neck. "Good for Rafaela Simone if she wants to win that award."

"So whoever wins is getting killed? Like, right on the stage?"

"Oh yeah, point-blank assassinated. They want this to be in front of the cameras."

"Is there any way to stop this from happening?" Marciano asked. Rafaela's request had suddenly become a whole lot more complicated. Even though he didn't want to sabotage his own mom's show, he wondered if it would be the only way to save her life. Then again, he didn't want to see anything bad happen to Rafaela. What a nightmare.

"If we take over the event, go backstage, and topple the assassin," Mauria remarked, laughing to herself as she said it.

"No, that's a brilliant idea!"

"You've had too much to drink."

"Speak for yourself! Mauria, you're brilliant."

"Oh . . . no one's ever told me I'm brilliant before," she said, and combed her long blonde hair with one hand.

"We'll all show up on Friday," Marciano excitedly told her. "We'll make it all undercover and top secret. Like, we'll make a plan. Elle told us there was a special reason we needed you on our side, and I think this is it. You need to help us on Friday night!"

"You're crazy."

"Look—we need to get back to my aunt's apartment. Will you come with me?"

"Not if you keep me locked up in a cheap bathroom."

"I promise we won't," he said. "Just come back. We'll get everybody together and work on a plan for the Thursday fashion shows, and for the Fabbies on Friday night."

"As long as you'll stay with me and keep me safe, I'll come back with you," Mauria said, and she wrapped her arm around Marciano.

"Uh ... okay, sure," he replied, somewhat awkwardly. He didn't know what to make of her hair tossing, batty eyes, and affectionate touching, but he figured it was all good as long as she was going to stay with them in Tribeca. And as she said, as long as Marciano was there, she'd stay.

When Marciano walked into Aunt Monique's apartment with Mauria Brown at his side, mouths dropped. Natasha had been running around the apartment all day like a chicken with its head chopped off. She even sent Enya to Woodsrow & Campertine to notify Monique, who was so stressed out by the news that she smoked about forty cigarettes on her way home.

When Marciano and Mauria arrived in the apartment, they were greeted by Natasha, Betty, and Enya. Monique was taking a spa bath in her master suite, and Max couldn't return since the sun was still out.

"I think I need to sit down," Natasha said to herself as soon as the door opened. She walked over to the dining room table and pulled out a chair.

"Everything's cool," Marciano said, closing the front door behind him. "Mauria went to her mom's apartment and overheard Candice talking about some really crazy plot to assassinate the winner of Best Designer at the Fabbies."

"Mom is nominated," Betty remarked. She was still standing beside Enya near the entrance.

"I know," Marciano replied. "Mauria doesn't want anything to do with this. She's on our side. We just need to figure out how we're going to handle Friday night."

"What a nightmare," Betty said, and put her hands to her head as she walked toward the dining table to join her younger sister.

"I have an idea—something we can do about Mom's fashion show," Marciano nervously told them. He looked at Mauria, and then back at his sisters. We can talk about it later when Max gets here, but I think I have a solution for the runway shows *and* for the Fabbies."

Natasha and Betty looked at each, and then to Enya, who was wearing her typical unemotional poker face.

"At this point, I'm open to whatever," Natasha said in dismissal. "But yeah, let's wait till Max gets back. And maybe Elle will call us—that would be a miracle."

"Hey, even though I'm not a hostage anymore, are you guys still gonna cook for me?" Mauria asked in the direction of Natasha and Betty. The sisters glared at each other.

Not long after the sun fell from the Manhattan skyline, Max rushed back to Tribeca. He was certainly surprised to hear that Mauria had escaped in his absence, and returned by her own will. He was even more surprised by how much Mauria was cozying up to Marciano, but that was another subject entirely.

Once Max was back and Aunt Monique was done with her spa bath, everyone gathered around the kitchen table to discuss options for later in the week. With no word from Elle, Maude, or Claude, the two-bedroom Tribeca apartment had become a hotbed of confusion. Mauria Brown filled everyone in on the conversation she'd overheard between Candice and Isabelle, and everyone agreed that they needed to attend the Fabbies and try to prevent the assassination.

What everyone didn't know was how to handle the runway shows on Thursday. Since the Fabbies were scheduled for Friday night, Thursday's runway shows were of critical importance. Maude and Rafaela Simone were both in the lineup, and their respective runway shows were going to be the deciding factor in the voting. Maude was the projected winner, but a catastrophic runway show would easily hand the Best Designer award to her nemesis, Rafaela.

Unfortunately, winning meant certain death at this year's Fabulous Fashion Awards. Natasha asked her companions if she thought they should tell Maude and the other nominees. If only Maude would answer her cell phone …

Betty countered with the next best idea: that they inform all of the event's organizers. This idea was crushed when Monique—in between sips (and spills, the amount of sips and spills being pretty much equal) from her martini glass—declared that Caligae oversees the Fabbies every year.

Once Betty's idea was shot down, Max chimed in. He asked if they should try to stir up problems within Caligae before Friday night. He hoped that if enough people got wind of Candice Brown's intentions, they could rise up and overthrow Isabelle, or maybe even cancel or postpone the Fabbies. Monique once again crushed the idea, and went on to elaborate about Caligae's massive bureaucratic system. Apparently it could take up to six months to legally and ethically remove a director. But they only had one week.

As more and more bad ideas flew around the table, Marciano was as quiet as could be. Rafaela's offer was exploding within his head like a DJ's sick beats at a South Beach circuit party. Suddenly he was faced with the opportunity to both fulfill Rafaela's wishes and keep his mom out of trouble. If he could sabotage Maude's fashion show, then Rafaela Simone would win the Best Designer award. Then he'd just have to work out a plan with the team to ensure that Rafaela lived past the Fabbies. The rewards could be great for him if he pulled it off. He'd both protect his mom, and get his own fashion line at a Manhattan boutique. On the downside, Rafaela's life was at stake …

"What if we sabotaged Mom's show?" he asked. The words slipped out of his mouth as if he couldn't hold his thoughts inside anymore.

"To keep her from winning?" Betty asked, and although Marciano was bracing for mischievous or angry looks from his siblings, they themselves wondered if it wasn't a bad idea. "She'd be safe from harm at the Fabbies."

"Then what—we're gonna put someone else in the line of fire?" Natasha asked.

"Someone other than Mom, yes," Betty answered. "We would still go and try to stop the assassination, but at least Mom would be safe. I mean, I'd hate to take this win away from Mom, because I really think she deserves it. But if it saves her life—"

"Would Mom rather have some award that doesn't mean anything, or her life?" Marciano asked, eloquently stating his position. "An award is just an award. It's not going to make her a better designer."

"Obviously she'd rather have her life," Natasha replied, although she wasn't sold on the idea of sabotaging the show. She really wished that her mom was there to weigh in on the conversation. "I don't know—I know that Mom's a good person too, and she wouldn't want to put someone else in harm's way. I feel like Mom wouldn't care about the award, but she'd care about putting someone like Rafaela in danger. Aunt Monique?"

"I've known your mom for thirty years, and no one knows her better than I," Monique replied, waving her fingers in the air as she spoke.

"So what do you think she would do?"

Monique stared blankly at Natasha, and then shrugged her shoulders: "What?"

"You said you know Mom more than anyone else, so what do you think she would do in this situation?"

"In what situation?"

"The situation we've been talking about for the past hour," Natasha said, narrowing her eyes at Monique, who shrugged again and flashed her long black eyelashes.

"Oh, baby, I tuned outta that conversation fifty-nine minutes ago."

Natasha shook her head in frustration, and glanced up at the table. Enya was sharpening her knife, Mauria was sharpening her nails, and about the only thing Max was doing was looking sharp. He hadn't said a word in a while, and wasn't offering any opinions about Marciano's idea.

"Let's just think about it," Marciano said, holding his arms out in front of him. He looked like he was trying to imitate a bad divorce lawyer. *I know he fathered three children out of wedlock, Your Honor, but come on, don't you think he at least deserves the house in Barbados?* Although Natasha wasn't fully sold on her twin brother's idea, she wasn't ready to dismiss it either. She wouldn't be able to live with herself if she shot down the idea, and Maude got murdered at the Fabbies as the result.

Natasha knew she'd forever feel like it was her own fault, and it would be so difficult for her to face her father and siblings afterward.

"And then when they announce the winner," Marciano continued, but before he could complete his sentence, a wicked idea came to him. He had been trying to connect the dots that explained why exactly they needed Mauria. Elle had foreseen some event, and said that Mauria was vital to their mission. Yet, it hadn't been clear what the mission was, or why Mauria's presence was so important.

"She'll freeze time," Marciano blurted out in excitement. "That's why we need her here. When they announce the winner of Best Designer, Mauria will freeze time so that we can stop the assassin as soon as they try to strike. That way if we sabotage Mom's show and Rafaela wins, there's still a huge chance that she'll be okay."

"That's actually not a bad idea," Betty chimed in. "Regardless of who wins Best Designer, we can harness Mauria's powers to help us. I'm sure the venue—hey, does anyone know where the venue is this year? Is it Madison Square Garden?"

"Central Park," Natasha answered.

"In February?"

"I guess they want to take winter fashion literally."

"Well there must be some kind of security room or tent where they monitor cameras on the premises," Betty said. "If you guys can get me back there, I can tap into the equipment and be your eyes from above."

"Enya can get you in there, and make sure no one disrupts you," Marciano said, beaming with excitement from the fact that his older sister was going along with his idea. "See, Natasha? This is a great idea. Mauria, how long can you stop time for?"

"Eh—it depends," she muttered. "It wears me out. I can only hold it for so long. Maybe thirty seconds to a minute at the most—I don't think I've ever done longer. You guys will have to be quick."

"We can be quick," Marciano replied, and then rested his gaze upon Natasha. She still had a skeptical look on her face.

"It sounds like a good idea, but I'm still not sold on sabotaging Mom's fashion show."

"Tash, it'll be fine," Marciano argued. "I think this plan will work. And there's zero risk for Mom if we sabotage her show on Thursday. Rafaela will win the award, and then we'll save the day. But there's always risk involved with everything. Are you willing to put that risk on our mom's life?"

Marciano's words stuck in Natasha's mind like chewing gum on a pair of Pradas. She didn't want to put her mom at risk, but for some reason the idea of sabotaging the Maude by Maude runway show just seemed dirty. She couldn't imagine if Maude found out that her own children were responsible for her losing the most important award in fashion. It's not like it was guaranteed that Maude would win, but she seemed to be the favorite against Rafaela. Winning the Fabbie for Best Designer would be a dream come true. How could Natasha deprive her own mother of that privilege—one that might never happen again?

"Let's think about it," Natasha diplomatically suggested. "We have until Thursday afternoon. We might even hear from Mom by then, and then we can go over this plan with her. I don't want to make all these crazy decisions too far in advance."

"I think you're right," Betty said. "We wait to hear from Mom before we decide what to do about the runway shows. But at least we have a solid plan for Friday night. And we have a whole week to refine it."

Everyone quietly nodded, and then got up from the table to go off and do their own thing. Mauria had already cut a deal with Monique to use her spa bathroom all week in return for a pair of Jimmy Choos. Since the rest of the houseguests lacked an endless collection of shoes to use as bargaining power, they were forced to loiter around the kitchen and crowded guest bedroom.

As Natasha stood up from the table, Max was quick to offer a comforting gesture. He wrapped his arm around her back, and leaned into her.

"You okay?"

As long as Max was wrapping his large, masculine arms around her, she was much better than okay. But she wasn't going to tell him that.

"I'm confused. *Really* confused," she admitted, and let her head hang down so that her eyes rested upon the dining room table.

"Let's take a walk."

"I thought it's not really safe to go outside?"

"It's not," he told her, "but if Marciano can do it, why can't we?"

Natasha turned to Max, and found herself within kissing range. *Kissing range* was like a minefield for Natasha. As soon as she'd get into that space with a guy, she'd find some way to detonate the mood. Maybe she'd watched too many cheesy movies where the girl and guy get within kissing range, and then the girl says something awkward, and the guy responds by laughing in an über-masculine way, before sweeping her into his arms and kissing her. Like these fictional girls, Natasha felt compelled to say something whenever she found herself within kissing range, although what she found was that real-life guys weren't quite like the fictional Fabios. Instead of a hearty chuckle and sweeping embrace, she'd end up with, "Uh—you're a weirdo," or her favorite, "When's the last time you brushed your teeth?"

Embarrassing for a girl. Mortifying for a girl who's about to get kissed. And so when Natasha looked into Max's eyes, she felt the pressure raining down on her.

"Is it wise to let a vampire this close to my neck?" she asked him, and then braced for his rejection.

"Yes," he replied, much more relaxed than she anticipated. "You're a Thirteen. If I bit you, I'd burst into dust. Actually, if your blood touches me it'll burn through my skin."

"I suddenly feel dangerous."

"Come with me," Max said, and he took hold of her hand as he walked to a window in the dining room. He unlocked it and pushed it open, allowing the cold winter air to burst into the apartment. Natasha didn't have a jacket on, and she had a feeling where this was going. But she stood by his side and braced herself as Max leaned forward, pointing his head of black hair toward the open window. "Ready?"

"Yeah," she squeaked. She felt like she was on a roller coaster that was about to take off. Natasha closed her eyes, and moments later she felt a yank, followed by a rush of cold air. The February winds completely absorbed her, wrapping her body in what felt like an icy blanket. It was cold enough that even though she was only in the air for a matter of seconds, each second felt like ten.

When Natasha's feet landed on a hard surface, she breathed in relief, and waited before opening her eyes. She wasn't sure if she'd be on top of the Statue of Liberty, or the Empire State Building, or on the ice-skating rink at the Rockefeller Center. But Natasha slowly opened her eyes and braced herself for a romantic scene.

"We're on the roof of my aunt's building?"

"Yeah, well—I can't fly that far," Max admitted, and shrugged his shoulders. The roof of Monique's building featured a semifinished deck that was accessible to any tenant, although February was a little too cold for most to venture upstairs. Max had laid out a blanket to sit on, plus some warm blankets to wrap themselves with—or at least to wrap Natasha with, since vampires weren't bothered by the cold. Natasha had to admit that it was cute. It wasn't the crown of the Statue of Liberty, but it was a start.

Max wrapped Natasha with a faux fur blanket as she sat down and crossed her legs. From the rooftop of Monique's building, they could see the lights of Tribeca extending down into the massive skyscrapers of the Financial District.

"Isn't it interesting—Manhattan? How these neighborhoods can look so different, and yet just blend into one another in ways that are supposed to make sense? Philly is a tiny version of this."

"Have you ever been to Paris?"

Natasha turned to Max and put her hand over her chest.

"I would absolutely love to go. Unfortunately we haven't traveled much at all—mainly, I guess, because my parents wanted to keep Marc and me safe. There's still so much that I haven't seen. Have you been everywhere?"

"No one's been *everywhere*," he replied. "But I've been a lot of places."

"From working for Caligae?"

"You could say that."

"So you were pretty quiet downstairs when we talked about sabotaging the fashion shows. Any thoughts?" Natasha asked him. She was interested in hearing his opinion. After all, she thought that he was going to come on board and become the de facto leader until Elle's return to New York. Instead he seemed to be taking more of the quiet approach, waiting for everyone to come up with a plan, and then being there to implement it.

"I'm not much of a strategist," he replied, and then closed his lips as he put an arm around Natasha. "Better at following orders."

"Well has your boss—this Dorina White—given you any orders? Or ideas?"

"As long as Candice and Isabelle are removed from power, then she's happy. She doesn't have a good plan other than to jump onto your bandwagon. If she did, she would've taken down the sisters a long time ago."

"Well, I guess I can't object to a cute vampire as added help," Natasha said, and turned to him with a little smile. "This still feels so overwhelming. We're having all these conversations about the Fabbies and Caligae and—I still can't even picture what Caligae *is*. I've been to the Fabbies before. My mom's taken me. But, like—all this talk about Candice and her sister and this ancient organization—"

"You remember that magical feel of Woodsrow & Campertine?"

"Yeah."

"Well apply that to the Pentagon, and you have Caligae. An underground, high-tech operation that keeps track of all supernaturals, and the entire fashion industry, all under one roof. Well, one roof per continent. And there are a bunch of agents like myself who fly around and maintain order."

"So, like—if Yves Saint Laurent comes out with an awful line of denim jackets, you'll intervene?"

Max shook his head in amusement.

"Not quite. More like major fashion conspiracies, or individual supernaturals who are causing trouble. You know—I was part of the team that took down a secret league of vampire designers when they released the V-neck. It was really controversial. They wanted to market a mainstream shirt that would expose more of the neck area for biting."

"Looks like they succeeded!" Natasha replied.

"Sometimes certain fashion trends are impossible to contain. The V-neck is popular now, but we fought it for a long time. We were worried that it would lead to more bitings."

"Where do you get your blood?"

"Animals or other supernaturals. Humans don't taste good. A good analogy for you would be like—if you were to eat dirt."

"That bad, huh?"

"Yeah, sort of a last resort, if you're starving," Max replied. "But we've been talking about me so far. Tell me something about Natasha."

"Well, I think your life is interesting," Natasha told him, looking deep into his eyes as she shrugged and bunched her lips together. "I haven't really done anything—traveled anywhere . . . I feel like I'm at the beginning of my story."

"Any guys in your life?"

"My gay brother," she said, and laughed. "Or my crazy French father. No, I don't have a boyfriend. I've never really had a boyfriend. And Betty doesn't help me out in that department, because she's more interested in computers and stuff—never really been one to date. I think she had an online boyfriend once, but they broke up after he killed off her character in a role-playing game."

"You're too pretty to be single."

"I think you have it the other way around," Natasha replied, laughing at his one-liners. "I'm too single to be pretty."

"What's that supposed to mean?"

"Exactly how it sounds. I've been way too single for way too long. I work in the fashion industry—well, I guess I don't have much a choice—but I love it regardless. And I know what pretty is. And you know what? I'm happy being me. I know I don't look like Mauria Brown, but I can still rock a pair of Manolos. You know, my mom might have a store up on Fifth Avenue soon."

"Really?"

"Yeah, if she wins Best Designer it'll be a sure thing," Natasha said, and instantly her mood plummeted. Something about being whisked up to the rooftop had given her a little burst of euphoria, but it was quickly replaced by the realization of the upcoming danger. "I haven't heard anything from them. My mom's not responding to my calls. My dad isn't. Elle doesn't even have a cell phone. She's probably the weirdest person I've ever met—old, blind vampire with a British accent. I don't know for sure that my parents are safe, or anyone in the office back home. Something tells me that they're safe, but I don't know for sure.

"I remember looking into my mom's eyes before we left for New York, when she told me about the potential store on Fifth Avenue. It was like her dream come true. And it was cool for me, to see my mom still dreaming at her age. To realize that she didn't have to have a store on Fifth Avenue in her twenties to feel successful. Instead of her twenties, it would have to be her fifties. It gave her such a rush, and that carried over to me. This was before I knew about the fashion industry—the *truth* about it. I just really want to see her win that award. She deserves it. And I want her to have a store in Manhattan."

"So you don't think we should sabotage her runway show?"

Natasha methodically shook her head no as she looked off in the direction of the Financial District.

"How could I take that away from her? Even if it means she's placed in extra danger, then we just need to be on extra alert."

"You realize who you're dealing with?" Max asked her, and his voice lost some of the warmth that it had just previously carried. "You can't even begin to imagine the power that Candice and Isabelle possess. Almost all of the ruling Colors will be at the Fabbies, and none of them are sympathetic to your cause. You have my help, and Mauria's, and maybe Elle's if she returns. But you and your brother are inexperienced."

"So you're saying we can't do it?"

Max shrugged, and turned away from Natasha.

"I don't know," he told her. He still had an arm around her, and he used it to gently rub her shoulders. Natasha leaned forward and sighed as Max's fingers massaged her upper back.

"I wish I could've met you in a produce aisle," she softly remarked.

"Never would've happened," Max replied. As cold air swept over their heads, they each smiled.

Chapter Eight

War erupted in the Tribeca apartment of Aunt Monique sometime between 2:00 a.m. and 2:15 a.m. on Sunday. Everyone saw it coming. The first warning sign was when Mauria woke up Monique in the latter's master suite, and proceeded to have a top-secret meeting that lasted all of five minutes. After the exchange of a limited-edition Gucci handbag, Mauria was given keys to the master suite, leaving Monique with nowhere to sleep except for her guest bedroom. The guest bedroom was already cramped: Natasha and her siblings had been uncomfortably cramming onto a queen bed. When they were woken up by Monique with orders to "sleep in the kitchen, honey," tensions flared. The late-night coup d'état of bedrooms, coupled with the ban on stepping foot in the living room, meant that the Philadelphians had to make due with sleeping bags on the kitchen floor.

This arrangement lasted for a total of about seven minutes. The siblings gathered together and negotiated a deal with Enya. Even though she didn't sleep, and therefore didn't care where anyone else slept, the living room ban had kept her from watching her favorite TV shows, namely courtroom dramas. In return for control of the TV, Enya promised to negotiate a deal for living-room privileges. And since Enya's idea of negotiation involved smeared mascara and broken arms, the siblings felt confident that they'd found the right diplomat.

Two seconds after Enya walked into Monique's guest room, the latter surrendered, and the living-room ban was over. The siblings would be able to sleep on sofas instead of hardwood floor.

The sofas turned out to be much better than a cramped queen bed, and even though Natasha had a lot on her mind, she found it slightly easier to sleep that night. When she woke up on Sunday morning, it was to the smells and sounds that resulted from her older sister cooking breakfast. Marciano was still passed out, and in the kitchen Betty was trying to teach Enya how to cook an omelet. Enya wasn't exactly delicate, so the minor issue of cracking an egg was challenging for her. Two cartons had been demolished before she finally got it right.

"Mmm," Natasha said loudly enough for her sister to hear her. Natasha didn't know how to cook, and had no interest in figuring it out. Cooking was different for Betty. She could control appliances with her mind, and so preparing four dishes at once was an exciting challenge. Betty was technical-minded, and liked the science of cooking. She liked to mix ingredients and observe what worked well, and what didn't work at all. Natasha was blessed to have Betty around, otherwise her mornings and nights would be dominated by restaurants and takeout.

"Good morning, pumpkin," Betty called out from the kitchen.

Natasha rose from the sofa like a zombie popping out of a coffin. And on top of that, she looked the part. Her curly hair resembled a greasy afro, and the upper half of her face carried a weary look.

"I need a shower."

"You need more than that," Marciano remarked with his eyes still closed. Natasha had assumed he was still asleep. Her twin brother was lying on one of the sofas, his headful of short black hair planted in a pillow. "Because of your disappearance with Max last night, Betty and I decided it's time to give you *the talk*."

"What talk? And we didn't disappear, we just—"

"Don't listen to him, Natasha," Betty countered. "I'm not giving you any talk. If you want to date—"

"It wasn't a date!"

"Obviously Mom never broke it down for either of you," Marciano told the girls. "Being the local expert on relationships and anatomy, I feel the need to interject here, before ... well, before there are little fanged toddlers running around Tribeca."

Natasha glared at her brother with a menacing pair of eyes.

"All we did was go up on the roof and *talk*."

"So that's what they're calling it these days, huh?" Marciano replied. "And by the way, your man left for Woodsrow & Campertine this morning with the princess of darkness."

"Stop it," Betty teasingly told Marciano. "Natasha, come eat breakfast. I'll make you whatever you—"

"Hold up, hold up," Natasha said. She arched her legs and spread her arms out, as if she were about to engage in a wrestling match. "There's no way that Mauria would wake up that early."

"While you were snoring and the rest of us were trying to sleep, we saw Mauria and Max heading out the front door," Marciano told her. "I asked them where they were going, and they said the department store."

"Yeah, because Max has been sleeping there during daylight," Natasha countered, but then paused as she pondered the circumstances. "So wait—Mauria went with him?"

"Yup. Probably stopped by Tempur-Pedic for a two-person coffin."

"Not funny," Natasha coldly replied, and a sudden weariness came upon her. Obviously Marciano was provoking her in order to get a reaction, and normally she wouldn't be so easily bothered, but there was something different about this incident. Why would Mauria wake up early to accompany Max to the department store? Lots of logical reasons popped into Natasha's head. Maybe Mauria wanted to go shopping, and felt safer if Max accompanied her. Maybe Max needed information from her regarding Candice Brown, and a shopping trip was the perfect opportunity for a private, long conversation. There were lots of reasons why they could have gone together, and yet, Natasha found herself not wanting to believe any of them.

"Do you think I should be worried?" Natasha asked, the words creeping out of her mouth in a methodical monotone. She sat down on the armrest of the sofa where she'd slept the previous night.

"No," Betty said, quickly dismissing Natasha's concerns.

"Are you kidding?" Marciano asked his twin sister. "I'm the one who should be worried. Mauria told me last night that she *likes* me. And not in the gay best friend kind of way. I'm ready to start drawing charts and diagrams to explain it to her."

"All this shows is that you really like the guy, and don't want anything to get in the way of a potential relationship," Betty warmly spoke from the kitchen.

"Duh," Marciano said. "What is this, Feelings 101? Listen Tashy Washy, you two haven't even held hands on a Ferris wheel yet."

"He just seems special to me," Natasha argued in her own defense. "I don't want anything to mess it up."

"Is it possible that your subconscious is creating an intense, monkeylike primal attraction for him in order to balance your mood due to your fears about this week, and its implications with our safety and that of our parents?"

"Or maybe I just like him," Natasha told her brother. "What's wrong with that? I just like him. And sure—it's nice to feel this during a dark time for all of us. Maybe it gives me a break from being stressed out."

"Not really, because now you're only getting more stressed out," Marciano countered.

He did have a point. Natasha wondered if her recent infatuation with Max was only causing more harm than good. Should she be focusing on more important things, like the safety of her family at the Fabbies? Or the fact that the wicked queen of plastic surgery, Candice Brown, was out to get her?

"Enya, what would you do about this?" Natasha asked their bodyguard-on-loan.

"I would kill both of them, just as I wish I could have killed this bacon while it was still alive," she replied without even looking up from the plates full of food that she and Betty had been preparing for the past hour. Enya was using a hunting knife to cut the bacon, and it was disturbing enough for Natasha that she momentarily forgot what they were talking about.

"Remind me not to ask you again for relationship advice."

"Baby girl, who needs relationship advice?" a frazzled Monique asked as she walked into the kitchen with her fake blonde hair up in curlers, a black eye mask covering her eyes, two cigarettes sticking out of her mouth, and a silk robe hanging off her shoulders.

"I do, Aunt Monique," Natasha told her, swinging around on the sofa to face her aunt. "I really like Max, and when I woke up today I found out that he went out to Woodsrow & Campertine with Mauria. Should I be feeling weird about this?"

"Who is Max?"

"Um ... the studly vampire who has been staying with us—"

"Oh him?" Monique asked, and stopped in her tracks just short of the kitchen. "Phew, girl, I thought the IRS had finally caught up with me."

Everyone—Enya included—blinked their eyes and tried to process Monique's revelation.

"Honey, you betta fight for yo man," Monique said as she put her cigarettes out in Betty's coffee, just as the latter was lifting it to her mouth. It wasn't on purpose, but disposing of cigarettes while wearing a black eye mask probably wasn't the smartest idea. "And I don't trust no one who would trade a Tom Ford–era Gucci handbag to have my bedroom for a week. I wouldn't trade that baby for nothing. Not even a real baby."

"Well, do you know why they might've gone together?" Natasha asked her aunt, who had grabbed the pitcher of coffee and was blindly pouring it into a mug on the countertop. About ten percent of the coffee made it into the mug, and Betty rushed to clean up the rest.

"Count Fangula has been sleeping in my boutique. If you go to the mall, I need you to return some pantyhose for me. And check up on that good-for-nothing mummy I hired to work the front desk."

"Okay, Aunt Monique," Natasha said. "Guys? Woodsrow & Campertine?"

"You sure it's safe?" Betty asked her, calling out from the kitchen, where she was wiping up coffee that had spilled all over Monique's robe, floor, and kitchen counter.

"We'll bring Enya," Natasha replied.

"Don't forget, baby, the department store is a safety zone," Monique advised her young niece. "Caligae isn't allowed to arrest people there. There hasn't been a fight in Woodsrow & Campertine in over one hundred years. In fact, I remember the last fight. Your aunt had three men fighting over her. An oil baron, a railroad tycoon, and a news media magnate."

"You had three men fighting over you?" Betty asked her.

"You say that with such surprise," Monique replied. "I've had men fighting over me since the dawn of time."

"And she means that literally," Marciano added.

"I look at three things, ya hear?" Monique told them, waving her coffee mug in the air. "First the shoes. Then the bank account. Then the health record."

"Why would you care about a guy's health record?" Natasha asked her aunt, whose lips scrunched up into a pink ball.

"Like I always say, don't waste your breath unless he's close to death. Now does Count Fangula have any kids?"

"Uh, you mean Max?" Natasha asked her. "Well, no—"

"Phew, nothing worse than money-hungry stepchildren," Monique said, and dramatically wiped her own forehead. "He got a car?"

"I think he can fly."

"Unless he got a Benz, you two ain't friends. This Egyptian *knows* better."

"I'll keep that in mind," Natasha nervously told her. "Well, I'm ready to head out. You guys coming?"

"Where, to the department store?" Marciano asked her. He made a loud grunt and slowly sat up from the sofa. "Hey Aunt Monique. Are there any consignment shops in Woodsrow & Campertine?"

"I'm gonna consign you if you ask me that again. Consignment store, meh."

"Please Aunt Monique, like half of your closet isn't secondhand Prada."

"You're crossing a fine line," she warned him, but he laughed anyway. "Listen—there's a market for all that stuff, but if you tell anyone I told you about it, I'll kill ya. It's called the Dutch Market."

"What about the department store?" Natasha complained, but her brother quickly shot her a look of accusation.

"Do you want to go to Woodsrow & Campertine to buy things, or to stalk your boy toy?"

"Stalk?" Natasha shot back at Marciano. "I'm not stalking anyone." She shook her curly brown hair, and did her best to seem convincing, but she knew she wasn't fooling anyone.

"Sis, I think maybe it's better that we go to this Dutch Market," Betty softly advised her younger sister. "You love consignment shops. It'll cheer you right up."

"Fine," Natasha reluctantly announced. "Are you going, Aunt Monique?"

"Honey, I've gotta do my hair. I'll tell ya where it is and how to get there."

"Oh, yeah?" Marciano taunted her. "If you're so opposed to this place, then how do you know where it is?"

Monique still had her black eye mask on, but Marciano could feel the malice coming from her covered expression.

"Is the Dutch Market safe?" Betty asked her aunt, who nodded in approval.

"Safe as my Tribeca apartment."

Aunt Monique's directions to the Dutch Market weren't exactly GPS quality. She drew a picture of Manhattan in crayon and spilled coffee on the destination marker. But after about an hour and several wrong turns, the young group of travelers arrived at the storefront that acted as the secret entrance to the Dutch Market.

The entrance was in a shop on Canal Street, in a dark, hidden room where shelves of fake designer goods covered every wall. The owner of the shop was a four foot eleven Chinese man named Wen, who was born and raised in Brooklyn but faked an intense Beijing accent in order to appear more authentic to tourists. He was buddies with Cedric, and the two used to be roommates in Hell's Kitchen until Wen got into some trouble with Caligae and was blacklisted.

Blacklisted supernatural beings were troublemakers who either disturbed humans or entered the ultra-taboo profession of selling counterfeit designer goods. Most of the peddlers of fake luxury products were regular humans, and the two-thousand-year-old curse that protected humans from supernaturals had unintended consequences: it protected a burgeoning illegal industry. Since supernaturals couldn't forcefully stop humans from manufacturing and selling fake jeans, handbags, and watches, they were stuck going through the regular court system. Every once in a while an angry supernatural would intimidate or bully a counterfeiter, but these incidences were rare. Instead, Caligae just kept a close eye on the illegal markets.

Wen got into the counterfeits market when he realized that he could use his extensive knowledge of fashion to make some extra money. He'd be able to tell which fakes were closest to the real thing, and therefore sell the best products. But selling fake Chanel handbags only hurt Chanel's brand image, and so although he made some quick money, he also made a lot of enemies among his own people. It wasn't long before Caligae caught him and blacklisted him. He was allowed to keep his shop under the condition that he spy on other counterfeiters and manage one of the secret entranceways to the Dutch Market.

The entrance to the Dutch Market could've been a lot more glamorous. A pile of knockoff luggage was stacked in front of a hole that looked like a giant sewer pipe. In fact, as soon as Natasha saw the entrance, she was reluctant to go in. A combination of fears sprang upon her, including claustrophobia and sewer rats. But Wen assured her everything would be fine. He also tried to sell her a knockoff bracelet spray-painted silver, but no sooner had the words left his mouth than Enya's clenched fist was hovering above his head.

Natasha, her siblings, and Enya ducked through the entrance, and after walking for ten steps they came to a rusty ladder leading downward. Enya went first, so that she could break the fall of anyone who might lose their grip. The tunnel was pitch-black, which added to the eeriness of their surroundings.

"Girl, you have the perfect hair for a rat's nest. You know that?" Marciano teased his twin sister. She nearly broke out into tears.

When they reached the ground, Enya helped everyone off the ladder. They were still in complete darkness, and couldn't see anything around them except for the ladder that had just led the group underground. The only noises were the sounds of their own breathing, coupled with the sound of dripping water.

"What was the last thing Aunt Monique said to do?" Marciano asked. Natasha's fear of rats made her forget any details that Monique had given them about the Dutch Market. Enya was clearly there for brawn, not for brains. Luckily, Betty had the answer.

"Someone just has to click their heels," she said, although her own shyness prevented her from leaping into the air and doing the honor.

"Well in that case—," Marciano remarked, just before bending down and crossing his arms in front of his belly button. He suddenly jumped into the air with the exuberance of a Broadway performer, clicking his heels twice and throwing his arms in the air. And as if a switch had been flipped, the entire room exploded in an eruption of light and noise. The sound of dripping water was replaced by the bustling sounds of an open market, and the thick darkness of the underground had completely disappeared. They were in what seemed like the center of a makeshift town, where a ladder ascended far up into a distant darkness. All around them were stalls and shops, and thousands of people, all moving without distraction. This was an entirely different scene from the old-world elegance of Woodsrow & Campertine. Instead of a massive department store, the Dutch Market was more like an open-air consortium of merchants. The market lacked coordination, but there was still something charming about the way it worked.

"I don't even know where to start," Natasha said to herself. Her fear of coming eye to eye with a New York sewer rat had totally subsided. She was ready for a serious session of retail therapy.

"No rush," Marciano told her, smiling at his twin sister. "We have all day."

"Rolex? Cashmere scarf?" Wen said with a heavy accent that was about as fake as the goods he was peddling. Shortly after he had helped the four young travelers reach the Dutch Market, a tall woman with ginger hair entered his storefront on Canal Street. There was something off about her. Maybe it was the pale skin, or the amber eyes underneath a silk headscarf. But Wen dealt with so many people on a daily basis that sometimes he was just more interested in making a sale than worrying about who was coming in and out of his shop.

"Only if it's *top quality*," the woman replied with a powerful, commanding voice. Wen knew exactly what this meant, and he led her to the hidden back room that housed all the best-quality counterfeits. It was the same room with the entrance to the Dutch Market, although he'd covered up the space since the young group left.

"Best quality back here," Wen enthusiastically told her. The woman took one walk around the little room, her white heels clicking with each step. "You want handbag?"

"I'm not looking for a handbag," she told him, and turned to face Wen. As he looked up into her amber eyes, something about them changed. They suddenly became paler, deeper, until all the light of the room was sucked into them. He tried to look away from her, but each time he averted his eyes it was as if he were blind to everything around him. He couldn't even see the handbags stacked on shelves right next to him. All he could see was the thin outline of the woman.

"What are you doing to me?" the words scrambled out of his mouth. He wasn't bothering to speak with the phony accent anymore.

"Did they go to the Dutch Market?"

"Who?" Wen replied. He toppled backward over a piece of luggage on the ground, and struggled to stand up.

"The boy and the three girls."

"What do I get out of telling you?"

The woman smiled, and bent down so that she was hovering above Wen. The latter finally stopped struggling, and looked back into her eyes. They held his gaze, mesmerizing him.

"I hate counterfeiters," she told him, and smiled to reveal long, white fangs. "If not for the great curse, I'd kill all of them. Especially the traitors like you."

"I made a deal with Caligae."

The woman laughed. It was a sadistic laugh, and one that sent chills racing through Wen's limp body.

"Do you want to know who sent me?" she asked Wen. "Candice Brown. And she doesn't honor Caligae's *deals*."

"Please!" Wen pleaded. "They're in the Dutch Market! I just sent them down there minutes ago. You—you—"

"Not only a counterfeiter, but also a rat," the ginger-haired woman remarked. "I think you should know that you've sold your last fake Louis bag."

"What, are you gonna make me work in a factory?" he asked, his face lighting up in fright, and he clutched onto the handbags scattered around the floor of the back room.

"No," she replied, and flashed her fangs once more as she moved within inches of his neck. "Something far worse."

"Bellissimo!" the Italian shop owner exclaimed as he presented Marciano with the most hideous, chain-covered, bejeweled leather jacket that the twenty-one-year-old had seen in his entire life. It looked like the result of Roberto Cavalli going to work for Harley-Davidson. The two were just not meant for each other.

"That's awful," Marciano bluntly told the shop owner, a rotund man with black skinny jeans, long white hair, and a mist of musty cologne that followed him around the small secondhand store. It was obvious that this guy was trying to offload his worst inventory on Marciano and the girls.

"What you think about this cloak, ay?" he asked Marciano. "Perfecto?"

"When I join a secret society and have a use for one of those, I'll let you know," Marc replied. "Betty, you've gotta help me over here."

"You know, I really don't like the intensity of these salespeople down here," she replied as she sorted through a rack of dresses. It was true that the Dutch Market had some intense salespeople. Betty assumed that most of them were working on commission, so it made sense for them to be as aggressive and outgoing as possible in order to make the most sales. The only problem was that the sales techniques were obnoxious and not customer-centered. Instead of trying to be helpful, these guys were just trying to pawn off hideous outfits that no one else wanted.

"Yeah, I can't breathe," her brother remarked, waving his hand to his face. "I have a four-foot Italian throwing patterns from the 1980s at me. I feel like I'm in a bad music video."

"Well, let's go try somewhere else," Natasha told her siblings as she tried to use Enya's rock-solid body to maneuver through the thrift store without getting verbally pummeled by salespeople. Marciano lifted out his arms and twirled himself like a whirlwind, all while the mustachioed shop owner followed after him with arms full of rhinestone-covered laptop bags.

"Get out!" Marciano shouted, practically leaping through the door. Enya and Natasha followed him, and Betty was the last to break free. No sooner had they stepped foot on the busy street than two young-looking beggars bombarded them with cotton socks for sale.

"I can't even compose a thought down here," Natasha complained as she scrambled to get away from the beggars, who were waving socks in her face in a desperate attempt to earn some money.

"Socks! You need socks!" one of the beggars cried.

"Um, I need my eardrums—," replied Marciano. He covered his ears with both hands as a look of grief overtook him. "Enya, can you do something?"

But before Enya had time to react, a shadow loomed over the four travelers that seemed to change the disposition of the beggars. In just a matter of seconds, they went from shoving thin pieces of cotton at Marciano and Natasha to slowly backing away from the twins. Natasha watched as the young beggars blinked their eyes repeatedly, and then scrambled off in separate directions.

"What the—"

Betty was the first to make sense of what had just happened. When she turned around, a woman was standing directly behind them. She was almost as tall as Enya, and was dressed in a black satin gown that flowed down to her white pumps. Her hair was ginger, and was wrapped into a silk headscarf. The woman's mouth was open just enough to reveal a pair of fangs, just beyond red lips of such a deep hue that if blood were smeared upon them, no one would ever notice.

Betty was struck by the woman's posture, her pale skin, and the calm aggression with which she had just intimidated the two beggars. Suddenly no one was bothering the young group of travelers. With the appearance of the woman, not a single salesperson was shouting at them or grabbing their arms and legs. The busy Dutch Market finally seemed manageable.

"Oh, look, it's the fairy godmother of thrift stores," Marciano remarked, but as usual, he was the only one laughing.

"On the contrary, I'm just someone who knows the market very well. Someone who saw a group of clueless young people and decided to lend a hand," the woman replied. She spoke with an intensity that befitted her perfect posture and piercing amber eyes.

"Thank you," Betty told her, nodding her head in appreciation. "I mean it. We were—"

"Ready to claw our eyes out," Natasha finished her sister's sentence, and grabbed her own curly hair in feigned frustration. "How'd you get rid of them?"

"Obviously you're new to the marketplace," the woman said, and smiled briefly with those red lips. "I'm Olympia."

She extended her hand, first to Enya, who firmly shook it. Betty followed, then Marciano.

"How ya do?" Marciano asked, adding a playful accent to his voice. His twin sister rolled her eyes.

When Olympia's hand touched Natasha, the two locked eyes, and the latter felt something that she couldn't explain. Olympia's hand was cold, like a patch of dirt on a winter morning. And there was something familiar about her. Natasha couldn't place where she'd seen her before, or *if* she'd ever seen her. Was it a fashion magazine? Everyone in the marketplace had to be somehow involved in fashion.

"You must work in fashion, huh?" Natasha asked, and predictably, Olympia grinned.

"I'm a buyer."

"Oh... our aunt is a buyer for Woodsrow & Campertine," Natasha replied. "Monique—has a little shop for mummies."

"Of course, Monique. How's she holding up?"

"No pun intended, right?" Marciano joked.

"She's doing well," Natasha answered.

"How about I show you the best, quietest little thrift store in the marketplace, and we can pick up the conversation there," Olympia suggested, motioning down the street with one hand.

"Sounds great to us," Natasha replied, and glanced at her companions for approval. Everyone seemed to agree that they needed a little guidance. Thus far, their luck with thrift shops hadn't been so hot, and they were beginning to regret opting out of going to Woodsrow & Campertine.

Olympia began to lead the way, and as she walked, street peddlers moved to give her space. Even some shopkeepers—standing outside to lure potential customers—ran into their stores upon seeing Olympia.

"How are you doing that?" Marciano asked her, and added a spring to his step so that he could catch up with the fast-paced walk of the older vampire.

"It's all in the eyes," she replied, and briefly smiled at him. She walked and talked like a high-powered executive. She didn't look like she belonged in the Dutch Market.

"You come here often?"

"Only on business."

When Olympia suddenly turned on her right heel and walked into a bookstore the size of a standard bedroom, the rest of the group paused. They certainly hadn't come to the Dutch Market to look for books. This was a fashion expedition. But they followed the woman inside, hoping looks would once again deceive them.

Once inside the bookstore, what they saw shocked them. Every single wall was lined from floor to ceiling with dusty, old books, and Olympia was carelessly pulling them off the shelves and tossing them behind her on the mud-stained burgundy carpet. A short, chubby shopkeeper was sitting on a wooden chair in one corner of the store, minding his own business as he read from a cream-colored newspaper.

"Uh ... are you sure you're allowed to do that?" Natasha asked, looking first at Olympia, and then at her twin brother, who was shaking his head in dismay.

"Ah, here's the one," Olympia remarked just as she pulled a thin paperback book from the shelves. Suddenly the front door of the bookstore slammed shut, and every single book in the shop bounced once before falling to the ground. Beyond the empty shelves were rows upon rows of clothing racks, a massive store compared to the smaller shops typical of the Dutch Market. Olympia banged a single hand on one of the wooden shelves that blocked their entry, and it fell to the ground, knocking out each shelf below it.

Olympia was the first to walk through the small opening that she'd created.

"We're here," she said, and held out her hands to present the grand store. The shopkeeper who had been sitting in the corner reading the newspaper grunted, and then slowly stood up to go man the cash register.

After the shock wore off, the group followed Olympia into the main store and stopped for a moment to observe the layout. There was nothing flashy about the store, and it certainly wasn't Woodsrow & Campertine. But the selection seemed endless.

"Womenswear is that way," Olympia pointed. "Men's over there. Shoes, accessories, jewelry—," she went on, pointing to each and every department, none of which clearly marked by any signs. "Enjoy."

"Wow," Natasha mouthed as she began to walk toward formal wear. Betty headed toward leisure wear, and Enya simply stood near the empty bookshelves with her arms folded, carefully observing the scene. The shopkeeper winked at her, but quickly lowered his eyes when Enya flashed her hunting knife.

As Marciano walked off toward men's shoes, he heard the sound of pumps approaching from behind.

"Hey, thanks for showing us this place," he told Olympia after turning to see her following him. "You come here often?"

"Like I said, only on business," she carefully replied. "You have a thing for shoes?"

"I do! I love shoes," he excitedly told her. "I have a ridiculous amount of them, and I hope it only gets bigger and bigger. A hot pair of shoes can make you feel great, you know?"

Olympia pursed her lips and cleared her throat, but didn't answer Marciano's question. When they approached a wall full of sneakers, Marciano instantly located his size and started to grab at the many pairs.

"So I assume you're visiting?" Olympia asked him. "New Yorkers rarely go to the Dutch Market."

"Yeah, just up visiting. Staying with our aunt and a couple friends. What do you think of these?" he asked, and held up a pair of mid-top sneakers that were mostly white with some light-blue patterns.

"Those are cute, aren't they?" Olympia said, getting momentarily distracted before snapping out of it. "Two friends, you said?"

"Yeah, we sort of just met them though. So I guess they're not *friends* friends, but you know how you can meet someone out and then they're your friend all of the sudden? I mean I don't know anything about Mauria, yet all of the sudden we're doing champagne mimosas in Columbus Circle."

Since Marciano was too preoccupied staring at the rows upon rows of shoes, he missed the sudden change in Olympia's expression. The woman had lost her playful smile, and it had been replaced by a look of both surprise and shock.

"And you're all staying together? Sounds like a crowded house."

"It is! One of them is a vampire, so he's gone during the daytime, but yeah, it gets crowded. It's nice though, to have company. I like being around people."

Marciano turned his head to smile at Olympia, but she was nowhere in sight. He quickly shook his head in either direction, looking around the store for any sign of the woman.

"That was weird," he remarked to himself, before returning to the stacks of sneakers.

Candice Brown was startled by the knock on her office door. After shouting in the direction of the doorway, she quickly minimized the solitaire game on her computer monitor.

"Ugh, a nerd?" Candice remarked, frowning as she glanced at the doorway to see a pocket-protector-wearing male executive with rimless, spherical glasses.

"Excuse me?"

"Nothing, you just didn't live up to my expectations," Candice disappointedly replied. "So who the hell are you?"

The executive hurried into Candice's office and occupied a seat in front of her desk. The old wooden junker had been trashed and replaced with a stunning metal desk crafted out of the aluminum of old World War II airplanes. Candice Brown impatiently tapped a pen on the desk as she waited for the man to speak.

"My name's Daniel, and I'm head of IT within Caligae's North American network. We've, uh—we've met several times, but I guess—"

"You don't have a memorable face," Candice bluntly told him. "But anyway, continue."

"I'm sorry," he nervously replied. "Um—"

"Well hurry up! I have *tons* of work to do," Candice added, and then peeked at the solitaire tab minimized at the bottom of her screen. She hoped this interruption wouldn't seriously affect the game's timer.

"Ms. Brown, we at IT run a report every month on Internet activity. It's highly discouraged that Caligae staff quote unquote *surf the web*. This has been one of Isabelle's strict policies."

"Yeah?"

"We give this report to the top managers of each department, showing who in their employ has violated the rule. The report also shows what websites employees have visited. This way the offenders can be reprimanded accordingly."

"Great rule, I love it," Candice replied, waving a single manicured hand. "Now what's your point?"

"Well, Ms. Brown, I went to run the report this morning and it crashed our servers," said Daniel as he lowered his slim glasses. "When we finally managed to pull the report, it was hundreds of pages long, and all pointing to only one user at headquarters."

"Someone in accounts receivable, right? They're the most corrupt in any organization."

"Frankly, Ms. Brown, it was you," said Daniel, causing Candice to frown. "Within just a couple of days in the office, you've managed to have enough Internet activity to actually jam our entire report. And there's quite an extensive list of websites. Online gaming, social networking, dating, message boards for rare stamp collectors—"

"Excuse me," she angrily replied, waving a finger in Daniel's face. "The gaming websites were all educational, and the networking was strictly professional."

"WealthySingleMen dot—"

"Okay, okay," Candice interrupted. "At least ninety-nine percent were professional. Look, I'm trying to cut a deal with my sister so that we can get an internal dating website for the entire secret society."

Daniel paused as he thought about Candice's idea, and after a few seconds his face lit up. "Why, that's an incredible idea! Most of us are overworked and single, and never have time to meet anyone. Why, you're brilliant!"

"Yeah, old news," Candice said. "So here's what you do. Just remove my computer from that little report you make each month, and in return, I'll have an internal dating website up within a week. Now get the hell out of my office."

"You've got it!" Daniel said, and he scrambled to get up from his chair.

Candice Brown rolled her eyes and then clicked on her game of solitaire. But just before she was able to resume playing, her cell phone rang. She moaned much louder than was appropriate, and angrily pressed a button on her phone.

"What?" her abrasive voice exploded into the speaker.

"It's Olympia. I found them. They're in the Dutch Market—"

"It's a safety zone, you dummy."

"I know. But—I know where they're staying, and with whom," Olympia proudly told her boss. "They have Mauria."

"They kidnapped her?"

"No. On the contrary, it seems she went freely with them."

Suddenly Candice Brown was filled with rage, and as she clenched her fists on top of her metal desk, she screamed into the cell phone.

"Bring her to me!"

"Done," Olympia replied, with a casual confidence refined over the course of many centuries.

As soon as Natasha stepped foot back on the streets of Manhattan, she knew something was wrong. Although she hadn't been keeping track of time while in the Dutch Market, she was a seasoned shopper and had an impeccable ability to judge the length of a shopping session. After all, this was a girl who had performed all-day shopping marathons. Once on a Black Friday weekend, she shopped for a record fifty-three hours. Sushi and caffeine kept her going.

If Natasha had to guess, she would say that they were only in the Dutch Market for about four hours. However, when the small group returned to street level, it was already nighttime, which would imply that twice as much time had passed.

"There's no way we spent that much time down there," Natasha said, voicing her confusion to her companions.

"I agree," Betty replied. "Something's fishy about this."

Marciano, whose judgment of time revolved around hunger, was quick to weigh in.

"You're right. We left after breakfast. If it was dinnertime, I'd be starving by now."

The group had exited the Dutch Market through a different entrance that led to a women's bathroom in a Broadway theatre. Luckily for them it wasn't intermission, and so they hurried out of the theatre and into Times Square, which was booming with life and lights. The smells of food carts taunted Marciano as they moved through the crowds, carefully avoiding the slew of promoters handing out business cards for comedy clubs. As soon as they left the part of Times Square closed off to auto traffic, the group waved down a taxi.

The ride down to Tribeca wasn't too intense for a Sunday night. Outside of the tourist areas, most residents were winding down in preparation for the coming week. There was an intense lineup of fashion shows to be held at Bryant Park between Monday and Thursday, culminating in the Fabulous Fashion Awards on Friday night. Every important person in the industry was going to be at the awards show.

When the taxi pulled up in front of Monique's building, everyone hopped out and hurried inside. The doorman buzzed them into the elevator, and the four of them squeezed themselves and their shopping bags into the tight metal box. Conversation had drawn to a halt upon hitting the busy streets of Times Square, but they were all still thinking about the odd passing of time that day. Well, everyone except for Enya, who was thinking about a jackhammer she'd seen in a Home Depot circular.

As soon as the elevator doors opened, Natasha held her breath. Something was wrong. She couldn't explain it, except that an intense feeling of nervousness spread over her entire body. She hurried out of the elevator, followed by her siblings and Enya.

"Marc, do you feel that?"

"Wasn't me."

"No, it's—what?" she asked him, turning and frowning at her twin brother.

"Oh, uh—nothing," he replied. "But I'd suggest getting as far away from the elevator as possible."

Natasha gave him a disgusted look, and then stomped off down the carpeted hallway toward Aunt Monique's apartment. However, she didn't make it very far before something unsettled her. The door to her aunt's apartment was practically hanging off its hinges, ready to topple to the floor at any moment. In the hallway just outside the apartment, scratch marks left by fingernails had made a disturbing imprint on the wall. Something terrible had happened.

Natasha rushed into her aunt's apartment. She wasn't thinking properly, and didn't even realize that there could still be trouble waiting inside. Sending Enya in first would have been the logical solution, but Natasha felt so disturbed that she needed to see for herself.

"Now she's gonna tie up the bathroom," Marciano complained as he, Betty, and Enya watched Natasha run down the hallway and disappear through the doorway.

"I don't think she's running to use the bathroom—," Betty quietly said, stopping dead in her tracks as her eyes fell upon the fingernail scratches in the wall. "Look at that."

"I've seen worse," Enya grunted, and clenched her fists.

"Maybe it's just art nouveau?" Marciano replied, drawing looks from both Betty and the Russian.

Enya was the next to storm down the hallway, followed closely by Betty and Marciano. They ducked under the busted door and hurried through the foyer into the living room, where Natasha was standing, facing Max. Monique and Mauria were nowhere in sight, and Max had a look on his face that insinuated something bad had gone down.

"Where were you?" he asked, addressed to no one in particular.

"We went to the Dutch Market," Natasha explained, almost defensively. "We were—we didn't mean to stay out this long. All of the sudden we came out and it was nighttime. I don't know what happened."

"Someone tricked you," Max quickly replied. "They must have lured you into a cursed shop. Did Mauria and Monique go with you?"

"No—no, they didn't," Natasha answered. She was shocked that he had no idea where they were. "You don't think—"

"As soon as the sun fell, I rushed back from Woodsrow & Campertine, only to find the door to the apartment busted, and your aunt's bedroom torn apart."

"How long ago did you get back?" Betty asked, stepping forward so that she was standing next to Natasha. She surveyed the living room and kitchen, both of which looked normal. Whatever fight occurred had spared Monique's precious living room.

"Not long ago—maybe ten minutes? Come," he said, and walked toward the hallway that led to Monique's master suite. The door to the bedroom was wide open, revealing Monique's king bed surrounded by an ensemble of candles expertly placed on two nightstands and on tiny shelves that poked out of the walls.

Max was right: the room was a disaster. And it wasn't just because Mauria had been staying in the master suite (although that didn't help). Clothes were thrown all over the room, a dresser had fallen over, a full-length mirror had been smashed, and two bottles of perfume were lying broken next to the bed.

"Oh my—," Natasha exclaimed, before covering her mouth.

"Terrible, right?" Max asked her.

"That this perfectly good bottle of Chanel Number 5 was smashed? Tragic," Natasha replied, and got down on her knees next to the bed so that she could dab her wrists in the spilled perfume. "And also tragic that—what the—!"

Natasha let out a yelp and jumped away from the bed.

"Something sneezed on me!"

"I think you inhaled too much of that perfume," Marciano replied, his arms folded as he shook his head at his sister's antics.

"Enya, can you go look under the bed?" Natasha asked the burly bodyguard towering over the small group.

"I will locate and destroy," she remarked, like a predator about to be unleashed in the wild. Even Max took a careful step back as Enya marched forward and shoved a hand under the bed. As the Russian struggled with whatever was under there, some muffled cries further alerted the others. Natasha stepped back until she was in her older sister's arms, and Marciano tried to replicate the same action with Max, to lesser success. No one could blame him for trying.

Everyone inhaled as Enya's muscular arm reemerged from underneath the bed. Was it going to be an assassin in waiting? A spy for Candice Brown?

The first thing they saw was straightened blonde hair wrapped around Enya's right hand. The hair was attached to the severed head of Aunt Monique, which Enya mercilessly dragged across the ground as the Tribecan mummy shouted "ouch" through pink lips.

"Pick me up, you big oaf!" Monique demanded of Enya, who scratched her own head, and then proceeded to lift her arm. She held Monique by her hair, allowing the dismembered head to dangle in midair. It was an unsettling scene for Natasha and her siblings, who had never been exposed to the undead in their most disturbing form.

"Aunt Monique?" Natasha asked, holding onto Betty for dear life. She blinked a few times as she stared at the dangling head. Aunt Monique frowned.

"No, it's the bogey monster," her aunt said, and stuck out her tongue while simultaneously going cross-eyed. "Oh no she didn't just ask me who I am. Honey, go find the rest of my body."

"Where is it?" Betty—easily the calmest among her siblings—asked.

"All over the place," Monique replied. "I think my torso is in the guest bedroom."

"Did they take Mauria?" Max asked her.

"Who?"

"Mauria—the pretty blonde that's been staying with us," he replied.

"Pretty?" Natasha replied as her head darted in Max's direction.

"I have no idea who that is," Monique answered. "All I know is that some redhead showed up dressed for summer, and she took off with a pretty blonde."

"So Mauria?" Max asked her.

"Who?"

"Oh, forget it," he said.

"I'm buzzing my head and getting blonde extensions," Natasha said out loud. "That's it."

"Let's all just calm down," Betty said, putting her hands up in the air. "If someone broke in and took Mauria, then our hideout is jeopardized, and we're no longer safe here. Let's put Aunt Monique together and get out of here as fast as possible. Is there somewhere we can stay? What about the department store? That's a safe zone—we'd be okay there this week, right?"

"Baby doll, I don't have enough room in my little shop," Monique answered. "Barely enough for Count Hunkula over here's coffin. We can stay with Cedric."

"He'll be alright with that?" Betty asked, and Monique nodded.

"Have you seen that boy's apartment? He has more space than Candice Brown has implants. Now there's a combination. Cedric's apartment and Candice's implants? I'd be a straight-up baller. *Sex and the City*, only without the sex. Or the city, for that matter. I'd sell that apartment and move to the suburbs. Me and my implants. Find a nice doctor from Greenwich. Uh-huh, girl."

Blank expressions dominated the group as everyone stared at Monique's talking head. Finally Enya took initiative and carried the mummy off to the guest bedroom to find the rest of her body. Natasha, Betty, Marciano, and Max stood around, unsure what to say or do. They knew the next step was to pack and get out of the apartment, but a silence had enveloped them. The realization of Mauria's kidnapping was starting to kick in. She was going to be a crucial part of their plan to prevent the assassination of Best Designer at the Fabbies. Her ability to freeze time could be the deciding factor in preventing the assassination.

Mauria's safety was another concern. Would her mother be furious about Mauria's defection? Would she be locked up in some Caligae prison all week, destroying any chances of her escape or rescue? Was Candice Brown capable of killing her own daughter?

When the four of them finally broke the silence and went off to collect their bags, there was a brand-new anxiety in the air, and a realization that nothing was going according to plan. With Mauria kidnapped, Elle still missing, and their parents nowhere to be found, the three siblings felt helpless. All that was left was for Candice Brown and her cronies to find and kill them before the Fabbies on Friday night, before the Maude by Maude and Haus of Simone fashion shows on Thursday. It was only Sunday night, and the next three days seemed too long and too scary to imagine. Not a single one of them had come up with a new plan, and no one was ready to start talking about revising their original plans. All they could do was pack, and get out of Tribeca as soon as supernaturally possible.

Chapter Nine

EVERYONE'S EYES WERE ON HER. NORMALLY, when Candice Brown or her sister Isabelle the Purple passed through the office floors or labyrinthine hallways of Caligae's headquarters, associates would avert their eyes. But this time was different. This time, Candice Brown's only daughter—her flesh and blood—had defected, and was being escorted in handcuffs by Isabelle, two armed guards, and a fully repaired and operational Bridgette #2.

Mauria hadn't slept since being violently abducted from Monique's Tribeca apartment by her mom's robot bodyguard. After being knocked unconscious, Mauria was thrown in a holding cell deep beneath Central Park, where she had been kept overnight.

At some point on Monday morning, Mauria's aunt showed up with Bridgette #2. Of the two wicked sisters who oversaw Caligae, Isabelle was much less confrontational than her larger-than-life sibling. Had Candice Brown gone to intercept Mauria and bring her to headquarters, there would have been a verbal shakedown. But Isabelle was more of the dry, dramatic type than one to get temperamental. Without a word spoken, she led the transfer of Mauria Brown from a twelve-cell prison to her own remote office.

Mauria had no idea where they were headed. She wasn't ready to confront her ill-tempered mother. She was dirty and exhausted from trying to sleep on a cold, stone floor, and she didn't like the fact that everyone in headquarters was staring at her. She felt like a circus animal being dragged onto stage. At least they could have given her a shower and dressed her up a bit.

"Say something," Mauria said to her aunt, speaking in a whiny voice. "What have I done to deserve this?"

"We'll talk when I get to my office."

"Why?"

"Because I don't want to make a scene," Isabelle remarked.

"Oh, and dragging me through headquarters in handcuffs isn't making a scene?"

"Just to ensure you don't try any of your tricks," her aunt replied. "Mauria, you have no idea how hard this is on me. I cried all night when I learned that you'd betrayed us. To think that you'd plot against your own mother and aunt."

Mauria frowned in response. There went her idea of claiming she was kidnapped.

"I wasn't plotting against anyone," Mauria exclaimed, with all the outrage of a spoiled princess. "I am a Color, and I'm part of the ruling family. It's an abomination that you're treating me like this."

"You know, Mauria, you should feel very lucky about being born into this family. And lucky that Candice is your mother. Candice and I had an awful relationship with our mother. She was a harsh, terrible woman."

"Yeah, too bad you betrayed Grandma before I got the chance to meet her," Mauria spat at her aunt. Isabelle's face instantly soured, and Mauria could tell she'd hit a nerve. While Candice could joke openly about the imprisonment of Cecilia the Red, it was a rather touchy subject for Isabelle, who always seemed to look back on the event with some regret.

Instead of shouting back at Mauria, Isabelle remained calm. She was always calm. She wasn't about to start a fight in the middle of headquarters. Once Mauria realized that her aunt wasn't going to take the bait, she let out a long sigh, followed by further minutes of silence as the small group walked along the twisted path that led to Isabelle's office.

"Is Mom here?"

"No," Isabelle quickly replied, practically under her breath. She hadn't told Candice about this meeting with Mauria, precisely because she wanted to give her sister some time to cool down. Candice Brown was still fuming over her daughter's betrayal. All Isabelle wanted to do was bring Mauria to her office and have a candid aunt-to-niece conversation about the assassination plot at the Fabbies, the future of Caligae, and Mauria's role within the organization and her own family. Isabelle wanted to handle the conversation in a civilized manner, without dragging her angry older sister into the mix.

As they neared the door to Isabelle's office, Mauria held her breath. She had no idea what to expect. Were they going to try to interrogate her? Would there be torture involved? At least Princess Leia looked fabulous for her *Star Wars* torture scene. Mauria was wearing yesterday's outfit, and looked like she had just got busted for a DUI. She looked about as sexy as a mug shot.

Just before Isabelle's palm fell on top of the fingerprint scanner, she paused and leaned in closer to the door.

"Do you smell that?" she asked, and then quickly turned to Bridgette #2. The robot shrugged. She had no sense of smell. The guards looked equally puzzled.

"It smells like chlorine," Mauria said, sniffing the air around her.

"Oh God," Isabelle moaned, and she quickly pressed her palm up against the scanner. The door slid into the wall, revealing not her office, but a long and narrow lap pool. The reinforced glass floor was missing, and the aquarium that had been built underneath her corner office had been extended. As Isabelle looked in astonishment at the ruins of her former sanctuary, a skeleton with a whistle was blowing on the silver instrument from a yellow lifeguard stand.

"My dear sister," Candice Brown shouted from the lap pool. She was wearing a pink one-piece swimsuit and a matching cap over her short black hair. While Isabelle stood at the edge of the pool with her mouth wide open, Candice used all the might in her cellulite to swim over to her sister.

"What happened to my office? Please tell me I'm in the wrong section of headquarters."

"No—I kind of demolished it. And a few other offices too. Nice pool, huh?"

"What happened to all my things?" Isabelle asked in frustration. The tense situation was causing her forehead to sweat. Isabelle wasn't the kind of person who welcomed change, and she certainly didn't like change being forced upon her. She rapidly fanned herself with one hand as she observed in horror the space that had once been her office.

"Threw all that junk in an empty conference room. Hey, care for a dip?"

"What about the fish?" she cried.

Candice stretched her plastic lips, and mouthed an *Uh-oh.* She then nodded her head twice toward the bottom of the pool. When Isabelle looked at the pool floor, she loudly shrieked, and then threw her hands in front of her eyes. The bottom of the pool was covered in lifeless, colorful fish, the same ones that once swam underneath Isabelle's feet in her former office.

"Had to do it," Candice said, as if she were talking about executing a mass murderer. "Probably should clean all the corpses out of the pool though."

"Candice, I need an office!" Isabelle cried out from beneath her slender fingers. "I've been coming here to work for years while you've been vacationing in the Maldives."

"Been there, done that, over it. The Maldives are so last year," Candice dismissively said. "And don't act so entitled. Think about all the starving people in the world who don't have an office."

"Well I'm not starving," Isabelle replied, finally removing her hands from her face.

"Girl, you have *crazy eyes* right now," Candice remarked, and shook her head.

"You killed all my fish and demolished my office!"

"Listen, sis—as always, I have the perfect solution. How about we put your office directly above mine. I know it's not on the main floor, but that room is just a big library now, and no one reads."

"Actually, a lot of people—"

"Just take the library," Candice said with the kind of grumpy expression that told Isabelle the conversation was over. "It's three times as big as your old office."

"Then why don't you take it?"

"Two reasons. First of all, I'd have to go up and down stairs, which is *not* happening. And second, I am the people's chosen leader. I need to be out there on the main floor congregating with those who love and serve me."

"I've never seen you congregate with anyone in Caligae," Isabelle replied, crossing her arms as she surveyed the wreckage of her former office.

"Tell me again why you are interrupting me? I'm getting a face-lift in an hour and want to look refreshed before my surgery."

"I brought your daughter," Isabelle said, and stepped out of the way so that Candice could see Mauria Brown standing in the doorway, flanked by Bridgette #2 and the two guards.

Candice's face grew red as soon as she laid eyes upon her daughter. "How *dare* you," she spat. "Wait—what'd she do?"

"She's been secretly working with the remaining Thirteens and feeding them information about the Fabbies," Isabelle quietly replied after letting out an uncomfortable sigh.

"Oh, yeah," Candice said. "Well why the hell did you do that?"

"I've always known that you were evil, but this is too much," Mauria replied. "Killing an innocent person just so you can create a publicity disaster and expose supernaturals? You're despicable."

"Well I don't know what that words means, but I'll take it as a compliment," Candice replied, placing her hands on her rather curvy hips.

"No, Mom, it means you've hit a new low."

"Well thank you, I cut my carbs two weeks ago."

"No, I mean in morality."

"I don't know what that words means either," Candice dismissively said. "Now I'm going to give you another chance. Not because I want to be a nice mom, but because I'm on so many presurgery painkillers that just *thinking* about possible punishments is beyond my mental capacity. And luckily for you, I need you to walk the runway on Thursday at the Haus of Simone fashion show. Isabelle, take her back to her apartment, but see that she's under house arrest. No one comes in, and no one leaves. I want video cameras in every single room. Not only am I going to keep an eye on you, but after I'm done taping I'm going to package the videos and sell them as a reality show."

"That's an invasion of my privacy!" Mauria whined.

"You were an invasion of my privacy for eighteen years, so consider this payback time. Isabelle, take her away."

Isabelle looked at her niece, whose emotions were toggling between the devastation of house arrest and the thrill of a bubble bath. And for a very brief moment, Mauria caught something in the way her aunt looked at her. Was it compassion? Sympathy? Empathy? There was something personal and intimate in the passing glance that Isabelle gave, before the latter's face reverted back to its typical stiffness.

Once Monique was put back together, Enya boarded up the front door, and the group left for Cedric's apartment in the Meatpacking District. There was a bit of a struggle getting there, considering Monique packed two months' worth of bags for less than a week's stay. Everyone arrived at Cedric's in a state of exhaustion, and those who'd had trouble sleeping were able to easily pass out.

Most everyone—including Betty, known for waking up at the crack of dawn—slept until noon. When everyone finally woke up, there wasn't much conversation. They were all in a contemplative state, and had too much going on inside their heads to want to chat with each other. After Betty prepared a late brunch, everyone split up.

Cedric's apartment was substantially bigger than Monique's, and so everyone was able to spread out and get their own space. While Monique soaked in the spa hot tub, Enya lifted weights in a makeshift gym, and Betty played around on one of the computers. Marciano was in a state of utopia as he tried on every single pair of Cedric's shoes, while the latter excitedly joined him. It was funny for Natasha to watch the two of them. Marciano got such a joy from fashion, and Cedric seemed to get joy from watching another fashion-obsessed guy go through his wardrobe. Every new cry of "Oh my God, you have these!" from Marciano was met with a big smile from Cedric.

But while everyone occupied themselves with their own various hobbies and interests, Natasha was the only one who wasn't sure what to do with herself. She wasn't in the mood to play dress-up, or surf the web, or work out with Enya. She certainly didn't want to get in the hot tub with Monique. She'd been seeing way too many bubbles coming out of that thing, and wasn't certain they were from the spa jets.

Instead of eating or sleeping, which were probably her two best solutions for boredom, Natasha sprawled out across an old leather sofa. There was a flat-screen television in front of her, turned to a news station, although she wasn't paying much attention to it. Hours flew by in front of the TV, until eventually Max woke up and joined her, sitting on a neighboring fabric sofa. Still, even with his presence, not a word was spoken between the two.

Natasha was lost in her own thoughts about the week ahead. And each time her gaze would fall upon the television, she couldn't help but wonder what this same news station would be playing on Friday night. Would they be showing footage of a vicious assassination at the Fabulous Fashion Awards? Would these same news reporters be talking about the death of her very own mom, and an investigation into an industry that she still didn't fully understand?

"You okay?" Max asked her, and Natasha turned to look at him. He was stunning, even in the morning (or *his* version of morning) with his bed head. He was wearing a plain white T-shirt and black nylon shorts, the kind that usually sport a college logo. This was probably the least amount of clothing that Natasha had ever seen him in, and his pecs and shoulders pushed against the cotton shirt to reveal a masculine, defined build.

"That's sweet of you to ask," she replied. "I'm not used to hearing 'you okay' from a guy. I'm doing okay. Well, not really."

"What can I do that will help distract you? You just need a good distraction."

"Can you distract me for three more days until the runway shows on Thursday?" she asked, and then laughed. "There's so much racing through my head, and I feel like I just can't handle any of this."

"You know, we don't have to make any moves at the runway shows. We can just show up to the Fabbies and keep with our original plan."

"But without Mauria? We really need her. She could be the deciding factor."

"True," Max replied. "I'm quick, but I can't slow down or stop time. Look, why don't we get out of here—get our minds off of this."

"Are you crazy?" she asked him. "Bad people are looking for us."

"If all of Caligae was after you, then you'd either be dead or in a holding cell by now," he said frankly. "And, I'm one of the people who would have been tasked to find you. I've never heard a single word, not even that there's a pair of Thirteens roaming around Manhattan. This tells me that Candice Brown isn't looking that hard. Either she's too busy with her plans for the Fabbies to bother or she's scared to make it known that you're still alive."

"Why would she be scared?"

"Not everyone in Caligae believes in genocide," he replied, and laughed as if it were the obvious answer. "We're talking about killing every single person of a single race. You think the whole organization is filled with people who think that way? We're not all like Candice."

"I'm sorry if I insinuated—"

"No, it's alright," Max quickly replied. "Hey, you're brand-new to this stuff. Just know that I'd never do anything to put your life in danger. Now how about we each get showered, put some fresh clothes on, and make the best out of tonight?"

Natasha looked deeply into his eyes, and finally smiled. What was it about him that was driving her so crazy?

"Okay," she said, and slowly stood up from the sofa.

"How does one acquire so much Lanvin at such a young age?" Marciano asked in amazement as he tried on a pair of boat shoes. Cedric's closet was unreal. He had amassed a collection of over five hundred pairs of shoes, spanning two walls in a room that had been designed to be the apartment's master bedroom. Instead Cedric used it as his closet, and settled for a smaller adjoining room as his bedroom.

"Well, I'm a lot older than you think," Cedric remarked. He smiled as he stood with his arms folded, watching Marciano slip into the boat shoes. "I've had a lot of time to collect."

"What kind of supernatural are you?" Marciano asked, and then paused. "Wait, am I allowed to ask that? Is it considered rude?"

"No, not at all!" Cedric replied, laughing. "That's totally appropriate. I'm a shape-shifter. But I'm also a Color."

"What, like Mauria Brown?"

"Yeah, she's actually a cousin of mine," Cedric replied. "My mom is Priscilla Black. She runs the European division of Caligae. We had a rough relationship growing up, and so I moved to the United States a long time ago to get away and do my own thing. I work for Caligae just because my family runs it, but my real passion has always been with makeup and styling. I guess because I can shape shift into other people, it helps me know what looks good on someone. If I can become someone who I'm styling, then I can literally put myself in their shoes and see how an outfit feels, fits, looks . . . I can make sure that the makeup looks right, that the hair looks right."

"So are you in your natural form right now?"

"Yeah, this is me. Although this isn't my natural hair color."

"This is the twenty-first century. Whose hair color is natural nowadays?" Marciano asked, which made Cedric laugh. "That's really cool, though. I wish I could shape shift. Is your mom a shape-shifter?"

"No, she's a sorceress, just like Candice Brown and Isabelle the Purple. There aren't many Colors in the world—less than twenty of us—and most of the ones that lead Caligae are sorceresses. That's just the old clan from back when they seized power. I think my mom was a little disappointed with how I turned out, though. She probably would've rather had a little sorcerer, or an oracle like Mauria."

"What's wrong with a shape-shifter?"

"Well, you know how supernaturals came to be, right? It started with one woman in Africa called Mother. She had thirteen kids, each with a different type of ability. You're a descendant of the thirteenth child. Her twelfth was a Color—a sorcerer, to be exact—who was stronger than all of the other children. And one of them was a demon—a child born badly deformed, but who had the ability to shape shift.

"The demons of ancient times gave us a bad name. It's because of their abilities, really. They could shape shift into people, things, and animals. They could possess the minds of the weak. I guess it felt to the old generations of demons that their powers were designed for wrongdoing, and so there were a lot of evil demons.

"After the great curse was placed, most demons joined Caligae, although some still roamed around, causing trouble for humans and other supernaturals. *Demonicide* became popular—the practice of killing a baby demon shortly after birth. Most are born with terrible deformities, and so I think a lot of mothers did it for that reason, but others just did it because they didn't want a demon in the family."

"That's really sad," Marciano replied. He'd stopped trying on shoes, and was sitting on the floor listening to Cedric's story.

"Yeah, it was really messed up. There's still some shame about being a shape-shifter. A lot of us won't admit it, and will pretend to be another kind of supernatural. I remember a dinner conversation just twenty years ago, here in New York. My mom had flown over to visit me, and we were having dinner with Candice and Isabelle, and some of the other Colors. Candice Brown had recently given birth to Mauria, her only daughter. And someone asked Candice if she had plans of having any more children. She practically spit out her drink. Then she looked directly at my mom, and said, 'Knowing that we have demon blood in our ancestry, I don't think it's worth the risk.' I'll never forget those words. I felt so ostracized."

"Did your mom stick up for you?"

"No, she didn't. I'm sure she loves me, but she lives in this totally different world that's so obsessed with appearance. I get that she privately hates Candice. I mean, who doesn't? But my mom wouldn't speak out against her. It would cause a civil war, and I don't think my mom wants to deal with that. It's easier to just let Candice be Candice, and allow life to go on."

"How does your mom feel about you being gay? Have you come out to her?"

"How do you know I'm gay?" Cedric asked with a surprised look on his face.

"Girl, you have like sixty pairs of Lanvin. Who are you kidding?"

Cedric laughed, and then nodded in affirmation.

"She knows. I came out to her a long time ago. I was born at the turn of the twentieth century, when the world was a totally different place. The '20s were some of the best years of my life. I practically grew up in the gay clubs of Berlin and London. I'd do styling and makeup for drag queens. When we weren't throwing lavish parties, we'd go to cafés, and we'd smoke and drink café au lait while talking about the way the world was changing.

"Then the world changed in a horrific way. Europe fell into a depression, and World War II devastated the continent. I lived with my mom in Paris during the war. She fought to keep Parisian fashion alive even after the Nazi invasion. Shortly after the war I moved to New York, and right before I left I told her that I was gay. I think the hardest part for her was that I wouldn't get married and carry on the bloodline."

"But you can get married in Iowa!" Marciano exclaimed. "And they have surrogacy, so you can still have kids."

"Well, back then the world was a different place. Homosexuality wasn't as accepted as it is today. My mom has gay friends whom she loves dearly. It's just a different scenario with her own son."

"And I guess you're the only child, huh?"

"Yep. One and only."

"Well, I'm sorry to hear that," Marciano said, speaking from his heart. "I'm sure that one day she'll come around."

"I think the only way it could happen is if she lets go of this *obsession* with image. If she left Caligae and stopped associating with Candice Brown, I think she could really lighten up. But I suppose one of the downsides of being attached to the fashion industry is that we're also bound to image."

"That's deep!" Marciano replied. "Will your mom be here this week?"

"Of course! She'll be in town on Wednesday night. I'm supposed to have dinner with her, considering she doesn't cancel again. Last time she came, Candice rearranged my mom's entire schedule. I only got to see her for a quick cup of coffee."

"Candice sounds awful."

"She's worse than awful," Cedric replied. "So are her henchmen. I heard about your encounter with Bridgette #2 in the subway, but I think Olympia is an even scarier threat."

"Who is she?"

"A menace. She's one of the oldest, nastiest vampires from the ancient world. She used to serve Candice Brown's mother, Cecilia the Red. In fact, Olympia and Elle were her two prized vampires."

"What does she look like?" Marciano asked, gulping as soon as the words left his mouth. "We met an Olympia in the Dutch Market."

"Tall, pale, ginger hair—"

"Oh, no—oh, don't tell me that. I totally blabbed to her."

"You have to be exceptionally careful who you trust, and who you talk to. You're part of a dying race, and there are a lot of people who would like to see the Thirteens become permanently extinct."

"Well—" Marciano hopped to his feet, and hurried to the closet entrance. He peeked out into the loftlike apartment, and then quickly closed the closet door. "Do you know this guy Max?" he asked in a quiet tone.

"I do."

"Do you trust him?"

Cedric lowered his eyes to the floor, and he softly bit his lower lip.

"There was a scandal," he whispered, "shortly after I moved to Manhattan. As soon as I got here, Isabelle the Purple gave me a job. It was a pencil-pusher job—I'd show up to an office at headquarters, and I had a title, but I didn't actually have to do anything. Still, I always listened, and kept my ears peeled for drama.

"Do you know the story of Dorina White?"

"Max told us about her," Marciano replied. "She's the one who was banished to Antarctica, right? Because she fought for the Thirteens during the War of the Colors?"

"No, absolutely not. Dorina White used to be *the* Candice Brown. She was the queen bee in Caligae, a merciless strategist, and a tactful leader. Cecilia the Red loved Dorina even more than her very own children. That's why Candice turned on her own mother. She was consumed with jealousy. And after the Colors managed to bury Cecilia, they turned their attention to Dorina White. No one was brave enough to fight her, not even Candice. Dorina is an oracle, just like Mauria. She has some wicked abilities. The Colors managed to trick her into accepting a position on the coldest, most barren place on Earth: Antarctica."

"So that's who's been making all those toys every December," Marciano joked.

"Yeah, although she's no Santa, and her henchmen are no elves. Dorina has amassed a whole legion of spies and mercenaries. In the '50s, shortly after I moved to New York, there was an attempted coup. A bomb went off in headquarters, detonated in an executive conference room. The bomb was meant to kill a slew of high-level Caligae members, including Candice and Isabelle. However, unknown to the assassin, the meeting had been pushed back by thirty minutes. There were only two people in the conference room when the bomb went off: Isabelle's husband and daughter. They had stopped by to drop off lunch for the executives who would soon be meeting.

"Isabelle was traumatized by the event, and built a new office for herself in a far corner of headquarters, so that she could be totally isolated from the other associates. An investigation into the bombing turned up three suspects, all linked to Dorina White. One of them was Max."

"No way!"

"Yes way. He had been dating Isabelle's daughter at the time. That's the only way he would have known about the executive meeting. Candice wanted to have him executed, but Isabelle vouched for him. She knew how much her daughter had loved him, and couldn't bring herself to believe that the entire relationship might have been a lie. And so they gave Max the benefit of the doubt. He continued to work for the organization, and life continued."

"He told us he's working for Dorina White."

"That's what your aunt said," Cedric replied. "Which explains why he's helping you. I have no doubt that he wants to bring down Candice and Isabelle. But Dorina White is worse than Candice. I don't trust anyone who claims to be one of her followers. And even though he may help you when the time comes, I'm terrified of what would happen if Dorina White was allowed on American soil."

"So what do we do about him?" Marciano asked, a hopeless expression on his face.

"We just wait."

"So what's it like to be a vampire?" Natasha asked as she and Max walked through the Chelsea neighborhood of Manhattan. "And why does every guy who walks past us stare you down, and then give me a dirty look?"

"You know you have a bad habit of asking me multiple questions at once, and leaving me unsure how to answer them, and in what order?" Max joked with her, and Natasha gently nudged into him. As her arm fell down at his side, Max affectionately brushed her hand with his ow. Instantly she looked up at him and smiled, but he kept his eyes on the rows of apartment buildings spanning either side of the block.

"Because I want to get to know you," she softly told him.

"Being a vampire is complicated, I guess. Sometimes I feel powerful, but other times I feel weighed down by the disadvantages. I haven't been in the sun in over sixty years. You know, the sun makes people happy."

"You don't think of yourself as a happy person?"

"Sometimes I do," he answered unconvincingly. "Sometimes I don't. Caligae weighs me down. And the curse. I feel like I could do so much more if I weren't bound to this curse."

"Yeah, but it's meant to protect people," Natasha said. "You don't want a bunch of vampires running around causing trouble. I mean—that's how I see it. Look at some of the stuff you can do, compared to regular humans. It creates an unfair advantage. The curse puts supernaturals in check."

"And makes it a disadvantage to be a supernatural."

"No, I think it just grounds you," Natasha replied, and turned to him again. "Imagine Candice Brown, as powerful as she is, with no checks and balances. She'd be out of control. Because of the curse, all she can really do is run clothing companies. That's not so bad, right? Better than trying to start wars with humans."

Max didn't respond, which worried Natasha. She didn't want to think that he was so ideologically different, or so affected, that he might actually share Candice Brown's disdain for the great curse. The curse seemed totally logical to Natasha. But then again, Max wasn't someone with a passion for fashion. Suddenly Natasha couldn't help but feel sympathy for this man. He was stuck working in an industry that he had absolutely no interest in.

"So you don't feel stuck?" he asked her, in a way that made it clear that he felt stuck.

"No, not at all. I mean, I was born into the fashion world. Look at my parents. I was raised on this stuff, and I just love it."

"You don't find it to be frivolous?"

"Frivolous?" Natasha replied, giving him an embellished look of shock. "No, I find it wonderful."

"Even six-hundred-dollar sweaters?"

"They always go on clearance at some point," she said. "Look, it's not about the price or the brand. It's just about having style, and being fashionable, and having fun with what you wear. It's about knowing who you are as a person, and dressing to match your personality. And it's about feeling beautiful. I don't know how else to describe it, but there's this feeling I get when I put on a really amazing dress, or some new sunglasses that really fit my face. It makes me feel good about myself."

"Well you should feel good about yourself regardless of what you're wearing."

"That's easily said, but not everyone is like that. Try looking at it this way: isn't there something that happens when you put on a tight-fitting V-neck that shows off your upper body, versus a baggy turtleneck? Don't you get a little rush when you look in the mirror?"

"I don't own any baggy turtlenecks," he replied.

"Okay, well do you get the difference? Even if the baggy turtleneck cost ten times as much as the V-neck, it's never going to look as good on you. Fashion is about the individual."

"So basically you're letting clothes define you."

"Okay, you're totally missing the point," Natasha replied, and playfully nudged him. "It's about figuring out who you are, and then having fun with clothes that reflect your personality. That's it. It's just about dressing up so that when you look in the mirror, you smile, and see yourself."

Max didn't respond, and Natasha could tell that he was pondering her words. She was amazed that someone with so much exposure to the fashion industry didn't quite understand it.

"I have a question for you," Natasha said, deciding to break the silence. Just as she asked, two middle-aged men in glasses and petticoats passed by with a pair of white Pomeranians attached to leather leashes. The men paused their conversation, looked at Max, and then raised their eyebrows at Natasha. "Does this happen to every girl you take for a walk?"

"What? Is that the question?"

"No, never mind. I was wondering when you got turned?"

"Turned into what?" he asked, slightly confused.

"A vampire."

"Ah, you have to be careful when you ask that. Not all vampires are turned. Many of us are born this way. You know, it's considered lucky to give birth to a vampire, because you're almost always guaranteed that your child will outlive you. But yeah, I was turned after I got back from fighting in the Second World War. I'd given up everything before the war because I didn't think I was going to come home. Then all the sudden I'm back in the U.S. with nothing and nobody.

"I wandered around a lot. I was a drunk. I had odd jobs to pay the bills, although somehow I never managed to pay my bills. One night I got so drunk in a Montreal bar that I blacked out. I woke up covered in my own blood. Something about my body felt different. I walked around until the sun started to come up, and the first beams felt so intense that I felt like a fire was burning underneath my skin. I remember banging on doors to see if someone would let me in. I ended up breaking into someone's house just to avoid sunlight.

"I had no idea what had happened. Usually Caligae finds newly turned vampires and werewolves, but it's hard to keep track of this. It can take months. I just remember wandering around for a long time until one night a woman found me, somewhere in between Calgary and Vancouver. She was dressed in all white, and had long platinum hair. The closer she came to me, the colder I felt. She told me her name was Dorina White, and that she was going to give me a special place in a lost world. She was going to make me powerful.

"Dorina taught me everything I know. She helped train me. She got me a job with Caligae. She's changed my life. I think if I hadn't met her, I'd be dead by now."

"Rough story," Natasha remarked, and let out a deep breath.

"At least it had a happy ending," he replied, and smiled. "Look at me now. I have a great life. Being a vampire has its ups and downs, but most of the time I'd rather be this than human."

"It must be sad knowing that you're going to outlive nearly everyone you meet, though," Natasha said.

"It's sad, but you learn to appreciate time. Everything's more precious," he said, and looked down at Natasha. "Like now, this very moment."

Max was a man of few words, but his few words had a way of melting Natasha's heart. She was totally intrigued by him, and it worried her a great deal. She still didn't know Max all that well, and there was so much more she wanted to learn about him.

"So what happens after this?" Natasha asked, as she began to think about his role in helping them.

"After what?"

"After this week. Let's say we save whoever wins Best Designer. Or let's say we don't. What happens to you?"

"That's a good question," he replied, and sat on it for a few seconds while he thought about the best answer. "If we're able to prevent the assassination, then Candice Brown's plot is foiled, and everything will go back to normal. I assume she'll really start to go after you and your brother at that point. And then you'll need me more than ever, to protect you, and to figure out how we can bring down the two sisters.

"And if the assassination happens," he continued, and then paused again. They turned a street corner, and he waited to respond until they passed a woman who was standing outside her apartment building smoking a cigarette. "If it happens, then we're all screwed. You realize what happens if humans find out about us, right? The curse is broken, and we all shrivel up and vanish."

He laughed after he finished his sentence, but Natasha could tell that there was some genuine concern.

"You really think the curse is like that, huh?"

"I don't know. Nobody knows. That's the scary thing about a curse. No one wants to be the first to test its limits. I guess Candice thinks that because of how quickly information spreads these days, she can make the revelation appear inadvertent and get away with it."

"But what if you just went up to someone—like that woman smoking back there—and told her you're a vampire?"

"Well, she'd probably laugh at me," Max replied.

"Okay, and you're right, she probably would. Either that, or she'd run back into her building. But you think you'd just burst into flames or something?"

Max shrugged, which made obvious the extent to which supernaturals really feared the great curse. Natasha had a tough time believing that the original supernatural would leave her own kind with such a violent curse. She could understand the rule for keeping within the fashion industry, and the rule that supernaturals shouldn't bother humans, but she was amazed that these people actually thought they might turn to dust if they violated any of the conditions. Even Candice Brown, as powerful as any supernatural, wasn't prepared to violate the curse in an overt manner. If the only way Candice would challenge the curse was to wait hundreds of years and craft an elaborate plot that required a technologically advanced society, then even she would be too afraid to go up to someone on the street and reveal her supernatural identity.

"Why risk it?" Max finally answered. "Even though I want to stop the assassination, I'm kind of curious what will happen if Candice Brown pulls this off. If there's some loophole in the great curse, then what happens next? Do we no longer need to stay within the fashion industry? Can we all just do whatever we want?"

"I guess that's what she's trying to find out," Natasha softly replied.

"Well, she's testing her limits. How far can she push the curse? No one knows. Even though sometimes I don't get the reasoning behind the curse, I do realize why we have it. And I'd rather see someone stable lead Caligae than Candice or her sister."

"That woman you mentioned, Dorina White."

"She would make a great leader," Max said, suddenly beaming with enthusiasm.

"But is the leader of Caligae kind of like the leader of all supernaturals? I'm confused."

"Not officially, but yes. Think of it this way: all supernaturals are bound by the curse. Caligae enforces the curse. Traditionalists like me will say that it is supposed to be a small organization that keeps an eye on supernaturals. Candice and Isabelle have turned it into a behemoth—a massive organization that reaches every continent, with lavish offices and tons of personnel. They've abused their own positions. It's nothing like what it used to be. Or so I've been told."

"So you think Dorina will restore it to its old form?"

"I do. Instead of being a massive *big brother* that spies on everyone and oozes into everybody's business, Caligae could be a small group that helps the industry. Something that helps supernaturals. I hope you get to meet Dorina someday. I think you'd love her."

"She sounds great, from everything you've said," Natasha replied. She kept one hand out hanging loose at her side, hoping Max would embrace it. It was one thing to walk through Chelsea with him, but hand-in-hand? What a magical distraction that would be from an otherwise absurd week. "What a world we live in."

"This is only the beginning," he replied, and slowed down as the two of them neared a quiet intersection. A couple locals on bicycles passed by, wrapped up in their winter coats. Max removed his hand from his coat, but instead of wrapping it around Natasha's small fingers, he placed his arm around her.

"Are you going to—," she began to say, until Max leaned down and kissed her on the cheek. His lips were cold, maybe more so than the winds sweeping through the streets of Manhattan.

"What were you saying?"

"I forgot," she replied, and laughed to herself. And at that moment, she felt like the prettiest girl in New York City.

Mauria paced uncomfortably around the kitchen of her Greenwich Village apartment as if she were awaiting a blind date. She fidgeted with everything she touched, and moved several small appliances back and forth until they looked perfect, before moving them again. The security guards positioned outside and around her building had called to say that someone was on their way up to the apartment. It wasn't clear who was coming, but Mauria guessed that it was her mother. She feared that her mom would be even crueler than she had been at headquarters. Maybe Candice didn't want to have a screaming fit in public, but there would be nothing holding her back from doing it within the confines of Mauria's apartment.

As the door opened, Mauria held her breath. She lost her posture and gripped the granite kitchen island with two hands, holding herself up with the strength in her arms. When the first sign of long, erect strands of auburn hair peeked out of the door, Mauria relaxed, and quickly marched around the kitchen island to greet her aunt.

"I didn't tell your mother I was coming here," Isabelle said as soon as she closed the door. She quickly took off a white fur coat and hung it on an antique rack beside the front door.

"Aunt Isabelle, you know that I—"

"I'm not here to talk about that," she quickly interrupted. She gave Mauria a quick peck on the cheek, and then took her niece's hand, leading her in the direction of the kitchen. "Do you have any wine?"

"The boxed stuff is in the fridge, for when my mom comes over. But there's a rack underneath the island."

She pointed awkwardly toward the small space where she stored her wine. She'd never known her aunt to be a drinker. Isabelle was the type of woman who would cradle one glass of wine over a long dinner, and then admit to feeling a mediocre buzz. Isabelle was renowned for being a sober drag, so Mauria actually hoped she'd get to see her aunt down a few glasses.

"Why don't you grab two glasses, and I'll get a bottle, and then we're going to talk," Isabelle suggested. Without saying anything, Mauria hurried toward the cabinet where she kept red wine glasses. She chose two particularly big Bordeaux-style glasses, and placed them on the counter, just as her aunt was uncorking a Châteauneuf-du-Pape.

Isabelle breathed heavily just before she poured two glasses. She glanced out the glass walls in the living room, looking out onto the terrace. It would have been a perfect place for them to talk, if not for the cold weather. Isabelle didn't want to put her coat back on, or risk spilling red wine on the white fur, and so she settled for an aluminum barstool at the kitchen island. She pushed a second barstool toward Mauria.

"Cheers," Isabelle said, raising the glass and toasting her niece. Mauria raised her own glass to meet her aunt's. She couldn't quite read Isabelle. The latter had an awkward expression on her face, which was clear from the moment she opened the door. It seemed like something was troubling her. Isabelle wore a deep look of sadness and uncertainty that was unusual for her. She was known for looking serious and pensive, but there wasn't usually so much grief behind it.

"Cheers," Mauria quietly said. She took a sip, although she was too distracted to enjoy the flavor. Isabelle smelled the wine before lifting it to her lips, and then closed her eyes as the red liquid poured into her mouth.

"Good choice," Isabelle said, although it wasn't clear whether it was directed to Mauria or herself. When she opened her eyes, they fell first upon Mauria, and then upon the granite countertop, which was an explosion of blues in an otherwise stainless-steel kitchen. "Are you happy?" she finally asked, which threw Mauria off guard.

But before Mauria had time to answer the question, Isabelle lifted her head and looked at her niece, who was sitting calmly in the aluminum barstool.

"Do you know anything about your grandmother?" Isabelle asked. "Aside from that she's buried in the English countryside by a powerful curse?" Mauria shook her head.

"Just her name. Cecilia the Red. I know she was a Color. I know about the war and all."

"But you don't know what she was like?" Isabelle asked, and once again Mauria shook her head. "She wasn't a very good person, so it's better that you don't know her, or weren't alive to meet her. You know—it's not like remembering someone who died twenty years ago. This was hundreds of years ago. Some of them short, but some of them very long. So long that you begin to forget things about people—certain qualities, maybe—and you start to make up your own. And one day your fantasy about a person has become your memory. I don't know how much of my memory of your grandmother is fantasy, and how much is actually true.

"But I remember that when I was young, I was terrified of her. She had a dangerous way about her that bordered on lunacy. I think that she had so much going on in her head that it was difficult for her to cope with the realities of life. She couldn't connect with people. She didn't trust anyone. And she was so brutal—if not physically, then emotionally. I resented the way she made Candice feel both unloved and unwanted. Your mother tried so hard.

"The night we fought and buried your grandmother, it was in a graveyard in a small town outside London. The air was damp, and the wind was painfully cold. I remember the spell I cast that forced your grandmother deep underground, and the harrowing look on her face—the helplessness in her eyes—as her body sank into the wet soil. I remember that Candice smiled, but when the two of us were alone she couldn't stop crying. For years I slept in the same bedroom as my sister, because she'd wake up in the middle of the night, screaming and sweating, terrified that our mother would somehow come back for her. Or maybe she was just terrified that Cecilia the Red would be the last and only woman to ever be a mom to us. She and I desperately needed someone to fill that role in our lives."

Isabelle reached out and placed a single palm over Mauria's hands, which were folded on the granite countertop.

"As wicked as your mom might sometimes seem, she's not Cecilia the Red. She's not your grandmother. She has a hardened way of expressing her love, and she's well aware of that. That's why she hasn't ever trained you to your full potential. Because she sees Cecilia the Red every time she looks in the mirror, and she doesn't want you to challenge her, as she did her own mother."

"How could you let her get like this?" Mauria asked, and as soon as the words left her mouth, Isabelle's face grew weak with sorrow.

"I know she's imperfect, but—when you love someone who is in the process of self-destructing, sometimes it's easy to perceive things as better than they really are. For decades, Candice felt so fragile that had I abandoned her, she'd have fallen apart."

Mauria narrowed her eyes as she listened to her aunt. It didn't seem like Isabelle was trying to have a conversation; rather, it sounded more like she was trying to convince herself of all the things she was saying. Her words felt like practiced lines that had probably been repeated over and over in her head.

"I was always attached to the private Candice. So while I consoled the private Candice, who each day displayed so much pain and fear resulting from our childhood, I ignored the public Candice, who grew cold and ruthless. As Candice slowly transformed into a version of her mother, I disregarded all the warnings. Because what I saw in private was so different—like another person entirely.

"One day your mother started to replace herself with plastic. It wasn't just about having voluptuous lips or fewer wrinkles—it was about replacing herself. It was about becoming a different person. This would be someone who, when she gazed into the mirror, didn't see any trace of the wicked woman who had raised us.

"And then suddenly she was a new person. My sister had become *Candice Brown*. She built a fashion empire, and muscled her way into the market. We stopped having those delicate and personal conversations. Everything became light. Everything was a joke. All of the sudden I was the serious one, and the personality that Candice invented for herself was no longer connected to me.

"Now my sister is barely human anymore," Isabelle said, and it seemed to be the hardest thing she'd said since sitting down with Mauria. As her eyes swelled up with tears, she blinked rapidly, the way someone would blink if light was flashing in their eyes. "And you've never had the chance to know the Candice that I knew. But I desperately want that old Candice back—both for you and for me."

"But why are you helping her with this crazy plan?" Mauria asked.

"Because I want my sister back, and I don't know what will make her happy enough to come back to me. I don't know what will be able to kill all that bitterness that's piled up over long centuries. But I'm willing to do almost anything to have her back."

"Including killing an innocent person?" Mauria replied. "How can you justify it?"

"I don't know," Isabelle said, lifting her eyebrows as she spoke. "Maybe I've grown so used to loss, that seeing someone die no longer has the same effect on me? Maybe I've been alive for so long that I don't appreciate the gift of life. I think about these things—I don't want you to think that I'm callous. I'm just—" Isabelle paused, and hung on the words for a long time. She used the opportunity to take another sip from her glass of wine.

"One of the last things my mother told me was that family is imaginary. I don't want to believe her. But I feel like abandoning Candice would prove my mother correct."

"We can stop my mom before she does this!" Mauria insisted, turning her palms over so that they were gripping Isabelle's hand. "That's not abandoning her. It's helping her."

"It's too late to stop her," Isabelle replied. "She'll make Friday night happen, no matter if I'm there, or you're there, or the Thirteens, or that fugitive vampire, Elle."

"So you won't even try?"

"What if it works?" Isabelle said, ignoring Mauria's question. "Maybe this will work. Maybe the assassination will ultimately lift the great curse. One life sacrificed to help many."

"It's not worth it. I don't know why you came here tonight. If it's not about stopping my mom, then why bother?"

"Because I just wanted to talk to someone else who loves her," Isabelle replied, choking the words out as a light shade of red enveloped her face. "We're the only ones."

"She needs to earn my love," Mauria stubbornly told her aunt. "Giving birth to me was not a guarantee. And if you're not going to stop her on Friday then I will."

Isabelle stared into her niece's eyes. Maybe she wanted to see if Mauria was bluffing, or maybe she was just looking for those missing parts of her own sister.

"If you won't cooperate, then I'm afraid I can't let you attend the Fabbies," Isabelle finally replied, adopting a colder tone. "You'll still walk the runway on Thursday at the Haus of Simone show, but then it will be back to house arrest."

"But I'm up for Best Supermodel," Mauria complained. She pulled her hands away from Isabelle's, just as her aunt reached for another taste of the red wine that she'd poured earlier. "And Mom is up for Fashion Icon. Since we're both nominees, we need to show up together on the red carpet."

"Your mom is almost always nominated, more as a friendly gesture. Not even the reporters on the red carpet are going to remember that she's nominated. It won't matter. I can't let you ruin this for your mother," Isabelle told her, delivering the words as gently as if she were telling a small child to clean up his mess. "I don't understand what it is, Mauria. What else do you want? You have your apartment, career, money, clothes, travel—anything anyone could ever want."

"What is it for *you*?" Mauria angrily asked, and stood up from the barstool. She was finished with the conversation, and as tears collected at the corners of her hazel eyes, she stared at her aunt, whose lips were closed and whose face looked numb. "You have your big job, your money, houses, summers split between the Hamptons and the Mediterranean. So why are you still so unhappy? I have a feeling it's the same for the both of us."

Before Isabelle could respond, Mauria stormed out of the kitchen. She was finished with the conversation. She was finished ruining a perfectly good night with conversations about her mother. Mauria had hoped that her aunt's unusual appearance meant Isabelle was going to talk about ways to foil Candice's plot on Friday night. But it was clear that Isabelle was dealing with even greater issues. She had allowed her beloved sister to spiral out of control, and as a result, Isabelle no longer had a grip on reality. She was just as lost as Candice Brown.

Mauria heard her own name echoing loudly in the background. It was unusual for Isabelle to raise her voice, so she was surprised to hear her name shouted down the hallway.

"What?" Mauria screamed without turning around. "Go away!"

Again she heard her name, repeated over and over as if it were coming from a speaker system.

"I said go away!" she yelled down the long white hallway that connected the kitchen to her bedroom. She stood in front of her bedroom door but didn't go in. It sounded like Isabelle was still calling out her name, yet Mauria's aunt wasn't in the hallway. She wasn't chasing after her. Why would she call to her from the kitchen? The whole thing was strange enough that it prompted Mauria to walk back to where she'd abandoned her aunt.

Mauria moved slowly through the hallway, but the voice didn't get any louder or softer. It was as if the words were coming from all around her, rather than a precise spot within the apartment. When Mauria peeked her head out of the hallway, the kitchen was empty. The two glasses were in the sink, filled with water, and the wine bottle was still sitting on the kitchen island. Isabelle's coat was missing, and the front door was closed. And yet Mauria still heard her name called out. Someone was looking for her.

She tried to relax her mind, although Mauria had never been properly trained as an oracle. She had many gifts—like her abilities to control time and space—that were largely undeveloped. She was like an untapped oil field that hadn't found the right investor yet. But from what little Mauria had learned on her own, she tried to focus not on the words, but where they were coming from.

Thursday, Haus of Simone, she repeated over and over in her head. *Help me.*

"Did Natasha tell anyone that she was leaving?" Betty asked, hovering above the sofas where Marciano and Cedric had taken the spots formerly occupied by Natasha and Max.

"She's missing?" was Marciano's dumbfounded response. Cedric just shook his head.

"Aunt Monique!" Betty called. "Hey, I'm pretty sure it's not safe to be in that thing for so many hours!"

Monique slowly turned her head, and stuck a pair of pruned feet out of the hot tub. She raised her flute of champagne with a single boney hand, loosely gripping the glass with two fingers. As she did so, the golden bangles on her arms clacked against the porcelain surface of the tub.

"She left with Fangorio. Cheers," she added, and saluted Betty with her champagne glass, before indulging in another sip.

"Enya?" Betty hopelessly asked.

"They went for a walk. I asked if they needed protection and they said no," the Russian firmly stated. "Enya does not beg. I ask once. You need bodyguard? No? Fine. I return to lifting weights. Or *Judge Judy*."

Betty bit her lower lip, and slowly turned on one heel until she was once again facing the boys.

"Is anyone else worried that she's out running around with Max? Why am I the only one who seems to care?"

"Because you're serious, and you're an older sister," Marciano bluntly told her. "But to tell you the truth, I'm a little worried too. Cedric had some interesting stuff to tell me about Max and this woman he works for."

"I'm not totally sold on him either," Betty replied, "and I'd love to hear anything you know. I can tell that Tash is really falling for him, and I don't like it. I don't know what his intentions are beyond this week."

"Well, what I told Marciano earlier—," Cedric began to say, just as Marciano stood up from the sofa to grab his cell phone, which was vibrating on the glass coffee table.

"Excuse me," he said, and quickly answered the call. "It's Rafaela," he told Betty, whose eyes darted in his direction with the hope that it was a call from their parents. "Hello? Miss Simone?"

Marciano knew what she was calling about, and so he hurried away from the living room in the direction of the kitchen, which like most of the rooms, had an exposed layout.

"Marciano, my darling, I had a dream about you last night." Rafaela's voice paraded through the cell phone with its usual stateliness. "Actually, I had two dreams. The first was that a monkey sold me a used car, and I took him to court after finding that there was a family living inside it. And the second dream was that you failed me."

"But—how did I fail you?"

"It wasn't quite clear," Rafaela replied. "I just remember seeing your face and the word *failure*."

"Ouch."

"Marciano, I need to know that I can trust you to sabotage Maude's fashion show on Thursday. I simply cannot win fairly. I'm not a fair person. I try to be fair, and I get a buildup of stomach acid. So tell me now, darling, whether or not I can count on you. Do you want to design a line for the Fifth Avenue Haus of Simone boutique, or not?"

"I do, I do," Marciano insisted. "But, there's also something you should know about the Fabbies—" He paused, and then looked back at the sofas, where Betty had taken his seat across from Cedric. His older sister was intensely listening as Cedric recounted the story he'd told earlier for Marciano.

"Spit it out, boy."

"Well... there's—"

"No, I'm talking to a homeless person. I just gave him a baguette, and now he's choking on—ah, there you go. You want multigrain? Well, beggars can't be choosers, now can they?" Rafaela said. "Marciano darling, as you were saying?"

"Rafaela, there's a—rumor—that something really, really bad—"

"Why are you talking like William Shatner?"

"Oh... I'm sorry."

"No, keep doing it. It's a turn-on," Rafaela told him, and then sighed deeply into the phone. "The one that got away."

"Uh... look, Miss Simone. Something really bad is going to happen to whoever wins Best Designer at the Fabbies. If I were you, I wouldn't even attend the ceremony."

"That's like asking a Jew to skip Ramadan!" she exclaimed. "How dare you ask me not to attend the most important ceremony of my life, on a night that I might be honored with fashion's greatest award."

"But what if your life depended on it?"

"My life depends on two things: money, fame, and winning."

"Actually, that was three things—"

"Marciano darling, I don't have time for the small details. That's why I have underlings like you. Sabotage Maude's fashion show and you become a star. Resist, and the only way you'll see your designs on Fifth Avenue is if you draw them in sidewalk chalk. This will be my last Fabbies before I hit menopause, and I want to go out with a bang at those after-parties."

"You can count on me," he whispered into the phone.

"I know. Goodnight Marciano darling."

Rafaela hung up, leaving Marciano in a state of confusion. There was no way that he'd be able to convince Rafaela to miss the Fabbies. In addition, his mom was missing, and he had no idea whether or not she'd turn up before Friday. He knew he'd have an easier time convincing her not to attend. Marciano wondered what would happen if

Maude won the award, but failed to show up to receive it. Would they just give it to someone else? Would Candice Brown change her plans last-minute, and murder the winner of Best Supermodel instead? No nominee in the history of the Fabbies had ever failed to show up for the ceremony. One year they even held the event in an Arizona rehab facility just so Marc Jacobs could attend.

There was no elegant solution for Marciano. He could save his mom's life and get a fashion line on Fifth Avenue by sabotaging the Maude by Maude runway show, or he could do nothing, risk losing his job, and put his mom's life at risk. The latter option was the most ethical, but there was a lot for Marciano to lose. He could justify sabotaging the Maude by Maude runway show by ultimately sparing his mom from danger, but Rafaela's plot seemed dirty and unpleasant.

By the time Marciano walked back to the sofas, Cedric had finished telling Betty about the scandal involving Max and the conference-room bombing. If Betty had been nervous before the conversation about Natasha and Max disappearing together, she was even more disturbed afterward.

"Why didn't we know about this sooner?" she asked Cedric. Marciano took a seat next to his sister on the aged leather sofa, which was made up of a vast assortment of browns.

"I had no idea that this guy was hanging around," Cedric replied, and shrugged his shoulders. "You just showed up with him last night. Monique wouldn't know this stuff. How long has he been hanging around you guys?"

"Since we kidnapped Mauria. The same day we met you," Betty added, and then let out a long sigh. "Meanwhile Natasha is head over heels for him," she said with a troubled tone to her voice. "Yesterday he and Mauria went to the department store together, and you would've thought that my sister had just lost the love of her life. She's going through an infatuation stage, and I don't like it."

"We'll all talk to her when she gets back," Cedric insisted. "Or when the sun comes up and Max is forced to rest. Then we'll get her full attention, and there won't be any awkwardness."

"Considering she makes it back tonight."

"Oh, don't even say that," Marciano quickly replied, and stuck his fingers in his ears.

"I'm sorry, I'm just worried. Not just about Max, but about a lot of things," Betty said, and placed a comforting hand on the back of her younger brother's head. "Everything okay with Rafaela?"

"She's good. Just, uh ... nervous about the runway shows on Thursday."

"Yeah, so let's talk about how we're going to handle that," Betty said, and quickly switched her attention to the new topic. "Since there's still no word from Mom and Dad, and I assume it's still very dangerous for us to be out in public—despite our sister's fearlessness—it would make sense to skip the shows, right? You had mentioned interfering with Mom's show so that she might lose to Rafaela on Friday night, but I'm not certain I want to put anyone in the line of fire. Especially if we aren't guaranteed to have Mauria with us."

"You mean you don't want to go at all?" Marciano asked his sister. "But that's like—sacrilegious!"

"I think your sister's right," Cedric told Marciano. "What good can come from showing up? It's not like you can go help out with your mom's fashion show while Candice Brown is looking for you. That's suicide. I mean, I love a good runway show, but I wouldn't risk my life for one."

"Why don't we stay indoors all week, and figure out a plan for Friday night," Betty calmly suggested.

"But what if Mom's runway show is a success and she wins Best Designer?" Marciano asked. "You're willing to take that risk?"

Before Betty could answer, the door swung open and shut, and all heads turned to the entrance. Without taking off her coat, Natasha hurried over to the sofas with a smile on her face.

"Where did you go?" Betty asked her, standing from the sofa to face her younger sister.

"Max and I went for a little walk," Natasha replied, and shrugged as if it was no big deal.

"While Candice Brown is out looking for you? That's appropriate. And where's Max?"

"He had to go do *Caligae stuff*, I don't know," Natasha replied, the smile fading from her face. "Why are you so grumpy tonight?"

"Grumpy?" Betty replied, revealing a thin smile. "I'm *worried*, not grumpy."

"Well please lighten up," Natasha told her older sister. "I like this guy. Stop being so serious. This whole weekend has been so serious, and I need a break from it."

"Right now is not the—"

"I heard Mauria's voice," Natasha blurted out, interrupting Betty.

"What did you say?"

"As we were walking back to the apartment, I began to hear Mauria's voice in my head, as clear as if she were standing right next to me. She's going to be at the runway shows on Thursday. She's walking runway for Haus of Simone, but she'll be sitting with her mom in the front row the whole time. She'll be allowed backstage for all of one minute to walk the runway, and then has to immediately return to her seat."

As soon as the words left Natasha's mouth, Marciano's eyes lit up.

"Will they be at Mom's show?" he asked his sister. "It's right before Rafaela's."

"I assume so. I don't think Candice would miss Maude by Maude. It's a big deal this year."

"Then let's save her before she even has a chance to walk runway," Marciano suggested, using his hands in an animated manner as he spoke to the group. "We can cause a diversion during Mom's show. Maybe set off the fire alarm or something. Max is super-fast—he can sweep in and grab Mauria, and we can make a clean getaway."

"You've been watching too many heist movies," Natasha replied, laughing at her brother. "This sounds much easier said than done. And I don't want to ruin Mom's show."

"What about that one-minute timeframe when she has to go backstage?" Betty asked the group.

"I agree with Betty," Cedric said. "Much less risky. We should try to pull this off without getting noticed by Candice."

"But you don't want to psyche her out?" Marciano asked Cedric. "Doing it in front of Candice would totally mess with her head in advance of the Fabbies. What a way to gain the upper hand! She'll be so nervous going into Friday night."

"What if it just makes her ramp up security, making it more difficult for us to break into the event?" Betty asked.

"Stop being so logical," Marciano said, which made his older sister roll her eyes. "We have the chance to gain—like—a psychological advantage over Candice Brown. And all we have to do is cause a diversion at Mom's show, distract Candice and the crowd, and then have Max sweep in and take Mauria backstage. She'll freeze time, allowing for us to get past backstage security, and then we'll hop in a car and be out of there. Mission accomplished. The Fabbies will be an utter failure without Mauria. We need to get her on Thursday. We have a small window of time to actually do it."

"Marciano is right," Natasha said, speaking up for her brother. "If we don't have Mauria at the Fabbies, we don't have a plan. We need to go to Bryant Park on Thursday and save her. I don't care how we do it. But I agree that psyching out Candice would give us an advantage."

"This all sounds pretty bold," Cedric remarked.

"Can we do it without ruining Mom's fashion show?" Betty asked everyone.

"Mom's fashion show should be the last thing we worry about," Marciano told her. "A fashion show is a fashion show. Mom's life is another thing."

His words struck a chord not only with Betty, but with everyone. Even Enya nodded approvingly from her weight bench across the loft. Marciano had gained everyone's vote of confidence, although he didn't feel so great about it. After all, he had a lot to gain from disrupting his mom's show. Not just his mom's life, but his own fashion line. He couldn't help but wonder if he was making the right decision.

"Natasha, do you know when Max will be back?" Cedric asked. "He's vital to this plan, so obviously we need to go over everything with him. I can arrange to get you and your brother backstage so that when Mauria freezes time, you can guide her out to the getaway car."

"Not sure, but he said before Thursday morning."

"The sooner the better. And if you're going to go through with this, then Enya and I need to spend two days preparing you," Cedric told them. "Candice Brown is totally irrational and violent. If she or one of her goons attacks you, you need to be prepared to defend yourselves."

"I agree with Cedric," Betty said. "We need to dedicate every single minute of the next two days to coming up with the perfect plan. No walks with Max, no playing dress-up—we need to be serious."

"I can't be serious all day long," Marciano replied. "I just can't. It's not me. I can be serious for about fifteen straight minutes and then I start getting giggly."

"Okay, well, try to be as serious as you can," she said with raised eyebrows. "Aunt Monique, does this sound good to you?" Betty called in the direction of the hot tub.

Monique raised her empty champagne flute in the air to toast Betty, and then raised it to her lips, only to be shocked by the absence of alcohol. Hastily she grabbed for the glass bottle and turned it upside down, patting it to see if there were any drops left.

"Refill!" she called from the hot tub, before moaning in exhaustion.

"She's in," Natasha quietly remarked.

"Then it seems you guys are in for an exciting couple of days," Cedric said as a nervous grin slowly appeared on his face.

Chapter Ten

"EXCITED FOR THE BIG DAY?" ONE OF THE LEADing members of Caligae asked Isabelle as they passed each other on the main floor of headquarters. Deep beneath the cold streets of Manhattan, where Bryant Park was bustling in anticipation for the final day of fashion week, the offices of the world's oldest secret society were stirring with nervous energy. By then, everyone of any importance in the fashion world was in New York, ready to see Thursday's fashion shows, and attend the Fabulous Fashion Awards on the following night. The number of supernaturals in New York City had exploded due to this fashion tourism, and Caligae—normally charged with keeping track of all supernaturals—was working day and night to manage to the massive inflow of their own kind.

Even Caligae headquarters seemed far busier than usual. Members of Caligae from other countries and continents had poured in to attend to the fashion shows and lend a hand to New York agents. The main floor, which normally could be described as a quiet mass of computers, personnel, and glass walls, usually bore more of a resemblance to a quiet accounting firm than the workplace of a secret society. But on Thursday morning, as Isabelle walked to her newly furnished office above Candice Brown's, she could only compare the scene at headquarters to a zoo that had let the animals roam free.

"You look great today!" someone said as they passed Isabelle in the hallway. She smiled, but didn't respond. She had dressed up for the day's runway shows, and was wearing a purple gown with cyan heels.

Unlike Candice, Isabelle was normally opposed to bling, but on this special day she brought the diamonds out in full force, in the form of a bracelet, earrings, and an engagement ring from her first and only marriage.

"Bella," a man said in a deeply accented voice, and he blew a kiss to her. Isabelle smiled again, although she raised an eyebrow upon realizing that he was wearing a construction hat. Not that she didn't see a lot of weird stuff around headquarters, but associates didn't normally wear hardhats to work. That fad only lasted for a hot second in the '70s.

As Isabelle got closer to her office, she saw another guy in construction garb, wearing a yellow hardhat and matching overalls. A third was munching on a doughnut just outside of Candice Brown's office. Isabelle couldn't see her older sister through the large glass window in front of the office, because the window had been replaced by a one-sided mirror. Candice liked her privacy.

"What's going on?" Isabelle impatiently asked one of the construction workers. As he bit down into his doughnut and jelly poured out onto his lips, his face squirmed into a sign of nervousness.

"You're not Isabelle, are you?" he asked.

"Chew your food and then speak."

"Sorry," he replied, his lips covered in powder and jelly.

"Oh dear God," she replied, and quickly passed him, walking directly into Candice Brown's office, which had been recently expanded by bulldozing the offices of two nearby executives. A miniature movie theater had been added, including a gym, a hot tub, three television screens, and a full kitchen.

"Flowers? From my seventy-eighth husband?" Candice moaned into her pink desk phone. "Oh, Olympia, just toss them. You know I hate to receive effeminate gifts at work. And why is he sending me flowers? I only want gifts with a resale value. Go see if you can pawn these off on some tourists."

Candice smiled and hung up the phone. Isabelle had to loudly clear her throat before Candice realized she had company in the office.

"What?" Candice said, glancing up from her desk with a look of exasperation. "Can't you see I'm incredibly bus—*ouch!*"

Seconds after Candice's loud shriek, a dwarf ran out from underneath her desk with a nail file and bucket of water.

"Get out!" she screamed, and then flung her right leg on top of her desk, which nearly made Candice fall off of her own office chair. "No one knows how to give a proper pedicure anymore. This remodel has created an environment of stress."

"Remodel? What's this about a remodel?"

"Uh—" As soon as Candice realized she'd made a poor choice of words, she gulped, and threw her leg off the surface of her desk. "Nothing, just, uh … added some extra space to my office, as you can see."

"Yes, I can," Isabelle unenthusiastically replied. She rolled her eyes, and then turned her attention to the spiral staircase that had been installed to connect Candice's office to Isabelle's. "Well I'm heading upstairs to get some work done before Maude by Maude."

"Uh … I don't really know if you uh—," Candice said, gritting her teeth as an uncomfortable look spread across her face.

"Candice, what did you do to my office?"

"Nothing."

"No, I know you did something to my office. Every time you get that constipated look on your face, I know you did something wrong."

"That's not true," Candice shot back. "I had curry for brunch."

"Candice—"

"How about you just take the day off," Candice suggested. "Go to Bryant Park, enjoy the runway shows, and relax."

"Candice—"

"Okay, alright, so I made some minor changes," Candice reluctantly admitted, waving her hands in the air. "I hired an interior designer to come in yesterday and give me recommendations on what to do with my office, and *she* told me that it was the new trend for powerful people to have two-floor offices."

"So having a lap pool, gym, and home theater isn't enough?"

"Don't forget about the tanning salon in what used to be the executive lounge around the corner," Candice reminded her.

"I knew you looked a little orange this morning," Isabelle disgustedly remarked. "So you're telling me that you've basically seized my new office on the second floor?"

"It's now a bowling alley with a dance floor and a robot DJ. Cool, huh?"

"Candice, I don't even—I—you know, I can't work like this. Everything was fine until you decided to start working out of headquarters. Why are you even here?" Isabelle said in frustration. "You don't work!"

"Hey, come take a look at this," Candice requested, ignoring her sister's whiney complaints. Isabelle methodically walked around Candice's desk and peeked at the computer screen.

"What's this?"

"Welcome to the interactive dating network for Caligae," Candice proudly told her younger sister. "It's a social networking site that connects us on every continent. Well, except for Antarctica and that white trash Dorina. But for everyone else, now they have a way to meet a potential life partner."

"So basically you're encouraging and promoting interoffice romance."

"Lighten up, dumpy."

"Don't call me that."

"Look, when's the last time you had a date?" Candice asked her.

"I actually have one today, at the runway shows. A gentleman is meeting me at Bryant Park. We're going to see the Maude and Rafaela runway shows, and then he's taking me out to lunch."

"Are you going to split the bill?" Candice asked.

"Why does that matter? Of course. Probably."

"Wrong!" Candice said, and pressed her finger against the aluminum desk as she made an obnoxious buzzing sound. "You're the one with loads of cash. Why don't you pay? It'll throw him off. I always pay for the first few dates. Then when he proposes marriage I suck his bank account dry."

"Nice," Isabelle replied, rolling her eyes as she spoke.

"Listen to me. I've been married close to one hundred times—"

"All of them tragic failures—"

"And—are you listening?" Candice hollered at her. "I have perfected the art of getting a man to propose."

"A brainwash serum?"

"No, it's all about the first date," Candice replied, speaking as if she were the world's foremost expert on the subject. "This is what you do. Today at the runway shows, don't talk much to this guy. It is a guy, right?"

"Yes," Isabelle said, feigning exhaustion with the conversation.

"Well, I just lost an office bet," Candice remarked, which led to a raised eyebrow from Isabelle. "But today, focus on the fashion, and don't speak much. Pretend you're really interested in the runway shows, and that they're more important than him. Then when he takes you out to lunch, here's what you do. If the date isn't going well, then order something quick and light, like a salad. Tell him that you have to be somewhere at a certain time—that way the date is guaranteed to end quickly.

"If you *do* like him, then only order an appetizer, and after a few bites pretend like you just got an important phone call, and split out the door. Toss a wad of cash on the table, enough to pay for the meal and then some, and jump in a cab. He'll feel like he owes you another date."

"Well, uh... what do we talk about on the date?"

"Talk about yourself," Candice suggested. "Tell him how important you are. By the end of the date, he should know how much you're worth, what kind of real estate you own, the number of shoes in your closet, and how much you've donated to charity over the past ten years. Drop a lot of A-list names of people you don't really know, but are pretending to. Just don't talk about religion. That's very taboo. Oh, and make sure you tell him how handsome he looks. But if he doesn't immediately reciprocate, throw a glass of water in his face."

Isabelle glanced at her sister with a surprised expression.

"Let me tell you something about men," Candice said with an authoritative voice. "Women never compliment men. They're too coy. So when you throw yourself at a man and tell him how attractive he looks, he'll be so preoccupied with the compliments that when you spend the whole date talking about yourself, they won't really be listening to you. They will, however, pick up the conversation at a subconscious level. I guarantee that on date number two, he'll remember everything you told him. It's a strategy that tricks the man into thinking he's more into you than he really is."

"I don't know, Candice; this sounds very complicated."

"It's really not that hard," Candice replied, waving a hand in dismissal. "Just remember that when you're on the second date, there's a small chance he might expect you to pay for it. Some guys are into powerful women. Especially the eighteen-year-olds."

"He's, uh... quite a bit older than eighteen."

"Good, more of 'em for me," Candice replied. "Well if this guy thinks you're paying, he might pull something shady and try to order like three martinis. The really expensive ones that cost as much as an entrée. Especially if he shows up drunk for the date."

"Why would he show up drunk to a date with me?"

"Exactly because he's on a date with you," Candice replied. "Now make sure he knows that you're only paying for one drink. He'll think you're being funny when you tell him this. If you tell him he's handsome right before you say you're only buying one drink, then it'll transfer at a subconscious super-psychological level. Oh, and tell him that it's either one drink or dessert, but not both. Not only would you be blowing your hard-earned money, but the caloric intake is just catastrophic."

"I'll, um... try to put your advice to good use," Isabelle replied, although she was somewhat skeptical of her sister's advice. "I'll be sure to let you know how my date goes."

"Yeah, I don't really care," Candice said, and shrugged her shoulders. "But I'll see you at Maude by Maude. You think those Thirteens are gonna show up?"

"I highly doubt it," Isabelle replied. "With all of us in attendance?"

"But you've confirmed a link between them and Maude, right?"

"Only them and Maude's close friend, a mummy who works in Woodsrow & Campertine. They told Olympia that she was their aunt, although we don't have any records of this mummy having siblings. And she's much too old for us to trace this sort of thing. All we know is that she's disappeared, and it's been a week since anyone has seen Maude or her husband."

"I find it very odd," Candice remarked.

"That Maude might not be at her own fashion show?"

"No, that you're still in my office. Get the hell out."

Isabelle shook her head and turned on one heel to leave Candice's presence. Without an office, there was no reason for her to stick around headquarters, and so she decided to head to Bryant Park. She had a long couple of days ahead of her.

"Cedric Black," he said, waving his credentials in the air as the two look-alike thugs guarding the backstage area nearly leapt out of his way. Even though Cedric was dressed like a traffic cone, in a blindingly orange sweater with lilac skinny jeans, his name commanded a certain level of importance. In an industry run by the Colors, he was one of them. And even though he was nothing like Candice Brown, Isabelle the Purple, or even his own mother Priscilla Black, Cedric had been born into entitlement. Fortunately, on the morning of the Maude by Maude and Haus of Simone runway shows, Cedric's entitlement worked in his favor.

As soon as the guards stepped aside, Cedric walked briskly into the backstage area of the massive tent erected within Bryant Park. Flanked by Natasha, Marciano, Enya, and Betty, all of whom were holding a coffin cleverly disguised as a boxed set piece, Cedric headed straight for the dressing rooms.

Cedric dressed the group in suits and dark sunglasses in order to give them a discreet and intimidating presence. Instead they looked more like tax attorneys. Not to mention that Marciano screwed up the group outfit by refusing to wear socks with his brown loafers.

Cedric quickly found an empty dressing room and hurried the group inside. There wasn't really enough room for all of them, but they squeezed together and managed to lightly rest the coffin on the floor. Moments later, the top opened, and Max peeked his head out.

"I felt all three of those potholes," he wearily said as his eyes scanned the small dressing room.

"When Enya drives, no one survives," Marciano remarked in an exaggerated Russian accent, and then glanced at the frightening Amazonian, who was staring him down. She lifted one hand and slowly clenched her fingers into a fist.

"So we're clear on the plan?" Cedric asked everyone, speaking lightly so that no one outside the dressing room could hear him. "I'll be in the getaway car waiting. Enya is backstage in case anything happens. She'll blend in as regular security detail. Max and Natasha hang out here until the first show starts—"

"No hanky-panky in the dressing room," Marciano said, which garnered angry glances from his sister and the studly vampire.

"And you, Marc, have the biggest responsibility of all," Cedric continued. "Are you absolutely *sure* that you can handle this? I mean,

I thought our plan was fine. I don't know why you changed it this morning, but—"

"I'll tell you guys after we rescue Mauria," he answered. "This is the right thing to do."

At that moment, all six of them looked around at each other. They had no idea if this would be the last time they all saw one another, or if it would just be the first step toward a victory at the Fabbies. But there was a general consensus that they were about to do the right thing. And nothing—Candice Brown included—was going to stand in their way.

"Get out of my way," Candice demanded of some lowly journalists as she stormed onto the scene of Bryant Park wearing her signature pink velour tracksuit, this time with a collar lined with cheetah fur. Her bulky sunglasses had a matching cheetah print, along with pink shades that complemented her black hair.

"But Candice—"

"No questions," Candice replied, throwing her hands up in front of her. "I just had a nose job and I'm heavily medicated."

"But aren't you always heavily medicated?" a journalist from a popular fashion magazine asked. Candice stopped in her tracks, turned to him, and slowly lowered her pink sunglasses. The entire crowd outside the New York fashion week tent became deathly silent as everyone waited for Candice Brown's response. The aged fashion mogul stared at the journalist with piercing eyes—probably the only remaining original parts of her body.

"Yes," she finally said, before repositioning her sunglasses and resuming her walk.

Candice had a front-row seat for two back-to-back fashion shows. The first was Maude by Maude, which was always a delightful show. Candice had been trying to invest in Maude's company for years, but the designer had repeatedly turned down every offer.

After an uncomfortable stare-off with Anna Wintour, Candice took her seat in the front row, sitting beside Isabelle, Isabelle's date (whom Candice didn't acknowledge), Bridgette #2, and a grumpy-looking

Mauria Brown. The same flood of reporters who had harassed Candice on her way into the tent had rushed down to the front row.

"Candice, who is your pick to win Best Designer this year at the Fabbies?" one of the journalists asked her.

"Whoever wins, I just know it's going to be to die for," she said, and then burst into a fit of laughter.

"Why is that funny?" one of the journalists asked her. When Candice realized that no one in the crowd was laughing, her smile faded into a snarl.

"*Why is that funny?*" Candice repeated, mimicking the voice of the reporter. "Obviously I'm the only person in the front row with a sense of humor—I mean, aside from my sister's date over here. You need the sense of humor for two people in order to spend an afternoon with her."

"Thanks, Candice," Isabelle wryly replied.

"Anytime. Now, to all of you lowlife journalist scum who can't afford the clothing you're writing about, why don't you crawl back up to the third row and start talking to people who actually need the cheap publicity you offer. I am Candice Brown. I own an island, a private jet, and all the toilets in my home are made out of gold. Maybe that last part isn't true, or the first part, or the second, but here's the real laugh: I put three-hundred-dollar pairs of sweatpants in my clothing stores, and people buy them. Now who's laughing at whom?"

As usual, the journalists smiled and scurried away from the front row with enough material to fill the following month's fashion magazines.

Candice first turned to her right, took one look at her daughter, and grunted. Mauria was sitting next to her with a scowl on her pretty face. Her arms were folded, and she was slouched in her plastic chair. Just as an assistant dropped off a bag of nacho chips in Candice Brown's lap, she turned away from her daughter to face her sister, Isabelle.

"So Maude's not going to be here, hmm?" Candice asked her sister, leaning in as she whispered with discretion. "You think that's an admission of guilt?"

"Do you realize you just insulted me a minute ago, and now you want to talk and pretend like nothing happened?"

"Oh, put a lid on it," Candice remarked, pulling away and adjusting her pink sunglasses. "You act like I've never insulted you before."

"Well, each time stings."

"Then get some Neosporin and get over it," Candice shot back. "Now what do you think about Maude?"

Isabelle raised her eyebrows, and then glanced up at the runway before returning her attention to Candice.

"Who knows what's going on in her personal life? If she turns up before tomorrow night, maybe we should bring her in to headquarters for a little chat. Make sure she's alright."

"As long as she doesn't win Best Designer, I can guarantee she'll be alright," Candice remarked, and then burst into laughter.

"Marciano darling!" The words hit him like a brick in the head. Marciano had just hurried into the main tent from the open air of Bryant Park, when he was spotted by the last person on Earth whom he had expected to see. Instead of being backstage preparing for her show, Rafaela Simone was sipping a cappuccino in a glass cup (probably stolen), lingering around the back of the audience to get a peek at her archrival's latest collection.

"Hi Miss Simone," he reluctantly said through gritted teeth. Marciano had changed out of the dark suit, and was wearing a black turtleneck with matching skinny jeans. He looked like he could be a member of the set crew, or an assistant to some cameraman covering the show.

"Marciano darling, where's your sister? And what is all this commotion coming from outside the main tent? Shouldn't everyone be inside by now? And why aren't you in the front row?"

"I just wanted to, uh ... to get a long-distance glimpse of the show. You know, make sure the clothing looks good from far away."

Rafaela nodded her head as if Marciano had just recited a complex algorithmic formula.

"I know exactly what you mean," she snootily told him. "In fact, one year I sent my models to the moon so that I could take pictures of them with a NASA satellite. I'm a firm believer in alien paparazzi, Marciano darling. If I'm showing up in extraterrestrial tabloids, my clothing better look phenomenal. That way when they invade Earth, they'll all want to buy my clothing."

"Well, I hope that when we're finally discovered by aliens, you get all of their couture business."

"I will, Marciano darling, and just hope you own stock in Haus of Simone when it happens," she remarked. "By the way, I just love your look today. Even though it's cheap and depressing, it reminds me of my childhood."

"That's comforting," Marciano silently replied, and gulped. In a quick fit of paranoia, he shot his head around to see if anyone was looking at him. If Candice Brown or any of her thugs were to spot and recognize Marciano, the entire plan could be foiled. "Um ... Rafaela, you really should leave Bryant Park."

"What, I can't watch my most hated rival's show, and hope that it's a complete and utter failure, thanks to a little saboteur work done by my employee, hint hint?"

"No, I mean—something bad is going to happen. Today and tomorrow. But—" He dropped his voice to a whisper and leaned closer to her ear. She balked a little at the physical contact, but listened anyway. "Someone is trying to murder the winner of Best Designer."

"Caligae protects against those things," Rafaela condescendingly replied, as if explaining a simple concept to a child.

"But what if Caligae is responsible? What if they're the ones who are going to do it?" Marciano whispered, staring his employer straight in her eyes.

"Marciano darling, you're not kidding, are you?" she asked him, lowering her voice so that she was whispering as lightly as he was.

"Can't you tell?" he asked, putting his hands over his chest in a motion of sincerity. His face was wrought with concern. "I know because they're after me."

"So they know that you're—" Rafaela paused, and then glanced around "—that number in between twelve and fourteen."

"Way to be discreet, Miss Simone, but yes. How'd you know?"

"Because I'm a telepath, and I could never read your mind," she said, and poked her own head with a single lean finger. "And although I'd love to see your mom's company deteriorate like ancient ruins brutalized by the cruel hands of time, she did send you to me in trust, that I would watch over you and protect you. I've always known you were special. Not just because you're fabulous and refuse to wear shorts, but because you're just strange enough that it would make sense for you to be a great fashion designer someday."

"Even if I'm sabotaging *both* yours and my mom's fashion shows today?"

"If I get that store on Fifth Avenue, you're designing a line for it," Rafaela proudly whispered to her employee. "Now—it seems I need to find your mom, and I think I know just where to look."

"Thank you," Marciano told her as a smile poured onto his face. Rafaela hurried toward the exit, but just before she could pass security, she tilted her head.

"Oh, and Marciano darling—go kick some ass."

No sooner had the words left Rafaela Simone's mouth than the lights dimmed within the tent. The noise of the room drew to a hush as lights sprang from the runway in narrow, cylindrical lines. A train track had been laid along the runway in a semicircle, and as spectators grew increasingly curious about how it would be used, the answer revealed itself in the form of an old steam-engine train. Maude's latest collection was inspired by the clothing of immigrants who voyaged to America in the early 1920s. The fashion designer had requested that the backstage be filled with water and a boat land at the foot of the stage, but the budget wasn't in her favor. And so she settled with a train.

The sound of a steam engine filled the main tent, just as a locomotive—painted white, with a picture of Maude's face on the front—rode out from the backstage at a snail's pace. As loungey electro-pop began to fill the tent, the first model stepped foot on the runway.

"She looks a little short to be a runway model," Isabelle whispered into her sister's ear as they watched the first model grow closer and closer. "She's not walking right either. Maude's gotten sloppy."

"Maude is never sloppy," Candice quickly retorted, and the expressionless gaze wrapped across her plastic-injected face twisted into a menacing scowl. Candice dug her hand deep into the bag of nacho chips sitting on her lap as she munched furiously on the food in her mouth.

When the model reached the end of the runway, she didn't stop and pose. She didn't turn on one heel. Instead she stood with her legs spread, arms at her side, chin up, and eyes directly on the woman sitting in the front row beneath her.

"Good morning," Natasha announced from the stage, loudly enough for everyone in the audience to hear her. Dressed in a couture cream gown decorated with pearls, Natasha's face was powdered, her hair was straightened, her lips were the color of a Fuji apple, and her demeanor was that of a woman who meant business. "This upcoming season's Maude by Maude collection celebrates the clothing of immigrants who pilgrimaged to America nearly one hundred years ago. The Haus of Simone's collection pays tribute to the clothing that New Yorkers would wear if King Kong attacked and ravaged the city. Since both of these collections have to do with people—or giant apes—landing on the streets of New York City, we have moved today's first two fashion shows outside to Bryant Park, to be presented to the public in the same open air breathed by New Yorkers and immigrants alike. The shows will resume immediately, just outside this tent."

Natasha didn't bother to look down at Candice; rather, she kept her eyes on the main entrance. She had worried that the crowd would be confused, but stranger things had happened in fashion. Especially with Maude and Rafaela Simone, both of whom were known for their peculiar artistic choices. Instead, everyone was pretty responsive. People left their seats and hurried to leave the tent and catch the runway shows outdoors.

Candice Brown sat still as everyone around her moved toward the exits. Her hands were digging through the bag of nachos fast enough to tear a hole in the thin layer of plastic. Her daughter sat quietly beside her with a thin smile on her face.

"Are you coming?" Isabelle's date asked her once he'd stood up from the front row. The Caligae director looked toward her sister. She couldn't see Candice's eyes behind the pink sunglasses, but could tell what was going on inside that troubled head. Things were about to get ugly. Isabelle stood up and followed her date toward the exit. She at least needed to get him outside before she reacted to the problems inside the main tent.

Max, hurry up, Natasha thought to herself as she looked around. The tent was clearing out, and the only people in their seats were Candice

Brown, Mauria, and Bridgette #2, all in the front row. Natasha could hear the crunching of nacho chips in the front row, rising over the noise of chatter as attendees cleared the exits.

"Cute," Candice finally remarked as she relaxed in her seat. She crossed her legs and folded her hands on her lap. "I'm going to ask you a question, and I want you to answer it as truthfully as possible. What do you hope to accomplish here?"

Natasha nervously looked down at Candice, and then at Bridgette #2, and then Mauria. She glanced up at Isabelle, who was walking through one of the exits, her head of ultra-wavy auburn hair turned curiously toward the stage. Natasha knew she wasn't going to accomplish anything unless Max hurried up. He was supposed to have swooped in already.

"I'm just making things even," Natasha finally responded to Candice.

"Did you really move the fashion shows outside?"

"Yes," Natasha replied.

"It's February."

"Fashion will assimilate."

Candice Brown crumpled up the bag of nacho chips and tossed it behind her. She unenthusiastically raised a bejeweled hand in Natasha's direction, and smirked from behind her giant pink sunglasses. "This is the end. This is where your race becomes extinct."

Candice flipped her outstretched hand so that the palm was facing the ceiling, and upon making a lifting motion with her fingers, the hundreds of plastic chairs in the evacuated tent levitated into the air. The faint light from the runway illuminated the rows of transparent chairs, held in midair by Candice Brown's unique ability to control plastic.

Natasha had never seen anything like it before, and it was terrifying. She gulped as she stared at the floating chairs, and her hands shook at her sides.

"Max, where are you?" she whispered.

"Run," Candice said, just before the first chair came flying at Natasha. She dodged her head, and then dropped to her knees as a second chair came toward her. Natasha kicked off the heels she'd worn down the runway and then jumped to her feet. Just as she neared the edge of the runway, two plastic chairs smashed into her, knocking the twenty-one-year old on her back. She coughed loudly as the shock of impact came and went.

On the ground in front of the stage, Bridgette #2 bent her legs, and with a single leap she jumped onto the runway. As soon as her brown alligator boots slammed against the stage, the wood cracked loudly, and splinters flew through the air.

"Your mother went out the same way," Bridgette #2 said with a touch of humor to her voice. The robot raised her leather boot above Natasha's straightened brunette hair, but seemed to be taking an awfully long time to stomp down.

"Do it!" Candice shouted. "What are you waiting for?"

Candice Brown finally stood up from her seat and walked toward the runway, where Bridgette #2 seemed frozen in time. Suddenly the entire runway shook, as if a rhinoceros was stampeding down its wooden surface. Enya stormed out from backstage and collided with Bridgette #2, sending the immobile robot flying through the air and into a dozen plastic chairs that were still floating above the ground.

As soon as Candice realized what had happened, she swung her head and snarled at her only daughter.

"Unfreeze her!" she demanded of Mauria, but the young supermodel stood up and walked toward the runway in a sudden bout of confidence. She pulled herself up onto the stage, so that she was standing beside Enya.

"Or else?" she asked her mom.

Isabelle had come back into the main tent, and was watching the entire scene with confusion. She didn't know what to do. She'd spent hundreds of years behind a desk, and hadn't seen conflict in a very long time. Nor did Isabelle want her reintroduction to conflict to involve a fight between her sister and niece—the only two people in the world who Isabelle was truly close to. Her eyes went back and forth between Candice and Mauria, but she couldn't make a decision.

"Or else *this*," Candice spat out. She raised both arms, and the three girls on the runway could feel the energy racing off of Candice Brown's body.

"I've got this," Enya remarked. She reached into a copper-colored fanny pack attached to her waist, and hastily removed the spray can that Cedric had given her. She sprayed her hair, creating a gray mist around her blonde ponytail.

Just as Enya's hair started to swing like the blades of a helicopter, the plastic chairs—suspended in midair—began flying onto the stage. First they came in twos, then threes, and then fours, swarming the stage in an onslaught of plastic. Enya leaned forward and sped up the momentum of her ponytail. When the first chair hit Enya's hair, it smashed into pieces. Then a second, and a third. Enya was shattering the chairs, but the sheer number of them was forcing her backward on the stage.

"Run!" she commanded Natasha and Mauria. The latter turned to hurry backstage, but Natasha quickly grabbed Mauria's arm.

"No, we can't just leave her!"

Just then, a chair collided with Enya's legs, knocking her backward. Two more hit her in the shoulders, and the Russian's heavy body slammed against the wooden runway. Mauria and Natasha turned toward Candice Brown just in time to see the rush of plastic chairs coming their way. There was nothing they could do. They held up their arms, but the chairs flew into them with savage force.

"I don't know what to do!" Natasha cried out to Mauria and Enya as she lifted her bruised arms in front of her head. "How do I use my powers?"

"I don't know," Mauria shouted. "I don't know!"

Mauria had lost control of Bridgette #2, and the robot was back up and angrier than ever. She leapt into the air and landed once again on the runway, ducking underneath the chairs.

"Where's Max?" Natasha shouted. "He's supposed to—" Before Natasha could finish, the back of Bridgette's hand smashed into her forehead. She rolled off the side of the runway and hit the ground with a thud. No sooner did Natasha hit the ground than Bridgette #2 dived at Enya. She hit the blonde Russian twice, knocking her backward into the steam engine that was continuing along its path. Enya hit the train with such force that both she and the small locomotive toppled off the runway, leaving Mauria all alone.

"You wouldn't hurt me," Mauria said to Bridgette #2, glaring up from a defensive position on the floor.

"Actually, I've been dying to," the cruel robot replied.

Just as Bridgette #2 stepped toward Mauria, a new voice shook the room.

"Candice!" someone called from the back of the tent. The fashion empress turned her head, and the swarm of plastic chairs paused. Even those that had collided with the stage and the three girls were back in midair, hovering above the ground like hawks ready to attack their prey.

"The other Thirteen," Candice said under her breath as soon as she saw the black-haired young man standing about ten feet from Isabelle. "It was idiotic of you to show up," Candice shouted across the room.

"Yeah, well you can't even spell *idiotic*!" he shot back. "And I hate your outfit."

"Bridgette, knock out Mauria, and then kill the female Thirteen," Candice ordered as she fumed over Marciano's comments. "And you," she said, turning back to Marciano and pointing an angry finger, "you're dead."

Candice flung both of her arms forward, and suddenly all of the plastic chairs hovering inside the tent flew through the air in Marciano's direction. She expected to hear screams, or cries for mercy, or the shouts of pain from someone being crushed by hundreds of chairs. But instead, there was silence.

Candice glared up at the chairs, piled in a spherical mess just inches from Marciano's body. In fact, she couldn't see him behind all the chairs, but she could still feel him there. She could feel that same scary feeling she'd felt hundreds of years ago when her people went to war with the Thirteens.

"Mauria, jump!" Marciano said, and the blonde supermodel quickly responded by rolling off the stage. By the time Bridgette #2 turned around, it was too late. The ball of plastic chairs came at her so fast that it not only devoured her body, but also the entire runway.

Candice looked back and forth in horror. Isabelle's hands were covering her mouth in shock. The sisters had no idea what had happened. All they saw was a triumphant Marciano, standing in the same spot with a grin on his face. His older sister, Betty, hurried through the entrance and passed her brother as she ran down to the demolished runway to check on Natasha, Enya, and Mauria. Candice Brown's eyes shifted between Betty and Marciano. The latter held his position, ready to respond to whatever Candice threw at him.

"Are they okay?" Marciano called down to Betty.

"I'll be fine!" Natasha called back amid grunts of pain as Betty inspected her younger sister. Mauria was already up on her feet, but was busy tossing her perfect hair.

"Enya?" Marciano called down. The Russian—sprawled out across the destroyed steam engine—managed to raise her arm and give a thumbs-up. "Candice—I'll give you one opportunity. You and your sister can leave the country and disappear before the Fabbies tomorrow night."

"Otherwise what?" Candice spat at him. "You think you can walk in here and ruin a lineup of fashion shows? You think you can destroy my robot, who cost countless millions of dollars and countless hours of research?"

Marciano shrugged his shoulders. "I guess you didn't count on your powers backfiring," he remarked.

"No, I didn't," Candice said, and bunched her bulbous lips together. "But I did know that you'd confront me at some point. And so I made sure that there's something—or someone—whom you couldn't count on."

Before Marciano had time to react, something hit him in the back of the head, knocking him unconscious. In a split second, Betty had also been knocked to the ground.

The last thing Natasha saw before a leather boot struck her forehead was that familiar set of blue eyes—the same pair that first enchanted her at the party at Mauria's apartment.

Chapter Eleven

"I KNEW I'D FIND YOU IN JERSEY," RAFAELA scoffed at her arch-nemesis. Miss Simone's black sedan was parked next to a Volkswagen bus in a parking lot at a busy New Jersey rest stop. Her driver's side window was rolled down, and so was the passenger's window of the adjacent vehicle.

"I thought I said no pickles?" Maude asked as she rummaged through a paper bag full of wrapped fast food.

"Honey, just pick them off," Monique replied from the driver's seat of the Volkswagen. Maude, who was in the passenger's seat, slowly picked off the pickles and tossed them out her window and into Rafaela's car.

"Oh, God!" Rafaela cried out as ketchup-covered pickles flew into her black sedan. "Can you stop that? I just had the interior steam cleaned after having to give a ride to my ex-husband."

"So are the rumors true?" Maude asked in her soft, French-accented English. She kept her eyes on a small packet of chicken nuggets in her lap.

"Yes, but I put a cream all over my body and they disappeared in three days."

"Wait—are you talking about your ex-husband or my children?"

"I'm talking about crabs," Rafaela sorely replied, "but on the subject of your children: they're locked up in a cold, damp cell, deep beneath Central Park."

"How much time do we have?" Maude asked, finally turning out the passenger's side window to look at her archrival.

"*We?* I somehow missed the memo that said I don't hate your guts anymore."

"Who sends memos anymore?" Monique naïvely asked before biting down into a double bacon cheeseburger.

"Rafaela," Maude softly began, "this is no time to fight. You can hate me now, and tonight at the Fabbies, and every day from here on out. But right now—I need your help. Elle and my husband went to New York last night in the cover of darkness. They're trying to arrange a secret meeting with Priscilla Black, to see if—after the Fabbies—she'll lead a revolt against Candice Brown and Isabelle."

"Would Priscilla do such a thing?"

"Only if she could be sure of her own success," Maude replied. "When the industry finds out what Candice and Isabelle are trying to do, I can assure you there will be a quiet revolution."

"*Trying* to do? You say it as if our safety tonight is guaranteed."

"If we save my children, Enya, and Mauria, then it will be. We need to go tonight. If we don't show up, they'll give the award to another nominee, who will be killed instead. Rafaela, tonight we both can be winners."

"Sorry to sound cold, but no one's giving me a trophy for rescuing your bratty kids," Rafaela shot back.

"And if I make you a trophy?"

"I want it to be twenty-four-karat gold, with a diamond."

"Copper, with a cubic zirconia," Maude replied.

"Well, it's more than I got from my ex-husband," Rafaela remarked, and after a brief shrug she smiled up into the Volkswagen. "See you in Manhattan."

Rafaela rolled up her car windows and stepped on the gas pedal, leaving a trail of dust and a few terrified children behind her.

"You think you can trust her, girl?" Monique asked as she rolled up one of the paper bags and tossed it in the back of the bus.

"No," she quietly answered, and then touched a button to recall the passenger's side window. "But one thing's for certain. She lives for the drama."

Maude turned to her best friend and smiled. It was time to go to New York.

"I'm surprised you left this room intact," Isabelle sarcastically remarked as she accompanied her older sister into an underground courtroom positioned between Caligae headquarters beneath Fifth Avenue and the prisons beneath Central Park. The courtroom was one of those relics of the past that had been built for the pure sake of building something. The monstrous room—crafted out of white marble—was inspired by the Lincoln Memorial on one of Candice Brown's rare trips outside a fashion capital. Upon her return to New York, Candice commissioned the construction of a courtroom with an absurd amount of Roman columns, larger-than-life thrones to seat judges, several fog machines, and a wicked sound system. Candice Brown's favorite part of the courtroom was the painted ceiling, which boasted larger-than-life images of her doing things like shopping, getting her hair done, and creating life.

Since Caligae had no formal court of law, and only enforced the great curse, there was absolutely no need for a courtroom. But Candice Brown didn't care about practicality. She was a woman obsessed with image.

"Of course I left this room intact," Candice hastily replied to her younger sister, and when Isabelle's back was turned, waved at a demolition crew to get lost. "Just because I expanded my office a little, doesn't mean I'm going to absorb all of headquarters."

"Well it sure seemed that way."

As Candice and Isabelle walked to their respective thrones, they nodded at the other women who occupied the seats reserved for judges. These women weren't, of course, judges. Rather, they were the heads of Caligae in the continents outside North America. A total of eight thrones sat proudly in the chamber: an extra-large one in the center, designed for Candice Brown, and an additional throne for each continent's leader.

Candice Brown had arrived late as usual, and all of the directors were already in their seats—except for Dorina White of Antarctica, who was banned from leaving her continent. But the rest were all assembled, in the world's most powerful and influential body of fashion industry magnates. These seven women controlled not only the global fashion industry, but had influence over all supernaturals. They wielded a tremendous concentration of power that for over four hundred years had been both deadly and unpredictable.

As Candice took her seat, all whispering among the other Colors came to an abrupt halt. It was rare enough that they had all been assembled in the same room, and was even rarer that the courtroom was the setting of choice. They seldom used the courtroom, and only did so when deciding on major, profound changes within the industry. None of them had been told what they would be deciding on that afternoon, but some assumed it had something to do with Mauria Brown. Rumors exploded within Caligae when Candice's only child was dragged back into headquarters with her arms and legs bound, and mouth taped shut. The fact that she had been captured after trying to assist two Thirteens was all the more dramatic.

"Does this have to do with the capture of the two remaining Thirteens?" Priscilla Black asked, leaning toward Candice. Priscilla sat directly to the right of Candice, as was appropriate for the director of Caligae's European branch. Europe was the envy of all Colors, including Candice Brown's very own sister, Isabelle. It was a territory that included Paris, Milan, and London: three of the world's greatest fashion capitals. As a result, the European branch was by far the world's largest and most glamorous. Priscilla Black was a cunning director who had fought alongside Candice in the War of the Colors. Although known to be an insufferable snob, her style of leadership was far more sensible and egalitarian than that of Candice or Isabelle, and this earned Priscilla a certain level of respect that was lost on her North American counterparts.

"No," Candice replied without bothering to look toward Priscilla. "It has to do with my daughter."

"Is this a trial?"

Candice smiled, bunching her pink lips together. She tapped a fake fingernail on a silver panel built into her armrest, when suddenly a large section of the ceiling—with its flamboyant images of Candice—retreated to reveal a dark hole. The other directors had never seen this before, and all eyes darted to the ceiling in amazement.

Slowly—painfully slowly—a plastic cage descended from the opening just as the courtroom's many fog machines covered the marble floors in a thick mist.

"Can you speed that up?" Candice shouted up to the technicians after five full minutes had gone by without so much as one-quarter of the plastic cage in plain sight. The cage stopped briefly, and then free-fell. Just as most of the directors were ready to leap out of their thrones in shock, the cage stopped abruptly at their eye level.

Inside the cage was none other than Candice Brown's daughter, Mauria. She was no longer bound and gagged, but was dressed in an Alexander McQueen straitjacket. Even in prison, Mauria managed to keep it couture.

"I have two things to say to you," Candice Brown's loud voice erupted within the courtroom. "First of all, love the outfit."

"Thanks," Mauria muttered, and tossed her blonde hair.

"Second of all, are you aware that your friends are all facing imminent death?"

"If I knew what *imminent* meant, then yes, I'd be aware of it," Mauria replied.

"Imminent is, uh . . . it means—Isabelle!" Candice shouted as she struggled for the definition. "Isabelle, tell her what it means."

"It means it's happening soon," Isabelle softly replied, and then suggested: "it might not be wise to use words in court that you don't understand."

"The only reason we're in this room, and I haven't killed her myself already, is because I've gained a recent obsession with courtroom dramas," Candice shot back at her younger sister. "So do I get to play judge or what?"

"Candice, is any of this really necessary?" Isabelle asked as she shook in discomfort. "That's your daughter in there. I would never put my daughter on trial."

"Reality check. Your daughter is dead," Candice told her, and Isabelle's face grew even paler than usual. "Look, Is—"

By the time Candice Brown realized she'd overstepped her boundaries, it was too late. Isabelle leapt off her throne and hurried through the fog until she was out of the courtroom. Within the chamber, the other five directors sat in total silence as they waited for Candice's next move.

"What—she can't take a joke?" Candice finally said, and nervously brushed her artificial black hair with one hand. "This isn't about me or Isabelle, it's about Mauria."

"You're disgusting," Mauria remarked from within the plastic cage.

"And you guys think I'm bad," Candice said loudly, turning her head as she addressed her fellow directors. "This is what I have to put up with every day! A whiny, spoiled child who doesn't know how good she has it. You could be a big homo like Priscilla's son, or have ratty hair like Jackie Gold's kids, but no—you're beautiful and powerful and wealthy, and yet you take it all for granted."

"Do you see the way she talks about you?" Mauria shouted at the other directors. "Insulting your children, right to your faces? And nobody has the nerve to do anything about it?"

Mauria looked hopelessly from behind the plastic bars at the blank faces of the directors. Priscilla looked both hurt and embarrassed by Candice's outburst, and Jackie was privately fuming. But not a single one of them said anything to contradict their velour-wearing leader.

"Then you're all cowards," Mauria said in exhaustion.

"My dear daughter," Candice said with a most wicked grin smeared across her face. "This afternoon, I sentence you to death. All in favor say *aye*."

"So, do we have a plan?" Maude whispered as she, Rafaela Simone, and Monique ducked behind a bench in Central Park. Anywhere else in the world, three middle-aged women squatting behind a park bench would warrant stares, and maybe even arrests. But this was New York City.

"I currently have a plan to make a plan," Rafaela exclaimed. She adjusted her turquoise-colored sunglasses. "What are those awful noisemaking things behind me?"

"They're either children or squirrels," Maude replied, but she didn't look back. Her eyes were focused on a dirty-looking homeless woman lying against a tree. The woman's face was wrinkly and tan from years of sun exposure, and she wore an outfit made out of black and white trash bags.

"Baby girl, when is she gonna move?" Monique asked.

"She's not," Rafaela answered before Maude could. "This woman has guarded the entrance to Caligae prisons for more than one hundred years. She is as clever as you are stupid."

"Oh no she didn't. Clever or not, trash bags were last season," Monique replied, and snapped her fingers in Rafaela's face. "Especially those white ones."

"She wears plastic as an ode to Candice Brown," Maude said. "She is a servant of darkness. There are only two ways to get past her. You can either feed her a newborn baby as a human sacrifice, or you can answer one of her wicked riddles."

"I didn't come here to think all hard and whatever—," Monique said as she caressed her thick, blonde hair.

"Your idiocy is destroying my immune system," Rafaela snapped at her. "The longer I hear you speak, the more pain I feel."

"The only reason you feel pain is because you crashed your BMW into a hot dog cart, flew through the front window, and landed on a couple of Korean tourists," Maude told her.

"Well I was hungry, and my car doesn't like foreigners. Don't worry about the Koreans, we already settled out of court. All they kept asking me was when I'd have a boutique in Seoul."

"So they can avoid it?"

"Avoid nothing, you fool!" Rafaela cried out. "Asia would be lucky to have a Haus of Simone on its geographical landscape."

"Keep telling yourself that," Maude remarked, which led to a sneer from her arch-nemesis. "We should all go in at the same time. That way we have three chances to get the riddle correct."

"Mommy, there are dead bears!" a small child shouted as he ran past the bench. Maude, Monique, and Rafaela swung their heads around.

"You think the fur coats were a bad idea?" Maude asked her companions, who simply shrugged, and returned their attention to the homeless woman at the tree. The plastic-wrapped prison guardian snorted and then spit on the dirt next to her.

"The most important question is, who here knows how to fight?" Rafaela haughtily asked.

"I've taken street fighting and kickboxing classes for the past ten years," Maude replied.

"So basically none of us know hand-to-hand combat?" Rafaela exclaimed.

"I just said that I do!"

"No, you said street fighting and kickboxing, which implies weapon-to-body and foot-to-head combat. I'm talking hand-to-hand."

"What's the difference, as long as we're beating up the enemy?" Maude asked, her tone suggesting that she was getting quickly fed up with Rafaela's attitude.

"The difference is—" Rafaela paused and thought for a moment. "Actually, you know, street fighting and kickboxing might just work."

"Girl, is that apple juice, or urine?" Monique asked, referring to a bottle filled with a questionable substance, tucked under the homeless woman's armpit.

"I don't know," Rafaela remarked, "but that color is totally going to be the inspiration for my next winter line."

"Let's go," Maude said, and suddenly sprang to her feet. She shook her enormous fur coat, and then walked through the dirt in her pair of white heels until she was just steps away from the homeless woman. Rafaela and Monique followed her, albeit at a more cautious pace.

The three of them stood there with their arms folded, their bodies enwrapped in plus-sized furs. They looked like an evil triad of mob wives who had been kicked out of North Jersey and unleashed on the streets of Manhattan. They shivered as the homeless woman's pale gray eyes looked up at them, and Rafaela even took two steps backward.

"Listen, you literal piece of trash," Rafaela exclaimed, waving a finger in the woman's direction. "We are going to break into Caligae's prison so that I can perform my one true act of altruism per year, before I go back to being a horrible person. We have not brought a vulnerable newborn for you to eat alive. Therefore, you plastic menace, you will ask us a riddle and we shall answer."

Rafaela jumped two steps forward, and then leapt back, before asking her peers, "How was that?"

Maude gave her companion an annoyed look.

"She didn't mean to insult you," Maude politely told the homeless woman. "We humbly request that you ask us a riddle, so that we can, uh—gain entrance to the prison."

The homeless woman stared up from her spot in the dirt. She opened her lips to reveal a dirty, toothless mouth, and then bent her head backward as she let out a hacking laugh. While the trio of fur-adorned women waited patiently, the guardian took her little bottle of yellow liquid, popped the cap, and poured some on the ground. Instantly the dirt and grass sunk into the ground like water spinning through a drain. The hole grew deeper and deeper, and dirt steps magically hardened to create a clay stairwell.

The homeless woman lifted out her hand, and nodded.

"So wait—what's the riddle, you dirty trickster?" Rafaela asked.

"Here's the riddle," the woman began, before breaking into a coughing fit. "Excuse me—the riddle is: what varies in size, shape, and color, and is used to go either up or down?"

The three women looked puzzled. Maude scratched her chin, Monique scratched her head, and Rafaela scratched at her cell phone (she still didn't know how to use it).

"I'm going to look up the answer online," Rafaela confidently exclaimed.

"A tree?" Monique asked. "Give us another hint."

The homeless woman's jaw dropped, and she stared at the women in amazement.

"If you have a home with three floors," she said, "then you use *this* to get to floors two and three."

"An elevator?" Maude asked, and batted her eyelashes.

"A parachute?" Monique guessed.

"Two beautiful men named Fabrizio and Fulhunkio?" said Rafaela.

The homeless woman was dumbfounded.

"You're kidding me," she said to them. "You must be the dumbest three people in the world. Look, I'm pointing to the answer to the riddle," she practically shouted as she waved a finger at the clay stairs leading deep beneath Central Park.

"Grass?" Monique asked.

"Would you use grass to go from the first floor of a house to the second?" the homeless woman cried.

"Honey, you can do a lot with some good grass," Monique replied, and laughed until she realized that the prison guardian was not laughing.

"A futuristic jetpack!" Rafaela said.

"A black hole," Maude guessed.

The homeless woman screamed and grabbed her thinning gray hair with her two bony hands.

"A black hole?" she screamed at the top of her lungs. "A black hole? I'll give you a black hole!"

The woman attempted to leap to her feet, but having barely moved in over one hundred years, her bones couldn't keep up with her excitement. She twisted on a single heel and toppled into the very hole she'd created for the three women, shouting grunts of pain each time a body part smacked against the clay steps.

"Oh, well," Maude said, and swung her fur coat as she looked at her companions. "We might as well take these stairs."

"If we never make it out of here, there's something you guys should know," Marciano quietly said. He, his sisters, and Enya had been placed in a high-security cell. There weren't any guards nearby, but an intimidatingly thick steel door prevented their exit. The metal was even too strong for Enya to penetrate, although she did unleash a barrage of punches, kicks, and body rams in an unsuccessful attempt.

The inside of the jail cell was certainly designed for a fashion criminal. Outfitted with Fendi bunk beds, Jonathan Adler lamps, and a full-size mirror, the cell was certainly a step up from federal prison. Still, the small group faced the very real prospect of death, and they had no idea when and how it would come. All they knew was that directly above their heads, crews were busy at work preparing for the evening's Fabulous Fashion Awards.

"Did you date my ex-boyfriend Jacob?" Natasha asked, spinning her head in Marciano's direction as soon as the words left his mouth.

"Kind of, and he wasn't your boyfriend, and that's not what I was going to tell you," Marciano replied from one of the top bunks.

"I knew it! And yes, he was my boyfriend," Natasha fired back from the opposite top bunk across the jail cell. "We held hands at the movies."

"Your hands ended up in the box of nachos at the same time," Marciano told her. "And then you spilled cheese all over his shoes."

"Well who wears open-toed sandals on a date?"

"Sis," Betty calmly interjected, "let's not talk about your dating life, please. The less I have to think about Max, the better."

As soon as his name was brought up, Natasha sunk into one of the bed's plush pillows. His betrayal had hurt in more ways than one. Not only did her forehead hurt, but so did her heart. Max was her shining knight during dark times, the only person who gave her a temporary escape from all the craziness that had engulfed her family's life over the past week. Even after he'd turned on her and foiled her plans, it was painful to think about him as a double agent.

"Rafaela Simone told me that if I sabotaged Mom's show yesterday, she would let me design a collection in her new Manhattan store opening up later this year," Marciano said, speaking quickly so that he could put his guilt out into the room. "Even though I changed the plan Thursday morning, that's why I was originally pitching to sabotage Mom's show. I mean, I cared about her safety too, but—that wasn't the only reason."

He waited in silence for someone to respond. Would Natasha holler at him? Would Betty scold him with that calm, motherly voice of hers? Would Enya grab him by the throat and slam his lean body into the stone floor?

"Uh ... does anyone have an opinion?" he asked.

"You didn't do it, and that's all that matters," Betty replied, much to Marciano's surprise.

"She offered you your own collection?" Natasha asked with a twinge of jealousy. "In a Manhattan boutique? How the heck is Rafaela getting a Manhattan boutique?"

"She has to be everywhere Mom is," Marciano answered, and raised his eyebrows.

"Geez, I need to go work for Rafaela," Natasha remarked. "Look at me, talking as if I'm going to be around for much longer. You think they got Mauria already?"

"I certainly hope not," said Betty.

"Yeah, me neither. I'm sure we would know if something happened. Watch her choose Marciano as her last meal."

"Oh my God," her brother replied.

"Oh, Marciano!" Natasha said in a high-pitched voice, attempting her best impersonation of Mauria Brown. "Oh, you're just so funny—you're like—oh my gawd—like, the perfect guy."

"You shouldn't make fun of people on death row," he replied.

"Yeah, well I'm on death row too," Natasha told him. "Enya, what is the code of ethics for death row?"

"I have been on death row in seven countries," Enya replied from a Poltrona Frau chaise a couple feet from the steel door. "Death row is the last frontier of man. He who survives, never dies."

"Enya, I don't think *survives* rhymes with *dies*," Marciano remarked. "Even with your thick accent, buddy."

Enya instantly shot Marciano a look that made him curl up into a ball. "Sorry!" he cried.

"Hey," Natasha spoke up, "so if we die today, does anyone have any regrets?"

"I regret that I haven't been able to share this whole world of supernaturals with my brother and sister until just a week ago," Betty affectionately answered. "I wish we could've shared this secret a long time ago. But I'm happy that at least now you know the whole story."

"I regret that I cut things off with Jacob because I was worried my sister would find out and be devastated," Marciano remarked, glaring in Natasha's direction. "Even though you two never dated—"

"We did."

"In your dreams," he replied. "But yeah, since you were so convinced that you two would be married with kids right after college, I couldn't bring myself to do that to my own sister. Even though he used to send me flowers and chocolates, and did my laundry every Wednesday."

"I knew you weren't doing your own laundry!"

"Of course not," Marciano said. "Every time I do a load of whites, they come out another color. What about you, Enya?"

"I have annihilated many a washing machine that has discolored my clothing," Enya firmly replied.

"No, I meant regrets. Do you have any regrets?"

"Never. I'm always right, and so I have no regrets," she proudly said. "Although, I did always want to be an equestrian."

"If you found, perhaps, a genetically mutated horse the size of an elephant, you would make a terrific equestrian," Marciano told her. A grin briefly appeared on Enya's face, before the Russian quickly shook her head and resumed her trademark icy gaze.

"I guess it's my turn," Natasha said, although she didn't know where the question would take her. She was pretty happy with the way her life had been going. There were things she would change, like maybe her difficult hair, or her height, or her average nose. She would have wanted more guys to be interested in her. Maybe she would have wanted to be better at flirting with guys. Natasha could think of a whole list of things, although none of them were really that important. She was happy with who she was. Natasha was a slightly dorky, fashion-obsessed twenty-one-year-old who couldn't sit through an entire movie without sketching dresses on a pad of paper. Her only regret was that she was being deprived of unleashing her designs on the world.

But just when Natasha was about to open her mouth and voice her sole regret about the brevity of time, an alarming noise came from the jail cell's massive steel door. They all held their breath, except for Enya, who jumped to her feet and prepared for one final fight. Natasha clenched the bed covers with her hands.

As the door was sliding open, Enya reached a single, muscular arm into the widening crack and grabbed hold of someone.

"Ow!" a voice shouted from behind the doorway, before its owner got yanked through the tight space and into the jail cell. Enya instinctively put the newcomer in a chokehold just as two women in fur coats rushed into the room.

"Mom?" Betty asked in shock.

Enya, who was one foul move away from breaking the newcomer's neck, looked down at the platinum-blonde head of hair.

"Maude?" the tall Russian asked, before lifting her employer up to her white heels. Maude wobbled on her thin legs, and her eyes wandered around the room. She looked dazed from the loss of oxygen.

"How did you break in?" Natasha asked as she leapt off the bunk bed. She and her brother and sister all hurried to hug their mother.

"The door was unlocked," Rafaela answered. "And there were signs pointing to your prison. This was a very difficult rescue mission, and it would have been much easier without your mother and aunt weighing me down."

Everyone—Enya included—embraced Maude and Monique. As an entire week's build-up of emotions poured out inside the jail cell, Rafaela rolled her eyes.

"You fools, you're standing around acting like idiots in the very headquarters of the enemy," Rafaela told them.

"Rafaela, you need a hug!" Marciano told her, turning his attention to his employer.

"Oh—no, dear God—you can't. I don't do hugs," Rafaela said as she backed away from Marciano, who was walking toward her with his arms held out in front of him. "This fur coat is actually a live, poisonous animal. It has rabies and dandruff. If you come near it—"

Before Rafaela could finish, Marciano wrapped his arms around her fur coat and squeezed. The cold fashion designer let out a long sigh.

"That's the first time a man has touched me in twenty years," she lamented. "The last one was my ob-gyn."

"We need to find Mauria," Betty reminded everyone, breaking up the emotional reconnection as she hurried toward the open doorway. "She has to be somewhere down here."

"Rafaela, can you track her with your mind?" Maude asked, pulling her attention away from her children for the first time since entering the jail cell.

"What? Nobody wants me for my beauty anymore?" Rafaela asked, and puffed her lips in an attempt to look smoldering.

"Baby, your good looks went the way of the dinosaurs," Monique replied. "A meteor came and blew the top off that a long time ago," she added, and simulated an explosion with her arms. Rafaela dryly raised a manicured eyebrow.

"She's in the jail cell next to us," the grumpy fashion designer declared, in the most unenthusiastic way possible.

"Did you pick up a telepathic signal or something?" Marciano excitedly asked his employer.

"No, I saw her just before we walked into this cell. I'm surprised these buffoons missed her. Well—maybe not completely surprised."

As soon as Rafaela's words sunk in, everyone looked at one another, and then darted out into the hallway.

"She looks different," Enya exclaimed with her deep, accented voice.

"That's because you're looking at a man," Rafaela remarked, taking her time as she walked out into the hallway. "The *other* adjacent cell."

Once again, everyone in the group looked at one another, and then rushed past Rafaela to the other neighboring jail cell. In a room stripped of its incarcerated luxuries (the cell at least had marble floors and a CB2 carpet), Mauria Brown sat on the floor, her cheeks red and her eyes wet from tears. At least her posture was still intact. But then again, Mauria was the type of person who was always in a pose.

"Mauria!" Natasha shouted, and ran up to the thick viewing glass that separated the two girls. To the left of the glass was the same massive steel door as was in Natasha's cell. She pulled on the door, hoping that it would be unlocked just like her own. "It's locked."

As soon as Mauria saw her friends through the glass, her eyes lit up with a mixture of nervousness and pleasant surprise. She jumped to her feet and shouted at them, rushing to the glass and banging on it with her fragile fists. Unfortunately, the jail cells were all soundproof, and her friends on the other side couldn't even hear the thud of her palms on the glass wall.

"Can she hear us?" Marciano asked.

"Dear God, you're not thinking of letting her go to the Fabbies looking like that," Rafaela muttered as she stood with her arms crossed, gazing into the jail cell. Mauria was helplessly banging on the glass. She was still wearing the straitjacket from earlier, although the arms had been untied, and they were bundled up around her elbows.

"Betty, you can control electronics, right?" Natasha helplessly asked as she looked back and forth between the steel door and an electronic keypad built into the wall.

"Yeah, but they usually curse these things to make it difficult for us engineers," Betty replied, offsetting Natasha's frantic energy with her usual calm. She walked up to her sister and placed a loving arm on Natasha's shoulder. "Mom, you want to give it a try?"

"You're an engineer?" Marciano asked his mom. He had been wondering what kind of supernatural she was. "I was hoping you'd be something cooler. Like a witch or something."

"She *is* a witch," Rafaela remarked, which drew a stern look from Maude.

"Yes, my love, I'm an engineer," Maude replied, lifting her arms as Monique took her fur coat.

"Is Dad a werewolf?"

"No, he just has an unusual amount of hair on his body."

Once Monique took her best friend's fur coat, Maude walked over to join Natasha and Betty. Maude was shorter than her daughters, and she cuddled in between them as she stared up at the electronic keypad.

She lifted one hand and slowly placed two fingertips on the device, but quickly recalled them as a small shock from the keypad startled her.

"It's cursed, huh?" Betty hopelessly asked her mom, who slowly shook her head.

"I don't know what to do," Maude quietly told her daughter. Mauria was watching from within her cell, and her expression sank as soon as she saw Maude's face.

"Well, at least we saved the rest of them," Rafaela muttered, ready to give up on saving Mauria. "I can handle one casualty. In fact, I could handle all five."

"Enya, what about those leather gloves that Cedric gave you?" Natasha said, and quickly looked up toward her Russian friend. Enya crossed her massive arms.

"I don't wear gloves."

"Yeah, but do you have them on you?" she desperately asked.

"Yes."

"Well didn't Cedric say you could punch through steel with those things?"

"Yes."

Jaws dropped as all eyes darted in Enya's direction. The rock-solid Amazonian frowned as she reached inside her jacket. She was dressed in a peculiar outfit: a skintight jumpsuit of metallic colors, with sable-fur trim around the collar. Over top the jumpsuit was a gold-colored jacket that was too small to button. Enya removed two gloves from the jacket's inner pocket and casually affixed them to her hands like a dentist slowly slipping into latex gloves before a root canal. Although Mauria couldn't hear what was happening, as soon as she saw Enya slip into those gloves she took three leaps backward.

"The glass or the door? Tell me what goes down," she commanded. Maude and her two daughters practically tripped over one another as they backed away from the cell.

"Um, can you destroy the glass?" Marciano asked, beaming with excitement as if he were a small child about to witness two freight trains collide.

Enya's frown loosened, which probably meant she was smiling. She stepped toward the glass, staring it down with an intimidating intensity. Mauria curled up into a ball in one of the far corners of the cell, and covered her ears with her hands.

As soon as Enya was close enough, the Russian giant lifted up her arms so that her palms—wrapped in the leather gloves—were touching the glass. She withdrew her palms just a few inches, and then shoved them into the glass wall. A loud crack echoed throughout the hallway. The entire wall of thick, bulletproof glass bounced out of place and cracked into several pieces, toppling onto the prison's carpet and marble floor. Mauria glanced up to see if it was safe, and then hopped to her feet. She carefully stepped over the glass as she hurried out of the cell.

"It took you long enough!" she exclaimed, before running into Marciano's arms, nearly causing him to lose his balance. Maude raised her eyebrows in surprise.

"Girls jumping into Marc's arms?" his mom remarked. "What's next? I'm going to see pigs flying?"

"Just give Rafaela a pair of wings," Aunt Monique joked.

The controversial designer gave a most wicked look in Monique's direction, before dramatically turning her head toward the exit.

"I will not surround myself with such tasteless trash," she announced.

"Oh, so you're selling your clothing company?" Maude asked, causing Rafaela's cheeks to beam red.

"I'm finished being your friend for all of an hour!" she cried, shaking in her fur coat like a feral animal on the loose in Manhattan. "I'm off to buy a dress for tonight's event. I don't want to see you or hear from you until the moment they call my name to win Best Designer, when I will stand up on that stage, thank myself, God, myself again, and then look you straight in your eyes—which by the way, are last season's blue—and say, *Thank you Maude, for being so inadequate*!"

Rafaela burst out into laughter, which quickly subsided after she reached her hands into the pockets of her fur coat. The rest of the group stared blankly at Miss Simone as her wicked laugh transformed into a troubled cough.

"So, it appears I misplaced my wallet," Rafaela spoke slightly, and then cleared her throat.

"You need to borrow some cash?" Maude asked.

"I'll pay you back tomorrow."

"All right," her arch-nemesis replied, before glancing at her friends and children. "If tonight is the night we bring down Candice, then we should all look absolutely ravishing. Fifth Avenue?"

"Is it safe?" Betty asked.

"My love, the best things in life are never safe," Maude replied, and blew a kiss to her daughter before walking down the hallway toward Rafaela.

Isabelle's Greenwich Village townhouse looked like it could be as old as she was. The younger sister of Candice Brown didn't really care for *modern*. She could appreciate modern fashion, modern art, modern architecture, but could never find a place for these things in her own life. Candice—in one of her haughty lectures to her younger sister—had once declared that Isabelle was stuck in the same time period in which she'd last been happy. Part of that was true. The world had moved on and changed so quickly after the death of Isabelle's daughter, but she herself yearned for little reminders of the days when she had a happy family.

And thus, Isabelle's townhome was a relic of the past, protected from the change constantly happening just outside her front door. There wasn't a single piece of furniture in her home that was less than sixty years old, and many of the rooms and walls were decorated with old outfits that held special meaning to Isabelle. One of the first dresses—enclosed in a glass case—to greet guests in the foyer was a mustard-colored *robe à la française* from the mid-eighteenth century. The stomacher was its best feature, made up of linen with black silk embroidery. The dress was on a white mannequin modeled to look like a Greek goddess. Candice always found the figure to be terrifying, whereas it put Isabelle at peace each time she walked through her front door.

Isabelle liked old fashion, and found it difficult to change with the times. Sometimes it seemed like fashion was moving too fast for her. She often opted to dress vintage at special events, shying away from modern couture. She wasn't a celebrity, so it really didn't matter anyway. Isabelle didn't get to walk the runway, and her candid photos didn't appear in magazines and TV shows like those of her sister. So what did she care if her dresses didn't follow the trends?

Among the seven gowns scattered across Isabelle's bed and bedroom floor, the youngest was about thirty years old. The orchid color made her think about the church in England where her mother was buried. Nothing grew there anymore. The same curse that had driven Cecilia the Red deep beneath British soil had polluted the land. Although Isabelle hadn't been there in four hundred years, she still remembered the color of the flowers just outside the church, in a garden that separated the building from a modest graveyard.

All of the gowns Isabelle had pulled from her closet were a shade of purple. She liked to dress her color. It was an outdated practice of the Colors. Being a Color was such a privilege—even during the times when the Thirteen ran Caligae—that they used to only wear clothes to match the hue of their namesake. Even Candice Brown did so once, a very long time ago.

As much as Isabelle loved the purple dresses that she'd selected as candidates for the night's gown, she struggled with her reluctance to try them on. Sitting on her bed, her slender legs folded in front of her, she thought about all the *things* she'd accumulated over so many years. She thought about how cluttered and routine her life had become. And the thought that scared her most was a nagging concern that she'd wasted the past fifty years not trying to rebuild a family.

There was something about Candice's brutality that had become too accepted in Isabelle's life. She thought about her sister's cruel comment earlier at the trial, and how she would have acted if someone else had said that to her. Surely Isabelle wouldn't have tolerated it. So why couldn't she stand up to Candice? Why had she been too slow to react when Candice was being attacked by the two Thirteens?

Suddenly Isabelle's life felt heavy. It felt heavy with things, guilt, and sadness. *Things*—like her gowns, or that mustard dress in the foyer—made her happy, but there were no relationships in her life that gave her any sense of joy. What worried her most was that if Candice's plot actually succeeded, Isabelle would be left with nothing. Isabelle feared what her sister would become if catapulted into a dangerous world where supernaturals were no longer bound to fashion. It was a surreal thought. There would no longer be a need for Caligae. Would Isabelle's life become totally obsolete?

The thought of having no one frightened her, and yet, she hadn't really had any true loved ones since the deaths of her daughter and husband.

"Why can't you just leave me," she said under her breath. She stretched out her legs on the bed, covering one of the dresses with her silk pajama pants and fluffy slippers. Then she nervously tapped a button on her house phone, which was set up beside the bed on an antique nightstand.

"Isabelle, I've been trying to reach you," Candice's unmistakably aggressive voice called out in the voicemail. "Look, I accept your apology for running out earlier. I, uh—will try not to bring up your daughter anymore. Don't worry, mine will be dead in a couple hours anyway, and then we can both commiserate. But look, you better be there tonight. Don't screw me over. This is the most important night of our lives. I'll see you there."

The voicemail ended with Candice yelling at someone in the background. Isabelle had listened to the message five times. Each time she'd listen, she'd look at her assortment of dresses, to see if any of them gave her enough excitement to start preparing for the big event. But after sitting in sadness for so long, and with so much on her mind, the dresses only acted as a reminder of how awful and monotonous her life had become.

Isabelle picked up her phone, but she didn't dial her older sister. She sprang from the bed, clutching the phone to her ear as she hurried to retrieve her suitcase.

"I need a plane to London, immediately. If the jet isn't available, then book a commercial flight. I'll be in a taxi to JFK in fifteen minutes, so you must hurry."

She hung up her house phone and tossed it on the bed behind her, as she prepared to skip out on the Fabbies for the first time ever.

"She's not answering," Candice complained as she stared at her cell phone. As a number of stylists worked diligently on the diva's hair and makeup inside her Upper East Side apartment, Candice turned her attention to the two vampires standing by the doorway. "She'll show up. Always does. You've seen her act like this before, right Olympia?"

"Numerous times," Olympia replied, revealing a white smile. Her mood was propelled by the destruction of Bridgette #2. Even though the two had been working together for years, Bridgette's death meant that Olympia was once again the top bodyguard in Candice Brown's employ. Since she didn't like to share success, this change was most welcome.

"See, I'm right. She'll show up." Candice hesitated as one of the stylists spread wax just under her eyebrows. "Max, did you make sure the Thirteens are locked up, and that there are ample guards down there?"

"Yes and yes," the tall vampire replied. "I can assure you there's no way they'll escape before execution."

"Perfect. And you know your role in tonight's events?"

"I do."

"Then don't disappoint m— Ow!" she yelled as the stylist ripped a strip of eyebrow hair from Candice's head. "God dammit! Go easy on the next one," she commanded. "As I was saying, don't disappoint me. You'll be backstage making sure there isn't any funny business."

"I've personally overseen that the two Thirteens and their friends are locked up, that the prison is well guarded, and that the executions will take place before the Fabbies even begin," Max told her. The vampire was dressed sharply for the night's special event, wearing a tailored navy suit with a white dress shirt and black tie.

"Is there anything we should be on the lookout for tonight?" Olympia asked her employer. "You seem more ... *nervous* than usual about this one."

"No," Candice quickly replied, and bunched her inflated lips together. "Nothing unusual. Just the regular old Fabbies. I just want to make sure that whatever is supposed to happen tonight, happens. No surprises," she added, and smiled. "Watch the backstage like hungry tigers. And get a nap before the event."

"There's no time for that," Olympia remarked.

"Well, it's daytime and neither of you have slept since the sun came up. You won't be crashing during the Fabbies?"

"This isn't my first rodeo," Olympia answered. She'd been around Candice long enough to give attitude without getting a swift and violent reaction. "I don't know about my *friend* here—"

"I'll be fine," Max answered, and glared at Olympia.

"You better be," Candice said. "Your life depends on it."

Chapter Twelve

Friday Night

"ONCE YOU GET INSIDE THAT CAR, THERE'S NO turning back," Cedric told the twins from within the garage of his apartment building. A black sedan with tinted windows was parked and waiting for them. This was the vehicle that was going to transport Natasha and Marciano to the Fabbies, although not to any red carpet. Instead they'd be hiding out in one of the dressing rooms, hoping to avoid event security, and lying in wait for the announcement of the Best Designer award.

Cedric would only be able to drive them to Central Park. After what happened at fashion week, Fabbies security would be checking each and every person who stepped foot in the dressing rooms and backstage area. Cedric wouldn't be able to smuggle them in like last time.

The large group had already split off. Enya, Betty, and Aunt Monique were in Columbus Circle, preparing to hijack the event's security control tent just before the start of the show. Mauria had gone off with Maude and Claude, all of whom were going to walk the red carpet. This left the twins alone with Cedric and Elle in the dark, dusty garage.

It was the first time they'd seen Elle since she rescued them from Bridgette #2. She was fresh from her and Claude's meeting with Priscilla Black, and judging by the look on her wrinkled face was not any more confident about the Fabbies than she'd been before the meeting. But Elle remained quiet, soft-spoken, and determined. After everyone else left, she accompanied Cedric and the twins down to the garage.

"I know what this means, but I kind of don't," Marciano said, breaking the silence as he and his sister stared ahead at the black vehicle. "Half of me is excited, and the other half wonders if this is it. If this is the end."

"I'm too young for this to be the end," Natasha softly replied. "I still want to be a designer. I want a line on Fifth Avenue. This is stuff I've been dreaming about forever. I probably have more sketchbooks than shoes—"

"Speak for yourself," Marciano remarked.

"Well I do! And if this is it—if this is the end, then I feel like I haven't been given a fair chance to do what I love."

"Then maybe it's not the end," Cedric told them, and offered a pleasant smile before he opened the back door of the sedan for the twins. Once the door was open, he walked around the car and sat in the driver's seat. Elle was still standing outside the car, her eyes shifting between the vehicle and the twins.

"I'm almost too afraid to let you go," she said, and fought back the rest of what she wanted to tell them. She had never wanted to get so emotional at that very moment, but it was hard not to. For centuries Elle had been protecting a dying race, and she'd been in hiding for just as long. She was Caligae's most wanted fugitive. She'd lost so many times in her attempts to protect the Thirteen from Candice Brown that the idea of winning seemed too distant to imagine. Elle had been waiting for four hundred years to release that massive exhale—that eruption of relief that her efforts had finally paid off.

"I suppose you should know what Priscilla Black told me. Like the other Colors, she's afraid to confront Candice. She said that if the winner of Best Designer is assassinated, she'll confront Candice using the European branch. She fears civil war, but she committed to it. However, if you prevent the assassination tonight, which hopefully you do, it may be difficult to prove that Candice was behind it, and then Priscilla won't do anything to help us. We'll be back on our own ..." Elle paused, and bunched her lips together, like someone might do upon biting into something sour. "But if you *are* successful, then tonight will be the beginning of a transition of power among supernaturals. Those who lead a life of evil will no longer be welcome in our community. If you can stop Candice Brown from killing a fashion designer tonight, then you can stop her at each and every turn.

"I've been alive for a very long time. Some might say too long. I've served both good and evil. I know the kind of darkness that you'll encounter tonight, because I've lived it. And I learned a long time ago that the honest and just don't always win. Good doesn't always conquer. Sometimes the bad guys win. Sometimes they win for a very long time, because the masses are afraid to challenge them.

"I would feel much better asking you to step inside that black car if I knew you had nothing to lose. But you do. You're both young—talented, smart. You have full lives ahead of you. They may not be normal lives, but if you succeed tonight, then you'll be one step closer to living in a world where you're not hunted because of forces beyond your control. You are Thirteens, and because of that, Candice Brown will come after you until either you're dead, or she is."

"Then let's get her," Marciano said, and grinned in a way that revealed not a single bit of fear. And even though Elle couldn't see the smile beaming off of his face, she could feel it, and it touched her in the most meaningful way possible.

"Four centuries, and I've finally found two people who aren't afraid of Candice Brown," Elle remarked as excitement spread through her. "Go get 'er."

As the sun fell on Manhattan, New Yorkers and tourists swarmed Central Park in order to see the evening's Fabulous Fashion Awards. The event was open to the public, but the crowds of people had to stand behind a roped-off area reserved for the press, the industry establishment, celebrities, and special guests. The audience included every single top name in fashion, along with many well-known people from entertainment, business, and politics. This was going to be the biggest Fabbies ever, and it was to be broadcast live on television for the entire world to witness.

There were two tents within reasonable distance from the stage, and they served all the production and event security needs. The bigger tent was set up with cameras, monitors, and production staff. A smaller one had been set up with equipment to monitor event security. Candice Brown's lackeys were running the tent, and they'd positioned cameras all over the premises. This tent, known as the control room, was essential to the plan to stop Candice. And so, thirty minutes before the start of the Fabbies, as celebrities poured onto the red carpet and onlookers swarmed the park, an attractive middle-aged woman approached the control room wearing a pair of sky-blue pumps and a smile.

There were only two guards outside the control room. Both were ghouls—an unsettling type of supernatural that were a step above zombies on the class ladder. In the old days, ghouls were afraid to go out in public because of their deformities, but ever since the advent of plastic surgery, many looked no different than an average human. However, one could always tell a ghoul by their thuglike appearance, limited intelligence, and terrible posture.

"Ma'am, this tent is off-limits," one of the ghouls told Aunt Monique, who was wearing a little black dress with a white, cashmere coat over top.

"Honey, I was told there's a buffet somewhere around here," she said, poking her head around to peek behind the guards. "That buffalo dip was the bomb last year."

"There's no buffet tent, and there's certainly no buffalo dip," the other guard sternly told her. "Now please, ma'am, go find your seat."

"I would but I can't sit down in this dress. Baby doll, do you see how tight this is?"

"Well maybe you should have thought about that before you left the house wearing it."

"*House?* What do you think this is, Greenwich, Connecticut? I live in Tribeca. Ain't no houses in my price range there. That's what I need, a man to buy me a house in Tribeca. I would be running the show. House in Tribeca—shoot. I wouldn't be sweating a bill at Christian Louboutin, that's for certain."

"Ma'am, you need to leave this area."

"Calm down, tiger. You tell me where I can find a nice man to buy me a house, and I'll be on my way."

"I honestly have no idea," one of the guards said, growing increasingly impatient with Monique.

"That's 'cause you're stuck working as bodyguards. You know how to get ahead in life, right?" Monique asked, and rested her hands on her hips.

One of the guards shook his head, and the other raised his shoulders in uncertainty.

"It's easy to get ahead in life. In fact, baby doll, I'll give you mine," she said, and lifted her hands to her neck. With a single push and a modest pop, Monique lifted her head off her body.

The ghouls reacted just as expected. Having never seen a mummy do that before, they dropped their guard for about three seconds as they stared in amazement at the headless woman. It was three seconds too long.

A green wellie flew through the air and collided with the head of a guard. A second wellie smashed into the other guard before he noticed that his partner had been taken down. Neither had time to stand up before Enya was hovering above them. The Amazonian swung her gloved fists downward, driving the heads of the ghouls deep into the dirt of Central Park.

As Enya stood up and slipped the green wellies back onto her feet, Betty came rushing out from behind a tree waving a finger in front of her mouth.

"Shh!" she whispered, and frantically looked around to make sure that no one was within earshot. They'd taken out the two guards outside the control room, but there were still any number of guards inside the tent.

"Baby, my head isn't going back on."

"Whisper!" Betty said as she ran up to Monique and Enya. "Whisper! Now, I have a plan—"

"There is no time for whispering or a plan," Enya remarked. With one swift move the Russian grabbed Monique's head and rolled it like a bowling ball under the tent's green cover. As soon as Betty saw Enya roll the head, she covered her mouth with both hands.

"Oh my God."

"Monique, how many are there?" Enya calmly asked.

"Ahh—four—ahh—," Monique managed to say between her own screams.

"Wha—wait!" Betty called as Enya stormed into the tent. She stepped aside just as a guard flew through the nylon flap. "Is it—okay—to come in?" Betty squeaked amid screams and gunfire. She didn't know what to do other than clutch a headless Monique and pull her out of range of any airborne guards.

After a full ten seconds of silence, Enya emerged from the front of the tent, dusting off her gold-and-silver jumpsuit.

"Coast is clear," the Russian remarked.

"Can you please follow the plan next time?" Betty asked in frustration, and hurried into the tent to prepare the equipment. "Now please clear out these bodies, and give Monique her head back."

"Do I have to?" Enya asked, glancing at Monique's body, which was stomping around in circles outside the tent.

"Yes!" Betty replied, just as she sat down in a computer chair in the control room. She took a long, deep breath, and just as she exhaled she mentally plugged into the room's computers. A quick wave of nausea overcame her, and she sat back in the chair and continued to breathe deeply. "Candice is on the red carpet."

"And the twins?" Enya asked as she lifted a dead ghoul over her shoulder.

"Exactly where they should be. Nowhere in sight."

"This is the coldest goddamn red carpet I've ever walked," Candice muttered to a journalist, "and I've walked the carpet with Anna Wintour."

"How is your relationship with her these days?" the journalist asked.

"Strained, ever since I took silver bullets to a luncheon in which she was in attendance. I'm sure we'll be best friends a week from now, and then by next season I'll be plotting her demise."

"Tonight you're nominated for Fashion Icon, and your daughter is nominated for Best Supermodel. Do you think the world will see a mother-daughter victory tonight?"

"Hell no," Candice replied with such contempt that her body shook within her pink velour jumpsuit and zebra-patterned fur coat. "First of all, I'm always nominated for that stupid award. And even though I think it would be gangbusters if my baby girl won, she sadly won't be with us tonight, or maybe forever, because she's been extremely sick. Yeah, we think it's life-threatening."

"She doesn't look extremely sick," the journalist replied with a confused expression.

"What do you mean?"

"Well, she's standing right over there. She looks fine to me."

Candice swung around so quickly that her hips nearly pulled out of place. She yanked the pink sunglasses off of her face (which was appropriate anyway, given it was nighttime) and stared in horror as Mauria walked the red carpet with a beaming smile. When Mauria finally turned around and caught her mother's glance, she smiled with her perfect set of white teeth.

All of a sudden the flashing of cameras, shouting of journalists, and screaming of fans came to an abrupt halt. The entire world around Candice and Mauria Brown stopped as the mother and daughter stared each other down.

Surrounded by lifeless bodies, paused in the middle of varying movements, Mauria slowly walked toward her mother, and when she got close, whispered a single, brief statement.

"Tonight, you better watch your big ass."

Afterward Mauria pulled back and smiled—her hazel eyes full of intensity. She carefully walked back to where she had been standing, and suddenly the world resumed. Cameras flashed, people shouted, and journalists called out to Candice Brown, who stood dazed and confused on the red carpet.

"Miss Brown! Miss Brown!" someone called to her, but Candice quickly swung her hand in dismissal. And without responding, she stormed down the red carpet on her way to the front row.

By the time Mauria unfroze time, Marciano and Natasha were already in an empty dressing room. The clever move had given them just enough of a window to get past the security guards watching over the tents reserved as the dressing rooms.

"Whose room is this?" Marciano asked. Natasha tried to answer, but was still panting from her nerve-racking sprint.

"I don't know, but if it's my lucky day, it'll be the dressing room of the Real Madrid football club," she responded.

"In a perfect world," Marciano replied, and laughed at his sister. "That would be a nice present for saving all of humanity. Like, Cristiano Ronaldo wrapped up in a box with a bow on it."

"I'd chew through that bow with my bare teeth," Natasha said, and the two of them chuckled. "I think you get Mauria if you save the world tonight."

"Oh, geez, I thought she'd get it for sure when I told her I'd seen Barbra Streisand three times in concert. Instead she started singing 'Hello, Dolly'."

"So that explains the loud screeching in Cedric's loft."

"Yeah, really," Marciano said, and shook his head. "I just need to sit her down and tell her flat out. The hints aren't working anymore."

"Well, if tonight goes anything like we're hoping, then you'll have plenty of—" Natasha cut herself short as soon as an unfamiliar coldness passed over her body. She cupped her hand over Marciano's mouth. Someone was near. She pulled her brother down to the floor and ducked behind three cardboard boxes piled next to a rack of dresses.

The flap to the dressing room opened, and a tall man wandered in, taking two steps and then stopping abruptly. He was dressed sharply, in a slim-fitting navy suit and black tie. He scanned the room as if he were expecting to find something. His lips were closed, and his face was expressionless.

After a few seconds that felt as long as full minutes, he turned around and left the dressing room, closing the flap behind him. Natasha finally exhaled. Being in the same room as him brought back a rush of emotions, but none more so than the anger of being deceived.

"He's here," she nervously whispered.

"Who?"

"Who do you think?" she turned to her brother and asked with a troubled look on her face.

"Oh," was all he replied. "Max."

Chapter Thirteen

THE FABBIES WERE UNDER WAY. EVEN IN THE cold of February, thousands were gathered for the outdoor event. Fortunately the weather wasn't too vicious on that particular night, and hundreds of heating lamps helped warm the seated guests. The crowds of standing onlookers had to make due with heavy coats and scarves.

"It's sad, the way she keeps looking over at that seat," Maude whispered in her husband's ear. Claude was on her left, and Rafaela Simone was on her right. Normally the two would never sit together at a fashion event, but since they were both nominated for Best Designer and both based out of Philadelphia, the organizers thought it would make sense to seat them together. Obviously the organizers didn't know their dramatic history.

"There's probably an invisible person whom only Candice can see," Rafaela said, butting her way into the conversation. "Probably a Martian. Or Jesus Christ."

"I think your brain is invisible," Maude replied with annoyance. Her soft-spoken husband waved his hand in dismissal; he wasn't going to get in the middle of the two women. "Who is missing from the front row?"

"Me?"

"No, you imbecile. Isabelle is missing. Candice's sister never showed up."

"If my sister wore a velour tracksuit to a fashion awards show, I wouldn't show up either," Rafaela remarked, her haughty voice carrying over into the second row. "Mind your own business, Ralph," the designer added.

"This may work in our favor," Maude whispered. "If Isabelle is missing, then that's one less ally of Candice involved in her evil plot."

"Oh, Isabelle wouldn't have helped anyway. That old bore. I went out to dinner with her once, and she put me to sleep reciting the menu. She's as irrelevant as salted peanuts on an airplane. Nobody eats that junk anymore, so why do they shove it in my face every time I fly cross-country?"

"Clearly, I can't talk to you about anything," Maude angrily replied.

"You can talk to me about anything that involves me," Rafaela told her, waving a hand for extra emphasis. "Anything that doesn't? Nope, don't really care."

Maude shook her head and looked up at the stage, into the cameras watching over the audience from the amphitheater. With each award, musical number, and runway preview, the announcement of Best Designer was drawing closer and closer. The nervousness that Maude had suppressed in order to look brave in front of her children was rushing back to her, and in a rare act of solidarity with her arch-nemesis, she grabbed Rafaela Simone's hand and clutched it affectionately.

"What on Earth—"

"Rafaela, whatever happens tonight, just know that it's been my pleasure to work across the street from you. And I really do wish you all the success in the world."

Maude might have expected a hug, a peck on the cheek, or a warm gaze. She certainly didn't expect to get slapped. But when Rafaela's lean hand landed lightly on her white cheek, the French designer practically jumped out of her seat.

"What was that for?"

"Have you gone mad?" Rafaela asked her. "Don't talk like that. You can't live without me, and vice versa. After all, what's a supervillain to do when there's no superhero around to counter her? The whole world would be out of balance. Or at least Philadelphia."

Before Maude could respond, someone from the fourth row tapped her on the shoulder. Maude slowly turned, and smiled when she saw her best friend.

"Long time no see," Aunt Monique remarked. As the audience stood up to clap for one of the night's winners, Monique quickly embraced

Maude, and deposited three small earpieces into her hand. "You, Rafaela, Claude. Put these in now. You're up soon. You okay, girl?"

"I think so," Maude said, unconvincingly.

"Best Supermodel is up next," Betty said to herself as she typed away at the computer. Enya was standing above her, arms folded, with one eye on the door and one rotating between the video feeds from the security cameras. "Why aren't Tash and Marc plugged in yet?"

"Give Cedric time," Enya calmly told her.

"How is it that you're patient when I need something done, but when you need something done you can't even wait for my input?"

"Because what I want is important, and what you want is less important."

"Thanks," Betty sarcastically replied. She shook her head and continued typing. "Tash? You there?"

"Here!" a clear voice resounded in Betty's ears. She excitedly adjusted her headphones and placed her elbows back on the computer desk. "Cedric just dropped in. We both have earpieces."

"Perfect," Betty replied. "Mom, Dad, Rafaela, Aunt Monique, and Mauria are all connected. You there, Marc?"

"Here. These earpieces are a little small, but I think I've got enough earwax to hold it in place."

"Gross," Betty said, and let out a long sigh. "Didn't need to know that. The Best Supermodel award is up next. I've been monitoring cameras backstage and guess who is creeping around?"

"Max," Natasha answered. "I know. He almost caught us in the dressing room."

"Whose dressing room are you in, by the way? Has anyone else come inside?"

"I don't know," Natasha said, as nervousness leaked into her words. "We've been going crazy waiting here, watching the door and hoping no one will burst in to start getting changed. Every minute feels like an hour. No one except for Max has come in yet, but—"

"Just hang in there. The Best Supermodel award is—I'm watching the cameras, and the host just went onstage to start announcing,"

Betty said. "Best Designer is up after this. Is there a musical number in between the awards? Enya, do you have the lineup?"

"No, but I can go get one from the production tent," the tall Russian offered.

"What, are you gonna just walk in and ask for a lineup?"

"I was going to ask with my fists."

"Let's not go there again," Betty replied, and turned her attention back to the monitors. "Mauria, can you hear me? Are you plugged in?"

"I didn't know this thing came with a plug?" said Mauria, her effeminate voice popping up on the network.

"No, I meant *connected*."

"But what about the plug? Monique didn't give me any plugs."

"No, there is no plug. I repeat, no plug," Betty replied in frustration. "Are they announcing the candidates for Best Supermodel?"

"Yes! Just called my name as a nominee."

Betty bit her bottom lip and glanced up at the monitors for the backstage security cameras. The backstage had been a circus of people all night long. No one seemed to know where they were supposed to go or what they were supposed to be doing. The entire show was operating on a heightened level of chaos, which wasn't apparent to anyone watching in Central Park or on television. But to Betty, who could see the entire behind-the-scenes production from the monitors in the control room, the Fabbies looked like one gigantic mess.

"What's this?" Betty remarked, talking to herself. It prompted some *huh*'s from her group members, who were all connected through the earpieces. Even Enya glanced over to see what had startled Betty.

Had one of the ghouls originally stationed in the control room been looking at the monitors, nothing would have looked unusual. In fact, all would have looked great. The backstage area was emptying out. Some security guards, dressed in all black and looking more like members of a SWAT team than local rent-a-cops, were clearing out the large space that connected the stage to the dressing rooms and press area. The chaotic scene was suddenly beginning to look manageable. The backstage was vacant. Even Max disappeared off the monitors.

"Something's wrong," Betty nervously said. She watched the monitors as security staff began to go from one dressing room to the next, ordering any inhabitants to clear the area. Some of them were half-dressed models and dancers, being rushed out of the backstage area as if a bomb were about to go off. The whole thing looked like an emergency evacuation. "Tash, Marc, hide."

"We've been hiding for—"

Natasha's voice cut off, and all Betty could hear were the sounds of her brother and sister breathing. Betty hoped that they were well hidden, or that the security guards wouldn't search too hard. On another monitor, three muscular men in black suits were approaching the stage-right exit.

"Oh my God!" Mauria's voice resounded through the network. Betty's eyes darted to the monitors showing the main stage and first few rows. She mentally activated the control room's audio, suddenly filling the tent with the cheers of thousands of people down by the stage. Mauria had won Best Supermodel. As she stood up from her seat in the second row and walked toward the stage, it looked as if she'd momentarily forgotten about the night's drama. Suddenly the Fabbies had become all about her.

"Tash, Marc, you okay?" Betty quietly asked. "Congrats Mauria, but be careful. There are three men standing where you need to exit, and the backstage just cleared out."

"We're good," Marciano replied. "They just opened the door, didn't see anyone, and left."

Mauria didn't respond, although Betty didn't expect her to. She had just walked up the stairs to the main stage, navigating the steep steps in a pair of white pumps. Mauria looked overwhelmed. She was on the verge of tears as she accepted the elaborate glass trophy from the presenter.

Betty shifted her attention to the backstage cameras. The entire area behind the curtains was vacant, save for the three suited men at the stage-right exit.

"Tash, Marc, I may need you to come out of the dressing room if something happens."

"What could happen?" Natasha fearfully asked. She didn't want *anything* to happen.

"I don't know, but there are three guys waiting to intercept Mauria. She's giving her speech now."

"Her mother looks proud," Enya remarked. The offhand comment surprised Betty, as she hadn't been following the cameras focused on the faces of those in the front rows. But when she looked at a monitor revealing all the members of the fashion royalty seated front and center, she could see that Candice Brown looked genuinely touched. Mauria's mother was smiling—not too heavily, but enough that it seemed sincere.

"Probably for the cameras," Betty replied. "Mauria, there are three men waiting to intercept you. I don't know who they are or what they're doing. Try to vibe them out as you're exiting. Tash and Marc are standing by."

After the words had left Betty's mouth, she zoomed in on Mauria's face with one of the stage cameras. Reality was beginning to set in. Mauria had just finished her speech, and as the audience cheered for her, the young model's expression transformed from a state of utopia to a guarded fear of what was in store for her. Betty watched as Mauria Brown glanced toward the stage-right exit, and then back at the audience. Suddenly her eyes were heavy.

Betty covered her mouth with both hands. Mauria was walking offstage, getting closer and closer to the suited men with each and every step.

"I'm scared," Mauria whispered, but loudly enough that it could be heard by those connected through the earpieces.

"Stay calm," Betty reassured her, but she herself was anything but calm. She watched the monitors, hoping that the suited men were merely going to whisk Mauria Brown off with the rest of the backstage crew. Maybe she had to go to a press tent or something to give a post-victory speech. Betty was thinking of every possible explanation for why the situation might turn out okay.

Betty grabbed her stomach as she watched Mauria walk offstage. The model passed the three men, who slowly turned to follow her. Mauria picked up her pace, walking quickly on her heels, unsure of where to go.

"Run! Heels off, run! Tash, Marc!" Betty shouted.

But it was too late. One of the guards hit her from behind, knocking Mauria to the ground and sending her glass trophy flying across the wooden floor, where the top half of it shattered into pieces. The same guard who hit her landed a swift kick to the back of Mauria's head, just as the other two guards began to shake within their suits. They were transforming. Betty had never seen a werewolf transform, but she watched in horror as the first two—and finally the third—exploded in size. Hair sprang from their bodies, and their skulls warped as long snouts erupted from their heads. They were hovering over Mauria, who looked like a piece of meat on the ground.

It wasn't long before the werewolves were joined by a tall woman, who casually walked onto the scene in a pair of red heels. Betty zoomed in with one of the backstage cameras, and was shocked to see the same ginger-haired woman whom they'd met in the Dutch Market. Her lips were bright red, and she was wearing an egg-white veil over a matching dress that looked way too light for the evening's temperature.

The woman said something to the werewolves, and instantly one of them picked up Mauria and threw her over his shoulder. The moment he did so, Betty's eyes shot up to Enya.

"Marc! Tash! Go to the curtains behind the main stage! Now!"

"Should I go?" Enya asked Betty, who looked frantic in her computer chair.

"Not yet," Betty answered between deep breaths. "I might need you for something else."

"Where are you going?" Natasha screamed after her brother. The two of them had darted out of the dressing room, but as soon as Marciano saw werewolves, he began to run in the opposite direction.

"I didn't sign up for this!"

"Get your ass back here!" she shouted, running after him until he slowed down outside a larger dressing room that had been recently vacated. The werewolves and the tall woman were headed their way. Mauria was slung over the shoulder of one of the werewolves, who looked particularly menacing.

"I don't know what to do," Marciano complained as his eyes welled up. He was hunched over with his hands on his knees, panting and looking ahead at the four people coming his way. "I don't know what to do. I don't know how to use my powers."

"Marciano," Natasha said, grabbing hold of her brother as a wave of courage came over her, one that she couldn't quite understand. "You were *amazing* when we confronted Candice. You killed that crazy robot with plastic chairs. You're probably the first person in history to kill anyone with a plastic chair!"

"Yeah, what's your point?"

"My point is that I don't know how to use my powers either. But I'm guessing if they start to attack us, something will just *happen*. And the more we get used to this, the more we'll figure out how to be Thirteens. But right now, we need to save Mauria. If she isn't awake to freeze time when Best Designer is announced, then our chances of saving the winner are *so* reduced."

"They're also reduced if we get killed by werewolves."

"You don't know that they're werewolves!" Natasha hollered, and pointed at the oncoming creatures. "Maybe they're like, werebunnies. Or werechinchillas."

"Bunnies carry disease, and chinchillas smell rotten."

"Well, they're obviously not wolves, I mean look at—" Natasha paused as the creatures grew dangerously close. "Okay, so maybe they *are* werewolves."

Marciano finally stood up, just as the ginger-haired woman and the werewolves came within a few yards of the twins. Both sides stood facing one another in silence. And although Natasha's heart was beating faster than it had all week, she could sense something when she looked into the eyes of the werewolves. There was something there—some emotion that she wasn't expecting to find. Was it fear? Could it be that these monstrous creatures, as much as two feet taller and substantially wider than Natasha and Marciano, were scared of confronting Thirteens?

"You're the woman from the Dutch Market. Olympia, right?" Marciano asked, breaking the silence.

"Good memory," the woman softly replied. There wasn't an ounce of fear in her eyes. Rather, she looked like she was ready for a fight. "This can go down one of a few ways. First, you can run. Second, I can order these werewolves to tear you apart. Third, *I* can tear you apart."

"How about option four," Marciano remarked. "You ditch the veil, and stop trying to be Madonna circa twenty-five years ago. Then you can give us back Mauria, and go tell Candice Brown that she's not killing anyone tonight."

"Killing anyone?" Olympia remarked in surprise. "Who's getting killed other than you and Mauria?"

"Best Designer, duh," Natasha replied, injecting some serious attitude into her words.

"What are you talking about?" Olympia asked. She seemed legitimately confused, which instantly surprised the twins. Had Candice not shared her plans with her own top staff? "Werewolves, devour them."

Olympia waved her hand at the twins as if she were dismissing unruly schoolchildren. The werewolf holding Mauria dropped the model on the ground, and the three creatures quickly surrounded the twins, circling them like a bloodthirsty school of sharks. Natasha and Marciano stood back to back, their fists up in a defensive pose. Not that they had any idea what to do, but they did their best to appear frightening.

"Do you feel that?" Natasha whispered to her brother.

"Feel what?"

"My body. It feels—something's different."

"Maybe it's just gas," he remarked.

"Ew. No, it's—I can't explain it," she said. "I feel—heavy."

Just as the word left Natasha's mouth, one of the werewolves sprang into action. He leapt at her, and Natasha's first thought was to duck or dive backward. But since Marciano was directly behind her, all she could do was lift her arms up. She saw the werewolf's sharp claws swinging toward her head, and in a frantic and desperate move, she threw her left arm upward to block him. She closed her eyes before impact, preparing herself for the pain of being slashed. But when the werewolf's claws connected with her arm, it was he who cried out in pain. When Natasha opened her eyes, she looked down at her own arm, held out in front of her. The entire appendage was draped in a layer of silver. Or maybe her arm had become silver. The other two werewolves looked on in shock.

Natasha seized on the opportunity. She leapt forward at one of the standing werewolves and swung her right arm. As she did so, the same layer of silver erupted over top her skin. She struck the werewolf in its snout, and the creature toppled backward, nearly falling into Olympia.

"Now I know how Enya feels," Natasha said between heavy breaths.

As Marciano watched his sister fight, one of the werewolves seized on his distraction. With a swift lift, Marciano was up in the air, held above the head of one of the werewolves, whose claws came dangerously close to piercing the young man's skin.

"Rip him in half," Olympia sadistically ordered, much too calmly for someone commanding one person to kill another. But when the creature tried to dig its claws into Marciano's body, it felt a hard surface rather than human skin.

Marciano drove two silver fists down into the werewolf's head. A loud crack resounded, and the werewolf fell to the ground, with Marciano falling on top of him.

The werewolf who had first tried to slash at Natasha was still gripping his arm in pain. As soon as his two comrades got knocked down, he leapt to his feet and took off running through the backstage area, leaving the twins alone with Olympia.

"Cute," Olympia muttered. She opened her lips just slightly enough to reveal long, white fangs. "But you're going to have a hell of a lot more trouble with me."

"Probably," Natasha replied, "but I can't wait to see how my body changes to kick your ass."

And with that, the twins began to circle the vampire.

"Here it comes," Maude nervously said. She felt like she was going to shrivel up in her seat, as if there were a black hole in her stomach that was sucking the rest of her body inside it. Her husband clutched her left hand. A presenter was walking up the stage to announce the award of Best Designer.

"Already back from commercial?" Rafaela Simone asked, and yawned obnoxiously. "Finally, an award that matters."

"I don't want to win," Maude said. Her breathing was frantic. She clutched her chest with her free hand. "Correction—I want to win, but I don't want to die."

"Reality check—nobody wants to die," Rafaela told her. "Except poets and suicide bombers."

"I'm talking to my husband."

"Yeah, well, you're sitting next to me," Rafaela boldly said. "And I reserve the right to join any conversation initiated within my earshot."

"Do you think the assassin is sitting among us?" Claude whispered, leaning in toward Maude and Rafaela.

"This is on television," his wife replied. "I don't want to look paranoid on TV. At every commercial I've been looking around, but I don't see anything."

The entire audience quieted down as the presenter leaned in to the microphone, which was on an ice sculpture acting as the podium. It was a beautiful sculpture of an angel with wide wings that sprang out four feet on each side. The microphone was positioned on the back of the angel's curly head of hair.

"Two awards left, but this is the one everyone has been dying to see," the presenter said. "Tonight we have five candidates for the award of Best Designer. The selections weave together a story of nominees from all walks of life, and all types of fashion. Among them we have two past winners, and three past nominees. Some of these nominees have stores in four continents, and others in just one. As everyone in the arts knows, an award will not make you a better artist, but it will give recognition where recognition is due. Winners of this prestigious award have seen their single-boutique businesses expand into global fashion empires. Other winners, already in possession of a fashion empire, have seen their sales skyrocket."

"Yawn," Rafaela whispered in Maude's ear, although the latter could barely hear anything except her own loud thoughts. Her nervousness was overwhelming her.

"Mom, they just called your name," Betty's voice resounded in her ear. "I turned off Marc's and Tash's earpieces but I'm watching them on camera. Mauria is unconscious."

There was no way that Maude could keep calm. Even if she wasn't awarded Best Designer, her children were in danger. She couldn't sit still knowing that Natasha and Marciano were engaged in a fight backstage. And since they and Mauria were supposed to be the ones locating and stopping the assassin, it seemed like the entire plan to stop Candice Brown was melting faster than an ice cube in a pot of boiling water.

To the shock of everyone in her row and behind her, Maude stood up and hurried past the people seated near her. Instead of turning toward the stage, she turned away from it, and began to hurry up the aisle. She needed to get to an exit, where she could go backstage and help her children.

Maude could no longer hear anything around her. The sudden explosion of cheers, Betty's voice, the announcer's voice—all of it was jumbled together in a confusing mass of noise. But when Maude looked up, everyone's eyes were on her.

"You won," she heard Betty repeat. It wasn't the congratulatory voice of a daughter excited for her mother, but the sober recognition that something awful was about to happen. "Run, Mom. Run."

Maude stood with her back turned to the front row, facing the mass of people in Central Park who were on their feet cheering for her. Slowly, she turned on one heel toward the stage.

"Where'd she go?" Natasha frantically asked, just before something collided into her back. She toppled forward into her brother, but instead of catching Natasha, he tried to swing at Olympia. She was far too quick. Within a quick flash she had appeared, rammed into Natasha, and disappeared. Her wicked laughing filled the backstage as Marciano swung his head around to look for her.

"Show yourself!" he cried.

"Tash, Marc!" Betty's voice screamed into their earpieces. "Mom just won! Mom just won! Wake up Mauria, now!"

Marciano turned toward Mauria, but Olympia was standing in front of him. She swung at him with the back of her hand. The bones in her fist felt like jagged rocks, and they sent Marciano off his feet. Natasha crawled toward Mauria, but Olympia kicked her with a bare foot. The impact caused Natasha to lose her breath, and she rolled onto her back as her arms flailed out on either side.

"Tash!" Betty screamed again. Natasha could barely breathe, let alone respond. She could hear her sister's frantic voice calling out to her, but there was nothing that Natasha could do. Olympia was too much for them to handle. Mauria was unconscious, and the twins would never be able to get to the stage in time.

Natasha closed her eyes and then reopened them. Olympia was standing above her. The vampire's amber eyes stared downward, and their gaze was piercing. Suddenly there was nothing around Olympia but a bright, blinding light. Natasha couldn't look away, couldn't close her own eyes. All she could see were those two small amber orbs.

"Betty—," Natasha mumbled. "I can't."

Back in the control room, Betty leapt up from the computer chair. She watched the monitors as her mom walked down the center aisle toward the stage, while people around her roared in applause. She was taking her time, doing her best to smile as her eyes fearfully glanced around, waiting for the moment when an assassin might strike.

"Enya, you have to get down there, now!" Betty cried out in despair. She grabbed one of the earpieces off the desk and handed it to the Russian. "Go! Please, go!"

Enya nodded, took the earpiece, and sprinted out of the control room, nearly taking down the tent with her.

"Monique, do you see anything?" Betty asked. Monique had moved to the aisle from her seat in the fourth row. On one of the monitors, Betty could see her aunt touching her earpiece and looking downward.

"Nothing, baby. Not yet."

"Stop her. Stop her from going up."

"But she's already there."

Betty suddenly felt like her heart had dropped into the pit of her stomach. She exhaled and looked up at the main stage monitors. Her mother was kissing the presenter on the cheek. The glass award was in her right hand, and she was ready to give her acceptance speech.

"Mom—," Betty whispered. And suddenly, all of the monitors in the control room went dark.

Natasha tried to stand up, but her body felt so heavy. She could hear the applause bursting into the backstage area, but each time she'd try to look away from Olympia she felt overwhelmed with nausea.

Marciano was back on his feet, and he charged at the vampire, but she moved so quickly that all he ended up doing was tripping over his sister. Marciano landed hard on his elbows. The whole time Olympia maintained her grasp on Natasha. The latter couldn't look away, even when her twin brother tripped over her. She was locked in a state of hypnosis, controlled by those amber eyes. Natasha tried to calm down. She didn't know how to fight a vampire. Her body had transformed rather obviously for fighting the werewolves, but nothing special had happened to combat Olympia.

"What now?" the vampire asked. A cold grin was spread across her pale face.

"Your hand!" Marciano shouted. Natasha couldn't look away from Olympia's eyes to see her own hand, so she had no idea what her brother was talking about, but he kept repeating himself. "Use your hand!"

Natasha didn't need to be told again. She lifted her arm and slammed it down where she thought Olympia's bare feet might be planted. Sure enough, the vampire let out a loud scream, and the intense hold she'd had on Natasha was suddenly broken. The latter's head was spinning, but when she looked down she was amazed at what she saw. Her hand looked dried and wood-like, and her fingers had grown at least six inches. Natasha's hand had transformed into a wooden claw, although the weight of it didn't feel any heavier or lighter than flesh. As she retracted her arm, and as Olympia stepped backward in pain, Natasha's fingers began to recall, and her hand slowly changed back to normal.

When the vampire opened her eyes again, wider than ever before, the blinding lights returned. They shined on Natasha and her brother with such intensity that it hurt them even with their eyes closed. Natasha lifted her hand, but she couldn't throw a punch. All she could do was try to block her own eyes with her arms.

Suddenly the twins could hear their mom's voice. She was giving her acceptance speech out on the main stage.

"We tried," Marciano mumbled. Natasha couldn't speak. She couldn't think of anything to say. The light was growing more and more intense each minute. There was a force coming from Olympia's eyes that seemed to pull Natasha toward the vampire.

Natasha soaked up each word that her mom said as if it were the last she'd ever hear. Maude's voice echoed on the speaker system. Natasha wasn't paying attention to the words, just the tone. The accent. The soft way that her mom spoke.

"I love you," Natasha finally said, letting out the words in a single, quick exhale. But what she heard next wasn't her mom or Marciano or the audience in Central Park. A bloodcurdling scream rose and fell in pitch, and when it ended the blinding light had disappeared. Lying on her back, Natasha looked up at Olympia. A wooden stake was peeking out of the vampire's egg-white dress. Behind her, hovering just a few inches above her, was Max.

He drove the stake in again, and Olympia fell to her knees. She was no longer grinning. She looked down at the tip of the stake, and then at Natasha and Marciano. Finally, she turned her head toward Max, but didn't look at him.

"So. Dorina," she managed to say, her voice choppy and deep. She looked back at Natasha with those amber eyes, causing the latter to flinch. Then she mumbled something in an ancient language, and her body fell upon the floor, exploding into a cloud of dust, as if someone had dropped an old book on a wooden table.

"Mom," Marciano said just before looking up at Max, who had no expression on his face as he gazed upon the twins.

"Go," he said, softly. Marciano sprang to his feet. Natasha did the same, but she watched Max's blue eyes as she did so. "Go," he repeated.

Natasha had so much to say, but there was no time. She ran, following her brother toward the stage. When she turned her head mid-sprint to look back in Max's direction, he was gone.

Marciano was the first one to reach the stage-right exit, and he was surprised to see Enya all the way on the other end at stage left. He nodded to her, and she made quick eye contact before returning her attention to Maude.

Their mother looked stunning. She was wearing a black dress from her latest couture line, with a gold belt and a chocolate-brown leather jacket. The dress was rather low cut, but as Maude liked to say, *legs, legs, legs*.

Natasha peeked from behind the curtain, looking out into the audience. Everyone's eyes were on her mother. Natasha looked for anything that might seem suspicious, or anyone uncomfortably close to the stage, but she didn't know what exactly to look for. She found herself watching every cameraman and front-row attendee with an unpleasant sense of paranoia. The assassin could be anywhere. It could be anyone.

As soon as Maude finished her speech, she turned to the stage-right exit and looked at her children. When she saw them she broke out into tears. Her pink lips formed a huge smile, and she dipped her head in their direction. Natasha and Marciano couldn't smile back at her. Their eyes traveled back and forth between their mom—who was heading their way—and the audience.

"She just has to make it off the stage," Marciano said, nervously talking to himself. His entire body was jittery, and so was Natasha's. Their limbs were shaking. Across the way, they saw Enya step out so that she could get a good look at the audience.

Although the twins couldn't stop watching the crowd, Maude maintained her eye contact. She was as nervous as they were, but if anything bad was going to happen, she wanted the last thing she saw to be her children. And so she watched Natasha and Marciano with all the joy and pride of a mother who dearly loved her kids, regardless of whether or not they came from her body.

"Faster, faster," Marciano whispered.

Maude was almost off the stage. Some cameramen were moving close, but otherwise no one else was nearby.

"A little more," Natasha said in between long breaths. She'd never been so nervous in her entire life.

Suddenly a tap on Natasha's shoulder made her jump. She and her brother spun around to see an older woman dressed in a green gown.

"Who are you?" Natasha demanded, stepping back to put some distance between herself and the newcomer.

"Oh, dear heavens, I'm presenting the Fashion Icon award," the old woman said after a loud gasp. "Oh, congratulations," she remarked as soon as Maude stepped off the stage. The woman quickly passed the mother and her children, but not before giving one more confused glance in Natasha's direction.

"Mom!" Marciano cried, and threw his arms around his mother. Natasha couldn't even speak. She just hugged her mom, and let out all the tears she'd been suppressing throughout the day. "You're okay!" Marciano said in excitement, as if he were telling Maude something she didn't know.

"I've never been so scared in my life," Maude exclaimed as the twins pulled her into the backstage area. Enya was quick to join them, although she didn't join the group hug. Instead, the Amazonian stood there with her arms folded, observing the scene.

"Is the network down?" Enya asked the three of them, who at first had no idea what she was talking about.

"Huh?" Marciano asked her.

"Betty isn't responding." Enya tapped her ear and then raised her eyebrows in confusion.

Maude, Natasha, and Marciano all looked at each other with a new sense of nervousness. Enya was right. Midway through fighting Olympia, and midway through Maude's acceptance speech, Betty had stopped communicating with them. They all reached for their ears and touched the earpieces, tapping them to make sure the devices were still working.

"Nothing," Natasha said, and then rested a hand on her chest. "Oh my God, you don't think—"

"The control room," Enya said, her deep voice echoing throughout the backstage area. "Maude, go get Mauria's unconscious body."

"Uh, sure," Maude said, unsure how to reply. "You don't think—"

"There is no time to think," Enya shot back. "Control room, now!"

"Mind if I take this seat?" Rafaela Simone asked a confused Candice Brown. As the Fabbies went to commercial and a new presenter walked out onto the stage to prepare for the final award of the night, Rafaela had abandoned her seat and snuck down to the first row. "I need to bask in some grievous solidarity with another loser."

"Did you just call me a loser?" Candice replied with shock in her dark-brown eyes.

"A Fabbies loser," Rafaela remarked. "I lost Best Designer, and every year you lose Fashion Icon."

"Well what if I win it this year?"

"You won't," Rafaela said. The designer then paused, dipped her brow and scanned Candice Brown's velour outfit, and then shook her head. "Yeah, you won't."

"I am Candice Brown. You are not in my league, and cannot just come sit next to me uninvited, in the seat reserved for my sister—"

"Who didn't show up," Rafaela bluntly stated. "It's okay, I'll be your sister tonight. I just have to hit up a vintage shop, and do my hair like a hooker, and I'll be one step below a celebrity impersonator. I mean seriously, your sister looks like the character actor who would play her on *Saturday Night Live*."

"Rafaela, you're getting on my last damned nerve," Candice spat in an angry whisper. "My sister was supposed to be here tonight for something *very big*. I don't know what happened."

"Maybe she got lost in time. Oh wait, that's every day."

Candice sighed, and turned her head away from Rafaela. Some of the other Colors were in the front row, and Candice considered trying to start a conversation with one of them. But before she could bother, one of the producers began to count down with his fingers, signaling that the show was coming back from commercial.

"The final award of the evening is being presented to this year's Fashion Icon," the old woman on the stage announced. "This is a relevant, life-changing award. I mean, hell, before I won it in the '90s, I used to be a huge slut."

The audience gasped.

"My reputation was worse than North Korea's. I once forced a *Times of Couture* reporter at gunpoint to write something nice about me. After a failed attempt to break into music, television, movies, radio, and blogging, I flew to Brazil and tried to change my face. I ran out of money midway through, which is why I look like this. But hey, I came back to the U.S., married a blind billionaire, dressed really well, and won the award for Fashion Icon. Now all I do is get drunk at fund-raisers and try to avoid my parole officer. So let's announce the nominees."

"*Love* this woman," Rafaela whispered to Candice Brown, who rolled her eyes.

"I was nominated the year she won," Candice whispered back. "You know, I was the favorite."

"Favorite to lose?"

"I don't know why I even bother talking to you," Candice remarked.

"Oh look, they just called your name."

"Excuse me while I look into the camera, smile, and then turn around and barf," Candice Brown replied. "Oh, and then I have to fake smile again when the award goes to some twenty-year-old actress who thinks Pucci is a knockoff brand."

"No," Rafaela said, looking her square in the eyes. "She called your name. You *won*."

Candice's expression went cold, and she slowly turned her head toward the stage. The presenter didn't bother to wait for her—she left the glass trophy sitting on the floor next to the ice sculpture and walked off while cursing about her arthritis.

As Candice Brown stood up from her seat, she turned around to face the audience. There were standing ovations, although not nearly as much applause as there had been for Maude and Mauria. But Candice took what she could get. She smiled for the audience, did a little bow, and began to walk up onto the stage to accept her award.

Candice managed to navigate the stairs without falling, and when she reached the ice sculpture she picked up her little trophy and held it in the air.

"Thank you!" she called out as the audience quieted down. "I've never won a Fabbie before. This is, uh—well usually I'm the kind of girl who can't keep quiet, and for once I don't know what to say. I know I'm not easy to like. I'm a loud New Yorker. I dress flashy. Some people say that I'm not very nice. I wouldn't say that I'm not nice. I just tend to think of myself as a realist. I cut to the point. Some people don't like that about me, but it's just who I am. I've been around fashion for a long time—longer than many of you know—and I've seen a lot of changes.

"I've seen trends come in and out of style so fast. I've seen people come and go. It's hard to always be what's *in*, and even harder when you become yesterday's news. That's probably why there are so many familiar faces at the very top. Those of us who you'd call fashion royalty—we're afraid to become yesterday's news. And sometimes I wonder if I deserve to be at the top, but this award shows me that you all think I do.

"I don't know who to thank for this. How can you thank other people for your own sense of style, right? But I do want to thank my sister, and say that I wish she were here. She was supposed to be here tonight, sitting front row with me. Isabelle, my dear, this is for you."

Candice Brown smiled one last time, and then a gunshot sounded under the glimmering lights of the main stage.

"She's not here," Enya said, stating the obvious as soon as she and the twins burst into the tent that served as the control room. The computer chair that Betty had been occupying was still swiveling, an unsettling indication that they'd just missed her.

"What do you think happened?" Natasha worriedly asked. Her brother rushed around the control room looking under tables, as if he were going to find his older sister hiding.

"Betty!" he called out.

"Quiet," Enya quickly said, and raised an index finger. "We don't need to attract any more attention than we already have."

"Is that Candice's voice?" Natasha asked.

"Huh?" Marciano said, only half-listening to her. He was still fumbling around the tent looking for Betty or any clues as to who could have taken her.

"Listen. Listen to the audio."

The three of them quieted down, and Marciano paused as he looked up at the many monitors in the control room. However, all of them had black screens except for one, which showed Candice Brown giving a speech on the main stage. The audio inside the tent was loud, and Candice's voice filled the room with a booming reverberation.

"She won Fashion Icon?" Natasha asked, but neither Marciano nor Enya answered.

"Isabelle, my dear, this is for you," Candice said. For a brief moment her eyes looked into the cameras, and it was as if she were staring right at Natasha. And then, suddenly, a gunshot exploded over the control room's speakers.

"What the—," Marciano remarked as the monitor quickly absorbed his attention. As gasps and screams erupted on the speaker system, Candice Brown fell backward onto the wooden stage. The last thing Enya and the twins saw before medical crew rushed in was a pile of blood leaking out from underneath Candice's lifeless body.

Chapter Fourteen

ISABELLE THE PURPLE KNEW SOMETHING WAS wrong as soon as she stepped off one of Caligae's private jets at London Heathrow Airport. As she walked down the airstairs, she kept her eyes on a woman in a black suit who was standing outside a limousine. The vehicle's door was open, waiting for Isabelle. She took her time, though, carefully navigating the stairs until she reached the paved ground.

"You're not the driver, are you?" Isabelle asked the woman, whose blonde hair was conservatively pulled up into a tight bun.

"No. European Caligae," she answered, speaking with a London accent. She held the door open as Isabelle stepped into the limousine. "We need for you to return to New York immediately. We have another jet waiting. Your sister was killed last night."

"Killed?" Isabelle replied in shock. Her black sunglasses nearly fell off her face.

"An assassin's bullet during her acceptance speech at the Fabbies."

"Wait—" Isabelle held out a palm, and took a deep breath. "She was giving an acceptance speech for what?"

"Fashion Icon. She won. At the end of the speech, a gunshot was heard, and a bullet hit her in the chest."

"Was this on live television?"

"Yes," the woman replied.

Isabelle fell back into the limousine's plush leather backrest.

"Oh my," she nervously said. Her fingers were tapping against the seat. "A bullet can't kill Candice. Her body is almost entirely plastic. Live television, you said?"

"Are you telling me that Candice Brown is still alive?" the woman asked.

"What's the situation at headquarters?"

"In New York? Chaos. There's no sense of control or leadership. FBI agents raided Candice Brown's home and her corporate offices in New York this morning. European and Asian police have done the same in the headquarters of her foreign affiliates. We've never seen anything like this before."

"Is Priscilla maintaining order?" Isabelle asked.

"She can't be in both Europe and the U.S. at the same time," the woman replied. "You have to tell me if you think Candice is still alive. If that's the case, then—"

"She's alive," Isabelle replied, and choked up as she was saying the words.

"Why would she fake her own death?"

The question puzzled Isabelle. Had all the talk about killing the winner of Best Designer merely been a big hoax? Had Candice never trusted her own sister enough to tell her the real plan? Or did everything change when Isabelle decided to bail on attending the event?

"I don't know," Isabelle softly replied. It was a delayed response. Isabelle was so lost in her own thoughts that she could barely maintain the conversation. "Maybe it was easier for her this way. To escape."

"Escape from what?"

"From everyone. Everything. Escape and watch everything crumble around her."

"But what does she gain if Caligae erupts in chaos?" the woman asked, intrigued by this new piece of knowledge about Candice's well-being.

"It's not about Caligae erupting in chaos," Isabelle remarked. "I mean, that will probably happen if this investigation into her death digs too deep into our industry's secrets. No, what will happen is far worse. The curse is going to fall apart. Supernaturals will be exposed. That's all she's doing, you know, is breaking the curse. Everyone in the world is now watching our industry with scrutiny. It's only a matter of time."

"She's mad if she wants to expose us," the woman exclaimed.

"She's mad in general," Isabelle replied, and raised her eyebrows. "Tell Priscilla Black that I'm not going to take her jet back to the United States. She can run North America and Europe until I return."

"But you don't understand," the woman said, and leaned in so that her eyes peeked into the back of the limousine. "Dorina White landed in New York City three hours ago."

Suddenly things had gone from bad to worse. Isabelle sunk within the limousine's plush cushions.

"I can't go back to New York," Isabelle said. She looked back as two members of the jet crew loaded her bags into the back of the limousine and then closed the trunk. Isabelle reached out to pull the car door shut, and the suited woman backed away. "Tell Priscilla that I'm very sorry, but I need to find my sister before Dorina does," Isabelle said, just before shutting the door. Seconds later, the limousine took off.

The mood was mixed back at Cedric's apartment. Everyone stayed up searching for Betty in and around Central Park until it seemed hopeless. Maude and Monique went to Woodsrow & Campertine late at night to see if they could locate someone who had seen Betty, and Cedric rushed to Caligae headquarters for clues, only to find absolute madness brought about in the wake of Candice Brown's murder.

The assassination was all over the news. It seemed like the only thing *on* the news. Social media websites were exploding with comments and blogs about the murder, and videos of the shooting had found their way onto file-sharing websites. Even people who hadn't watched the show on TV and didn't know much about fashion were getting involved. As rumors poured in that the assassination was an inside job, the entire fashion industry began to look like a sideshow ripe for investigation.

"She's not dead," Elle said as she listened to the news coverage. The old vampire crossed her arms and gently shook her head. It was early on Saturday morning, and no one had been able to sleep much, if at all. Natasha and Marciano were seated next to her. Mauria, Cedric, and Enya were on another sofa. Maude and Claude were already on their way back to Philadelphia with Monique in an effort to gather friends and employees to help put the word out about Betty.

"Who isn't? Candice?" Cedric asked. As soon as the words left his mouth, Mauria's teary eyes quickly turned in Elle's direction.

"Yes. Somehow I just know," she replied. Elle leaned forward and stood up from the sofa.

"Do you think Candice has Betty?" Marciano asked, but Elle quickly shook her head.

"No, she'd have no reason to take Betty. I don't think anyone in the world knows where Candice is. Maybe not even her very own sister. But I think that whoever took Betty knew what was going to happen last night. And for some reason they want an advantage over us."

"Why would they need an advantage over us?" Natasha asked. She was so tired from lack of sleep and from everything that had happened before and during the Fabbies that her words came out slow and exhausted. She looked like she could pass out on the sofa at any moment.

"Because for some reason they know everything about us. Details that I doubt even Candice knew. They know that you're formidable, and a threat to whatever it is that they're planning."

"You must be talking about a Color?" Cedric asked her, and Elle nodded.

"Who else," she remarked. "Cedric, I need you to watch Caligae closely over these next couple weeks. See what happens. See if anyone tries to assert power. With Candice gone, politics may change drastically."

"Is there anything we can do?" Marciano asked.

"Yes, there is," Elle replied, and she smiled briefly. "Marciano, Natasha, Mauria, and Enya, the four of you have astounded me with your bravery and capability. This past week has been a trial unlike anything you've ever faced. I'm afraid Candice has won this round, but it doesn't mean that you can't still defeat her. I need you to form a team, and go and find Candice Brown. You must bring her back to New York either by force or coercion. I think that dangerous things may come out of all this attention being drawn to the fashion industry. If we can show Caligae and the world that Candice Brown is still alive, we can avoid a hazardous situation. As long as she's presumed dead, I fear that as each day passes, the outside world will grow more and more suspicious of the secrets that hold this industry together."

"You think we'd be exposed?" Cedric worriedly asked her.

"I do."

"I don't know if I can handle my mom being alive," Mauria admitted. "All night I've been dealing with the idea that she died. Now you're saying she might still be out there somewhere. I'm sick of my mom monopolizing my emotions."

"Wow," Marciano remarked, "good word choice."

"Thank you," Mauria replied, and flashed him a white smile.

"My dear," Elle continued, "bringing your mom to justice may be the first step in gaining inner peace. She has caused trouble for other people for centuries. Now you have the chance to put that trouble to rest. Find her, and bring her back to New York."

"I need to look for Betty," Natasha said.

"No one is going to hurt Betty, I can guarantee you. If she has been kidnapped, it's only because someone is using her to protect themselves from all of you. Bring Candice Brown back alive, and we'll be one step closer to finding Betty."

"Are you going to come with us?" Marciano asked her.

"An old, blind vampire would just weigh you down," Elle softly admitted. "I can't run around the world anymore like I used to. But I'll be there when you need me. You can think of me as your guardian angel."

"Wait—," Marciano remarked, and held his hands up in the air as he processed the thought that had just sprung into his head. "I've got it! We'll be the Elle's Angels." As soon as the words left his mouth, he turned to his twin sister, who was looking back with the same beaming smile.

"Elle's Angels, that's perfect!"

"Like, oh my God!" Mauria exclaimed.

"Okay, I didn't say you had to come up with a team name," Elle remarked, but it was already too late. Mauria and the twins had approved. Even Enya gradually nodded her head. "Oh dear, so be it. Elle's Angels."

"Hey, where do we start looking for Candice?" Marciano asked.

"Excuse me a second," Natasha said, and bunched her lips together as she stood up from the sofa and walked off toward the bathroom. She felt weary and exhausted. Even though the mission to find Candice Brown should have seemed exciting, she grew worried that she'd been thrust into too much, too quickly. She had almost died at the hands of Olympia less than twenty-four hours ago, and already she was being sent back out on behalf of the forces of good. Natasha needed a break from *good*. She needed a break from everything. Whatever happened to her job back at Maude by Maude? Whatever happened to her crowded Philadelphia apartment, and her TV shows that she'd been missing? Whatever happened to her life?

Natasha closed the bathroom door behind her. Wearily she walked to the sink and turned on the water. She stared at herself in the mirror. This was worse than a morning look. This was a *stayed up all night* morning look.

Natasha dipped her head down into the sink and washed her face with cold water. She'd never gone very long without seeing her older sister, and feared that this kidnapping would hang over her for however long it lasted. Elle seemed confident that no harm would come to Betty, but that wasn't a given. Anything could happen, as was proven at the Fabbies. Natasha wondered if their entire plan had served any purpose at all.

Natasha jumped when she raised her eyes back up to the mirror. She clenched her eyelids together and quickly shut off the water.

"I'm going to open my eyes, and you won't be here," she said, but when she reopened them, Max was still standing behind her, looking down upon her with a look that suggested both sympathy and deep desire. "What if I had walked in and pulled my pants down to pee?" she asked him. "Did you think about that?"

Max grabbed Natasha's arm and spun her around, and before she could say anything else he kissed her. Natasha tried (not very hard) to pull away, but couldn't. Maybe because he was strong, or maybe just because he was such a good kisser. Natasha imagined what he was saying to her through each kiss. That he was sorry. That he had to betray her in order to save her later. That she was all he could think about, every waking moment. Maybe Natasha was getting carried away, but she was having fun with each passing thought.

When they finally pulled a couple inches away from each other, Max held Natasha with both arms.

"I have to go, but I'll come find you soon," he whispered in her ear. "I love you."

Natasha looked into his eyes one more time before letting her arms drop to her sides. She closed her eyes, and when she reopened them Max was gone. Aside from thinking that Cedric needed better security in his apartment, Natasha wondered when she'd see Max again, and why she was so quick to forgive him. He'd saved her life, but he'd done so in such a complicated way. She wanted to sit and think about it and try to put all the pieces together. There was so much that she wanted to ask him, and yet the idea of being around him worried her. Not just because of her feelings for him, but because he was so deeply and ambiguously integrated into a world that Natasha still knew very little about.

When Natasha turned back to face the bathroom mirror, something about her face startled her. She quickly ran two fingers along her lips, which had become as dark as Brazilian cherry wood. The sensation wasn't warm, rather her lips felt hard and jagged. She quickly recalled her fingers after one of them caught the edge of a splinter.

"Oh my God." Natasha stared alarmingly as the darkness retreated from her lips, being replaced in a matter of seconds by a more natural pink color. "I'm a Thirteen," she whimpered.

Betty woke up abruptly, shaking with cold. The temperature seemed nearly freezing. The small, dark room in which they were keeping her hadn't been the slightest bit cold when she was first thrown in. In fact, it had been pretty warm. But upon waking, the cold air around her felt so brutal that she could feel her jaw shaking. Betty backed into a corner and bunched up her legs on the stone floor.

She could hear noise outside the room's single door. It was an old rusty thing, and made her think she was probably in a warehouse or abandoned factory. She could be anywhere. Betty had no idea what time it was. Everything, including her clothes, had been taken from her, and she'd been left with nothing more than a pair of thin pajamas.

The distinct sound of heels startled Betty. She perked up, poking her head upward in the direction of the door. She tried to feel around the immediate area with her mind for electronic equipment, anything that she could use to relay a signal to her friends and loved ones. She found nothing.

When the door handle began to turn, Betty pulled her knees into her chest and wrapped her arms around them. She didn't know if she should be excited to be potentially leaving the cold room, or scared of what might be in store for her. She couldn't think of any reason why she'd been kidnapped, unless Candice Brown had been successful at the Fabbies. But Betty didn't want to think like that. She didn't want to think that her mother, and possibly her brother and sister, could all be dead.

The first thing that Betty saw was a pair of white heels on slender, pale legs. Betty followed the legs up to a white cashmere coat that led to a long neck, and platinum-blonde hair that fell beyond a face hidden by the room's darkness. The woman's presence had made the room even colder than it was before the door opened. Betty was shaking, both from the temperature and fear. This was no henchman of Candice Brown.

"You must be—Dorina White," she mumbled as she struggled to keep her hands steady around her knees. Even in the darkness of the room, she could see the woman smile.

"We're going to go for a little car ride," the woman said in a voice that swelled with old Hollywood glamour. She sounded like a starlet from the 1950s, or a society woman who never learned to pronounce words like a normal person. "And you're going to tell me *everything* you know about your brother and sister, and what they're capable of."

"My family's alive?" Betty asked.

"Every one of them. For now."

"Twenty missed calls?" Candice Brown muttered as she glanced at her cell phone. "You'd think she'd have given up by now."

As Candice sipped on a piña colada with one hand, she grabbed her cell phone with the other and tossed the small device behind her. It flew over the deck of the yacht and made a small splash in the water. She smiled, and stretched her legs out on the cushy daybed.

"Laurent!" Candice shouted. She wiggled on top of the mattress, and then placed the piña colada down on a stool positioned next to her. Within seconds, an older, attractive man with a full head of gray hair who looked like he belonged in a Ralph Lauren ad campaign stepped out onto the deck.

"Yes, dear?"

"How long do you think this whole thing is going to take? You know, breaking the curse?"

The man smiled and shrugged. He lifted his arms into the air and turned to look at the seemingly endless miles of water around them.

"Out here, who cares," he remarked, speaking softly and with a French accent.

Candice nodded. She fidgeted with her pink sunglasses, moving them up and down her nose.

"Enjoy yourself," the man added. "You don't have to go back to New York for a long time. Everything will be fine. It's not like Dorina White is going to come back while you're gone."

"You don't think—," Candice began to say, before cutting herself short. She suddenly grew very serious, enough so that the old man lifted his hand in a show of apology.

"I didn't mean to get you upset," he said. "Please—everything will be fine."

"She wouldn't come back, right? Even if they think I'm dead, Caligae still—I mean, there are rules in place—"

"Please, please, I'm sorry for upsetting you," the man said. He smiled at her the way old lovers do, and then turned to head back inside the main cabin.

Laurent's apologies were too late. The idea was creeping through Candice's mind like a fast-working virus, pushing aside every other thought or idea that had popped into her head that day. She grabbed for her piña colada and began to rapidly slurp on it. When some ice got jammed in the straw, she stuck the glass to her mouth and began to dump the frosty liquid down her throat.

"Oh my God," she said as soon as she pulled the glass away from her lips. It slid out of her hand and shattered on the deck of the yacht. She threw both hands in front of her cheeks and slid them upward. Her manicured fingernails caught the edges of her sunglasses, pushing them off her face. She began to breathe heavier and heavier as her thoughts became consumed with the last person on Earth who should have been on her mind. That one name that had been a thorn in her side for hundreds of years.

"Get a grip on yourself," Candice said under her breath. "It's not like she knows where you are."

Candice took a long breath, and then looked off to her right. She watched the quiet way that the waves moved, and listened to the gentle sound of the yacht gliding effortlessly through the sea. She exhaled. Everything was going to be all right.

Just as Candice Brown stepped off the daybed to retrieve the scattered shards of glass from her piña colada, an explosion rocked the deck of the yacht, sending clouds of smoke pouring up into the blue sky, and leaving a trail of screams abandoned in the seclusion of the sea.

THE END

Also from inGroup Press

Talbot Mathias has always felt a little different. He's never been able to really connect with his adoptive parents, has had difficulty making friends at school, and has been tormented by his sexuality ever since entering Mariner High School. As dark visions begin to consume Talbot's nights, his days grow worse and worse with vicious treatment at the hands of bullies. But what neither Talbot nor the bullies know is that a haunting transformation is seeping its way through his veins.

ISBN 9781935725091
inGroupPress.com